OUR DEBTS TO THE PAST

DI ROB MARSHALL
BOOK 8

ED JAMES

OTHER BOOKS BY ED JAMES

DI ROB MARSHALL SCOTTISH BORDERS MYSTERIES

Ed's first new police procedural series in six years, focusing on DI Rob Marshall, a criminal profiler turned detective. London-based, an old case brings him back home to the Scottish Borders and the dark past he fled as a teenager.

1. THE TURNING OF OUR BONES
2. WHERE THE BODIES LIE
3. A LONELY PLACE OF DYING
4. A SHADOW ON THE DOOR
5. WITH SOUL SO DEAD
6. HIS PATH OF DARKNESS
7. FEAR OF ANY KIND
8. OUR DEBTS TO THE PAST (coming 2025)

SGT RAKESH SYAL POLICE THRILLERS

1. FALSE START
2. FALSE DAWN
3. FALSE HOPE (coming 2025)

Note: 1 is set before Marshall 1, 2 between Marshall 6 & 7.

POLICE SCOTLAND

Precinct novels featuring detectives covering Edinburgh and its surrounding counties, and further across Scotland: Scott Cullen, a rookie eager to climb the career ladder; Craig Hunter, an ex-squaddie struggling with PTSD; Brian Bain, the centre of his own universe and bane of everyone else's.

1. DEAD IN THE WATER (revised 2024)
2. GHOST IN THE MACHINE (revised 2025)
3. DEVIL IN THE DETAIL (revised 2025)
4. FIRE IN THE BLOOD (revised 2025)
5. STAB IN THE DARK (revised 2025)
6. COPS & ROBBERS (revised 2019)
7. LIARS & THIEVES
8. COWBOYS & INDIANS
9. THE MISSING
10. THE HUNTED
11. HEROES & VILLAINS
12. THE BLACK ISLE
13. THE COLD TRUTH
14. THE DEAD END

Note: Books 2-8 & 11 previously published as SCOTT CULLEN MYSTERIES, books 9, 11 & 13 as CRAIG HUNTER POLICE THRILLERS and books 1, 14 & 15 as CULLEN & BAIN SERIES.

Book 10 is a new book starring Craig Hunter combining a new story with expanded material previously given to mailing list.

DS VICKY DODDS SERIES

Gritty crime novels set in Dundee and Tayside, featuring a DS juggling being a cop and a single mother.

1. BLOOD & GUTS (revised 2024)
2. TOOTH & CLAW (previously SNARED; revised 2018)
3. FLESH & BLOOD
4. SKIN & BONE
5. GUILT TRIP

DI SIMON FENCHURCH SERIES

Set in East London, will Fenchurch ever find what happened to his daughter, missing for the last ten years?

1. THE HOPE THAT KILLS
2. WORTH KILLING FOR
3. WHAT DOESN'T KILL YOU
4. IN FOR THE KILL
5. KILL WITH KINDNESS
6. KILL THE MESSENGER
7. DEAD MAN'S SHOES
8. A HILL TO DIE ON
9. THE LAST THING TO DIE
10. HOPE TO DIE

Other Books

Other crime novels, with *Lost Cause* set in Scotland and *Senseless* set in southern England.

- LOST CAUSE
- SENSELESS

"We can pay our debts to the past by putting the future in debt to ourselves."

— John Buchan, Lord Tweedsmuir

Address to the People of Canada on the Coronation of George VI on May 12, 1937.

1

Then

25 years ago.

Saturday, 3rd of June, 2000

Heather sat back in the passenger seat and let the wind blow through her hair. Windows down, shades on – might be evening but it was as bright as Gary's Tartan Techno was loud. Felt like the deep beats oomphing out of the speakers were shaking the car, under a layer of tuneless bagpipe drone.

And she hated bagpipes.

She took off her sunglasses and looked around the countryside, the grass rising up this side of the Eildons. Everything was bright and green and lush. The old Melrose station passed by in a blur on the left, which was now a nursery on this side and that fancy Italian restaurant on the other side. Her parents were going to take her there for her birthday dinner soon...

Heather took a sip from the bottle of wine and savoured the sweetness.

Gary turned down the music, then looked over to her. 'So then, birthday girl – do you want to go to the pub now?'

He was sort of on the borderline between good-looking and *weird*. His forehead was too short and that goatee made him look like a sex case. But his eyes twinkled with mischief and mystery – when he looked at you, you knew all about it.

'The Ship?' Heather blew a blast of air up her face. 'What do you think?'

'I'm driving and it's your birthday – you have to choose.'

'I hate choosing...' Heather turned around to look at the back seat. 'What do you guys think?'

Georgina was snogging that guy Heather didn't know. Seatbelt unbuckled and practically in his lap. She broke off and locked eyes with Heather, her red face shrouded by frizzy black hair, then grabbed the bottle back and took a sip. She snogged the bloke and passed the wine to him through the kiss.

Gross.

Heather turned the music even further down until she couldn't hear the bagpipes, then loudly cleared her throat. 'I said, do you want to go to the Ship?'

Georgina broke free again, only to frown at Heather. 'Huh?'

'The Ship? Now?'

'Not yet!'

'But we might not get in if we leave it any later.'

'Shh. Drink up.' Georgina forced the wine back into Heather's hands. 'Birthday girl.'

Heather looked at it and all she could think about was backwash. Sod it – she wiped the end with her hand, then took a long drink.

Georgina laughed, that braying rattle. 'Darren knows the bouncer, anyway.'

Ah, Darren – that was his name.

'Listen, we've got this wine.' Darren wrapped his arm around Georgina like he owned her. His stubble was so patchy and that baseball cap perched on top of his head like a peanut on the Eildons. 'Let's at least finish that, eh?'

'Suit yourselves, then.' Gary blasted past the turning for Melrose and headed towards the main road.

Heather took another sip of the sickly-sweet wine then handed the bottle back to them.

'Oh, I totally forgot... Got a little something for you...' Georgina pulled out a shiny CD-R from her bag, then leaned forward, swaying as she tried to insert the disc.

'Careful, Georgie!' Gary swung around the roundabout, making her wobble a bit.

She eventually slid it into the player and it clicked and whirred.

'Have you not got your—' Gary headed north. 'Put your fucking seatbelt on!'

Georgina scowled at him, still leaning between them, her sweet wine breath lashing over them. 'What's it to you?'

'If I have to brake and you go flying through the window, then that's one thing. But if you rocket into the back of my *head...*'

'Killjoy wanker.'

Gary tapped the brake and she jerked forward. 'See?'

'*Fine.*' Georgina sat back behind him and snapped in her seatbelt. She sat back, arms folded. 'Arsehole.'

Dirty, cheesy rock blasted out of the speakers. Old people's music.

Georgina rocked along, making devil horns with both hands.

Heather scowled at her. 'What the *hell* is this?'

Georgina scowled right back. 'It's Alice Cooper!'

'Who the hell is she?'

'*He.*' Gary laughed. 'He's a he. My dad's a massive fan.'

'I mean, it's better than the tartan techno, but...' Heather shook her head. 'It's not exactly my music, is it?'

Gary snorted. 'Remember that song "School's Out" we played on the last day of school?'

Heather shrugged. 'Kind of.'

'This is also by him.' Gary thumbed behind her. 'I asked Georgie to put it on the mix. It's called "I'm Eighteen" – just like you...'

Heather sat back and nodded. Aye, the tuneless tartan techno had been much better. 'Right.'

'You're being such a drag, Heath.' Georgina scowled at her. 'What's up?'

'Just... Nothing. I'm fine.'

'Come on. What's up?'

Heather sat back and looked out of the window, watching the Leaderfoot Viaduct pass on the left.

Rather than head up to Earlston, Gary pulled off onto the wee road over on the right, then looked across to her.

She made brief eye contact with him, then looked away again.

Gary stopped at the junction, indicating left, then turned up the music and leaned over. 'Seriously, are you okay?'

'Totally fine.'

Georgina reached forward to turn the music back down. 'Seriously, what's up with you? It's your birthday and you're being so square.'

Gary turned around. 'Put your seatbelt back on!' He set off along the road.

'What's got in your knickers, *Dad*?' Georgina did her braying laugh again. Got ten times worse when she was drinking – made Heather want to scream.

Gary frowned at that, but he didn't say anything.

'I'm fine, Georgie.' Heather ran a hand through her hair. 'Just... Hell of a lot on, you know?'

'Here we go... Exam results... Uni stress... Blah blah blah.'

Georgina rolled her eyes. 'You'll get into Edinburgh, don't you worry.'

'Easy for you to say. Doesn't matter what happens to you at uni, does it? If you mess up, your uncle will just give you a job at his company.'

'Wish it was that simple...'

Gary slowed as they approached Scott's View. A long row of parking spaces, giving each car a share of that glorious vista across the Tweed to the Eildons, which kind of loomed over Melrose so close it was hard to make them out sometimes, but here they were like a camel with three humps.

He pulled into a space. 'Now, isn't that a cracking view, eh?'

Heather looked around. Only a VW camper van and another car there.

No sign of Sinead or the others.

'This is a great spot for shagging.' Darren pointed at the VW. 'That camper van's notorious.'

Georgina scowled at him. 'Notorious with who?'

'The lads at work. Usually parked down at the William Wallace statue car park. Right, Gary?'

Gary scratched his cheek. 'Wouldn't know, Daz.'

Darren and Georgina got out of the car, leaving Heather with Gary.

Gary rolled up the windows, having to reach into the back to get Georgina's. He looked over at Heather with those mischievous eyes. 'You look very pretty tonight.'

'No, I don't.'

'You do.'

'Course I don't.' Heather held his gaze. 'Are you trying it on with me?'

Gary shrugged. 'Maybe.'

'I'm flattered, but no.'

Gary's wee forehead crumpled a bit. 'Sure about that?'

Heather nodded. 'Sure.'

'Cos of my dad?'

'Nothing to do with him. Or what he does. Just waiting to find the right guy, that's all.'

'Okay.' Gary laughed. 'And *Mark Henderson* was right?'

'Mark was very wrong.' Heather shut her eyes for a few seconds. 'He made me realise I should set my sights a *lot* higher.'

'Well, the offer's there.' Gary threw his arms up in the air. 'Think about it. We could be good together.'

'I will...' Heather opened the door and got out. She felt relieved to be out of the car, with that stiff summer breeze blowing the frizz back into her hair – she'd spent so long straightening it out.

Darren and Georgia were sitting on the wall, drinking the wine and snogging.

Sod that.

Heather leaned against the wall, but kept a good distance from them. Actually started feeling a wee bit sick.

Gary walked over, slowly, eyebrows raised. 'Listen, I'm sorry—'

'Are you sure you're happy not drinking?'

Gary frowned, taken aback by the change of direction. Then he sat next to her and smiled. 'Totally fine with it. Much prefer driving. I like being in control. Besides, I could do without a hangover tomorrow. Got to drive the old boy down to Stranraer tomorrow.'

'*Stranraer*? What for?'

Gary shrugged. 'He won't tell me.'

Drugs...

Everyone knew the family were into something dodgy...

And Gary wondered why Heather didn't want to go out with him...

'Absolute pain in the hoop.' Gary leaned next to her, scrawny arms folded across his pigeon chest. 'You know what?

Forget what I said – I'd much rather be getting wasted with you lot. Not sure when I'll be back, either.'

'Are you going to Northern Ireland?'

'Nah. Think he's meeting a guy about a greyhound or something.'

'Right.'

Definitely drugs, then.

Gary tilted his head to the side. 'Are you sure you're okay?'

'I'm fine. Just…' Heather sighed. 'Birthdays…'

'They're supposed to be fun.'

'And they are. And I love the fact everyone's come out for me. Well, most of everyone. It's just…' Heather looked up at the clouds in the blue sky. One looked like Homer Simpson throttling Bart. She looked back down at Gary – he was such a good listener. 'It's just a lot of pressure, you know? I hate being the centre of attention…'

'Tell me about it. Much prefer being a back-seat driver.' Gary laughed. 'Except when I'm *actually* driving.'

Heather smiled at that, then took in the view across to the Eildons. Those rolling hills climbing from the river, stuffed full of trees.

Gary put an arm around her.

She leaned in a bit.

He felt safe.

Georgina and Darren were laughing at something, but for once it wasn't them.

Heather looked over at Gary. 'Have you got your mobile with you?'

'Aye, sure. Why?'

'Can I borrow it to make a call?'

Gary un-holstered it from his belt, like it was a handgun. 'Don't have that many minutes left, but seeing as how it's you…'

'Just be a couple. And I'll pay you back…' Heather took the brand-new Nokia and tapped in a number from memory, then hit the wee green button and put it to her ear. 'You're the only person I know who has one of these things.'

'Total game-changer, Heath.' Gary grinned. 'Mark my words, everyone will have one soon.'

'Hardie house, Andrea speaking.'

'Hi, Andrea Speaking. It's Heather Calling.'

Andrea sighed down the line. 'Oh. It's you. Happy birthday.' She sniffled. 'How's it going?'

Heather watched the other car drive off, leaving just them and the camper van now – still no sign of Sinead. She locked eyes with Gary. 'It's going okay.'

'What are you up to?'

'We're out and about. We're still going drinking in Melrose. Meeting all the others in a bit. Never guess what – Georgina's being a bit annoying...'

'What else is new, eh?'

Heather laughed. 'Just calling to see how you are.'

'I'm sick as a dog, Heath. Stinking cold. Sad I can't make it.'

'Yeah, it sucks. You're okay, though?'

A long pause, each tick of the clock costing Gary his precious minutes. 'Take it you heard I broke up with Gary.'

'I did, aye. That why you're not here?'

'I am genuinely sick.'

'Come on...'

'I mean it. But me not being there will make things much easier for everyone, right?'

Heather felt Gary wrap his arm around her again. 'What's that supposed to mean?'

'I'm not daft, Heath. You're talking on a mobile. You don't own one. But I know who does.' Andrea paused. 'Just... Be careful. Okay?'

Heather looked around at Gary, but he was staring at the camper van with an impish grin on his face.

Truth is, she did fancy him. A bit. He was a bad boy. And she liked bad boys.

'Wouldn't dream of it, Andi.'

'Been there, done that. Believe me, you don't want that T-shirt.' Andrea sniffed hard. 'Where are you? Melrose? Gala?'

'Eh, Scott's View.'

'And you're there to snog him, right?'

'Hardly. There's a gang of us here.'

Gary looked over at her, tapping his watch.

'Listen, I better go. Love you loads, Andi.'

'Love you too. Have a great night.'

'Will do. Bye!' But Heather didn't know how to hang up the phone, so she handed it back to Gary.

He pressed a button then re-holstered it. 'How's Andi?'

'She's sick.'

'Ah, right.' Gary rubbed at his neck. 'Shame she couldn't make it.'

'Aye.' Heather looked hard at him. 'Said you broke up with her?'

Gary held her stare. 'That what she told you?'

'Well, that you'd split up.'

'That's more accurate.' Gary sucked a deep breath in through his nostrils then let it out slowly. 'She dumped me, Heather. Told me I'm not good enough for her.'

'Always two sides to the story, eh?' Heather stared at him, locking eyes again. She could get used to that. 'How do you feel about it?'

'Her choice, not mine. Trust me, it was her doing. I'm the loyal type.'

Just then, a car pulled up and parked next to Gary's.

He broke off from the hug, like he didn't want to be seen with her.

Sinead got out first, followed by David, who grabbed her hand. Both dressed in black hoodies with those stupid big jeans and keychains. And Sinead was kidding nobody with that dye job – she was as ginger as Heather.

Then Kat and Ian got out, practically shagging. Fingers and hands everywhere.

Heather watched them all and did the sums in her head.

Three couples.

Plus Heather and Gary, who were both single...

Like it'd been set up.

Heather walked over to them, where they were laughing and joking, but she had to drown it out – they were all much more drunk than her, except for Sinead and Gary.

Georgina glowered at them. 'Wasters.' She grabbed the bottle and drained it, then hoyed it over the side, down into the thick gorse. 'Whoooo!' She watched it go.

It didn't make a sound.

Georgina sighed. 'Disappointing.' She walked back over to Gary's car and got out a second bottle of white wine. She swigged it and passed it over to Darren.

And the truth of it was – Heather was *bored*, even though it was her birthday. Should be a lot more than this – even going into Edinburgh or down to Newcastle or *some*thing, not the usual Friday night of going to the Ship in Melrose and maybe the club in Gala.

Heather looked across the valley again. Aye, there was more to life than this. More than Melrose and Gala.

That Alice Cooper song started playing again.

Heather let out a deep sigh as she focused on the camper van.

Darren was leering at her. 'That's pretty famous. Lad I know said it belongs to this prostitute and she shags blokes in it.'

'Shut up!'

'That's what he said...'

Heather saw it move a little bit.

So someone was in there...

Sod it.

Heather walked over to the camper van and knocked on the door.

No answer.

'We know you're in there!'

Darren joined her, holding the bottle of wine. 'What's up?'

'Saw it moving.'

'Know what the boys at work say, eh? "If it's rocking, don't come knocking".' Darren laughed like it was the funniest thing ever. And seemed a bit disappointed he didn't get a laugh from her. He pushed the side, rocking the van on the suspension. 'Come on, you hoor! Out you come!'

Heather joined him and they rocked it back and forth a few times.

Then Kat and Ian ran over, laughing and giggling, and joined in from the other side. They got it rocking from side to side, the suspension crunching and grinding.

Heather felt a bit crap about it now, so she let go.

Georgina grabbed Darren's arm and stopped him. 'What the hell are you doing?'

Darren nodded at the van. 'Seeing if the hoor's in there.'

'Come on. Imagine if that was you?'

'I'm not a hoor, though!'

Gary laughed.

Sinead giggled, despite being sober.

Gary took the bottle from Ian, then handed it to Heather without taking a sip.

'Thanks.' Heather took a deep drink. Sod it, she should get pissed – it was her eighteenth, after all.

She looked back at the VW.

The van door opened. A man stepped out – cap and shades, thick jacket, hood up – then ran away, jumping the wall in a flash and barrelling down the hill.

Heather rushed over to the gate and tried to follow his path, but she lost him in the thick gorse below.

'What the fuck?' Gary was the only other one who noticed – the rest were playing air guitar. He nudged the camper van door open to its full width and had a wee nosy inside.

Heather joined him.

Gary stopped her with his hand. Then turned around, eyes wide. 'You don't want to go in there.'

'Don't tell me what—'

'Seriously.' Gary reached for his phone on its holster. He put it to his ear. 'I mean it, Heather.'

Heather pushed past him and stepped into the back of the camper van. It stank of sweat and toasted marshmallows.

A woman lay on the mattress.

Tongue lolling out. Red marks around her throat. Eyes bulging, but staring right through Heather.

Dead.

Fuck.

All Heather could do was scream.

2

Now.

25 years later.

Thursday, 5th June

Duncan Brown hated waiting in line anywhere.

In the grocery store, in his car, anywhere. But this place right here was the worst of all possible worlds – immigration at Edinburgh Airport.

Some sort of performative cruelty, where they made a bunch of planes wait for just three openings. And the other two lines were getting through *way* faster than his.

Always the way...

They don't tell you when you join the lines how the others will go much quicker, do they? And it wasn't like being stuck in traffic on a freeway and being able to cut in and out of different lines, was it?

Another false signal – the immigration officer held the dude back again. He'd been next to Duncan on the plane, a fat guy in his forties who just played a video game the whole flight. The *whole* flight. Who does that?

Duncan took a deep breath.

There we go – the fat dude waddled off and the immigration officer beckoned Duncan forward.

His turn.

Finally.

Duncan took it slowly, easing over. Nothing to stress about. Everything was totally okay. He smiled, not too much, not too little, and handed over the navy passport with the Canadian coat of arms proudly on the front.

The officer took it and examined it slowly, like there weren't hundreds of folks behind Duncan. A big guy, kind of spilling out of his uniform. Needed a shave. Needed a wash. He snorted. Picked his nose. Sniffed. Examined what he'd excavated from his nostril. Then looked up at Duncan. 'Edwards Air flight from Toronto, right?'

'Makes you think that, pal?'

The immigration officer frowned. 'No need for the attitude, sir.'

'Sorry. Force of habit.' Duncan gave an embarrassed laugh. 'Grew up here.'

'Oh? Where?'

Duncan flashed a smile. 'Down in the Borders.'

'Ah, beautiful spot.' The immigration officer sat back and grinned. 'Whereabouts?'

'St Boswells.'

'Don't know it. Go to Melrose for the sevens every year, mind.'

'It's not far from Melrose.' Duncan smiled again. 'Just a few miles.'

The immigration officer nodded then went back to the passport. 'Are you still a British citizen?'

'I... I am, aye.'

'This is a Canadian passport, sir.'

'Aye, sorry. The British one's out of date. Got a Canadian one after I got dual citizenship.'

'Got you.' A deep yawn. 'When did you leave?'

'2001.' Duncan coughed. 'Haven't lost the Borders accent.'

The immigration officer looked at him like he'd gone insane. 'Sure.' He leaned forward and stroked his chin. 'What's the purpose of your visit, sir?'

'To see my mother. She's, uh, got dementia.'

'Sorry to hear that, sir. Where are you staying?'

'With her. In St Boswells.'

'Okay. And how long are you planning on staying?'

'Honest answer is I don't know yet.' Duncan let out a slow breath. 'Have to see how bad things are with Mom. Could be a short visit, but it might turn into something longer. The care home hinted that she wasn't in a good way, so...'

'I get it.' The immigration officer looked at something on his screen, then sat back and folded his beefy arms. He reached over and stamped the passport, then handed back his papers and looked past him. 'Next.'

'Thank you.' Duncan hefted up his suitcase and carried it, rather than wheeling it.

The doors opened and he eased through, out into the airport.

And he stopped, standing on British soil. On *Scottish* soil. First time in a quarter of a century. Just a few miles from home.

He took a deep breath, then blitzed through the airport and out down a long corridor into the Scottish summer.

Rain and clouds. The air wasn't so much cool as icy – might be June, but this was Edinburgh.

The whole place had changed a lot in the time he'd been away. Much more built up. And was that a *tram* stop – when the hell did they come back?

Asshole – should've done more research before hopping on a plane...

Okay. Focus – where the hell was the rental place?

'Sir.'

Duncan swung around.

A police officer charged towards him.

Everything clenched inside Duncan. He scanned the area – plenty of places to run to, nowhere looked good enough to get away, though...

Despite the cold, Duncan felt a trickle of sweat down his back. He tried a smile, but it felt fake. 'Can I help?'

'You dropped your passport, sir.' The cop held it out to him.

'Ah. Thank you.' Duncan took it back with a wide grin, more relief than warmth. 'Honestly, I'd lose my head if it wasn't bolted to my neck.'

'Take better care of both, then. Have a nice trip.'

'Will do.' Duncan nodded his thanks, then walked along the front of the airport and followed the signs over to the rental place. Walking like he belonged there, trying not to attract any attention.

He'd expected a fancy building with a receptionist behind a desk and fresh coffee, maybe even pastries, but it was just a wall filled with lockers. Yellow and brown. And a few touchscreens in the middle. He got out his cell and found the email.

Scan the QR code.

He pinched and zoomed until it filled the screen, then made it brighter.

Where the hell was the reader?

Ah, there – he held his cell up to the camera, then the screen flicked green.

Thank you for choosing to hire your car through Travis Rental.
Your keys are now available in F18.

F18?

Where the hell was F18?

What the hell was F18?

He looked outside at the rows and columns of parked cars, but that couldn't be right, could it? He needed keys... Even now, when your key didn't do anything and was just a box to control a computer.

He spotted a drawer had flapped open, like in an escape room.

F18.

Right. He reached in and took the Nissan key fob.

Okay...

A deep breath as he looked back the way to make sure the cop wasn't following him – or watching – then he walked across the parking lot to the car parked in F18. A big Nissan SUV. Perfectly anonymous. Or he hoped Scottish cars were basically the same as in Canada, and everyone drove these big-ass things.

He opened it, then dumped his case in the trunk. A deep sigh as he checked to see if he *definitely* hadn't been followed, then he got behind the wheel.

Only, he was on the wrong side.

So he had to get out and switch around to the ass-backwards side he'd learnt to drive on all those years ago. Been driving on the right for twenty-five years, except that trip to Turks and Caicos seven years ago, which was a total disaster.

And of course – it wasn't an automatic. He hadn't driven stick since... 2000?

Take it slowly – he really couldn't risk drawing attention to himself.

He tapped St Boswells into the satnav and it locked in on the location. He put the stick into first and drove off.

~

Duncan took it slowly through St Boswells and, unlike Edinburgh Airport, this place hadn't really changed. Still the same fancy houses set back from the main street, lined with trees. The kink around the town hall, then the shallow climb. Some minor changes, though. Was that a Morrisons? In St Boswells? Just a small one, but still.

And was that a *bookshop*?

Duncan had to pull in to let a car past outside a hardware shop where there'd been a gallery. Driving on this side was still a bit weird, but the gears were all coming back to him. Left foot in. Left hand controlling it, though this one had seven gears. Five he could get, but *seven*?

He drove off, but pretty quickly he had to pull in again.

There it was.

His parents' home. The place he'd lived for the first act of his life.

He'd somehow forgotten it was on the corner, with a lane leading up the back. Stone-built and sturdy. Felt like a feature of the landscape – hard to imagine someone building it.

He sucked in a deep, deep breath, then got out and walked up to the front door. His ancient house keys were ice cold in his hands. He put the mortice in and – holy shit – it still worked.

No breath he took could be deep enough.

He opened the door and stepped inside.

Smelled all damp and musty. And freezing cold, even though it was June. They'd never got around to installing central heating, then. Dad had talked a lot about it. He pressed a hand to the giant night-store heater in the hall – cold. The fireplace in the living room was empty, no wood or coal stacked up and ready.

Duncan tried a light switch and, wonder of wonders, it turned on – the electricity was still working. A good thing, though it meant Mom was paying for a house she didn't live in.

He stood there, taking it all in.

All those memories hit him like a hockey stick to the head.

A wee boy, running up and down the stairs.

Last day of school.

First day of university – driving up that stupid road to Edinburgh, but he was determined to run a car, wasn't he? Meant working in the store to pay for it. But he didn't mind hard labour.

Then when he was working, he'd pop back here every few weeks to do some washing and see them. But never for too long.

And then the day he left for the final time. Or so he thought.

Someone knocked on the door.

Duncan wheeled around but all he saw was a misty shape in the glass. He opened the door again and peered out.

A woman stood there. Fifties, with a horrible scowl on her face. Fringe too short. 'Can I help you?'

Duncan frowned at her. 'Excuse me?'

'I live next door. Do you mind telling me who you are?'

'Oh, I'm Mrs Radford's nephew.' Duncan offered a hand. 'Duncan. Duncan Brown.'

She didn't shake it and her scowl deepened. 'She never mentioned a nephew.'

'She never talked about Margaret? Her sister?' Duncan spotted the picture was still on the wall. He pointed at it – two middle-aged women at Niagara Falls, both hugging him as the frozen water hissed and sprayed behind them. 'This is them. A while ago, now. That's me there with them.'

'Oh, aye. Margaret. She moved to Canada, right?'

'Right. Exactly. I'm her boy. Hence the accent.' Duncan gave her a broad smile. 'Can probably tell I'm Canadian.'

'Thought you were American.'

'Which is why we always point out we're Canadian.'

Duncan laughed but she didn't join in.

Instead, she wrapped her arms tight around her torso. 'What are you doing here?'

'My mom heard her sister went into a nursing home. She isn't well enough to make the trip herself, but she's well enough to send me to see if I can help my aunt.' Duncan smiled as he held out the keys and let them dangle. 'Mom gave me these and I can't believe they still work.'

Something softened in her. 'Ah. Okay.'

'I'll be staying here while we sort out her affairs. Mom has power of attorney, or whatever you call it here.'

'Right. Right. We call it that too.'

She wasn't someone he recognised from years ago, otherwise he'd already be putting on the gloves.

'So you live next door?' Duncan pointed left and right. Eyebrows raised.

She pointed to her left. 'That side, aye.'

'Oh, so you must've bought it from Keith and Moira?'

'We did, aye.' Her frown was back. 'How do you know them?'

Ah shit...

Duncan ran a hand through his hair. 'Oh. Auntie Pat talked about them a lot. You know how older people get, right? They tell you all about their friends' lives as if you knew them. And Mom's the same.' He held her gaze. 'How long have you lived here, then?'

'Seventeen years now.'

Duncan winced. 'Oh, that's not long before my Uncle John passed away, right?'

She looked away. 'That's right, aye. Hit your aunt hard.' Using the term meant she was buying into the story... But she frowned at him again. 'Why isn't her son here?'

'Colin?' Duncan looked away. 'I'm afraid he moved away. Mom hasn't heard from him in years.'

'Oh. I'm sorry to hear that. Patricia talked fondly about him. When did he die?'

'He didn't die. Just haven't heard from him in years.'

'I get it. He moved to Canada to stay with her, right?'

'Stayed with us for a bit, eh? But he worked in the petrochemical industry. A refinery up in Alberta. I didn't understand what he did.'

'Oh, Pat said he worked in a factory?'

'I think that's how he explained it to her, but it was pretty complicated stuff.'

She nodded. 'What happened to him?'

'No idea. Haven't heard from him in about twenty years.'

'Do you think he died?'

'Maybe.'

'I'm sorry to hear that.'

Duncan frowned. 'You been in to see my aunt at all?'

'Once a fortnight.' She pointed inside the house. 'Been looking after this place too. Water the plants, check for post. Can't get the electricity company to stop the supply, so I'm glad someone's dealing with it. I suspect you'll sell it?'

'Not sure, to be honest. Sorry. I need to see what they've got to say at the home.'

She nodded, but couldn't look at him. 'Well, Pat's not doing well, so I can't see her coming out anytime soon. And those places...' She looked back at him. 'You know how these people are, right?'

Duncan shook his head. 'Haven't had to deal with them.'

'Care home managers?' She gave a dark, dark look. 'Scoundrels, every one of them. One hand on your shoulder, the other in your pocket. My mother was in one a few years ago and it was depressing. And expensive.'

'I'm sure they're not all bad.'

'I guess not. It's just... It's the *money*. People save all their lives to pass money on to the next generation, then it all goes to bloody care homes.'

'Oh, totally. It needs to be reformed.' Duncan checked his watch. 'Actually, I'm running late, so how about we catch up later?'

3

DCI Rob Marshall drove far too fast along the road, full of twists and turns – he wasn't quite used to this new car yet but it was a dream compared to the old monster. Ancient trees lined both sides of the road and the weather made it feel like autumn rather than late spring or early summer, depending on how you measured it.

And he needed to be there an hour ago…

'—not happy with this, Robert.' Superintendent John Ravenscroft's voice boomed out of the dashboard speakers. 'Not one bit. You need to close this down. Now.'

Marshall took a final corner and was on the straight now, with the clear view across the Tweed marred by the imminent threat of rain, billowing dark clouds above the blue sky. 'Will do, sir.'

'I mean it, Robert. No ifs, no buts, no maybes. Shut. It. Down.'

'Just about there now, sir, so I better go and shut it down for you.' Marshall killed the call and let out a sigh. 'Wanker.'

He took it slowly along the road and had to check he'd actually hung up – this new car had a mind of its own. Ravenscroft hated him enough without him making his antipathy towards the arsehole obvious.

All the spaces at Scott's View were full, with a long row of cars blocking even them. And continuing on past it, lining the road like a sporting event was taking place. He trundled past, slow enough to catch a glimpse of a woman talking to cameras and journalists. He spotted a gap, but he arsed up the parallel park so badly he just pulled in and got out, then hurried back along the road. Had to zap his car's hoojie to make sure it actually locked.

Marshall didn't know what he'd done in a past life to deserve a series of shonky cars, but it must've been selling used cars or something. He stopped at the edge and took in the scene.

Heather McGill was talking to the cameras. Red-haired and fiery, her green eyes piercing the overcast afternoon. Speaking into a microphone plugged into a little guitar amp, but it was more than loud enough to carry. 'And that's why now, more than ever, it's important the police give us all closure on the murder of Sharon Beattie. This case has haunted every one of us for the last twenty-five years.' She lowered the microphone, then looked around, spotting Marshall and turning away.

DI Andrea Elliot stood next to her, looking frazzled and angry, despite the wide smile. The stiff breeze plastered her long fringe to her forehead and cheek.

Heather raised the mic back to her lips. 'Sharon was twenty-one when she died. That's no age. I was here on my eighteenth birthday when we found her. Twenty-five years ago, almost to the day.' She reached down into a box and pulled out a giant photo, then held it up – a woman, young and happy, with a "Rachel from *Friends*" haircut. 'This is Sharon. She lived in Galashiels. Her dad raised her after her mum passed away. You might've walked past her in the street or in Tesco or sat next to her on the bus or whatever.' She pointed to the side. 'She was murdered right there. A few minutes before we found her body.'

Silence for a few seconds.

Nobody moved.

Elliot adjusted her fringe and spotted Marshall.

He stepped forward, shuffling between two reporters tapping into phones rather than onto paper.

Heather looked deep into the nearest camera, with BBC signage on but not the most recent. 'In those days, everyone said she was a prostitute. Now, you'd call her a sex worker. Sharon used to park her camper van at various locations nearby to service her clients. Those men are the people who should be ashamed of themselves. Not her. They're the criminals, not her. That night, it just so happened to be parked here at Scott's View.' She looked down at her feet.

Marshall stepped forward again, just a few paces away.

Heather looked back up with a coy smile. 'But everyone knows everyone in these parts and they all knew Sharon's reputation. And the joke was, "if the van's rocking, don't come knocking". I'm ashamed to admit it, but we rocked it. We rocked the camper van from side to side. Thinking it was all a big laugh. I've felt so ashamed by what we did. We were young and stupid and ignorant. I didn't really have a sense of empathy. Nobody does at that age. Maybe some do, but we didn't. And maybe everyone was a lot crueller back then. I don't know.' She shut her eyes. 'But we found her body.' She reopened them and looked at the Sky News camera. 'Sharon had been strangled. And the killer was never caught.' She brushed a hand through her bright-red hair. 'One thing I've kept going back to about that night is we saw her killer. Well, I did. A friend did too. That animal sneaked out a few seconds after we'd stopped rocking the van. He'd been hiding until the coast was clear. But I'm worried he has done this before. Or since. And I'm worried he's still capable of doing it, which is why we need to find him.'

Marshall stepped closer to her.

Heather noticed him again, giving him her full attention.

Elliot held up her own microphone and punched in: 'But the good news is, we've unearthed some potential leads in the case.'

'This is DI Andrea Elliot of Police Scotland.' Heather looked at Elliot and smiled wide. 'The police have agreed to reopen Sharon's case.'

Marshall felt the stress hit like a pickaxe between the shoulder blades. He pushed between them and held out his hand for Elliot's mic, then waved at the reporters. 'Good afternoon, I'm DCI Rob Marshall.' He smiled for the cameras. 'Just wanted to add to Heather's moving speech there that Police Scotland acknowledge the evidence and agree the case will be reopened. There's some debate internally about whether it goes to our central Cold Case Unit or if it'll be allocated to the local Borders Major Investigation Team, which I lead. We will, of course, confirm which in due course, but I want to stress we have already devoted active resources to take over Heather's work.'

Heather nodded along with it. 'I insisted the police looked at Sharon's case again for the twenty-fifth anniversary and, wonder of wonders, some "lost" evidence was uncovered. No wonder they didn't stand a chance of catching the animal who did this to Sharon.' She gave a bitter shake of her head.

Marshall raised a hand. 'Evidence from under Sharon's fingernails was misfiled after the postmortem.'

'Misfiled...' Heather gave another shake, then stared at the BBC camera. 'But the killer should know one thing – the cops have his DNA, taken but never analysed. And DNA recovery techniques have got a *lot* better since then. Mark my words, this will provide an identity for the killer or, at the very least, a relative we could speak to. And I mean the police.' She stared down the STV camera lens. 'Someone should be feeling very nervous right now. The noose is closing on them.'

Marshall stepped in again. 'Does anyone have any questions?'

A BBC journalist Marshall knew raised his hand. 'When do you expect it to be announced whether it's the MIT or Cold Case?'

'I understand the decision is imminent.'

'How imminent?'

'Very imminent.' Marshall smiled. 'My understanding is senior officers are meeting this afternoon to agree the final decision, which will be communicated on Monday morning.'

That guy from Sky raised his hand next. 'Is there any truth in the rumours of the Borders MIT being folded into the Edinburgh one?'

Marshall gave him a polite smile, but the anger fizzed in his gut. 'I don't deal in rumours, only facts.'

The Sky guy nodded, though his eyes were tightening. 'But it's a fact you never found the body in that recent case down in Hawick, aye?'

'The fact is we were able to convict the killer, ensuring the safety of the local community.' Marshall gave a broad smile – this DCI role came with so much stupid bullshit on top of the actual job. 'And that's all we've got time for, folks.' He stood there, smiling for the cameras.

And it started raining.

4

Galashiels seemed to have withered since Duncan had last been here, like grape vines diminishing in a drought. All the shops seemed to have gone too. And it used to be full of people, now it was just cars – and traffic. Not the kind of busy he was used to back home in Canada but—

Huh.

Weird to think Canada was home now. Not here.

Felt like someone was sitting next to him on the passenger seat. He even had to check there was nobody there and that he was alone.

A train whizzed past on the right – when did they come back? Like the trams in Edinburgh. Still, the roads down from the airport had been a joke – single carriageway between Edinburgh and Newcastle? Like a second-world country...

Duncan set off from the roundabout and headed across the bridge, down towards some traffic lights. The pub on the corner used to be a wild one he'd gone in for a dare a few times, but was shut now – and looked like it'd be permanently closed. Opposite a new curry house that used to be a bank years ago.

God, he hadn't had a curry in *years* – not something Canada was good at.

The lights switched to green, but a bus still swung around from the right, almost clipping his rental car. He had to bump up onto the sidewalk.

That could've been nasty.

Duncan set off, heading out of Gala and towards Peebles – maybe that was still nice. Maybe it had a train too.

He took a sharp left up the hill, past the boxing gym in the old church he used to go to, then drove up past where they were refurbishing a decrepit block of flats.

Ah – he came to the shortcut through the town and realised he should've cut off by that church on the way in and avoided having to drive through the town.

Lesson learned for next time...

He took the right onto a back street and there it was on the left.

Butler House.

He pulled in between two giant gateposts and drove across the parking lot.

Perfect space, hidden under a canopy of trees.

Duncan sat there while the engine cooled, sucking in deep breaths. First time in twenty-five years...

He got out and it started raining. Great. He jogged over to the front door and stepped inside.

The place smelled like duty-free – a riot of perfumes and fragrances. A young nurse was behind the desk, working at a computer. Tiny little thing. Hair almost black. She looked up with a kind smile. 'How can I help, sir?' Weird accent, maybe Eastern European?

Duncan smiled at her. 'Here to see Patricia Radford.'

'I see.' The nurse looked at her machine. She was even younger than he thought. Even smaller and even more attractive.

Duncan smiled as he put his hands into his coat pockets and touched his gloves. The rough leather against his fingertips. 'Mind if I take your name?'

'Zuzana. Zuzana Svoboda.'

'Is that Czechoslovakian?'

'That's a good guess. But my country has not been called that for very long time. Was Czech Republic when I was born but is now Czechia.' Zuzana focused on Duncan. 'I'm afraid Patricia doesn't have any appointments booked.'

'I received a notice from the manager here? April Johnston?' Duncan looked over his shoulder but there was nobody there. He'd feared this but the reality was he was going to have to use his old name here... 'Listen, I've just flown in from Canada to see her.'

He hadn't been Colin since the name change and he wasn't sure how far along his mum was – or if she'd recognise him.

Better to be honest, but he needed to confine Colin to here at the care home.

Duncan leaned forward. 'I'm her son. Colin. Colin Radford.'

'Aha.' Zuzana smiled and it lit up the whole room. 'Patricia talks about you a lot.'

Duncan tried to smile but he was quaking inside. Everything seemed to shake and throb. 'All good, I hope?'

'She says you're the best son anyone could have.'

'Stretching things a bit.' Duncan coughed. 'Not proud of the fact I lost touch with her a few years ago. More to do with Dad than Mom, but it's what happens when people have to take sides. And she took his. Families, eh?'

'Is not easy.' Zuzana got to her feet. 'Do you want to see her?'

Duncan grinned. 'That'd be great.'

'This way, Mr Colin.' Zuzana led him along the corridor. She was so young and there was hardly any of her. He probably weighed three times what she did. At least.

He wanted to put the gloves on but fought the urge...

She opened a door and showed him through into the TV lounge.

Duncan's heart pounded in his chest as he stepped in.

Needn't have bothered – his mother wasn't there.

But an ancient woman was, her face lined and scored. Thinning grey hair. But those fierce eyes.

Jesus...

It was her.

And time had ravaged her.

'Archie!' She was in a wheelchair, almost tipping over as she reached over to grab something from an old man sitting on the sofa. 'Let me have it!'

'I want to watch my programme!' He held the remote control out of her reach. 'It's always on at this time!'

Somehow she managed to snatch it from him then bounced back. 'I'm watching the news, Archie, and that's the end of it!'

'Come on, guys.' Zuzana prised the TV control from Mom, her grip as weak as a newborn's, then passed it back to Archie. 'There you go.'

'Thank you, Susie.'

Mom punched her on the thigh. 'But I was watching that!'

'You've got a visitor.' Zuzana pointed at Duncan. 'Your son's here to see you.'

Mom barely looked at him. 'I used to have a son.'

'You still do, Patricia. Colin's here now.'

'Don't be so thick. Colin lives in Canada. He's such a nice wee laddie.' Patricia winked, then whispered, 'He's a stone-cold killer.'

Duncan swallowed hard – fuck.

This was worse than he feared.

Zuzana gave him the eye.

'I'm...' Duncan raised his hands. 'I'm not...'

'I know you're not.' Zuzana laughed, then leaned in close and raised her voice: 'Patricia, this is your son, Colin.'

Mom looked over at him now. Those fierce eyes. Not a shred of kindness, just hard biblical judgment. 'That's not my son!'

'It's me, Mom. I'm Colin.'

'Colin who?'

Duncan let out a deep breath. He could've stuck with Duncan – she was further gone than he'd expected. 'Colin Radford, Mom. Your son. Colin.'

'If you say so.' Patricia frowned at him. 'Why are you saying "Mom"?'

'Because I've lived in Canada, Mom.' He smiled at her. 'Mum.'

'That's better.'

Zuzana leaned away from her. 'Some moments, your mother's quite lucid, but others... Not so much...'

'That's not my son. It's John. John Radford. My husband.'

Duncan crouched in front of her. 'I'm Colin. Your son.'

'Colin!' She reached out with her arms.

Duncan cuddled her and it was like hugging a bag of bones.

She actually smelled like her, though.

He broke off and had to rub his eyes. 'How are you doing, Mum?'

'Well, aside from these bastards trying to kill me...'

'Come on, let's go to your room.' Zuzana grabbed the handles, then wheeled Mom through the house.

Her room was just behind the reception desk and seemed pretty nice. Bright enough and with a nice view across some gardens to a wall. Despite the rain, a gardener was mowing the lawn.

Hardly any stuff in the room, just a single bed and a wardrobe.

Zuzana switched on the TV in the corner but the reception was all fuzzy. Some things never changed.

'See? It's broken.' Mom pointed at the screen. 'And I'd much rather watch in here than sit next to Archie through there. He smells of smegma.'

Zuzana laughed. 'That's not very nice.'

'Exactly. He's awful. Can't believe you let him stay here without washing.'

Duncan went around the back of the TV and started fiddling around with the cables. It was all coaxials and SCARTs. Where were the HDMIs?

'He's as entitled to our care as you are, Mrs Radford.'

'Well, he smells like a fox died inside his pants.'

There we go. He plugged the box into the TV using the HDMI, then checked the screen.

Black. He pressed the input button on the remote and it went onto BBC1 in full HD. Or maybe not quite full, but it was crystal clear.

Zuzana's eyes went wide. 'You're a miracle worker.'

'Not really.' Duncan shrugged. 'I just plugged it into the correct input.'

'Well, you're a god in my eyes.' Zuzana smiled at him and her gaze lingered. 'It's tea time soon so it's best not to overstimulate her with a longer visit, so try and keep this to about ten minutes?' She patted his arm and gave another smile. 'I'll leave you to it.' She walked off out of the room, letting her hair hang free.

She was old enough to be his daughter.

Hell, there was that lassie in school who'd possibly have a granddaughter by now.

Lassie…

Duncan chuckled – maybe the old words weren't so deeply buried.

Mum sat there, one eye on the telly. 'You look just like my John.'

'I'm your son, Mum. Colin.'

'Are you?' Mum looked over at the TV.

A newsreader sat in a studio. '—police in the Scottish Borders have announced the reopening of the investigation into the twenty-five-year-old murder of Sharon Beattie at the local beauty spot known as Scott's View. Detective Chief Inspector Rob Marshall had this to say.'

'Police Scotland acknowledge the evidence and agree the case will be reopened.' A big guy stood out in the fierce wind, a fake smile plastered over his face. 'We have devoted active resources to take over Heather's work.'

A woman appeared next. Red-haired, fierce eyes. The caption read:

Heather McGill
Justice for Sharon Beattie! campaign

'It's important the police give us all closure on the murder of Sharon Beattie. This case has haunted us all for the last twenty-five years. But the killer should know one thing – the cops have his DNA, taken but never analysed. And DNA recovery techniques have got a lot better since then. Mark my words, this will provide an identity for the killer or, at the very least, a relative we could speak to.' She stared down the lens. 'Someone should be feeling very nervous right now.'

Duncan stood there, arms folded.

Fuck.

He'd no idea.

Such a jack ass – he'd walked right into a perfect storm.

Hard to believe it was twenty-five years ago – things had changed so much.

He'd changed so much.

And nothing had been done on that case. No wonder he'd been safe.

Fuck…

'I'll let you in on a wee secret.' Mum leaned in close. 'My Colin murdered a girl and I helped him get away with it. Poor wee bastard never stood a chance, except for me.'

Fuck.

A double whammy.

Not only were the police reinvestigating it, but Mum was leaking his secret to anyone who listened.

How her stone-cold killer son killed a girl and she helped him get away with it.

This was a mistake.

He should run away. Get the fuck out of this stupid backwards country. Head back to Canada. Ignore all of this.

But his mother was sitting there, smiling at him. All proud of her lad.

His mother… Her brain might be going but she was still her. Didn't he owe her everything?

Duncan smiled at her. 'That's not what happened, is it?'

'How would you know?'

'John sent Colin away because they didn't get on.'

'John didn't know Colin killed that girl.' Mom tapped her nose. 'That was our little secret.'

'I didn't know you were in here, Mum. I swear.'

'I miss John.'

'John died, Mum.'

'I want to die too. I want to go home and die in my own house.' She looked at him with fluttering eyelashes. 'Will you help me to die, son?'

5

Marshall stood in the rain, just getting wetter and wetter, as he watched Heather talking to the BBC reporter.

One thing was abundantly clear – she didn't care what she did. She just wanted to get her own results and bugger the consequences.

'Well, that went even worse than I feared.' Marshall looked over at Elliot. 'Ravenscroft is going to slice open my liver.' He checked his phone. 'Surprised he hasn't called me yet.'

'Probably just sharpening his knife.' Elliot ran a hand down his arm. 'Cheer up, Robbie. This is the worst that can happen and it's not that bad, is it?'

Marshall wanted to disagree. Strongly. 'Feels like you wanted this.'

'No way.' Elliot raised her hands. 'Feels like an accusation.'

'Might feel like one, but it's not one. It's simply a question.'

She wagged a finger at him. 'Nuh-uh-uh.'

The second-hand teenage sass annoyed the fuck out of him. 'I'm serious, Andrea. If you and Heather engineered this whole—'

'Of course we didn't.' Hand on hip, like that added any credence to the possibility of her telling the truth over this. 'And that's the honest truth.'

Marshall didn't believe her for a second. 'Well, then, that's all I needed to hear, but if—'

Elliot's phone rang.

She fished it out of her coat pocket, then checked the display. 'Really need to take this, Robbie. That okay?'

'Go for it.' Marshall nodded and watched her walk off.

'Sam, are you okay?' Her voice was soft and maternal. Always surprised him that she had a speed other than annoying as hell.

Marshall focused on Heather again and felt like someone was now hacking away at his shoulder blades with that pickaxe.

Aye – he was getting angrier about it all.

Still, the crowd were finally dispersing, leaving just a couple of TV journalists doing pieces to camera. A handful of influencer types talked to their phones, mounted on those gimbal things to keep them steady.

When did some random idiot sitting in their car outside Home Bargains become news?

Looked like Heather was finally wrapping up – she looked over at Marshall and made eye contact with him, but then kept on talking to the guy. Maybe not wrapping up, after all. Or just playing for time.

Marshall recognised the guy – Alexander Vickers. He'd recorded a podcast with a serial killer a few years ago. And got himself deep into the investigation. Deep enough to be really, really annoying.

Elliot came back, stabbing her finger off her phone and clenching her jaw tight. 'Well, my darling daughter was supposed to come home for the weekend and has just cancelled on me.'

'Sorry to hear that.'

'There's this thing happening on Saturday night I really wanted to go to and Sam was going to babysit her brothers... And my folks are away.' Elliot laughed as she sorted out her fringe, plastered to her face by the rain. 'Have to say, Robbie, *I* wouldn't come all the way back from Glasgow for *that*...'

Marshall was still watching Heather, still waiting for a chance to jump. 'What's the thing?'

'Speaking of Glasgow, how's Cal Taylor doing?'

'You mean at Gartcosh?' Marshall shrugged. 'Haven't heard from him.'

'His first week in a new job and you haven't checked in with him?'

'Texted him to give my best wishes and offer a chat, but you know Cal. Even with a shattered foot, he's still determined to be a cop.'

'He's working for the NCA, Robbie, that's not being a cop.' Elliot laughed, all loud and braying. 'Not a real one. Sitting in an office, feet up, looking at spreadsheets and messing up convictions.'

'Do I detect a note of derision there?'

'Dealt with the NCA a few too many times. I like Cal and I tried to warn him about them. He's a good cop. Or was. Until he let that boy shoot him in the foot.' Elliot winked at him. 'You've played a blinder in moving him on, though.'

'I didn't move anyone on.'

'You did, Robbie. Let you make Jolene full DI now. And you're still not full DCI yourself.' Elliot cracked her knuckles. 'Leaves the door open for me.'

Marshall looked over at her now. 'Are you sure you can step up?'

'What, because of my colourful home life?' Elliot gave him a hard stare, then broke off into a grin. 'I feel the lightest I've ever felt, Robbie. Didn't realise how much shit I was going through until I stopped going through it. Then I could sleep again.' She looked over. 'Hang on.' She hurried off towards Heather, but an older man blocked her path and started speaking to Heather.

Elliot stopped and waited, clearing her throat and fiddling with her fringe. 'Sodding hell.'

Marshall joined her. 'Not like you to not barge in.'

'Trying to be all Zen these days, Robbie. Show people some respect, you know?'

The man scowled at Heather, then stormed off, shaking his head.

Elliot didn't waste this opportunity and went straight for her.

Marshall took it a bit more calmly, keeping a decent distance.

Elliot was in her face. 'Who was that?'

'He's just someone from the community who helped me out.' Heather clicked her fingers. 'Can't remember his name.'

Elliot gave a flash of her eyebrows. 'He seemed pretty annoyed with you.'

'Problem with something like my campaign is everyone feels like they own a piece of it, so they all want to be the one calling the shots.'

'And which shots does he wish he was calling? Which pieces does he think he owns?'

'All of it.' Heather clenched her jaw. 'And he feels like I'm jumping the gun.'

Elliot glanced at Marshall. 'He's not the only one.'

'I'm pissed off at how *slowly* this is going.' Heather shifted her gaze between them. 'This anniversary only comes around once. Of course I had to force things! That's how it works in social media – you get the spotlight and you keep it on you. And you don't let go. And you keep on pushing.'

'I understand all that.' Marshall stepped between them. 'But this press conference wasn't the right way to progress things. It's just as well DI Elliot was nearby as I was in Edinburgh attending a meeting.'

Heather rolled her eyes at him. 'This again...'

'We have a process, Heather, which is much more likely to get answers to what happened than—'

'—actually doing something?'

'Look.' Marshall fixed her with a tough look. 'Arranging a guerrilla press conference like this is forcing matters. It means things can get rushed.'

'I don't believe this...' Heather looked up to the skies and laughed. 'You're going to pin someone on me, aren't you?'

'No, Heather. I'm just being clear.'

'Are you saying you lost the evidence back in the day because things were rushed?'

'I'm saying we don't want to repeat that.'

'Listen to me, Rob. I have over fifty thousand followers on social media.' Heather prodded herself in the chest. '*I* got you the DNA lead, not you lot.'

Marshall tried to keep calm as he wiped the bead of her spit from his chin. 'That's patently not true. It was our officers re-examining the old files who found the missing evidence.'

'Because we had copies of the crime scene reports, so we could point out the bits of evidence you'd—' Heather made rabbit ears. '—"mislaid".'

'And you shouldn't have them.'

'Maybe not, but there are plenty of ex-coppers in my legion of supporters who want justice for Sharon. The fingernail clippings were in the report, but somehow they got lost after the postmortem, because somebody was hiding things.'

'Nobody hid anything. They were all in a big box, with all the tiny evidence in hanging files. Whoever put that item in there missed the hanging file, so the bag slid down into the bottom of the box. It was still sealed and still intact. Sure, nobody looked for it and nobody remembered it was there, but it didn't come from you or your followers, it came from the forensics services scientists in Gartcosh.'

Heather looked away from Marshall, chewing her cheek. 'Should be investigating whoever was in charge on that case.'

'The officer responsible is long dead.' A sigh escaped Marshall's lips. 'Not a bad guy, by all accounts, just over-stretched.'

'So you're *defending* him?'

'They didn't have the resources we do today. Got to remember, Heather, this wasn't Police Scotland. And it's before forensic services were centralised too. There were no Major Investigation Teams in Lothian and Borders and there were only a handful of detectives down here. None of them were murder specialists. That case just had Edinburgh detectives moaning about driving up and down the A68 every day. Nowadays, my team would lead it.'

'That sounds like a lot of words to agree with me and say he was inept.'

'That year, there was a spate of murders across the territory. It's no excuse, but it's certainly an explanation.' Marshall held up his hands. 'But I get it, Heather. You carry a tremendous amount of guilt over what happened.'

'Don't you fucking dare suggest this is my fault.'

'I'm not. But that was a long time ago and I bet it's played on your mind since you found her body.'

She looked away, snorting.

'But you don't need to push things so hard, okay?'

'I'm not.'

'I mean it. If this is to work, we need to be on the same page over this. Okay? Let it take its time.'

Heather laughed. 'I can do this myself.'

'Okay, you might *think* that but, as far as I'm aware, for all your social media followers you can't afford to process the evidence in a private lab, can you?' Marshall narrowed his eyes. 'And nobody else has come forward, have they?'

Heather bit her nails, then focused on Elliot. 'Andrea, are you coming to the anniversary thing on Saturday night?'

And now Marshall knew what Elliot was up to...

But letting this all play out was the smartest move – that way he'd learn how deep Elliot was in on this.

Elliot was frowning as she tugged at her fringe. 'Remind me what that is?'

'Jesus Christ. It's twenty-five years since it happened, Andi, so we're going to celebrate the case being reopened.' Heather glanced around. 'We can use it to talk to people we haven't seen in years and see what they can remember after a few glasses of truth serum.'

'I'll see what I can do, but I've got three kids and I'm on my own.'

Heather glowered at Marshall. 'So Police Scotland won't help us?'

'I wouldn't be there in an official capacity, anyway.'

Heather looked back to Marshall. 'See? You don't care about it.'

'Look, you can't push people into—'

'I'm just planning on asking questions. People might be there who hadn't heard of Sharon until this.' Heather pointed at the few remaining reporters. 'I might not be able to afford a private lab, but I can certainly afford to have a celebration of her life and see what shakes out.'

Marshall didn't know what to do.

She was beyond obsessed. Beyond guilty. And worst – she was avoiding seeking help in the right way and instead was determined to funnel her energies into this campaign, and all just to assuage her feelings of guilt over what happened.

Which wasn't her fault.

Hard not to feel sympathy, but still...

'Are you doing all that for her...' Marshall narrowed his gaze. 'Or for you?'

Heather's mouth hung open in an O. 'I can't believe you're asking me that!'

'It's a straightforward question.'

'You think I'm some traumatised weirdo, don't you?'

'I think you enjoy the attention.'

'Wouldn't you be traumatised by something like that?'

Marshall felt that deep stabbing in his guts. She didn't know about his past, so he let it ride. 'Is there anything else you're hiding from us?'

'Eh?'

'Well, this news conference was sprung on us. Now you're talking about this celebration. What else is there, Heather?'

'There's nothing else.'

'That's the full truth?'

'Completely.'

'Because if someone does come forward, it'd be a police matter. It'd be obstruction to withhold their information from us. Even if you're the only one they trust.'

'I know that.' Heather sighed. 'Look, I get messages all the time from creeps at, like, three in the morning. Drunk or high or whatever.'

'Has anyone got in touch over this?'

'No.' She held out her mobile. 'But I've just been on nationwide TV so my phone's melting down with the number of people who are contacting me through Facebook after that. Haven't checked my messages yet, but I suspect it'll be the usual cranks, perverts and nutters. You wouldn't believe the number of penises I get sent to me.'

'I would, actually.' Marshall held her stare. 'But you need to make sure you pass on any leads to me or Andrea, Heather.'

'Of course.'

'I mean it.'

6

Duncan knocked on the care home manager's office door.

The door opened and a woman appeared. Mid-sixties, silver hair, dressed professionally in a pant suit. Beatific smile. 'April Johnston, hi.' She shook his hand, soft and gentle. 'Mr Radford, thank you for your patience.'

'It's not a problem at all, ma'am.'

'Well, I don't like to keep people waiting. In you come.'

'Sure. Sure.' Duncan followed her into the room.

Two chairs in front of the desk. He took the left one, but it felt like there was someone next to him. Someone who'd talk to him and tell him all the shit he was doing wrong.

How they were going to catch him and bring him to justice.

How he should run back to Canada.

But the seat was empty.

'Have to say, I love your accent.' April perched behind her desk, her posture erect. 'We don't get many Americans here.'

'That because you can't distinguish Canadian from American?'

April raised her hands, palms facing out the way. 'Oh heavens, I'm sorry.'

'Oh God, I was joking. Not many people can tell them apart without living there.' Duncan laughed. 'The apologies are all mine for this bastardised accent.' He winked at her. 'The Canadian bits will soon wash out.'

'Oh, so you're planning on staying?'

'I got a one-way ticket here and I can stay up to six months without a visa. I'll be here as long as Mom needs me.' He coughed. 'I mean, *Mum*.'

April smiled at the correction. 'That'd be great for Patricia, but you have to prepare yourself for the reality she may not last six months.'

'Oh. I hadn't thought of that.'

April sat back and fussed with her hair. 'When did you move away?'

'A while ago. Early 2000s. Had a career opportunity over there. Didn't look back, really.'

'That's a long time. Before your father died.'

'That's correct. Didn't see eye to eye with him. Didn't even know he'd died, to be honest. Always meant to return, but... Well, that's why I need to do this now.' Duncan leaned in close, trying to ignore the feeling someone was sitting next to him and judging every word. 'Listen, when you called me, I honestly didn't know how bad Mum had got. You said on the phone how she's failing? Have I come back to Scotland to say goodbye to her?'

'I'm afraid the outlook isn't positive. She can no longer walk and has trouble with her hands as well. It means she needs to be fed and changed by my staff. And that's not even the worst part – her heart is weak.'

'How weak are we talking here?'

April nibbled at her bottom lip. 'Put it this way – we've had to bring her back twice already.'

'Oh, Jesus.' Duncan pinched his nose. 'Didn't she have a DNR?'

'No. That's the thing. We need her family to sign one to avoid lifesaving measures. If that's her wish.'

'It is.' Duncan nodded again, but his throat was thick. 'I saw how bad she's got.' He grunted away the thickness. 'She doesn't seem to be all there. And the things she's coming out with... Is that normal?'

'You mean, in my expert opinion?' April sighed. 'Well, your mother's not quite the worst of our residents, but you saw the condition she's in, right?'

'I did.'

'By this stage, half our residents think they're spies or royalty or something else equally whacky... We help them refocus them on the here and now.'

'Are you saying it's Alzheimer's?'

'Most likely. There still isn't a single test to determine it. Some of the scans and procedures are extremely upsetting to the client, so our policy is...' She sat back and shook out her hair. 'Why put them through all that just to slap a label on it? The care's the same.'

Duncan could see the logic in that, though it seemed pretty open and shut. 'How bad is it?'

'It's far enough along to be causing issues here. About sixty percent of our residents have some form of dementia, in various stages. In your mother's case, her heart condition is far more likely to be her end, I'm afraid.' She gave him another flash of that beatific smile, like she was some angel of mercy. 'Your father was a resident here.'

'I... I didn't know.' Duncan looked away. 'We had a difficult relationship.'

'I see. He was a challenging individual, I hope you don't mind me saying. Your mother, on the other hand, is a saint. She was in here every day to see him.' April sighed. 'And now she's the patient. Everyone here loves her. Despite the occasional outburst, she's as good as gold. And those are down to the condition.'

'How long has she been here?'

'She was in BGH after her first heart incident and she said she wanted to come here. Said it would be nice to be in the place where your father got such good care.'

Sounded like PR bullshit rather than his mother's words.

All the same, Duncan smiled. 'Thing is, I honestly didn't realise she'd got this bad, otherwise I would've come over earlier. Much, much earlier. So this is my fault. I should've checked up on her. I feel so *guilty*.' He swallowed down the lump in his throat. 'But thank you for calling me and letting me know what's happened.'

'We had tried a few times. She kept going on about her son and Zuzana found a name in her address book.'

'I appreciate it.' Duncan splayed his hands on his lap. 'Thing is, Ms Johnston, I—'

'Please. April.'

'Nice name. I wonder if it'd be possible to look after her at home.'

'Well.' April sat back and thought about it for a few long seconds. 'Your mother came here of her own volition, helped by Dr Japp.'

'Not... Not Dr Alan Japp?'

April nodded. 'He's still her GP.'

'Wow. He must be ready to be a patient here himself...'

'He's not quite that old!' April laughed. 'But what I'm saying is it's in Patricia's gift to decide whether she stays here or not. Do you honestly plan on caring for your mother at home?'

'Certainly plan to.' Duncan shifted on his seat. 'The house is just sitting vacant, after all.'

'Your father died in 2015, right? And he'd been in here for a few years, hadn't he, so Patricia would've been there on her own for a number of years.'

'Is that a problem?'

'No. Not at all. Just thinking out loud. I suppose it'll be familiar to her, but I wonder about the effect caring for her everyday needs will have on you, Colin.'

'It's what she wants. She told me. And I feel like I have to honour her wishes.' Duncan laughed, but it faded. 'I'm serious – I feel bad for drifting. I want to make up for lost time. I want to stay here and help her.' He hung his head. 'And I have to say I'm a bit embarrassed by what she's been saying.'

'Some of the things don't bear repeating. And I've heard some wild ones over the years I've worked here. But they all get a bit paranoid, even those still with all their faculties. We're not supposed to play along with their paranoia but we tend to deflect it and let them get it out of their systems.' April consulted her notes again. 'Thing is, your mother keeps threatening people with death. Saying her son will kill them. "Wouldn't know it looking at him, such a sweet boy, but he definitely has the devil in him".' She shook her head. 'I don't know where half the stuff comes from.'

'I can assure you it doesn't come from me!' Duncan gave her a kind smile. 'I won't be murdering anyone.' He paused to let her react. But she just stared into space. 'Is there anything that can be done about it?'

April frowned. 'What do you mean?'

'Medication. Anything to help with the outbursts?'

'The sad fact is, she's been getting worse. More agitated and she spends much of her day crying... the hydromorphone helps at a therapeutic level but Dr Japp has concerns over raising the dosage.'

'She's on morphine?'

'No. Hydromorphone. It's even stronger.'

'Bloody hell. What kinds of concerns does he have?'

'That it'll negatively impact her respiratory function. Coupled with her heart ailments, it might hasten her end.'

Duncan saw a solution start to form...

April gave him a smile. 'Dr Japp is coming in first thing in the morning to review her situation.'

'Is that routine?'

'I'm afraid not. We needed to heavily sedate her the other day and, if it doesn't improve, we will put her in the... section for violent residents.'

'You have a segregation unit here?'

'That's a bit harsh, but I suppose the idea's the same. Unfortunately, your mother requires a robust care plan to curb these... issues.'

Duncan nodded slowly. 'Thing is, I had a chat with her and Mum was adamant she wanted to live at home.' He gave a bitter laugh. 'Or, in her words, die at home.'

'It's a common request.' April looked out of the window, dotted with raindrops, across the parking lot. 'A lot of them want out of here. They seek the familiar. Your family home was hers for a number of years.' She checked her notes. 'Are you *sure* that's an option?'

'Was never sold. From what I gather, a neighbour looks in every so often.'

'And you know what's involved in caring for someone in your mother's condition?'

Duncan nodded again. 'I do.'

'You've done it before?'

'Not personally. Had buddies back in Canada who went through it. Helped them out a few times. It ain't easy, but Mum gave me the first twenty years of my life. So I want to be there for her last few.'

'That's very noble of you, Colin, but it'll be a lot of work.'

'Hard graft hasn't been something I've shied away from in

my life. Moving to Canada was a big thing. Thriving there was tougher.'

'Well, let's see what Dr Japp thinks tomorrow, then we can explore this further.'

'Thank you.' Duncan got up. 'Listen, do you mind if I'm here for the appointment?'

'Of course not. In fact, it'd be a great help.'

'Thank you.' Duncan shook her hand again, then left her office and walked off through the care home.

He stopped by the TV lounge.

His mother was on her own, happily watching the news like she always did. She looked over at him but didn't seem to recognise him and went back to her show.

Duncan sighed and walked off.

Aye, he wasn't in control of this situation.

The tiny receptionist wasn't there anymore, so he didn't even sign out and just stepped outside into the cooler air.

He didn't know if he was doing the right thing here.

He walked over to the rental car.

John Radford stood there, dressed in a funeral suit. 'We had a difficult relationship, did we?'

As he approached, Duncan could see bits of his face were rotten. His hair and nails were long. Mud covered him and dusted his clothes. And he was almost transparent. 'You know we did.'

'You need to buck up your ideas, son. This visit started off as one of mercy. See your mother, say goodbye and bugger off back to Canada.' Dad leaned in close and grabbed his lapels. 'Her little slips are going to give the game away, aren't they?'

'She doesn't know what she's doing...'

'That's understating it a bit.'

'Dad, she loves me – the whole reason she stuck me on a plane back then was to save me.' Duncan sat behind the wheel and put the key in the ignition.

'Think about that press conference, son...' Dad was sitting on the passenger seat, popping a cigarette out of a packet. 'That lassie's threats about the DNA...'

Duncan swallowed hard. 'I'm not giving mine up.'

'No and that's wise. But your mother... When she dies, they'll take it... Won't they?'

'Fuck.'

'You should get on a plane now, son. Do they still fly direct to Toronto from Edinburgh? Like that time we went to visit your Auntie Margaret. Or when your mother put you on that plane after you killed that hoor? You should do that again, Colin. Or go to New York or Chicago. Get you close enough to home, but a fuck of a long way from here.'

'I know, I know... It's just...' Duncan looked over at the care home. The wind rocked the trees and blew a branch off. 'I need to make sure Mum's quiet.'

'You mean kill your mother.'

'No. Just that she stops blabbing about what happened.'

'Why?'

'Canada has an extradition treaty with here, right?'

'Guess so. Both part of the Commonwealth. Same king.'

'Exactly.' Duncan sat back and thought it through. 'Maybe I do need to kill her.'

'It's not much of a life in there, is it? It'll be easy, son. Very easy.' Dad sucked at his cigarette – Duncan could smell the smoke. 'And much, much easier than silencing that Heather lassie, eh?'

'You don't think I—'

'You need to, son.' Dad exhaled slowly. 'Kill her, then get the fuck out of Dodge.'

'Fuck.' Duncan reached into his pocket for his phone and powered it on. He popped the second SIM card into the slot, then waited while the phone attached to the network.

No.

He killed the mobile data, then started up the VPN app and selected a location in Vietnam.

The phone thought about it for a bit, then said he was secure.

He connected it to the care home's wi-fi using the card Zuzana had given him.

Good. He was under control again.

He opened up the browser and went to Facebook, then entered his bogus email address and password from memory.

Jim Smith.

He found the campaign page:

Justice for Sharon Beattie!

A blurry photo of a young woman with a Rachel haircut.

Thousands of followers. The most recent post was a link to an item posted on the BBC News site just that afternoon. It was gaining traction…

Duncan tapped on the message icon, then started typing:

> I have some information relating to the murder of Sharon Beattie. I was there that night. I feel bad about not coming forward until now, but I've been out of the country. Let me know if you'd like to meet up. Best, Jim

He sat there, reading. And re-reading.

Then he hit send.

7

Marshall sat in his car, drumming the steering wheel as he waited.

The view from Clovenfords... You'd never get bored of that. Looking across the start of what they called the Tweed Valley, despite the river having another fifty or so miles to run to Berwick and the sea – including weaving past Scott's View...

Muscular hills spread out either side – the nearest was getting the slowest haircut as they removed the forest, tree by tree, leaving a pale skinhead.

Everything Everything played over the stereo and he could almost make out the words, but they didn't make any sense to him. He looked at his phone. The track was called "No Reptiles", but that didn't explain what he was singing. Still, it took a lot to get Marshall's thumbs moving and *holy shit* that was a chord change. Gooseflesh ran up his arms.

A text popped up from Elliot:

> Sorry Robbie I should of told you about the thing on Saturday Andi x

Marshall didn't know which he was more annoyed about – the 'should of' or the complete lack of punctuation or the fact she didn't tell him...

He sent a reply:

Let's discuss tomorrow. Have a good evening.

Clipped but friendly enough.

He sat back and listened to the tune. Aye, they were good.

Someone rapped on the window.

Jen was peering into his car.

Marshall killed the music, then got out into the sunshine. 'Didn't see you there.'

'Nope, but I saw you.' A cheeky flash of her eyebrows. 'On the telly.'

'Oh. That. Not my finest hour. And they say the TV adds twenty pounds or whatever. I've already got a head start on that.'

'Nonsense.' She held her arms out wide. 'C'mere.'

Marshall hugged her. 'How are you doing?'

'Usual. Thea's still difficult, but at least she's not at home.'

'Eh?' Marshall frowned. 'Thought she came back from uni?'

'Aye, she did, but now she's off to Camp America for two months.'

'What's that?'

'Didn't you have it at Durham? You go to these summer camps in the States. Means you've got a good job for the summer where you earn a decent amount of cash but you get to see the country for a bit afterwards. She's already talking about doing her third year over there.'

'Wow.'

'I mean...' Jen shrugged. 'Trying to just let her be.'

'Good idea.'

'So, where is she?'

'It's a place a few hours from Chicago, which apparently is really close. Her father's heading out to see this Club World Cup thing with a couple of mates and his new floozy, so he's going to drop by.'

'You're on good terms with him then?'

'She is. I'm not.' Jen gave him a broad smile. 'So, let's see this place, then.'

'Okay…' Marshall took a deep breath as he led her down the drive to a Seventies house. Another deep breath as he pressed the bell and it chimed inside.

Sort of sunk down from the road but probably just so people on the other side of the street got the view over the house.

Marshall wasn't sure about having someone looking over his house…

His house…

Hadn't even stepped inside and he was already taking ownership of the place…

Jen finished her external survey of the front garden. 'South-facing garden.'

Marshall looked over at her. 'That's a good thing?'

'It's where the sun goes, Rob.' She traced its arc through the sky from east to west, where it currently was – hovering over the hills on the Tweed Valley he couldn't name but had walked up. 'Jesus, Rob, how long have you been doing this?'

The door opened and an old woman looked out at them, silvery streaks in otherwise dark hair. 'Oh, you must be Mr and Mrs Marshall. How lovely.' She opened the door wide and stepped back. 'Come on in.'

Marshall followed Jen inside. 'We're not—'

'Do you have children?'

Jen smiled at her. 'I've got a daughter.'

'Oh.' The owner gave a stern look of harsh judgment. 'I see.'

'I'm his sister. I live in the village. I'm helping Rob find a place for himself.'

'Ah.' And now she smiled at them. 'Well, I want this to be a family home like we had. We raised three boys here. But my husband's no longer with us and, I have to say, I'm nowhere near ready to join him so I want to enjoy what's left of my life.' She patted Marshall on the arm. 'I'll let you have a look around yourself.'

MARSHALL HELD the door and tried to visualise it being *his* door. Maybe it could be. He smiled at the owner. 'Thanks for your time, Mrs Hegarty. My solicitor will be in touch either way.'

'I'll await that. Have a lovely evening.' She shut the door behind them.

Marshall walked up the drive after Jen. 'Thanks for giving me a second opinion.' He glanced back at the house as they walked towards his car. 'What did you think?'

'I'd ask if you fancied a drink in the pub, but it's still shut.' Jen grimaced. 'Besides, we've got that thing tonight so we'd better make a move.'

'Good point.' Marshall got in the car, then started driving them back to Jen's, even though he could see it from here. 'Not sure I'd like being so close to you, mind.'

'Well, you're in the flat above my garage just now so it's further away.'

Marshall put the car in gear. 'True.'

'But to answer your question, Rob, I thought it was nice. Needs a ton of work but you've probably got the money.'

'I do.' Marshall drove off. 'Or I probably do. Depends how much it goes for.'

'But do you want to live on an estate like this?'

'What's wrong with it?'

'Nothing. It's nice. But you just strike me as a "cottage in the wilderness" kind of guy.'

'I'm not that bad, am I? I lived in London for a decade.'

'Suppose.' Jen looked over at him. 'What do *you* think, Rob? After all, you're the one who's got to live there.'

Marshall stopped at the roundabout – a heavy flow of traffic from Peebles stopped him from scooting across. And the truth was, he hadn't processed the house... 'I think I liked it. Big rooms, in the main. I'd knock two of the smaller bedrooms together to give a better master one on the darker side of the house. And a big en suite bathroom.' He gave a mock shiver. 'But Jesus Christ – that fireplace.'

Jen laughed. 'Didn't it remind you of Grumpy's old one?'

'A bit.' Marshall pulled off and crossed over the roundabout, then took the first left. 'I do appreciate you coming with me to look at it.'

'Quickest way to get you out of my house, Rob.'

Marshall laughed. 'You're the one who wanted me to stay there.'

'True.' Jen looked over. 'You ever hear from Kirsten?'

'No. Why?'

'Nothing.'

Marshall frowned at her. 'What's happened?'

'Nothing, Rob. I was asking if you'd heard from her recently. What with you still working together but not being an item.'

'Well, we don't work together, really. And she even moved her team up to Howdenhall, away from the Gala nick, so I don't see her very often. And I never hear from her.'

'Getting dumped by you will do that.'

'I broke up with her, sure, but the relationship had run its course. It'd been dead for a long time.' Marshall pulled up outside Jen's house. 'It just took me a while to realise that.'

His phone rang through the stereo.

Ravenscroft calling...

'He's finally got around to calling me, eh?' Marshall sighed. 'I better take this.'

'See you inside.' Jen got out and walked over to the door, but was nosy enough to look back at him.

Marshall leaned back in his seat. 'Evening, sir.'

'Robert, I'm really not happy about that shit show tonight.'

'I'm the same, sir, but I'm—'

'Miranda's seething.'

'I'm sure she is. But the truth is, Heather hid this from me.'

'Did she.' Ravenscroft sighed and it sounded like a rainstorm. 'I gather Heather's friends with DI Elliot, right?'

'Went to school together, aye. Apparently, Andrea would've been there that night, but she was unwell.'

'I see. I don't need to stress that this is the sort of thing that makes Police Scotland look bad.'

'The good thing is it was Lothian and Borders back then, sir. They didn't have an MIT down here.'

'Is that a dig at me?'

'No, sir. Just a statement of fact.' Marshall shook his hand in the universal gesture for wanker. 'I'd like to assign surveillance to her.'

'To Heather?'

'She's made herself a public figure over this. If the killer is—'

'That's not going to happen.'

'But she's putting herself in the spotlight.'

'Robert, I don't have the bodies. Besides, the optics of the police following a private citizen who most recently embarrassed us? Not good. Not good in the slightest. We'd need her permission and, from what you've said, it wouldn't be forthcoming.'

'I know, but...' Marshall sighed. 'Okay, sir. I take your point.'

'Have a good evening, Robert. Let's pick up tomorrow.'

'Look forward to it, sir.' Marshall ended the call then sat there, making a dickhead sign now.

Marshall knew he really should grow up, but that guy...

He got out of the car and headed inside, shaking his head.

Jen was in the kitchen, filling the teapot from that stupid hot tap thing she'd got installed. 'That call go okay?'

'Worse than I feared.'

'Oh.'

'I hate working for total bloody—'

Marshall's phone again.

'Bloody hell.'

Heather McGill calling...

'I need to take this one.' He went into the living room and answered it. 'Hi, Heather. You okay?'

'Rob, you got a minute?'

'Sure.' Marshall sat on the leather sofa. 'Are you okay?'

'I'm fine. Just calling to say I've been through the messages and, like I thought, most of them were wasters. Either time wasters or just wasters. But only six cocks.' Heather laughed down the line. 'And one of them was actually flaccid.'

'I'm sorry to hear that.'

'Hate it too. Cost of doing business, Rob.'

'Shouldn't have to accept that kind of thing.'

'If it means I have to put up with that to get a result, I'd do it a hundred times over.'

'That mean you've got something?'

'Maybe.' Heather paused for a few seconds – seconds that felt like hours. 'I've got one from a guy who says he was there that night.'

'Okay.' Marshall sat forward on the sofa, clutching the phone tight in his hand. 'Did he say anything else?'

'He's asking to meet up.'

'And are you going to?'

A long pause. 'I'm trying to suss him out.'

'Okay, that's a good idea. Heather, you know that I need to be there, right? Me or Andrea. But one of us definitely does. Okay?'

'Of course. I'll pass the details on to you once I set it up.'

'Let me know the very second you hear. Okay?'

'I'll text when I've got a time and place.'

'Heather, you need to call me too, okay?'

'Right. Sure.'

'I'm concerned about your safety, Heather. You've got to be very careful.'

'And I am. I have been.'

'This is a different thing. When you go on TV, the reach increases dramatically. That means more non-consensual nudes. But it also means more potential threat.'

'I can handle myself.'

Marshall sighed – everyone thought they were invincible, didn't they? Until they proved they weren't... 'We should talk about surveillance again.'

'No fucking way.'

'I'm serious, Heather. We could—'

'I'm not having some cops sitting outside my house, watching me have a shower and going through my bins.'

'Heather, I mean it.' Marshall stayed sitting on the sofa. The leather was warm now. 'We need to protect you.'

'Jesus Christ.' Her sigh was full of exasperation. 'I hear you, Rob. I do. But no.'

'Just don't do anything stupid, okay?'

'Of course I won't.'

'Call me when you know more.'

'Will do.' And she hung up.

Marshall didn't feel right about it, but he put his phone

back in his pocket. He got to his feet and looked at himself in the mirror – he looked shattered. And that angry spot on his chin was so damn sexy...

Jen came through with a mug of tea for him. 'Have this, then we need to get changed for the gig.'

8

Heather parked at Scott's View and scanned around – no other cars there, but it was a miserable wet summer evening, so no bloody wonder.

She looked across the river valley to the hills, soaked in rain and hidden behind thick mist. It all felt so different to twenty-five years ago – and she didn't. Like no time had passed since that birthday…

Didn't even celebrate it two days ago. Forty-three… How had *that* happened? Where had the time gone?

A few years ago, she'd changed the date on Facebook to the same day in May and then kept nudging it back so it never appeared in anyone's feeds – it was now in January.

Heather wasn't one of those people who wished people a happy birthday. Not that she didn't love her friends and wish them well – she didn't want to be reminded of what'd happened on hers all those years ago.

She got out her phone while she waited and went through her messages.

HEATHER:

How do I know this is legit?

JIM SMITH:

I was there. Heard you all singing along to that Alice Cooper song. It has to be tonight.

Why tonight?

Don't want to be a dick about it but I'm only here today. Heading back to Orkney in the morning.

Okay. Tonight it is.

She hated lying to Marshall, but she really didn't trust the police. Those pricks lost that evidence – her killer would've been caught if it wasn't for their incompetence.

A car pulled up at the other end, parking across two spaces so it pointed right towards her. A man behind the wheel, hard to make out.

He flashed the lights, the heavy raindrops catching in the beam.

Here we go...

Heather opened the door but didn't get out, just let the rain thunder down on the tarmac.

Maybe she should call Marshall...

She'd been through this so many times in her head – if Jim Smith got spooked, he might never talk.

Was he the sort to run?

Heather squinted as she focused on him and tried to make that assessment.

An older gent. Looked harmless. Seemed 'normal' compared to the weirdos. Those freaks seeing her on telly and thinking that sending photos of their ding-dongs was the natural thing to do.

None of them were exactly pretty penises and a few of them

looked like they needed medical treatment – all of them needed psychiatric help.

Sod it. She sat back and sent a text:

> Rob, I'm meeting him tonight. Seems harmless. H x

She sent it then gritted her teeth and got out of the car. She left the engine running and the door open.

Jim Smith got out of his too. Mid-fifties. Not that tall. Not that big. Not that anything. Just a bloke. Even limped as he walked over to her. 'Heather?'

'Depends on who you are.'

He smiled at that and he actually had a lovely smile. 'Jim Smith.'

'So how do I know it's you, though?'

Smith kept his distance, respectfully. 'Like I said in the messages, Heather, I've got some information you might like to know.'

Weird accent. Maybe it *was* Orcadian, but she wouldn't know. Sounded a bit American.

Orcadian – that's what they called people from there, right? She'd been there a couple of times for work and the accent was weird. Or was that Shetland?

'Go on, then.' She stayed right by her car. 'What's the information?'

He walked a bit closer but stopped a respectful distance away, then ran a hand across his chin. 'I was there that night.'

'So you said. Doesn't mean you were.'

'True. I was in one of the cars.' Smith pointed at her space. 'The camper van was right there, wasn't it?' He waved around the panorama. 'The view here's still gorgeous, isn't it? Probably hasn't changed that much since Walter Scott's days. Not like you can see the A68, is it? Can sure hear it, though.'

Heather really didn't feel right about this. She grabbed the doorframe of her car – she should just get in. Lock it. Drive off. Didn't even need to put her seatbelt on, like fucking Georgina that night. 'There weren't any other cars around that night.'

'There were.'

'One drove off.' Heather scowled at him. 'You weren't here, were you?'

'I was.' He pointed behind him, over the far side. The opposite from where the camper van had been, behind where he was parked tonight. 'We were over there.'

'We?'

'I was here, Heather.'

'I didn't see you.'

'I know that. But I saw you. You and your pals. Two cars. And you were drinking, weren't you?'

'How do you know it was me?'

'You're pretty distinctive, Heather. Red hair like that.' He pointed at her head, then looked over to where the van had been. 'You know, I'd ask you why you care about Sharon, but it's because you blame yourself, isn't it? I saw you rocking the van.'

Heather avoided eye contact with him – the shame and guilt were like constant companions, total bastards who whispered in her ears. Sometimes they shouted at her – reminding her of what she'd done.

'It's true, though. I mean, repenting your sins is no bad thing, Heather. Quite the opposite, really. It's noble.'

'You said we. Who were you with?'

'Me and my girlfriend at the time. We'd come here to just sit and chat, especially in the summer. Here or the William Wallace statue just down the road. Both have incredible views.' He swallowed then sniffed. 'Haven't been here in a while – it really is breathtaking, isn't it?'

'You were just sitting there?'

'We weren't having sex, if that's what you mean.'

'Sure.' Heather gave a flash of her eyebrows. 'That's a weird accent, you've got.'

'I live in Orkney.'

'Long way from here.'

'Lived in Edinburgh for a while. My girlfriend lived down here. In Galashiels. I moved to Canada a few years ago. But now I'm back and living in Orkney.'

She felt it was true, but the best lies had an element of the truth to them, didn't they? 'Thank you for messaging. Takes a lot.'

'It really does.' His breath misted in the heavy rain. 'Truth is, Heather, I didn't think much about that night for years until I saw your thing on the BBC today. Guess that's what you wanted, right? To remind someone like me?'

'I suppose so. Thing is, I get a lot of random weirdos sending me stuff at all hours.'

'What kind of thing?'

He's another one...

'Dick pics. Wind-ups.'

'Honestly?'

'Honestly. And I get way more than my share of time-wasters, too.'

He scowled at her. 'Why do people do that?'

'Think about it. When we found her body twenty-five years ago, it was all over the papers and the telly. But the news fades. And now I've managed to explode it out so it's a huge news story again. It's on the national news. UK-wide. And the police have opened the case again and so they're all covering it. STV, BBC, Sky News, they were all here.' She swallowed. 'So for the weirdos, it's a chance to get attention. Apparently, in all big police investigations you get people phoning in to confess to doing it.'

He shook his head. 'People are weird.'

'A lot of people wouldn't message, you know? They'd just sit with it. But you came forward. A bit late, but maybe you hadn't seen anything until now. Hadn't even thought about it, like you said.' Heather licked her lips. 'Why did you message me?'

'Because it felt like the right thing to do.'

'A lot of people wouldn't.'

'Like I said, it hadn't crossed my mind until I saw your piece. That was the first time I'd even heard a woman was killed here.'

'Even though you were here that night?'

'Even so. Been very, very busy since.' He scratched his neck. 'My job was insane back then too.' He laughed. 'Girlfriend was worse. Thing is, she had a boyfriend and she was cheating on him with me.'

Heather nodded – this felt like the actual truth. 'So. You said you had some information?'

'Right. The BBC said only two people saw the killer. Yourself, Heather, obviously. And a friend. Gary, is it?'

'That's right.'

'Well, there's now me. I can describe what he looked like.'

'You mean, you saw him running away?'

'No. Not just that. I saw him going into the camper van with Sharon.'

'What?'

'We'd been here a while. I got a good look at him.' He left a long pause, pregnant with hope and potential. 'Thing is, Heather, if you live around here, you would've heard all about Sharon's reputation. And it's all a joke to people, right? Heard one of your lot shout, "if it's rocking, don't come knocking" right before you started doing that.'

Heather looked away.

'I read the stories about her life. She had to do that because she was desperate. And he murdered her.' He shook his head. 'Who knows what she did to him to deserve that.'

A bitter laugh burst out of her lips. 'Are you being serious?'

'Must've had his reasons. Did you see where he went?'

Heather nodded. 'Did you?'

'I did.' Jim Smith walked over to the edge and pointed down. 'He went down there, right?'

Heather looked around – the place was still empty, just their cars and the teeming rain.

She could run away.

But she really needed to know what he knew. After all, the whole point in her campaign had been to get someone like him to come forward.

Heather joined him by the edge and looked down for the first time in twenty-five years. Not a long drop, just a flight of stairs down to a grassy patch with a couple of benches, spread out so they looked like they'd fallen out with each other over something. Then the gorse he'd lost himself in – hard to tell if it'd grown any in that time.

'It's a pretty steep climb down to the river, but it's doable – you'd disappear very quickly.' Jim Smith pointed down. 'Then you just needed to cross the Tweed and you could be in Earlston in maybe thirty minutes or Gattonside, if you went the other way.'

Heather looked at him and tried to figure out what to do. But this was beyond her. Rob bloody Marshall was right – this needed to be official. 'I want you to go to the police.'

'I'm not sure that'd be helpful.'

'Why not?'

'It's just… I can't.'

'Look, it's got to be worth the shot, though. Right?' Heather stepped forward, trying to assert dominance over him. 'Here's how we're going to play this. I'll pass on your information to the police and they can either meet you at home in Orkney or get local cops there. And they can do one of those identikit things, right? Pick the guy out of a crowd of similar people. Or they can age him up and stuff like that. Then they'll issue a press release.

And I can share it on my socials. I've got a network of people who spread the message far and wide. Come on, Jim – someone might recognise him.'

He stood there, thinking it through. Forehead twitching like he might be ready to agree... Then he gasped. 'Trouble is, Heather, the girl I was with that night wasn't the only one cheating. The lassie I cheated on is now my wife. And I'm not sure the little bit I saw is worth throwing away my marriage over.'

'He killed her, Jim. Someone knows him. Someone knows everything about him. Someone will recognise him. Don't you think Sharon deserves justice?'

He had his hands behind his back. 'Let me think about it.'

'Please. But it'd be really good to go out there with something. If you were to add in a witness description, it could really help our cause. And we've got all these new forensics now.'

'You said you had that. What have you got?'

'We've recovered her fingernail clippings.'

'Why would that be important?'

'Because it looks like she defended herself and scratched him. They're going to process them. They think they can recover his DNA from it.'

'Right.' Smith looked away, his Adam's apple bobbing up and down. 'I see.'

The rain got even heavier, a rattling as it battered off the tarmac.

'But I totally understand.' Heather smiled at him, then patted him on the arm. 'Thank you for getting in touch. And for meeting. Please think about whether you'd want to go to the police with this.'

'I already have.'

Hope fluttered in Heather's heart. 'And?'

'I don't want to.' Jim Smith grabbed her around the throat, his gloves digging into her skin and squeezing so hard. She kicked back against him, tried to scratch his face, but he was much stronger than her and pressed her against the wall.

She couldn't breathe, she couldn't even hold herself up anymore.

Her lungs burned, she needed air that wasn't coming.

Her vision narrowed and she closed her eyes.

Heather's last thought was she hadn't noticed him putting on the gloves.

9

PC Sheila Crawford took it slowly as she drove north from the Old Melrose roundabout. Just about getting dark, but it'd soon be light again – even this far south in Scotland, it never got dark. 'What do you mean?'

'I mean...' PC Liam Warner was in the passenger seat, gripping the handle above the door. 'I mean, I only ask you because of your great experience in the job but—'

Sheila glowered at him. 'Liam, are you saying I'm old?'

'Well, you do retire soon.'

'Liam!'

'What?'

'Have you ever heard of tact?'

'I'm tactful. When I need to be. Some people just can't face the truth.'

'The *truth*?' Sheila laughed but it really wasn't bloody funny. 'Maybe some people just don't want to face the truth. Think about that, eh? I've got my thirty, Liam, but I don't want to be reminded how bloody old I am.'

'Just asking if this is all there is.'

Sheila sighed. 'What, policing?'

'Yeah. And life. Is this all I'm going to see in this career?'

'I can't comment.' Or be arsed dealing with his daft pontificating...

Liam sat there, nodding like that meant something. Or anything. Daft wee laddie. 'Level with me here – do you think I'm cut out for this?'

'And you want the truth, right? No, Liam. You're not cut out for this work.'

'And you say I lack tact?'

'The truth stings, eh?' Sheila looked over with a grin. 'There are other jobs out there, Liam. Thousands.'

'I became a cop to help people and it feels like... This can't be all there is to life. Can it?'

'Liam, I've raised two laddies and a lassie. That's rewarding. Maybe you should have kids.'

'I've got kids.'

Sheila blinked hard a few times. '*You*'ve got kids?'

'Paul and Connor. Five and eight.'

'I had no idea.'

'They're a pair of nightmares. Each of them.' He laughed. 'So I've got four nightmares.'

Her phone rang.

She picked it up and checked the display.

Isla calling...

Sheila sighed, then tossed the phone to Liam. 'It's Sarge... Can you answer?'

'What did your last slave die of?' Liam answered the phone. 'Hi, Sarge, what's up?' He yawned. 'She's driving.' Another yawn. 'Okay. Okay.' He put it on speaker, then held it out. 'Here we go.'

'Sheila, it's Isla.' She sounded distorted through that crappy old phone's speaker – Sheila had only dropped it in the bath twice... 'I've just had someone pop into the station. Said there's a suspicious vehicle at Scott's View. Are you able to attend?'

Liam frowned. 'Suspicious how...?'

'Motor running, driver's door hanging open, nobody around. If you remember, there was a press conference there this evening, Liam. Need you pair to head over.'

'Come on, Sarge.' Liam slammed himself back into the seat. 'We're just about off shift.'

'And I can see you're currently going through Earlston, so I guess that means you're going to attend for me?'

Sheila sped up. 'On it.'

'Thank you.'

Liam ended the call. 'Can do without this...'

Sheila took the turning for Scott's View, then shot down the road. 'This is the job, Liam. You get asked to attend a scene. You do it until you get relieved.'

'Got to be more to life than this. Got to be.'

She looked over at the moaning daftie – that big scratch across his forehead still looked sore. 'I worked the old case. The one on the news, where they found that girl murdered at Scott's View.'

'That was years ago.'

'Twenty-five, aye. Like you just said, I'm ancient.'

'I didn't say that... Or I didn't mean it that way... Just... I wanted your wisdom, that's all.' Liam slotted her phone into the holder on the console. 'What happened?'

'Sex worker found in a camper van. Picked her up a couple of times too.'

'For sex work?'

'Drunk and disorderly, mostly. Drugs too. Her and her pal were a pair of nightmares.'

'See? It works. But you didn't pick her up for prostitution?'

'Nope. Policy was to turn a blind eye to that kind of thing.'

'How woke of you.'

'Liam...'

'Just saying. Would've thought you would've been all about arresting sex workers.'

'This is when things started to change.' Sheila turned the corner and took it slowly as they passed Scott's View. Dark and empty, except for a single car parked at the far end.

Driver door open. Engine running, pluming smog into the spitting rain.

Aye, not hard to see why they'd been called out...

Sheila did a three-pointer, then drove back and pulled in a couple of spaces away from it. 'Well, that does look suspicious.'

'Agreed, but can we get away soon?'

'We go when we're finished.' Sheila got out and put on her cap, then clicked on her torch and shone it at the car. 'Why drive all the way to Gala to report it?'

But Liam was still in the car, texting someone.

Sheila rapped on the window.

Liam looked over and frowned. Then went back to finishing his text.

What a laddie...

Finally, he got out. 'Alright, alright.'

'Honestly...' Sheila led him over and shone her torch inside the car.

A bit messy in there. Newspapers and documents, mostly. Nobody in there.

'Liam, can you run the plates for me?'

He stomped his foot like a petulant child. 'Come on...'

'Do you need me to show you how to do it again?'

He pointed at the car. 'Can't we just shut the door, stop the engine and leave the keys at the station?'

'Liam, you've got a bloody job to do!' Sheila rested her hands on her hips. 'Until you quit, you better bloody well do it to the best of your abilities.'

'Yeah, yeah, yeah...' Liam grumbled then put his Airwave to

his ear. 'Control, this is BPC-523. Can you run plates on a car for me? Zulu Alpha sixty-eight Sierra Romeo Lima. Over.'

Sheila walked over to the edge and could just about make out the sleeping Sphinx shapes of the three Eildons. Just past it, the sun was setting through the miserable rain.

'A Vauxhall Astra.' Liam looked over at her. 'Does a Heather McGill mean anything to you?'

'It does. Can't place it, though.'

'Lives in Earlston.'

'Still nothing.' Sheila shone her torch down into the darkness and just caught gorse. Tons and tons of the stuff, all spreading out down the hill.

Then her beam caught a bench in the middle of the grass.

Her beam flashed over something under the bench.

A leg.

10

The support act finished their song in a blaze of lights, white noise and crashing cymbals, the guitarist and bass players' arms like saws, lashing back and forth.

Then silence.

Then rapturous applause, roaring out.

The singer grabbed the mic, with his guitar now hanging free. 'Thank you, guys. Remember, we'll be at the merch desk where you can buy our records and T-shirts and all sorts of other shit we have to sell to make ends meet. We'll even sign body parts... Just not... *That*. Goodnight and enjoy Everything Everything!'

More rapturous applause.

Then the house lights came up.

Marshall hadn't been inside the Assembly Rooms before – certainly not that he could remember. Not the biggest venue in Edinburgh but it must be the prettiest. He'd no idea when the decor dated from, but it was ornate – intricate plasterwork and giant gilt-edged paintings on the walls. Not that the curved black speakers or the metal-framed stage exactly matched it.

He checked his phone again, still nothing. Bloody Edinburgh reception.

Jen looked around at him. 'They were good.'

'Really good.' Marshall smiled as he pocketed his phone. 'Thanks for encouraging me to do this.'

'You didn't exactly have a youth, did you? Spending all your time studying...'

'While you were inventing new forms of Jägerbombs...'

'Don't knock it. I've left behind a legacy.'

Someone pushed through the crowd and wrapped them both in big hugs. Cath, grinning wide. 'There you are.'

Jen looked her up and down. 'You're looking well.'

'Feel like shit. Sobriety sucks balls.'

'Sorry to hear that. But it's a good look on you.'

'Don't believe that for a second. Listened to a podcast where the guy said the first six years are awful so I've got, what, five and a half years to go?' Cath shook her head. 'Still, I've lost half a stone and it turns out I actually like doing yoga.' She sipped her cola. 'Didn't bring my car, because I forgot I wasn't drinking anymore.'

Jen laughed. 'It's okay, we can all get the train. We're getting a cab from Gala.'

Marshall pointed to his sister. To his twin sister, not his half-sister. 'I was just saying to Jen, thanks for inviting me along.'

'No problem.' Cath took a sip of cola from a big cup, rattling with ice cubes. 'I might be an idiot and a total fuck-up, but I've got good taste in music. And I'm saving a packet by not drinking, so I've bought a fair few of their albums on vinyl now.' She laughed. 'Not that I've got a decent record player.'

Marshall frowned. 'I could lend you my old one, if you wanted?'

'It's fine. I'm getting a new one.' Cath downed the rest of her cola and looked at their glasses. 'Can I get you a drink?'

Jen frowned. 'Are you sure?'

'Sure I'm sure.' Cath nodded. 'My treat.'

'Well, in that case.' Jen raised her almost-empty one. 'Red wine would be great. But two's my limit.'

'Nice to know someone in the family has a limit.' She threw her head back and bellowed with laughter. 'Rob? You want anything?'

'The IPA, thanks.'

'Coming right up.' Cath disappeared off into the crowd.

Jen watched her go. 'I think she just might have ADHD…'

Marshall sipped at his beer. 'What makes you say that?'

'I see it a lot. I'll mention it to her at some point.'

'Right…' Marshall raised his eyebrows. 'You know some people don't want to be diagnosed.'

'And some need to be.'

Marshall checked his phone. One bar of 4G. Finally.

A text from Isla Routledge:

> You got time next week to chat about Liam Warner? x

No, he really didn't…

But Marshall tapped out a reply:

> Is he still thinking he could be a detective?

He spotted an older message, from Heather and sent a couple of hours ago.

> Rob, I'm meeting him tonight. Seems harmless. H x

Fuck.

Marshall called her but it just kept on ringing.

Shite, shite, shite…

Jen frowned at him. 'You okay?'

Marshall shook his head. 'No. I'm really not.'

Then his phone started to ring.

Ravenscroft calling...

11

Marshall got out of his Uber and leaned back in. 'Thank you. Safe drive back to Edinburgh.' He shut the door and walked along to Scott's View, chewing on extra strong mints.

Twenty past ten but it was still not quite dark.

The place was even busier than for Heather's impromptu press conference earlier. A few patrol cars but more than a few with the battered look of pool cars.

A Subaru pulled up in front of him and DI Jolene Archer got out. She fanned out her blonde hair and gave him a nod. 'Boss.'

'Jolene.'

'You were in Edinburgh?'

'Right. At a gig with my sisters. Had to get an Uber back as the trains were cancelled.' Marshall yawned into his fist. 'Hopefully if they do extend the line to Carlisle, it means they'll finally staff it properly. Feels like they should put the cancelled trains in the timetable beforehand.'

She laughed at that. 'Could've picked you up in Stow or something.'

'Just as easy to get the cab here. Bloody expensive, though. Need to see what sort of mood the boss is in to know if I can expense it or not.' Marshall yawned again, then tried to shake it free. 'Jen and Cath are still at the gig.' He checked his watch. 'Probably finished now.'

A figure the approximate shape of Kirsten Weir in a Tyvek crime scene suit scurried away from them.

Marshall moved to follow her.

Jolene stopped him and gave him *that* look.

'Right.' Marshall cleared his throat. 'Shall we have a look at what we've got?' He led over to the crime scene.

PC Liam Warner was managing the outer locus, beefy arms folded over his puffed-up chest. A pink scar still ran across his forehead. Absolutely dripping from the rain but didn't seem to mind it or seek the refuge of a brolly. 'Sir.' He passed over the clipboard, somehow completely dry. 'Been meaning to ask every time I see you, how's your sister doing these days?'

Marshall looked away. 'Still sending her apologies.'

'For what?'

'For scratching your face, Constable.'

'Oh, that. I'll get over it.' Warner giggled, high and shrill. 'See, I already have!'

'Good man.' Marshall handed him the clipboard. 'I'll let her know you were asking after her.'

'Evening, all.' Leye Anotade took the clipboard and signed in. Not many people Marshall had to look up to, but he was one. He smiled at Marshall, but there seemed to be some sadness in it today. 'I'm here to inspect the body.' He looked around the area. 'But I don't see one.'

'It's down the hill.' Warner pointed to the gate just past the display showing a map of the area. 'There's a sort-of path down there.'

'Thanks, Constable.' Leye handed back the clipboard. 'Give me a few minutes with the body, Rob, then we can have a chat.'

He walked over but the gate was blocked by the crime scene manager.

Marshall didn't want to go there, so he headed over to the wall and looked down.

Forensic services had already erected a tent, glowing in the gloaming from arc lights placed around in a circle. Some suited-up figures milled around down there, but it was like they were trying to seem busy.

Leye emerged at the bottom and started chatting to the crime scene manager. He grabbed a Tyvek suit from the pile next to her, then started suiting up.

'Hiya, Rob.' Sergeant Isla Routledge was walking over, tucking her cap over her bun. Might be cold and wet, but she was just wearing a standard-issue T-shirt to show off toned arms. 'You come here often?'

'Sadly this is my second time today.' Marshall smiled at her. 'Isla. Listen. About your text, we—'

'Let's chat on Tuesday.' Isla smiled at him. 'This is a bit more important, right?'

'Agreed.' Marshall sighed. 'Gather PC Warner spotted the body?'

Isla's turn to sigh. 'No. Sheila Crawford did.' She pointed back at a Vauxhall Astra. 'Responded to a suspicious car. Which they found.' She pointed at the ledge. 'Then she had a wee peek down there and saw her leg poking out from under the bench.' She winced. 'I've been down there, Rob. It's Heather McGill.'

Marshall felt like the air had been kicked out of his lungs. 'You're sure?'

'They ran the plates... And I recognised her name from the telly. Forensics recovered her ID from her pocket. It's her alright.'

'Shite.' Marshall ran a hand through his hair, already damp from the rain. 'This is a complete mess.'

'Have to say, Rob, that whole thing looked really stressful. That impromptu news conference...'

'Aye... And then some.'

Down below, Leye entered the tent – so they were hopefully close to answering some questions.

Maybe.

Seconds later, a female figure emerged, tearing off her mask and goggles. Elliot stared up at them. 'Robbie.' She cast them into the discard pile. 'Can't be her. Just... *can't*.'

Marshall felt hope fluttering in his guts – not that someone else had been killed, but that it might not be Heather. 'Are you saying—?'

'No.' She looked at him with fire in her eyes. 'It is her.'

It hit Marshall like a nuke dropped from a plane. A flash of light, then searing heat burning up his arms.

Fuck.

He turned to face Isla and Jolene. 'Heather sent me a text this evening... Said she had a lead... That she was meeting someone. But I was with my sisters at a bloody gig in Edinburgh. And you know what the reception's like there. All those stone walls...'

Isla nodded. 'Who were you seeing?'

'Everything Everything. Except I had to leave to come here before they started.'

Jolene shrugged. 'Never heard of them.'

'I like them.' Isla smiled. 'Well, that "No Reptiles" song anyway.'

Elliot appeared at the gate, trailing her Tyvek suit behind her like a wedding train.

Jolene sniffed. 'You know who Heather was meeting?'

'Nope.' Marshall shoved his hands deep in his pockets. 'Said it was some guy who had information about the case. She'd promised to call me and give the location so I could attend. Or Andrea could. Then she... She just seems to have done it anyway.'

'Guessing she's lied to you, Robbie.' Elliot looked like she was struggling. Maybe even going to cry – very rare for her to show any emotion, but the death of a childhood friend seemed to be it. 'This is fucked up.'

'I know.' Marshall patted her on the arm. 'How about you and I go and tell her family, eh?'

12

Elliot drove really fucking fast.

Made the dark road blur around them, twisting the trees into supernatural shapes.

If he'd been behind the wheel, Marshall would be taking it really slowly at this time of night – but she wasn't. He couldn't see any oncoming headlights but that made it feel worse – it was so dark he couldn't see the road as it twisted and turned around the sharp bends. Trouble with the Borders was the roads had to fit into the contours of the land, not the other way round. 'Driven this way during the day a few times, but it's pretty hairy at night.'

Elliot slowed for a bend, then shot through it. 'Wimp.'

'Are you sure you're okay?'

'Sure.' Elliot sighed. 'It's just a bit of a shock, you know?'

'I get it.' Marshall looked over at her but she was focusing on the road. 'Take it you guys were close?'

'Years ago, maybe. Heather was a good pal at school. Sat next to her in maths and French and physics and...' Elliot laughed. 'How the hell can I still remember that all these years later?' She grimaced, then looked around at him as she hurtled towards another bend. 'Can't believe it, Robbie. After what they all went through... I mean, that night...' She ran a hand through her hair, splaying out her soggy fringe. 'That was Heather's eighteenth. No wonder it fucked her up, eh?'

'It'd leave a scar, I'd imagine.'

'From what I heard, she's the one who started rocking the camper van. She went over and knocked on the door, for sure. And she saw Sharon's body in there.' Elliot drove them in awkward silence, punctuated only by the angry sounds of the car as it responded to her driving. 'Should I even be on this case?'

'You weren't there that night, were you?'

'No, I'd drifted apart from most of them. I had this stinking cold. Turns out it was hay fever. Can feel it building up in my system now. Need to take so many antihistamines it's *unreal*. Weirdest thing – Heather spoke to me just before they found Sharon's body. Borrowed a friend's phone. Bloody hell, it's weird to think nobody had them back then and now we're all addicted to them.'

'What was she like back then?'

She had a long sniff, sounded all wet. 'Heather was wild.'

'Wild, how?'

'Ach, just the same way we all were. Up for parties and exploring the world. Meeting new people, seeing what nonsense we could all get up to.'

'I get it.' Marshall gripped the handle that bit tighter. 'But you know the people who were there, right?'

'Most. And some more than others.'

'That could play to our advantage. You being friends.'

'She wasn't a *friend*, Robbie. We were close-ish back then, but we drifted apart when she moved away to uni. Then she came back a few years ago.'

'Where did she study?'

'D'you know, I can't remember?' Elliot shook her head.

'Can't believe I can remember sitting next to her in French, maths and physics, but not which fucking uni she went to or what she studied there.'

'But you've obviously seen her since she came back, given she came to you, right?'

'Right. Had a dinner with some of our mutual friends not long after. Told us she was looking to reconnect with her parents, but I think her dad died not long after. Then she was starting this campaign and just sort of latched on to me.' Elliot pulled up on the main street in St Boswells, facing towards the village centre. 'You wanting me to lead here?'

Marshall nodded.

'Probably better I do.' Elliot got out and stormed up the path.

Marshall took his time getting out. By the time he reached the door, it was opening.

A woman in her late sixties stared out at them, squinting. Dressed in her nightie and dressing gown. 'Is that you, Heather?'

'Sorry, it's Andrea Elliot.' Elliot smiled at her. 'Sorry. You'll remember me as Andrea Hardie.'

'Andrea? Wow. It's been years. Are your folks still in Lauder?'

'Still there, aye.'

'What's up?'

'This is official business, I'm afraid.' Elliot put on a serious face. 'Listen, can we have a word with you inside?'

13

Barbara McGill's kitchen looked out across a well-lit garden. Mature trees swayed in the breeze. A washing line dripped with rain, but was empty of clothes – a basket full of bedding sat by the back door, ready to go upstairs.

'I can't believe it.' Barbara wrapped her hands around the mug. 'It's *definitely* her?'

'Saw her with my own eyes.' Elliot nodded, but she hated it. Made her neck feel like it was filled with ground-up marbles. 'Found her purse on her.'

Barbara stared into her cup.

Elliot sipped some of her tea, then looked over at Marshall. 'I really hate this, Mrs McGill.'

'Please. It's Barbara to you, okay?'

'Okay.' Elliot laughed. 'Obviously, DCI Marshall and myself are going to do everything we can to identify her killer, but it'd be useful to know a few things about her.'

'Where do I start? My daughter may have been many things, but she was a difficult teenager. A right tearaway. Drove me and her father demented.' She focused on Elliot. 'You know all about that, Andrea, eh? But that discovery... Sharon's body...

It left a deep impact on her.' Barbara took a dainty sip of tea. 'Not so much on the group she palled around with, eh?'

'Do you remember who she was with that night?'

'The usual crowd, I think. That Georgina lassie.' Barbara scrunched up her face. 'That lassie was feral. Name like that, you expect a bit of decorum, but nope. Feral. And Sinead, of course. She wasn't too bad. Crazy for her car. And I've no idea who the laddies were. Heather would never give me any names.'

Marshall made a note in a spare notebook he'd cadged from the pool car. 'Gather she'd moved back here recently?'

'That's right. She left the Borders after school, like many do.' Barbara frowned at Elliot. 'You stayed, didn't you?'

'I actually left, but not for long. And I came back.'

'Aye, well. Heather moved to Edinburgh. Studied tourism and hospitality at Napier. And she didn't come back.'

'That's it. Couldn't remember it.' Elliot clicked her fingers. 'Don't think I saw her until a couple of years ago. Remind me what she did after uni?'

'What didn't she do? She was a holiday rep, which was mostly partying. Worked all across the Med. Algarve, Majorca, Crete, someplace in Turkey. Then she moved to Japan to teach English. Then to South Korea.'

Marshall pushed his cup away. 'You see much of her in that time?'

'I went to visit a few times, but she rarely returned to the Borders, no.' Barbara took another sip. 'Like she was running from what happened, you know?'

'I can well imagine.' Marshall shifted his gaze between them. 'Did she say why she came back?'

'Well, it was her father. After his first heart attack. She moved back to be closer to us. But he didn't last much longer. It'll be five years in November.'

'I'm sorry to hear that.'

'I'm used to being on my own now, of course. But...' Barbara sighed. 'Took a lot of adjustment at first. My girl was there for me.'

'And Heather lived locally, right?'

'She bought a place in Earlston.' Barbara took a long drink, finishing her cup, then topped it up from the pot. 'Thing was, Heather was always restless. Like she needed to run. But then she started doing this campaign a few months ago and she became a different person.'

Marshall frowned. 'How do you mean?'

'She had focus for the first time in her life. Seemed settled.'

'Does she work nearby?'

'She's freelance. She got into writing when she was living in Seoul. Did these travel and lifestyle pieces for some internet thing. She was going travelling a lot, still, but... Well, she did, anyway. Then her causes started taking over.'

Elliot took the pot and filled up her own cup, then put some into Marshall's cup, but he didn't look like he was going to drink any. No sign of any milk, though. 'Do you know if she was seeing anyone?'

'Not that she told me. Did she say anything to you, Andrea?'

'It never came up, no.'

'I see. Heather kept herself mostly to herself. Back in my day, being in your early forties, unmarried and childless would be a rarity, but now... Having three kids like you do, Andrea... That's the rare thing.'

'Aye, it's a sair fecht, that's for sure.' Elliot gave a polite smile – Barbara had no idea what she'd been through... 'Do you know if Heather reconnected with any of the old crowd?'

'Just Georgina and you. But you were the closest.'

Elliot felt that like a punch in the kidneys. 'Me?'

'She spoke highly of you, Andrea. How your friendship deepened in recent months.'

Elliot let out a deep breath – it wasn't her understanding of how things had been between them.

'You were doing some good with this project, weren't you? I didn't see my daughter becoming some kind of social media activist, but she did. Spent most of her waking hours trying to solve wee problems in the community. Had all these followers who'd come to her with issues. Said she had over fifty thousand, just on Facebook. And there's Twitter and all the rest.' Barbara stared at Marshall. 'Is what happened related to her campaign?'

Marshall pushed his cup away again. 'Given the location, it seems prudent to investigate that avenue.'

'You said her body was found at Scott's View. Where the incident happened all those years ago. So of course it's connected.'

'We're considering it. Naturally. But we wondered if there were any other possibilities.'

'I can't think of anything.'

'Do you know why she'd be there at night?'

'I know Heather often parked there. Not sure what she was doing. Probably just thinking through what happened.' Barbara shook her head. 'I've no idea why she'd be there at night, no.'

Marshall made another note – Elliot had no idea what he was writing down. Maybe his shopping list. 'When did you last see her?'

'At the weekend. I was supposed to see her yesterday. We'd sometimes go for a tea and a scone in the bookshop café, but she cancelled.'

'Did she give a reason?'

'Said she was too busy with her campaign.'

Marshall nodded again. 'Was that the last time you heard from her?'

'No. I spoke to her yesterday after you announced you were reopening the investigation. She was pleased as punch.'

Marshall smiled at that, like he was pleased she'd had some joy in her last few minutes alive. 'Did she mention meeting anyone last night?'

'Meeting someone?'

'About the investigation. Someone who'd come forward, maybe?'

'Not to me, sorry.'

'Do you have a key for her house?'

'Of course. I water her plants when she's away. Which is often!' Barbara got up and shuffled over to a drawer.

Elliot leaned over to Marshall and whispered, 'I can stay with her for a bit – see what she's got to say.'

Marshall smiled. 'Good idea.'

Barbara shuffled back and handed him the key. 'I want that back, of course.'

'Naturally.' Marshall scraped the chair leg back as he got up. 'We'll look after your daughter's property for you.'

'That's all I ask.'

Marshall gave Elliot a final look, then left them to it, getting out his phone as he went. 'Hi, Jo, it's Rob. Could you pick me up?' The door shut behind him.

Leaving Elliot and Barbara alone.

The clock by the cooker ticked out a beat.

'I knew this whole thing was going to be the undoing of her.' Barbara looked around at the closed door, then shook her head. 'What the hell was she playing at? It's what happens... You poke a bear and it bites back.'

'Did she tell you that?'

'No, but...' Barbara finished her tea, then poured yet another cup from the pot. 'You were all there and you didn't all have to do this, did you?'

'I wasn't there.'

'Oh?'

'I was ill. Thought it was a cold but it was hay fever. Still get it every June and July. It's brutal, no matter what I take for it.'

'Well, I thought you were with them but I'm happy to stand corrected.' Barbara offered her another top-up. 'Wee spotty hotty?'

'I'm good, thank you.' Elliot raised her hands. 'After the press conference, she spoke to a man. Any idea who he might be?'

'If you showed me a photo, maybe.'

'Haven't got one, but I'll bear that in mind.'

Barbara rested the pot down then tucked in the tea cosy like she was fussing over a baby. 'I bet that whole press conference went down well with your lot.'

'It wasn't ideal.'

'I can't believe this.' Barbara shook her head again. 'Can I see her body?'

'It'll be a while before it's taken to BGH.'

'Okay, but that's where she's going?'

'Absolutely. Eventually it'll be released to the funeral director.'

'Can you take me there, Andrea? I need to see her.'

'Of course. I'll call ahead and make sure our pathologist knows.'

'Thank you.' Barbara took a long sip of tea, then let out a deep breath. 'Will you find her killer?'

'We'll try.' Elliot locked eyes with her. 'That's all we can promise.'

'I understand that. Do you think it's whoever killed Sharon Beattie returning to finish the job?'

'We don't know.'

'It's obvious, isn't it?'

'We'll see.' Elliot patted her arm. 'Now, let me make that call.'

'I might make some scones.'

Elliot frowned at her. 'At this time?'

'Never a bad time to make scones, Andrea. Besides, I've got enough flour to see me through the next ice age.'

14

The dashboard clock read half eleven but it felt much later.

Marshall sat in the passenger seat of Jolene's car, doing one of those yawns that just kept on coming. 'Thanks for picking me up.'

'All part of the job, right?' Jolene drove them off the A68 in Earlston.

The wee town was already asleep – even the pub was hunkered down for the night. Marshall visualised it as a sister village to St Boswells, the way they both ran east from the A68, but Earlston was the earthier of the two – no upmarket bookshop or gun rooms here.

A cat darted across the road ahead of them, then ran through the big town square, but they headed south past workshops and garages.

Jolene pulled up outside an address on Station Brae, but the nearest train line ran up the next river valley.

Still, at least that was closer than it being in Edinburgh – when the service actually ran.

A car flashed its lights at them.

Marshall got out into the thin rain.

Trev Pienaar unfolded himself from his car, but seemed to get his jumper caught on something. He tugged at it, then joined them. 'Alright, mate? Glad you guys finally showed up.'

'Sorry for the delay – we had to get the keys from the victim's mother.' Marshall dangled them in the air. 'Need some help from us?'

'It's not a crime scene, but if we keep it limited to us three, that's a tolerable exclusion sample.' Trev gestured inside. 'Lead on, my friend.'

Marshall snapped on some nitrile gloves as he walked up to the door, then stood there, listening hard.

No lights on.

No sounds from inside.

He slotted the key in the lock, then opened the door and held it open.

Not even a cat waiting.

Still no sounds. No, 'Is that you?'

Marshall stepped into the house. 'Hello?'

No reply, just his words echoing through an empty home. Pale blue walls, oatmeal carpet.

Pine smells came from the giant bowl of potpourri by the door. A key bowl next to it, empty – perfect sign she did live alone.

'Right, I'll have a bit of a mooch around and see what I can find, yeah?' Trev walked deeper into the house, humming a tune Marshall couldn't quite place.

Marshall looked at Jolene. 'Okay, let's have a—'

An alarm started blaring out.

Then the landline started ringing.

Probably all connected up.

Marshall stuck his fingers in his ears. 'Jo, can you get the code from Andrea?'

'Will do.' Jolene put her mobile to her ear then picked up

the phone handset and slammed it down. 'Andrea, it's Jolene. Can you get the alarm code for Heather's house?' She walked off, phone to her ear.

Marshall went into the kitchen, where the alarm was a bit quieter. Or at least it didn't feel like someone was sticking knitting needles in his lugs.

Very clean and tidy. Organised. No dirty plates sitting out. All the crockery and cutlery away. The only sign of a life in here was a notepad on the table, but Marshall couldn't decipher what she'd been writing on it in her elliptical scrawl.

Handwriting was becoming a dying art and he knew that more than most.

He snapped a couple of pages to see if anyone at the station could get a better read of it.

Next door was the sitting room. Two purple sofas at right angles, artfully stacked with cushions and a neatly folded throw. A small TV rested on the wall above a fireplace. Books on three tightly packed shelves. Two lay on the coffee table, one open. Seemed like it was for effect.

Marshall checked the cover – a book about maps for countries that no longer existed, which fitted in with her travel writing.

He tried the next door, expecting a bathroom but getting a study.

And here it was – mess. Chaos. *Stuff*. Signs of life, that someone actually lived here.

A giant oak desk ran wall to wall, with a Mac laptop hooked up to a monitor at one end. An open notebook sat at the other, with stacks of files between. Six rows of bookshelves filled the other three walls, stacked with box files and books, mostly on travel.

The alarm stopped blaring.

Marshall let his fingers go then looked at the notebook through here, a black Moleskine at least A4. Similarly hard to parse her handwriting on these notes, but Marshall took some more photos anyway.

Jolene appeared in the doorway. 'Mum had the code. Thank God Heather hadn't changed it.'

'Thank you for that.' Marshall flicked through the book, but couldn't make out more than one in four words – he hoped Heather could understand her own handwriting and make sense of any of it. 'You find anything else?'

'Nothing upstairs.' Jolene started sifting through the papers. 'Two beds and a bathroom. All clear. One was hers, but her stuff was all tidied away.'

'Seems to be the way of it. Obsessively tidy.'

'Wish my house was a tenth as tidy.' Jolene looked around the room. 'So it does look like she had many causes on the go at once, not just Sharon's death.' She held up a file. 'Dog crap in parks, immigration, the cost of lettuce in Tesco, teens playing music through phone speakers on trains and buses.' She looked over at him. 'You know that's called "bare beating"?'

'I didn't but I do now.' Marshall smiled at her. 'Should be a mandatory twenty-year sentence for that.'

'Tell me about it. Everyone just became so selfish during lockdown, right? I mean, how many people do you see walking around with massive headphones like a Cyberman on *Dr Who* but you still get psychopaths blasting Facebook Reels through their tinny phone speakers?'

Marshall nodded along with every single word and didn't want to think back to that time. He gave up on the notebook – maybe someone else would have a better read of it. 'She's got her fingers in so many pies, but none of them seem particularly likely to link to why she was killed. Except the obvious one.' He tapped the laptop keyboard and the monitor put up a password request – he hadn't expected anything else, but at least he knew it was her machine.

Jolene tapped the screen. 'I'll get Ash Paton to work through this.'

'Ash?' Then it hit Marshall. 'Forgot she trained in IT forensics.'

'It's good to still have it on our side of the fence, right? People have everything on their phones.'

'Especially Heather. It'd be good to recover it.'

'Asked them to prioritise it, but there's no sign of it, Rob.'

Trev appeared in the doorway, inspecting the hole in his jumper. 'Listen, guys, I don't think there's much here for me to process but I'll get my team out.'

Marshall frowned. 'Your team?'

'Haven't you heard? Kirsten's left. She starts over at Gartcosh on Monday.'

Marshall raised his eyebrows. Felt like someone ran a cold ice-pick down his neck. 'I didn't know that.'

'Why should you? You haven't been going out for a few months, have you?'

15

Jolene drove along the back way towards the murder scene. 'I mean, shouldn't you have known?'

'Probably.' Marshall leaned back in his seat. 'Seems like it's breaking news.'

'Don't you speak to her?'

'It didn't end that well between us.'

'Really?'

'Really.'

'So, one minute you're buying a house together and the next you're... not? What happened?'

'I broke up with her and she didn't take it well.'

'I know that. I mean why did it end?'

'We just drifted apart, I guess. We didn't want the same thing – we would've bought the house a long time ago if we did. Any house. We saw most of them in the Borders.' Marshall nibbled his fingernail. 'But she kept delaying things. I'd sold my flat in London and we were staying at my mum's while we found someplace and... She was supposed to be staying there too but she kept spending the nights at hers, even though she was based down here and…' He sighed. 'The whole thing was a mess, Jo. I just needed to get out.'

'Sounds rough.'

'It was.' Marshall gave a deeper sigh. 'You know what? She asked if I wanted to be fuckbuddies.'

'*Fuckbuddies*?' Jolene laughed. 'Seriously?'

'Right.'

'Jesus. How old is she?'

'Trying not to judge…'

'Sex positive, eh?'

Marshall laughed. 'Thing is, I'm a pretty simple guy. I'm just looking for an uncomplicated relationship. Someone to settle down with. Someone who makes me smile and laugh.'

'But Kirsten just wanted the release of sexual energy a couple of times a week? And maybe going to the cinema once a month?'

'Something like that. And this is between us.'

'My lips are sealed.' Jolene grimaced. 'Have you thought about Andrea?'

'Eh?'

'She's single. You're single. Why not?'

'No fucking way is why not.'

'She's not that bad.'

'No, she bloody is. For starters, there's no attraction, either physically or emotionally. And she has three kids. Plus she's a train wreck and a complete arsehole.'

Jolene laughed. 'Sure you should be saying that about a direct report?'

'You're a direct report now, Inspector, and this is a personal chat.' Marshall waited for a smile. 'And she might've got better, behaviourally, but she's the last person in the world I'd want to get into something with…'

'Just saying… I think she likes you.'

'Well, please don't say that or think that.'

'I'm winding you up, Rob. But I'm sorry it was so tough with Kirsten. I had no idea.' Jolene slowed as they neared on Scott's View.

Seemed to be even more vehicles here, despite people supposedly being out and doing work.

Marshall stifled a yawn. 'Right, now my private life's been dissected, let's see what we've got.' He got out and walked over to the outer locus.

Warner stood there, grinning away as Marshall signed them back in. 'Any idea when I'll get off, sir?'

Marshall handed back the clipboard. 'That's a matter for Sergeant Routledge, not me.'

'Thought so. Tried calling her but she's not answering.'

'If I see her, I'll let her know.' Marshall fixed him with a hard stare. 'But stay here until you hear, okay?'

Warner glowered. '*Fine.*'

'And from someone of a superior rank, okay?'

'I'll sort it out.' Jolene smiled at him. 'Should really be someone from the night shift running it now, right?'

Warner nodded enthusiastically. 'Pre*cis*ely.'

The gate creaked open and Leye wandered through, yawning even harder than Marshall was doing right then. 'Rob, my man.' He shook his hand. 'How you doing?'

'Should be on the train home having just seen Everything Everything playing in Edinburgh, but I'm here with a dead body and no clues.'

'Cheery as ever.' Leye thumbed behind himself. 'I've finished with her body and she's just being readied for transport to pathology.'

Marshall nodded his thanks. 'How's it looking?'

'She was definitely strangled, then pushed over the edge. Sustained some injuries from the fall and there's an obvious displaced fracture of the cervical spine. But the contusions from strangulation are obvious and those other injuries appear to be postmortem.'

'Any similarities with Sharon's murder?'

'Hmmm.' Leye clicked his tongue a few times. 'Both were strangled, but I'll have to acquaint myself with the case file.'

'Could she have been killed elsewhere and dumped here?'

Leye considered it for a few seconds. 'Not likely. Lividity is fixed and appears consistent with her final resting place being here, just after her death. If she'd been moved here or killed prior to this, it'd be set differently. And her car's still there, isn't it? Not that that means anything definitively.'

'I'm glad there's something straightforward in this whole thing.' Marshall sighed. 'Got a time of death?'

'An indicative one, yes. Based on the core liver temperature, I'd say she was murdered at half past eight, give or take fifteen minutes.'

Marshall groaned – that wasn't long after she'd sent that text. The one he'd missed. If he'd read it... He was in Edinburgh, sure, but he could've sent anyone from here. 'You're sure?'

'Are you asking if I know how to do my job?'

Marshall smiled at him. 'No need to bite my head off.'

Leye snapped his teeth together, then gave him a wide grin. 'Yes, Rob, I'm sure. I pierced a thermometer into the victim's liver and measured her core temperature, then extrapolated back by using the ambient temperature to arrive at the time of death. The body was found just over an hour later.'

'Sorry, I'm just tired and grumpy.'

'This is a tricky one, my friend.'

'Just find it hard that she was lying there for the best part of an hour.'

'Still, who's visiting here at that time of night in these conditions? And of that vanishingly small number, who's looking over the side there? Once you've seen the sun go down over the

Eildons, it's just darkness. Any psychological theories you wish to investigate?'

'The killer is acting spontaneously. No weapon, no trace evidence, no clear victimology, no witnesses.' Marshall stood up tall. 'You got anything else for me?'

'Maybe.' Leye clicked his tongue a few times. 'I think the killer wore leather gloves.'

'You think?'

'Well, they left the pattern visible in the strangulation marks as deep impressions on the skin.'

'Putting on gloves isn't entirely consistent with it being spontaneous.'

'Spontaneously putting on gloves. And that's now your job to find the killer.'

Marshall frowned. 'How does that tally with the original case?'

'I *think* that didn't have gloves, but I don't remember there being any prints on the body. But I'll dig into it and let you know.'

'Cheers, Leye.' Marshall gave him a smile. 'Let me know when you can do the postmortem.'

'It'll be tomorrow now.'

'Obviously.' Marshall smiled. 'But cheers for doing it so quickly.'

'See you tomorrow.' Leye walked off towards his car.

Marshall looked around and spotted Kirsten.

She made eye contact with him and actually smiled at him. Then she walked off, then got into her car and drove off.

Aye, Marshall really should speak to her. Clear the air. But mixed messages were her MO...

'Rob!'

Marshall swung around.

DS Douglas Crawford was waving at him. Tall, with jacked-up muscles and thick stubble peppering his jawline. 'You got a minute, mate?'

Marshall acknowledged him with a wave and walked over.

Crawford was with Sheila. 'You've met my mum, right?'

Marshall smiled at her. 'We've met, aye.'

'Mum found the body, right?' Crawford cleared his throat. 'And she was at the initial crime back in 2000.'

'Spooky, eh? Finding one of that lot dead... And now this?' Sheila was staring into space, her forehead creased. 'Got a year left, then they'll turn me into glue.' Her laugh was cold and bitter.

'I'm sure you've still got tons left to offer.' Marshall smiled at her. 'Such as coaching Warner.'

'That laddie...' She laughed again and it had some warmth in it. 'I mean, he's not a laddie, is he? He's got two kids.'

Marshall felt his head jerk back in surprise. 'Has he?'

'Not sure he knows how he got them...' Sheila snorted. 'Anyway. We're supposed to be off shift now, so I'm going to relieve him.'

'Did Isla approve that?'

'She did, aye.' Sheila walked off towards Warner. 'Come on, Liam...'

'So.' Crawford folded his arms. His polo shirt had been carefully chosen to show off his guns. 'Do you want me to pick Mum's brains on the old case? Show us what's relevant in the file?'

Marshall frowned at him. 'Was she a detective?'

'Uniform.'

'I mean, sure, ask her what she remembers and get the gen on the detectives – find out who was good, who was bad, who's even still around – but I'm not sure what she could add.'

'Sure, of course. And what else do you need from me?'

'First, I'm putting you in charge of the door-to-door.'

Crawford scratched his neck. 'Eh, there's not much nearby, sir.'

'We're near both Earlston and St Boswells... Plus a few wee villages. Get people out, asking if anyone saw anything. Another car. A man walking here. Anything. And interview the guy who reported it to the station in Gala.'

'Sure. Of course.' Crawford stood there, shoulders low. 'And after that five minutes is up, I'll make the tea and scratch my balls.'

'No need to be like that, Douglas. This is important work.' Marshall narrowed his eyes at him. 'Need someone to run digital forensics on the laptop.'

'That'll be Ash Paton. I'll get the team to run down any leads from that, I suppose.'

'Good man. And if you could find the man who approached Heather after the news conference too, that'd be great.'

Crawford looked at Marshall like he'd gone insane. 'What man?'

'Someone spoke to her afterwards. Might've been a pretty heated discussion. He was older than her.'

'You think this guy's killed her?'

'Not sure, but we clearly need to speak to him. Can you go through the footage and check?'

'What, the stuff that was broadcast?'

'Not just that. The cameras would've stayed rolling after. See if they've caught him. It's possible he's her killer. Or he's someone else entirely. But I want him tracked down and spoken to.'

'On it, sir.' Crawford strode off with some purpose now.

Marshall knew he had an issue there – one of those cops who sought glory but it tried to avoid him.

'Rob?' Isla stormed over to him, fists clenched. 'Did you say Liam and Sheila could go?'

'Me? No. I explicitly told them to speak to you. Sheila said you'd let them go.'

'Fuck's sake. Why do I keep getting saddled with *liars*?'

Marshall smiled at her. 'You're welcome to become a detective.'

'That mean you want me?'

'Could do with you, aye.'

'Rather be a real cop, Rob.' Isla laughed. 'That said, I've got a few too many improper ones.'

'Tell me about it.' Marshall held her gaze and neither of them was looking away. 'Are you heading back to Gala soon?'

'Why?'

'Could do with a lift.'

'You don't have that stupid American truck anymore, do you? The one Liam scored when parking his car...'

'Was that him?'

'Oh shit...'

'Well, I managed to get shot of it, so I've just got a normal car now.'

'Well, to answer your question – yes, I'll be heading back once I've toasted Liam's nuts and Sheila's ovaries, so I could drop you back.' She gave him a cheeky salute. 'Sir.'

'Less of that.'

She gave him a crafty wink. 'You ready now?'

Didn't seem like anything else needed his attention, so Marshall smiled at her. 'I'll wait for you by the car. You need to borrow my toasting fork?'

She laughed as she walked off.

16

Despite the only other cars on the road being taxis going as far over the speed limit as Elliot had been, Isla drove carefully and precisely. And they didn't seem to care about a police car creeping up behind them, just kept blitzing through the night. 'I mean, the pair of them were just taking the piss.' She scowled. 'They *definitely* told you I'd let them go?'

'Definitely.' Marshall looked over at her, but she was locked into driving mode. 'That's what they said. Sheila, anyway. And Liam was moaning about it.'

'She's a wily fox. And he's an idiot. Our shift rotation finishes tomorrow and we're heading to hers for drinks afterwards, which puts me in a bit of a spot.'

'In what way?'

'If she's taking the piss and buggered off early, then I've got to give her a doing, don't I? A real carpeting. And then it'll be bloody uncomfortable, won't it?'

'I get it. The pressures of rank.'

'Can't imagine you deal with the same shit, Rob.'

'Different shit, but the same smell. At least your inspector's a good guy, right?'

'True, but word is he's got a job in Edinburgh.'

'Is that an opportunity for you?'

'I'm fine where I am. Except when people lie to my face.' Isla weaved into the station's car park and slotted into the space. 'Okay. Let's hope they're still here.' She looked over and locked eyes with him again.

He didn't look away. Becoming a bit of a habit. 'Let me know how it goes, okay?'

'Will do.'

'I mean it. If you need a mentor or anything?'

'A *mentor*?' She snarled the words, then the derision seemed to soften into something else. Like a laugh. 'I do need something, that's for sure.'

'I'm serious. It's important to have someone you can discuss this stuff with. I've got a chief super at Gartcosh who listens to me and my noise. Helps me make sense of it all.'

She grinned. 'I'll bear that in mind.' Then frowned. 'Now, given I couldn't find them at Scott's View, I need to find both toasting forks and shove them right up their arses.' She got out and marched over to the station, sticking her cap on as she went.

Marshall got out and yawned. God knows how someone like Isla managed to handle shift rotations – a nine-to five-broke Marshall. Not that he wasn't always in the station before seven and after nine at night...

An Audi pulled up. And Marshall knew the owner...

Detective Superintendent John Ravenscroft got out. Despite the rain, his silvery fin of hair stayed precisely sculpted. '*There* you are, Robert.' At this time of night, his Scouse accent turned wild.

'Here I am, sir.' Marshall gave as big a smile as he could

muster, which wasn't much. 'Have you just driven down from Edinburgh?'

'Sadly. I was out for dinner with the better half and some friends. Mrs Ravenscroft wasn't particularly impressed when I got the call and then had to spend the rest of our meal slipping in and out to answer follow-ups, but it's the nature of the beast.' Ravenscroft cracked his knuckles, narrowing his gaze. 'Let me get this straight – we've just reopened this investigation, launched that campaign and now this happens?' He shook his head. 'Miranda's spitting teeth, Robert. This isn't good. Not good at all.'

'I'm assuming this is connected to the Sharon Beattie case, sir. I told you Heather said she'd been contacted by someone. I was supposed to meet them with her, but she jumped the gun.'

Ravenscroft sighed. 'Wouldn't exactly be the first time, would it?'

'I did get a text message from Heather, sir. Didn't receive it at the time, thanks to the crap mobile reception in Edinburgh.'

'Edinburgh? What were you doing there?'

'I was at a gig with my sisters. But I doubt I would've deterred her.' Marshall put his hands in his pockets – the safest place for them. 'Spent the trip down from Edinburgh thinking about how I could've saved her. Time of death was roughly when she'd sent the message.'

'I see.' Ravenscroft ran a hand down his face. 'Well, there are things we tell ourselves to salve our consciences, right?'

'What? You're the only one who's allowed to make social plans?'

'That's not what I'm saying in the slightest.' Ravenscroft gave him a hard stare, then broke off to look away. 'So, what's the plan here, Robert?'

'Just do the usual, sir. Follow the leads until they get us somewhere.'

'Don't get cheeky with me, okay?'

'I'm not. This is a murder case. We've got processes and procedures in place for a reason. It's possible Heather McGill was killed by the same person who murdered Sharon Beattie. But I'm not about to leap to conclusions here. We're going to do everything we can to nail it down.'

'That's what I like to hear.'

Another car parked. Seconds later, Elliot trudged over, hands in pockets. 'Speak of the devil.'

'Which devil? Me or him?' Ravenscroft laughed and plastered on the face for when he was in company. 'And what were you saying to the devil about us?'

'The usual.' Elliot sighed. 'I've just dropped Barbara off at BGH.'

Marshall frowned. 'But Leye's only just left and the body's still at Scott's View.'

'I know. I spoke to him. The poor woman was desperate to get there. Baked a batch of scones while I was waiting and was going to do another one. I told her she won't see the body for a while, but she just wants to sit there with her kid. It'll be ten times worse when she sees her.' Elliot yawned. 'I'll go back to pick her up, then maybe get her to sleep.'

'Good stuff.' Ravenscroft pointed at Marshall. 'Robert and I were just discussing a strategy. Were you a cop at the time?'

'Excuse me?' Elliot put her hands on her hips. 'How old do you think I am?'

'It's not that!' Ravenscroft raised his hands. 'It's just... The local thing.' He frowned. 'Isn't there a connection?'

Elliot scowled at him, like she was trying to decide how hard to slap him. 'I was at school with Heather, if that's what you mean.'

Ravenscroft nodded as though that's what he'd meant. 'And were you there that night?'

'No, sir. I wasn't. Should've been, but I wasn't well.'

'Right.' Ravenscroft focused his attention on Marshall. 'Have we got the old file back at the station yet?'

'This is the issue, sir. I've had a couple of DCs in Andrea's team poring over what we can get from the old case file from the system, but the full original is still with the Cold Case Unit at Tulliallan.'

'But I agreed to reopen this?'

Elliot nodded. 'You did.'

'So why's the file not here?'

'I requested it, but they're playing silly buggers and saying this should be their case.'

Ravenscroft stared up at the sky and that quiff still stayed vertical. 'Cold Case Unit is Whitehead, isn't it?'

'Where they send old detectives to turn into lumps of wood, aye. But hopefully it'll be here soon.'

'I'm not a man to put much weight into hope.' Ravenscroft sucked in a deep breath. 'Can you get someone to head up to Tulliallan, then grab the file and bring it back here?'

Elliot shrugged her shoulders. 'If you approve this case sits with Rob's team, sir, then sure.'

'Consider it done.' Ravenscroft checked his watch. 'Right, it's midnight now. Suggest both of you go and get a few hours' sleep while I cover things here. Let's reconvene at seven, okay?'

17

Friday

Marshall pulled into his space outside the station and yawned hard. Might as well have not bothered trying to sleep. And the coffee wasn't exactly working.

Half five but the sun was already way too bright, especially this early.

He grabbed his travel mug from the holder and got out into the sunny morning, then took a deep drink and hoped the second one of the day would shift this.

Everything felt heavy.

He yawned again and it just kept going.

'Watch it – that yawning's contagious.'

Marshall looked around and saw Isla teasing her hair out of a bun. Surprisingly long, and the curls had eased out a lot – maybe she'd had them put in.

Marshall smiled at her, but another yawn kicked in. 'Oh, hey. You just coming off shift now?'

'Finally.'

'That's a long backshift, right?'

'Very long. I'm just thinking about the OT.' Isla frowned at his mug. 'This you coming back on?'

'Ships that pass in the night, eh? Managed a couple of hours of lying on my bed while my brain went crazy thinking through this case.'

'Antihistamine.'

'Eh?'

'Old-school antihistamines. The ones that say "drowsy" on the box. They knock you right out.'

'That's a good recommendation.' Marshall smiled. 'Aye, sadly I need to be non-drowsy today.'

'Supposed to be back on tonight for night shift, so I'm off to the gym now, where it's going to be ridiculously busy, then I'll try your technique of lying on my bed while my brain goes crazy.'

'Sod antihistamines – that's how the professionals do it.'

She laughed. 'Try not to solve the case by then.'

'No promises.' Marshall smiled. 'Did you manage to speak to them? I mean, Liam and Sheila.'

'Found them just as they were leaving. Thick as thieves and blaming everyone else, including Sheila's son. Then they tried to make out like *I*'d told them they could go. So I punished them by forcing them to take a few hours of overtime.'

'Tough boss.'

'The toughest.' She grinned at him. 'Catch you later, Rob.'

'See you, Isla.' Marshall entered the station, wondering if she flirted with everyone like that or just him. He swiped through into the incident room, then lugged his coffee mug into his office, which felt like it weighed a ton – he felt like he weighed about sixty.

Ravenscroft sat behind his desk, working away on his laptop. Took a few seconds for him to stop typing and notice Marshall. That, or he was playing power games. 'Ah, Robert.

Perfect timing.' He closed the lid. 'Just about to head off.' He frowned. 'Didn't we say seven?'

'We did, but I need to get up to speed before I brief the troops.' Marshall took a slurp of coffee. 'Unless you solved it overnight?'

'Sadly not. I've pushed out a media release – the vaguest stuff I could find words for – and I've notified the upper echelon. Crawford's completed the preliminary canvass as well. A big fat zero, I'm afraid to say, and one so big you could see it from space. Not that I expected anything, hence sending you for some kip.'

'Thanks, sir.' Marshall yawned again. 'Not sure it did me any good.'

'Hopefully that coffee will sort you out.'

'Hope so too, sir.' Marshall took another sip. 'First one didn't, mind.'

Ravenscroft blinked hard as he packed his laptop away – he looked like a zombie. 'Listen, Andrea's already in but she seems a bit manic. I've asked her to focus on getting hold of the sodding case file – she's sent someone called McIntyre up to Tulliallan to get it.'

'Good. Jim's one of the better officers we've got here.'

'Right, right. Listen, I'm really not a fan of bunfights like that. When things get political, it doesn't serve anyone, does it?' Ravenscroft lugged his laptop bag over his shoulder. 'I mean, I know people call me "the scythe" behind my back, because I slice through departments like one, but I'm more of a scalpel. I'm precise. I just want things to run efficiently. I want police officers doing police officer things. And driving to Tulliallan and back isn't the most police officer thing, is it?' He shook his head. 'Cold Case should be on the same page as us, willing the file to us to investigate and not selfishly holding on to it.' A sinister smile filled his face. 'Maybe I'll take my scalpel to them next.'

Marshall hoped he would and wondered which God he had to make sacrifices to in order to make that happen. 'Have you gone public with Heather's name yet?'

'Still awaiting approval on that score from above. Gone out with the usual vague emptiness. "Police Scotland are investigating a suspicious death tonight in the Scottish Borders near Melrose". The usual holding statements and bugger all else.'

'I think we should get her name out there, sir.'

'I've just gone with us holding back the victim's identity pending family notification, which we've obviously done, but that's to give us a bit of breathing room.'

'For what, though? Surely that's going to play better out there?'

'Robert, think it through, would you? You're the one who said Heather's now a public figure, remember? She's been murdered so we should expect a media firestorm the moment the news hits. We're talking national-level headlines and rolling coverage. To that end, I've been carefully crafting a set of nested press releases. I'll issue the first one after I've had some beauty sleep, then do a full briefing. We know the media are going to go crazy over this, so we need to maintain full control of the narrative. "No suspects yet", "ongoing investigation", "premature to speculate on any linkage" and all that jazz.' Ravenscroft walked over to the door, then paused with his hand on the door. 'Oh, and I think it's prudent for me to take Andrea for media liaison.'

Marshall nodded, but slowly enough to hide his excitement at having her off the case and away from him. 'You don't want her working on this case, then?'

'I don't think she can, Robert. Not least because of her existing relationship with the deceased. So she shouldn't be directly involved, but I think she can help us by being the face of this. Local cop, local woman, lost a friend. Having her standing next to me with her local accent and my… less so local. All that stuff. It'll give us good optics.'

'Of course, sir.'

'Good man.' Ravenscroft clapped Marshall on the arm like he was a good boy and deserved a biscuit. 'Have a good day, Robert. I'll call in once I've had some kip, okay?'

'Of course, sir. Do I need to brief DI Elliot?'

'Already done.'

'Okay.' Which meant Marshall was probably going to face a backlash on the level of a nuclear detonation from her at some point. 'We'll try and solve it for you.'

'Always under-promise and over-deliver.' Ravenscroft grinned, then buggered off out of the office.

Marshall shut the door, then sat at his desk, feeling a bit icky that the seat was already warmed. He stayed there, drinking his coffee and staring into space.

A final yawn, then he had an hour or so of work to get through before it was time for the briefing.

18

'Gather around!' Marshall stood at the front of the room, waiting for them to congregate. He shut his eyes, trying to will himself into action. The third coffee of the day was starting to have some effect, but it took finding his AeroPress in the bottom of his drawer to get him up to speed. He wasn't exactly feeling ready to attack this, but boy did he need to.

He reopened his eyes and saw thirty-odd cops staring back at him, with his direction their only way forward. 'Okay. Thanks to those who've been in overnight. Check with your supervisor whether you're still needed, but you can get home and get some sleep. It's massively appreciated.' He locked eyes with Crawford and got a nod back. 'Okay, so let's summarise where we've got to. Heather McGill was murdered at around half past eight last night at Scott's View. And this room might be pretty small, but it contains an elephant.' He walked over to the wall where someone had fortunately stuck up photos from the case summary, then tapped on one. 'The Sharon Beattie case.' He pointed to the big publicity shot of Heather, looking all determined. 'And the murder of Heather McGill last night.'

The room was silent.

'Both cases happened at the same location, almost exactly twenty-five years apart. Similar MOs. Heather was there that night. She discovered Sharon's body. And she was killed just after Sharon's case was officially reopened. That means there's got to be some connection. Right?'

Crawford nodded. 'Could it be suicide, sir?'

'Nope. She was strangled. Leye said the injuries sustained in the fall appear to have happened just after her death, which is consistent with someone murdering her and then pushing her over. He also spotted the imprint of a pattern made by the stitching of some gloves. There should also be a ligature near her body, but there isn't. Therefore, the means left the scene of her death, which means we're dealing with an inflicted injury.'

Crawford tilted his head from side to side, like he was weighing up both sides of that equation. 'Was she killed by the same person?'

'Now that we don't know.' Marshall shook his head. 'But it's the elephant in the room, right?' He looked around the room. 'I want us to focus on two possibilities. First, we need to consider whether she was randomly attacked or murdered for some other reason than her connection to Sharon Beattie's murder. After all, Heather was obsessed by Scott's View. Given what happened, she visited frequently so it's possible she just stopped there at the wrong time or someone knew she'd be there and killed her just because.'

Elliot scowled at him. 'Feels like way too much of a coincidence.'

'Agreed. Which is why I think this is linked to Sharon's murder.' Marshall tapped the photos on the wall. 'We have several factors connecting the dots here. Obviously, they occurred at the same location and, superficially, there are similar MOs to both cases – namely strangulation. There's no indication Sharon's killer wore gloves...'

Elliot nodded. 'That's right. Manual strangulation, but they didn't recover fingerprints. Or good enough ones.'

'The biggest factor for me is that Heather was involved in the incident back then.'

'She was.' Elliot grimaced. 'Her and a few others rocked that camper van back and forth. You can chalk it up to the stupidity of youth all you want, but it was a pretty crass thing to do. If any of my kids did that, I'd absolutely batter them.' She held up a hand and looked around the room. 'Metaphorically speaking.'

Marshall smiled, but he didn't see any humour in it. 'Andrea, you being so close to the victim could be useful for us. I want you to pull together a list of all those involved and, Douglas, can you get them all spoken to ASAP?'

Crawford nodded. 'Will do, sir.'

'Aye, aye.' Elliot thumbed towards the back of the room. 'Already given a list from memory to DI Archer.'

'Excellent. But that's not a full inventory, is it?'

'With insight like that, you could be a detective one day, Robbie... Jim McIntyre's fetching the original case file from Tulliallan – it's got a complete list of everyone spoken to.'

'Okay, good.' Marshall focused on Jolene. 'DI Archer, can you also get a team looking into Heather's interest in the case? Not just her personal involvement, but the campaign as a whole.'

Jolene nodded. 'Will do, sir.'

'Eh?' Elliot frowned. 'Why's that important?'

Trust her to ask the annoying question...

'Because we've got to consider that Heather poked a hornet's nest, as it were. She called me last night to say someone had been in touch after we reopened the case. Then she texted to say she was meeting up with the person last night.' Marshall looked around the room, trying to swallow down the feeling of guilt he had over it. 'It's fair comment to say Heather's had form in hiding details from us. The reopening of the investigation, for instance, was caused by her going off-piste. So we need to find out who she'd been in touch with.' He focused on Crawford. 'Getting her phone and the records would be a great starting point. How's that looking?'

'Already requested the records, sir.' Crawford had his arms folded. 'Ash pinged her phone and it's off. Last-known location is centred around Scott's View, but the radius is massive. Possibly the killer could've thrown it, but we'll search for it, sir. We'll find it.'

Marshall looked around for DC Ash Paton, but she wasn't there.

Crawford did a similar thing, covering it with a cough. 'But forensics have secured a laptop from the house and hopefully we'll have a picture by lunchtime of any messaging she's done.'

'Sounds good, but…' Elliot pointed to Heather's photo on the wall. 'Thing is, Heather was a demon on WhatsApp. One of those people who's always online. Always first to reply. And *always* last.'

Crawford narrowed his gaze to her. 'Not sure what you're saying?'

'I'm saying, Sergeant, that you might not find much in the way of texts.'

Crawford held her gaze for longer than was strictly necessary. 'I'll bear that in mind.'

'Brilliant.' Marshall rested a finger on the map pinned to the murder wall. 'Scott's View is a symbolic place for Heather. Whether it's connected or not, we don't know.' He looked at Jolene. 'Jolene, I need you to focus on why she was there. Who she was actually meeting.'

'On it, Rob.'

'Good. Good.' Marshall focused on Crawford. 'Have you found the man from the press conference yet?'

'Not quite.'

'What do you mean by that?'

'Well, we've found who you mean.' Crawford handed Marshall a photo of a man talking to Heather.

It was the right guy, but Marshall didn't recognise him.

Crawford pinned it to the wall. 'Sky gave us that. Had a lot of B-roll of her talking to that guy. It's in our canvassing packs for today and I've sent the photo as widely as I can. Someone has to recognise him.'

'Good work, Douglas.' Marshall looked around the room but there was nobody from forensics. 'Okay. Let's reconvene later, but please focus on the fact we're ahead of the game here. That means we have a lot of things in our favour. We'll catch this guy – and maybe it'll lead to finding Sharon Beattie's killer too. Maybe it won't, but let's keep our eyes and ears open. Dismissed.'

The crowd dispersed.

Elliot stood off to the side, already on her phone to someone.

Marshall slipped back into his office, then sat at his desk. He got out his phone and called Kirsten.

She bounced it straight away.

Great.

'We're sorry but the number you dialled is unavailable. Please leave a message after—'

Trev walked in, clutching a coffee and looking shattered. 'Sorry I'm late, Rob.'

'There you are.' Marshall ended the call and dropped his phone onto the desk. 'You missed an *enthralling* briefing.'

'Just finished up at the crime scene.' Trev sat down and grunted. 'You want my update now?'

'Sure.'

'Team are working hard, Rob.' Trev sucked deep on his coffee. 'Completed the forensics in the car – we don't think the killer got in with her, but we've got a lot of samples to run. Leye thinks she was killed outside, then pushed over the edge. Timing works. So that's been our focus.'

'That means she trusted whoever she was meeting, right?'

'Right. And he then strangled her. So you're looking for someone strong enough to overpower her and manually strangle her to death. No defensive wounds too, so your guy's likely to be very strong. Heather was small and light, but it's possible he carried her a reasonable distance to dispose of the body there.'

'You got anything backing that up?'

Trev held up an evidence bag. 'Found a button that matches a missing one from her raincoat.'

'How far are we talking?'

'Like three metres. But still, carrying another person any distance at all takes strength.'

'Leye said she wasn't moved?'

'No, he said she died where she was placed. Rigor mortis set in with her in that location. I think it appears she was attacked in the parking space, choked to death, then he carried her clear of any passing vehicles and deposited the body under that bench.'

'Got it.'

And all those comments stacked up – a strong guy who knew precisely what he was doing.

Someone knocked on the door.

DC Ash Paton waltzed into the room. Her shaved head was growing out to stubble now, but still made her look beyond hardcore. 'Morning, Trev.' She held up a bagged laptop – the same one Marshall had seen in Heather's office. 'Thanks for liberating this from her house inventory. I've managed to get in.'

'That was quick.' Marshall leaned forward. 'You got anything?'

'Started by extracting her internet history to see what sites she's been on. Can't get into Facebook, but there's enough text stuff for the team to get on with.'

'What about WhatsApp or text messages?'

'Sadly it looks like her texts might be on her phone, but she's got the WhatsApp app on her laptop.' Ash grinned. 'Sorry, that sounds very clumsy.'

'It does.' Marshall grinned back, but he wanted to know what the hell she'd found. 'Anything in there?'

'Good news is all her personal stuff seems to be in WhatsApp. Trouble is, there's a syncing issue, so the messages are out of date by a few hours. Back to three o'clock yesterday.'

'Before the press conference.' Marshall groaned. 'Why did it cut off then?'

'It needs to come from her phone and that needs to be online. Probably something as simple as turning it off so no calls would interrupt the press conference.' Ash gave an impish smile. 'But there are still plenty of messages on here. And some are particularly interesting.' She tapped the laptop. 'Looks like Heather had recently broken up with a boyfriend. And he didn't take it too well.'

19

Marshall drove them up the A68, stuck behind a column of traffic, even at this hour. A beautiful morning now, but it'd no doubt turn into rain again at lunchtime. He glanced over to Elliot in the passenger seat. 'I need to talk to you about—'

'So Rebel is just hacking into people's laptops now?'

'Rebel?'

'Rebel Rebel. Not sure if she's a boy or a girl. Ash Paton.'

'Jesus.' Marshall shook his head. 'You seriously need to stop doing that.'

'It's good for morale, Robbie.' Elliot sniffed, then crossed her arms. 'Trev's a good lad, though. Better than your ex, right?'

'My ex?'

'Kirsten. You aren't going out together anymore, not that you actually told me. Where I'm from, that makes her your ex, at least as far as I remember how these things work.'

'Right. Sure.'

'She was a right bugger for not helping out.'

'Maybe it was the way you asked.' Marshall looked over again. 'Or threatened.'

'You know me, Robbie. I'm results-focused.'

Marshall had to brake hard as an overtaking car pulled in right in front of him. 'Dickhead.' He even had to slow to give the berk some space.

'You sure you should be calling me a dickhead, Robbie?'

'Not you, him.' Marshall waved at the idiot in front. 'Has Ravenscroft been in touch?'

'First thing, aye. Said I'm being seconded to work for him. To focus on *media*.' Elliot grabbed her thighs like anyone else would headbutt someone. '*Media*? Fuck's sake, Robbie. I'm your best investigator and you're letting him use me for media?'

'I wasn't given a choice. And besides, you're too close to the investigation.'

'Eh? Where do you get that from?'

'The fact we're going to see a friend of yours from school right now? I mean, you shouldn't really be here, so be thankful.'

'Even so, you're the one who's losing out...'

'Once we've cleared this, you'll be back to normal.'

'Sure? Because these things tend to be a case of who touched it last.'

Hard to disagree – and Marshall didn't think that losing Elliot would exactly be the *worst* thing in the world...

'Talk to me about Mark Henderson...'

'What's there to say, Robbie?' Elliot sighed. 'Him and Heather were an item back in the day, so he's already on the list for Jo's team to speak to. Like we said back at the station, I'll do the intros and then bugger off to do media.' She refolded her arms. 'Just didn't know they were seeing each other again.'

'Mark and Heather?'

'Aye. Obviously less close than I thought. Thought we were pals, but it seems we were barely acquaintances these days.' She nibbled at her thumbnail. 'Feels like she was just trying to get the gen on how to kickstart the investigation from me. Pretty hard to take, you know?'

'I get it. But you still helped her, didn't you?'

'Eh?'

'You schooled Heather on that whole press conference.'

'If I said no, would you believe me?'

'Probably not.' Marshall sped up just as they saw the first sign for Lauder, one of those fancy ones with pictures to make the place look tempting for tourists – hard to avoid when the main road between Newcastle and Edinburgh went right through it. But it was a nice wee high street, with cafés, restaurants and a gallery. 'Look, I've never disagreed with reopening the case, but how it happened is suboptimal.'

'Suboptimal?' She coughed out a laugh like she was coughing up a lung. 'My *friend's* dead!'

'It's pretty obvious that she's poked a bear here and we're having to find her killer. I'm not saying it's your fault, Andrea, but I just wish you could've talked your friend down instead of up.'

Elliot sniffled again.

Aye, he'd pricked a nerve there...

Time to change tack.

'What's Henderson like?'

'Marko?' Elliot let out a slow breath. 'Barely seen him in the best part of twenty-five years.'

'You both live in Lauder but you haven't seen him in all that time?'

'I mean, I've seen him a few times, but not to speak to. Think he works in a garage now.'

'What was he like?'

'He was okay. Quiet. Never one to be the centre of things, you know? Lot of people like that. Me, I want to be in the heart of things, leading from the front.'

Aye, she really did want his job, didn't she?

And she really thought she was good enough to do it.

Marshall pulled up outside Mark Henderson's home on the

main drag through Lauder. On the ground floor and looking pretty run down – a broken bench outside with some smashed flowerpots. Rotten windows. 'You want to lead here?'

'Wouldn't want to cramp your style.'

'Andrea, the whole reason you're here and—'

'Aye, aye. Of course I will.' With that, she got out.

Marshall followed her out and walked over to the buggered front door. Flaking paint showing more filler than wood.

At least Elliot had rung the doorbell.

Didn't look like anyone was inside.

Marshall looked back towards Gala. 'Think he's at work?'

'I called there and he wasn't in yet.'

The door opened and a man scowled out at them, like the day was already too bright. And he just looked broken. Overweight and drawn. Shaved head, patchy and grey. Stubble lanced with silver. Dressing gown stained with egg yolk and brown sauce. Maybe sixty, so not Mark Henderson. 'Hello?'

Elliot smiled at him. 'Remember me?'

'Should I?'

'I'm the one who had your baby.'

'Andi?' He grinned at her. 'Andi Hardie?'

'It's Andrea Elliot now, but aye.' She opened her arms. 'Come here, you.'

He let him hug her, then broke off to look her up and down. 'Been a while, eh?'

'Hasn't it just.'

'That song, though...' He laughed. 'Remember dancing to that song with you in that club in Gala...'

'Then you blink and it's twenty-five years later and I've got three kids.' Elliot glowered. 'And I'm now a cop. DI Andrea Elliot.' She pointed to the side. 'This is a DCI Rob Marshall. Rob, this is Mark Henderson.'

Marshall was reminded once again how some people just aged harder than others...

He shook Henderson's hand, stained with nicotine. Had the look of the kind of guy who smoked a *real* cigarette rather than woke vaping. 'Need to ask you a few questions, if you've got a minute?'

Henderson shifted his gaze between them. 'Any chance this could wait?'

'Nope. And it's easier if we do it inside.'

Henderson winced. 'It's a bomb site in here.'

Marshall smiled, then thumbed at the road behind them. 'Easier in a bomb site than on a doorstep on the A68.'

'Fair enough.' Henderson stepped back to let them past.

Marshall followed Elliot into a grungy living room – and not in a good way. Henderson was right – it was a bomb site in there. The complete opposite of Heather's pristine home.

Games consoles sat under a telly in the corner of the room. A stack of games, all mixed together – PS4, PS5, Xbox One, Xbox Series X, Nintendo Switch. A brand-new Switch 2 sat on the box in the middle of a coffee table, the screen showing *Mario Kart World*.

That had only just come out – good to have a hobby...

The sink overflowed with filthy dishes. Food wrappers piled high, but only half of them looked like takeaway boxes. Some beer cans on the counter and some smaller tins of mixers next to own-brand bottles of spirits.

Probably from last night – Marshall wondered if he was someone drinking away what they'd just done...

Elliot took a seat at the kitchen table. 'Nice place.'

'Really?' Henderson plumped down opposite her, then his face straightened out. 'Still a sarky cow, eh?'

'Your dad lived here, didn't he?'

'Left me it when he died.'

'Sorry to hear that, Marko.'

'Heart attack. Should've seen it coming. Drank and smoked like there was no tomorrow. On top of a Scottish diet.'

Henderson patted his nostrils. 'And he liked the white powder.'

'That'll do it, eh?'

'Exactly. Three years back. Lived here since. Was staying in Gala before that. Should really sell up to be closer to work, but can't bring myself to part with the place. Still full of his stuff, you know?'

Elliot nodded as she looked around. 'Where do you work?'

'Mechanic in Gala. Max Power over by Aldi.'

'Right. Right.'

Henderson looked at Marshall, then back at Elliot. 'What's this about, Andi?'

'Heather McGill.'

'Right-o.' Henderson sighed. 'What about her?'

'When was the last time you saw her?'

'Few weeks back.'

'Oh?'

'What's that supposed to mean?'

'You didn't meet her last night?'

'Eh? No. I was in the pub. Pool league.' Henderson gestured at the empty cans. 'Things got a wee bit out of hand and a few lads came back here after for a game of cards.' He raised his hands. 'Nothing illegal. Just a few rounds of Uno.'

Elliot laughed. '*Uno*?'

'Rock and roll, eh? Good laugh once you get into it.'

Elliot held his gaze. 'But you've been speaking to her, haven't you?'

'O-kay.' Henderson looked away. 'Guessing you've got some evidence to suggest I have been, right?'

'Want me to go into it?'

'No, you're good...' Henderson collapsed back in his chair. 'Aye, so I was seeing her. Punching above my weight there. That's what all the lads said.' He grinned, then took a deep breath and bit his nails. 'Then she broke up with me.'

'Sucks, doesn't it?'

'Ach, we weren't much of a couple, though. Went out on a few dates.' Henderson laughed. 'She ended it about two minutes after I brought her back to this place.' He waved his hands around. 'See what I mean about it being a bomb site?'

'Just needs a tidy, that's all.' Elliot looked around, then focused on him. 'Maybe less pool and more snapping on a pair of Marigolds, eh?'

'Maybe.'

'So how did you get back together, then?'

'Mind how we went out together as kids? Whole thing fizzled out, almost as quickly as it started. I wasn't part of that group... The ones who... You know...'

Elliot narrowed her gaze. 'You mean, you weren't involved in the incident at Scott's View twenty-five years ago.'

'Correct. We'd broken up ages before. Soon as that happened, I was persona non grata with the rest of them.' Henderson gave a hard stare. 'Same thing happened to you after you ended it with Gary, eh?'

Marshall looked over at Elliot, but now wasn't the time to question her about it. He scribbled down a note to that effect.

'That was a massive mistake.' Elliot rolled her eyes. 'Haunted me ever since.'

'We were all such fuck-ups back then. I wanted to leave school after fourth year, but Heather persuaded me to stay on to do my Highers. Said it'd be good for my career, but I was *toiling*. Not academically minded, you know? Then she broke up with me in, like, October and I wasn't going to waste a *whole* year, was I? So I left school. Got a job. Still have the exact same one.' Henderson looked off into the distance, not that there was anywhere to look – the windows were smeared on both sides. 'Heather, though... She left for uni in Edinburgh and never looked back.'

'But she did come back, right?'

'Aye. Be... five years, maybe? Bumped into her in Gala Tesco's, of all places. Said she'd bought a place in Earlston. Folks were still in St Boswells.' Henderson frowned. 'Maybe her dad had died, actually. Anyway, her mum was still there. And we went out for a coffee a couple of times.'

'But?'

'Andi, I always harboured feelings for her, even when she was away. Mind that Christmas, when the arsehole had a party.'

'The arsehole?'

'Georgina.'

'I didn't know you called her that.'

'Not just me. But she was.'

'Still is.'

Henderson laughed. 'Well, she was back from uni. Final year in St Andrews. Mummy and Daddy were away at a cousin's in Australia for a few weeks or something, so she had a massive party at their place up in the hills. Mind it?'

'Vaguely rings a bell.'

'Got totally out of hand. Load of lads from Gala piled in. Total nightmare.' Henderson glared at her. 'That was the last time I saw you, Andi.'

'Sure I've seen you in the street.'

'Never spoke to me, eh?' Henderson snorted. 'I thought Heather would've been there at the party, but she wasn't. And I got totally wasted. Huge mistake. But then she did show up and I was absolutely guttered. Out of my skull. She ended up snogging some idiot. Broke my heart, to be honest.'

'But you managed to get back with her, right?'

Henderson cleared his throat. 'We chatted on Facebook a bit over the years she was away. Just little messages every few weeks and... then our relationship rekindled slowly.'

'Rekindled how?'

'Actually went on a date. I was terrified. That fancy restaurant in Melrose, by the hotel. Dean thingy runs it.'

'Mark, your memory's shocking.'

'I know. Never forget a face, but names? Absolute disaster zone for me.'

'You said it took time to build up?'

'Aye. Heather had changed a lot. She was pretty guarded. Used to be an open book, right?'

'That's how I remember her, aye.'

'That incident changed her. When she broke up with me, when she went to uni in Edinburgh... felt like she was running away.'

Elliot nodded. 'So you asked her on a date?'

'Aye. Thought I was going to make an arse of everything, but it just exploded into life. Got a taxi back to hers that night. Mad passion. Like way crazier than when we were kids. We shagged all the time. Even...' Henderson swallowed hard. 'Even did it once in her car at Scott's View.'

Marshall sat back. That was pretty messed up. 'What happened?'

Henderson looked over at him, blushing like he'd only just realised Marshall was there. 'What do you think happened? I put on a condom, shagged her on the reclining seat in her Astra and she drove off.'

'Who suggested it?'

'Neither. We just went there. Sat for a bit. Talking and taking in the view. Then we started kissing. Then it just... happened.'

'What time of year was it?'

'Eh, last October. Why?'

'Was that the only time?'

'Well, there, aye. But not the only time we shagged in her car, no. Did it in the car park by the Wallace statue just down the road. A few back roads. Elibank.' Henderson didn't seem to mind telling all this to two cops – he came across as quite the Lothario. Or wanted to seem that way, anyway. 'But it just fizzled out again. And I'm serious – it ended when she saw this place.'

Elliot looked around again. 'Hasn't made you tidy up, has it?'

'What's the point?'

Marshall waited for eye contact. Took a few seconds. 'Did she say why she was ending things?'

'Too busy.'

'She say what with?'

'Work. She was freelance. Writing stuff. Magazines and papers and that. Don't really understand that.' Henderson frowned. 'Why are you so interested in her?'

'It's taken you a while to consider that, hasn't it?' Marshall smiled at him. 'If the cops came into my house first thing in the morning to ask me questions about an ex-girlfriend, I'd be asking what'd happened to her.'

Henderson snarled, 'What's going on?'

'We found her body at Scott's View last night.'

Henderson got to his feet and stomped around. The empty tins rattled. 'What the *fuck*?'

Marshall waited again. There. Those dark eyes were filled with rage. 'We're going to need to speak to your friends in the pub last night.'

Henderson pleaded with Elliot. 'Come on – you can't think I did this, can you?'

'It's not about that, Marko. We're looking to exclude people.'

'Fuck's sake!' Henderson slammed himself down on a chair. 'I haven't seen her in *ages*.'

Elliot nodded. 'Thing is, you might not have seen her, but you'd been bombarding her with messages, hadn't you?'

'Eh?'

'Fifty-seven over the course of a fortnight. And not a single reply.' Elliot raised her eyebrows. 'That's harassment territory there.'

'I...' Henderson buried his head in his hands. 'I only did it when I was pissed.'

'Seems like you were pissed most nights, then?'

'Pretty much.' Henderson sighed. 'Look, I heard Heather was dating someone she'd met on the internet. And it melted my brain. She'd been using those apps, you know? Hinge and Bumble and all that. She was always on her phone when we were together. And it's... She was two-timing me, right? She was using her phone all the time, but now I know what she'd been doing on it...'

Elliot frowned. 'Any idea who she was seeing?'

'Sorry, no. I've no idea.'

Elliot pulled out a photo. 'You recognise this guy?'

'Let me see.' Henderson glanced at it. 'It wasn't him. He's ancient.'

'Okay, but do you recognise him?'

Henderson gave it a more careful inspection. 'Sorry, no.'

'He was at the press conference yesterday. Spoke to her afterwards.'

'Sorry. I've never seen him in my puff.' Henderson frowned. 'How did she... die?'

'Someone strangled her.'

The frown deepened. 'Like what happened to that Sharon lassie?'

'Similar, aye.' Elliot nodded. 'You know a lot about that?'

'A few of my mates were there when they found her body, so of course I do. Gary was pretty traumatised, if I recall. Made me glad I wasn't there.' Henderson sighed. 'Look, I'm not a killer. I loved Heather. Thought things were maybe going someplace. But then she just ended it and it completely broke me. If I've been sending too many messages, then I'm sorry. I was a mess. I wish I could apologise to her.' He looked out of the window at the passing traffic. 'But when she said this campaign was taking over her life and she didn't have space for me... Not great, is it? But I know when I'm beaten, so I just stopped.'

And he really did look defeated.

20

Duncan sat in his car, waiting. In all the time he'd been away, he'd remembered Scotland as a land of drizzle and misery. One season all year, unlike the four distinct ones you got in Canada – glorious summers but stiff winters with the shitty cycle of heavy snow for a few days, which melted away... Only to repeat the cycle again.

He looked over at his mother's care home. Butler House, like that made it seem grand.

And he was late for the appointment. He'd been early when he got here, but he'd sat there thinking about it. And now he was late.

Like making a decision by default.

'You need to go.'

Duncan looked over at Dad in the passenger seat. 'I can't abandon her.' He sighed. 'I can't let her die alone.'

'She won't be alone, son. They've got staff in there.'

'I know, but it's not the same thing. When you died, she was there for you. If I go, she won't have me.' Duncan sighed again. 'I don't know what to do.'

'You do, though. You should've already gone. You could be

halfway to Canada now, son. Or somewhere else. But you need to silence your mother, don't you?'

'Maybe.'

'Come on… You silenced Heather last night. You've taken so many, son. What's one more life?'

'She's all I've got left,' Duncan snarled. 'And I owe her for what she did for me.'

'Ah, here we go. Truth is, you still crave forgiveness from her, don't you?'

Duncan punched the wheel. 'Fuck you.'

'You really need to silence her, my boy. Or just go. Sitting here's not doing anything for anyone.'

Duncan punched the wheel again, then got out and crunched across the gravel to Butler House. He skipped up the steps, then entered the front door.

Zuzana was behind the desk, scribbling at some paperwork. 'Just a moment.'

Duncan watched her work and felt an urge… Deeply buried normally, but it was surfacing like a deep-sea diver.

Zuzana looked up. 'Yes?'

'Hi, don't know if you remember me but—'

'Mr Radford.' Zuzana pointed to the side. 'They're in Ms Johnston's office.'

'Thank you.' Duncan walked over and knocked on the door.

The place reeked of beetroot, that earthy musky smell.

'Just a minute.'

Duncan leaned closer to the wood. 'It's Colin Radford.'

'Can you take a seat?'

'Sure.' Duncan sat down. Fists clenched – he should be in there, but instead he'd sat outside talking to his dead father…

Talking about cracking up.

Focus on the fact you're sane…

'They'll be talking to the cops, won't they?' Dad was on the next chair. 'You should've run away.'

Duncan rolled up his sleeves – scratches covered both forearms, fresh blood welling.

'Ah, yes. The day after Sharon. After she'd scratched you…'

Duncan looked again but his arm was clear.

'You're way too experienced now, aren't you? Too good at getting away. They don't get a chance to scratch you now, do they? Heather was stunned by your speed and power. But Sharon got you back then, didn't she? Got you good. And there've been others, haven't there?'

The door opened and April smiled at him. 'We're ready for you now.'

'Thank you.' Duncan got up and followed her in, rolling down his sleeves as he walked.

Dr Japp was sitting there, next to Mum. Taking her blood pressure, pumping that cuff wrapped around her arm then watching the needle drop.

Last time Duncan had seen him, he had a full head of dark hair, but now it was mostly bald with patches of silver. And he really did look old enough to be in there as a patient…

Mum was staring into space. 'Poor boy goes off like fireworks when the wind blows the wrong direction. Father was the same. Best thirty seconds of my life, then he's off to sleep like a light.'

Japp laughed at that.

Mum looked over at Duncan but stared right through him. 'Who the hell are you?'

'This is your son, Mrs Radford.' April smiled. 'This is Colin.'

'Is it? Looks just like his father.'

'Not a bad thing. He was a handsome man.' Japp stood up and put his equipment away. 'Can I have a word, Mr Radford?'

Duncan smiled. 'Sure.' He followed Dr Japp back outside into the corridor.

Japp shut the door behind them. Then coughed. Hard. A

few times. He wiped his lips with his handkerchief, dotted with blood. Poor guy… 'It's been a while, Colin.'

'Years.' Duncan cleared his throat. He didn't have a hanky to wipe his lips clean, though. 'How's Mum doing? Honestly?'

'Honestly?' Japp rested a caring hand on his arm. 'Seen it all in my career.' He laughed and almost coughed again by the looks of it. 'My very, very long career.'

'I remember you. Surprised you're still practising.'

'What else am I going to do? My wife left me. My children don't speak to me. I hate golf. Too old for tennis. All I'd do is sit around drinking and, as a physician, I can tell you how bad that is for you.' Japp smiled. 'You used to work on the rigs, didn't you?'

'Based up in Aberdeen, aye.'

'Remind me what you did?'

'I was an engineer. Made sure all the rigs were working. Supposed to spend most of my time in Aberdeen but the reality is I was out in the North Sea, fixing issues. Nightmare. And it was a bugger of a commute, at the best of times. I didn't come back here too often. Most of my onshore time, I used to go camping up north.'

'Everyone calls it wild camping nowadays.'

'Everything old's got to be something new, right?'

'Exactly. Ex-actly.' Japp coughed. Just once, but so violently it was like he was going to bring up a lung. 'What do you do for work in Canada?'

'Nothing at the moment. On a leave of absence. Open-ended until I see how Mum's doing.'

'That's not answering my question.'

'Right. Sorry. Work at a place called Atlas Steels. I'm an engineer. Focus on automating stuff in the factory.'

'Always thought you were a brainbox. Chip off the old block.'

'Dad wasn't smart.'

'I mean your mother! She was a clever cookie.'

'Guess she was. When I heard she was in here, I spoke to my boss. We're between projects so he said I can take a sabbatical. Unpaid, of course, but this is why you have savings, right?'

'Of course. Of course. The fact you've come back to Scotland to sign your mother's DNR is an immense kindness.'

'Least I could do.' Duncan shrugged. 'Anyone would, wouldn't they?'

'I'm not so sure. Thing is, Colin, it might be needed sooner rather than later.' Japp fixed him with a hard stare, cutting through those rheumy eyes. 'I'm afraid your mother's dementia is only getting worse. Coupled with both her breathing difficulties and heart ailments, she's becoming increasingly fragile.' He leaned in close. 'You probably saw me measuring her blood pressure in there. It's stunningly low. Almost impossible to measure, in fact. And at that level, it greatly increases the risks of falls and then you're looking at broken hips and so on.'

'Right.' Duncan swallowed hard. 'I didn't even know.'

'She might only have a few months left, Colin. With severe dementia, the sufferers essentially forget how to swallow properly and that makes them prone to lung infections. She'll have difficulty breathing. And the hydromorphone can ease her urgency to breathe. It's a perfect storm. Trouble is, without a DNR we'd have to perform lifesaving measures on her again and, mark my words, it'll be required soon. As you know, that isn't what your mother wants and the bare facts are she isn't legally competent to make the decision for herself.'

Duncan ran a hand down his face, but it didn't wipe away the stark reality. 'I'm sorry.'

'Oh, it's not your fault, Colin. And it isn't hers either. It's just nature. With most sufferers, the condition expresses as confusion and, quite often, as anger which can tip over into violence. Paranoia's also common. One minute, people are out to get her and the next she's saying her son's a killer.' Japp nudged his shoulder. 'We take it all in our stride, of course, even the comments about sexual proclivities, which are none of our concern nor taken as factual.'

Duncan laughed. 'Maybe she's confusing me with my Dad. He was a violent man.'

'Who the *hell* are you to say that?' Dad glowered at him. 'And to *him* of all people? Look at him! Just look at him!'

Duncan ignored him and focused on the doctor.

'I do know what you mean.' Japp laughed, then wiped his lips again. 'I can see why you left the country!'

'She's held your secret for years, son, but now the dementia's loosening her lips. You should run away.'

Duncan smiled politely. 'I'd never have left, except a job came up in Canada. Hated to go but it was impossible to turn down. And I've been so busy. I'd no idea how bad she got.'

'How could you? You were on the other side of the Atlantic, weren't you? They can seem fine, but then you find them walking around Morrisons in their underwear.'

Duncan nodded slowly. 'Do you think I could look after her at home?'

'Now you're asking...' Japp blew air up his face, then scowled at him. 'She's getting the best care here. Why on earth would you want to?'

'She asked me. I feel like I owe her. If she doesn't want to live in a place like this, then—'

'A place like this?' Japp scratched his head. 'This is one of the best in the Borders. In all of southern Scotland, in fact.'

'But she wants to die at home.'

'That...' Japp puffed up his cheeks. 'A lot of people want to die in their own homes. Not all do, mind. Far from it. When the Grim Reaper visits, they'll mostly be in a hospital or a hospice, but...' He sighed. 'But with a condition like your mother's, I suppose that giving her familiarity could be a good thing.'

Duncan stepped back as Zuzana walked past, giving a wide

smile, then he watched her go, before looking back at Japp. 'So, could I do it?'

'Well, it's a tall order. The staff in a care home like this are experienced with such matters as your mother's going through. Whereas you're not.' Japp gave him a stern look. 'Colin, you need to ask yourself some searching questions. Such as, can you provide twenty-four-hour care for your mother?'

'Of course I can. She did it for me when I was little.'

'Do you have children yourself?'

'No.'

'Well, that's a shame.'

'I'm fine with it.'

'No, it's just that you'd be used to wiping someone else's arse.' Japp fixed him with a stern look. 'Ninety percent of it will be about keeping her clean. Also, taking her out for a walk to get some fresh air in her lungs and to stimulate her mind. And as high a protein diet as she can tolerate. The care staff here will give you her medication, of course.' He looked deep into his eyes. 'This matter's entirely up to you, Colin. I'll support where I can.' He gripped his shoulder. 'Do you want to do this?'

'Like I said, I owe her.'

'But are you *sure* you want to?'

'If she only has a couple of months to live, like you're implying, then it's the least I can do. I'm a pretty smart guy, so I can learn. If I have questions, I'm sure I can call in here for some advice. Or ask yourself. Right?'

'Of course. Well, then.' Japp gave him a curt nod. 'You're a good son, Colin.' He opened the door. 'Okay. Let me speak to the manager here to finalise her release.'

Duncan watched him go, trying to ignore the person sitting in the chair to the side.

Dad shook his head, slowly and balefully. 'What the *fuck* are you playing at?'

21

The station car park was virtually empty for once. A good sign – people were out and doing the doings. And Ravenscroft wasn't here for a few hours, meaning Marshall could focus on some work. He killed the engine and opened his door.

Elliot stayed where she was.

Marshall looked over at her. 'You okay there?'

'Just fine and dandy, Robbie. Why?'

'You've been silent all the way back. Which is very unlike you.'

'Saying I'm a gobshite?'

'You denying it?'

Elliot laughed. 'It's just...' She sighed. 'Seeing Marko after all that time was really weird. Talk about a blast from the past.' She sniffed and rubbed at her nose. 'He was quite a lively kid, you know? Not the smartest and he definitely shouldn't have stayed on for his Highers. But now... He's just a complete *waster*, isn't he?'

Marshall raised his eyebrows. 'That's a bit harsh.'

'Don't you think he is?'

'Because he didn't go to uni and works in a garage?'

'No, because he's a useless alcoholic. Barely functioning. And all those games consoles. That Nintendo thing's just come out and my youngest is being a nuisance about me getting him one. Marko's lucky he inherited that place from his dad.' Elliot glowered at him. 'But you think I'm a snob, right?'

'Maybe a bit of one, aye...'

'Rich coming from you, Robbie.'

'What's that supposed to mean?'

'Not all of us went to school with Little Lord Fauntleroy at Gattonside.'

'Balfour Rattray? He was a fucking bully!'

'Even so. Posh school for posh snobs like you.'

'That place was hell. I'm glad they shut it down.' Marshall needed to get her off this topic – she was a dog with a bloody bone on that one. 'You seemed surprised Mark and Heather had been an item again.'

'Would you go out with someone you'd been involved with as a seventeen-year-old?' Elliot winced. 'Sorry, I didn't mean that, Robbie.'

Marshall felt his pulse racing. 'It's okay, Andrea.' He swallowed down the sour taste in his mouth. 'Most people I know aren't seeing the same person since they were seventeen.'

'Right. Thing is, Heather always had bad taste in men. All about the shag, not the morning after. She was like a typical bloke... And mostly with laddies older than us. Lads with their own cars. You know the sort, right?'

'Describing my sister there.'

'Well. Mark was the only one our age I can remember.'

'But the fact he pined for her for years after...'

'The one who got away, right? Some blokes are crazy for shit like that, right?'

Marshall shrugged. 'Guess so.'

'Like you and that wee princess. Liana, was it?'

'She wasn't one and she didn't get away. Just a colleague.'

'Aye, aye. I believe you.' Elliot gave him a flash of her eyebrows. 'Is he a suspect?'

'You're not on the case, remember?'

'Sure, okay, but you brought me along.'

'Because you know him and you could get him to open the door. And you did, but that's all.' Marshall stared her out. 'What do you think?'

Elliot looked across the car park, clicking her tongue so it went up and down in pitch – not annoying in the *slightest*. 'Nah, he's not got it in him. Besides, he was stinking of booze so he'd clearly been on one last night.'

'Doesn't preclude him from getting to Scott's View to strangle her, then getting blotto.'

'True.' Elliot held out the print of the photo. 'Fucked if I know who this guy is, mind.'

'Can you ask Heather's mother?'

'Thought I'm not on the case...' Elliot sighed. 'Guess Ravenscroft will want me to add it to my media liaison remit.' She pointed out of the window. 'Here's laughing boy.' She got out and hurried off.

DC Jim McIntyre was just winching himself out of a pool car he'd parked too close to the wall. He rested a box on the roof, then finally freed himself and walked off.

Then he went back to collect the box.

Marshall followed her over.

Elliot stopped by the pool car's boot, blocking him in. 'You got the case file, Jim?'

'Eh?' McIntyre looked around, frowning. Then he spotted her and hefted up the file. 'Aye, got it.' He chuckled. 'Swear you can see the finger marks from the Cold Case DCI still clinging on to it.'

'Useless pricks.' Elliot grabbed it from him without a thank you and started poring through it. In the car park. 'Ah, here we go.' She read a sheet of paper. 'The list of people in both cars.'

Marshall scanned it over her shoulder, because one thing she loved was people doing that. 'Sinead Paton, David Limond, Kat McNish and Ian Smith.'

'Don't do that!'

Marshall stepped around. 'Are they on Jolene's list?'

'Of course. I think they all moved away, but Jim here will search for them, won't you, Jim?'

'I'll try my best to find them, aye.'

Marshall took the page from her and kept reading. 'According to this, those four drove off right after they found the body?'

'That's what I remember hearing, aye. Sinead freaked out and drove off. Total cowards. Says they were spoken to but claim they didn't see anything.' Elliot shrugged. 'Whether that's actually the case...'

McIntyre nodded. 'I'll make sure, boss.'

Elliot gave him a fist bump. 'Good man.'

'In the other car, we had Heather herself, plus Georgina McAllister, Darren Fox and Gary Hislop...' Marshall raised his eyebrows. 'I've heard people talk about a Gary but I didn't know it was *that* Gary.'

Elliot looked at McIntyre. 'Can you get on with it, Jim?'

'Will do, boss.' McIntyre took the box back off her, then buggered off into the station.

Elliot watched him buggering off and didn't look anywhere near Marshall. 'Robbie, I disclosed this all to Pringle and Standards a few years ago. Sure, we were an item when we were at school, but we'd split up by this point.'

'Okay.' Marshall leaned against the car and tried to make eye contact, but she was having none of it. 'I'm comfortable with you having a direct link to one of Scotland's biggest drug dealers and I'm prepared to let it slide, but only as long as you still have nothing to do with him.'

'Of course I don't.'

'And you're going to tell Ravenscroft, aren't you?'

Elliot frowned. 'Doesn't he know?'

'He should do.' Marshall smiled. 'But you're going to remind him, specifically noting how Hislop was part of the original case.'

'Of course.'

Marshall kept an eye on her – there was something going on there, that's for sure. 'Are you still in touch with Georgina?'

'*Sadly*. Lives in Melrose now. She's one of the organisers of this silver anniversary thing.'

'What thing?'

'Tomorrow night? Heather organised it and I think Georgina put money into it.'

Marshall nodded slowly. 'Okay, I'll get someone on Jolene's team to get her story.'

'I can help.'

'You're media liaison, remember?' Marshall shook his head, then smiled at her. 'Okay, so that's all of the people you know, except for Darren Fox.'

'No idea who he is.'

'But he was with them that night, wasn't he?'

'I think he was Georgina's boyfriend. Didn't know him, mind.'

'You ever meet him?'

'Once or twice. Really didn't like him. Got that creepy vibe off him.'

'Was he at school with you?'

'No. One of those guys who knew someone and who turned up occasionally. Think he's from Penicuik.'

'Another task for Jolene, then.'

'She's got a lot on her plate. Think she's up to it?'

'She's good, otherwise I wouldn't have fought for her promotion. But I'll see if I can spread the load a bit, seeing as how you're media liaison now.'

Elliot scowled at that. 'Heather already tried finding Darren Fox, Robbie. As far as we can tell, he dropped off the map.' She took a deep breath. 'But I know a man who might know him...'

22

Jolene turned off the A68 at the main junction. The Buccleuch Arms was doing a brisk trade – and no wonder. The old coaching inn looked inviting to hungry travellers – just gone on the market but surely someone would snap it up soon.

Marshall wasn't quite starving yet, but he'd need to eat soon enough.

Jolene drove them through St Boswells, the big open green lined with trees, with a row of mansions set back. Main Street narrowed at the town hall and they passed a corner shop and the Borders gun room on the left – because this was one of those places, where shooting wasn't just for toffs – then they twisted up the hill, past the wee Morrisons and the titular bookshop, then St Boswells Hardware.

Jolene waved a dismissive hand at it. 'Spreading like Covid was five years ago...'

'Sadly there's no vaccine against Gary Hislop...'

Jolene laughed. 'Lethal injection might work.' She did a three-pointer, then doubled back and parked outside the chip shop. 'You going to be long?'

'Few minutes, I suspect.'

'Just as well I brought my phone, eh?'

'See if we're getting anywhere, eh?' Marshall got out into the sunshine and it actually felt pretty hot. Any warmer than this and he'd turn into a sweaty puddle. A heavily sunburnt sweaty puddle. Made him glad he wasn't in the Met anymore – summers in London were dry and hot. He crossed the road and entered Main Street Trading Co. bookshop.

Might be just ten o'clock but it was rammed. Hardly any tables free in the café, plus a load of customers browsing the books, including a couple of young kids causing mayhem by running around and playing tig.

A big fat bloke was handing over a box of books to the woman behind the till and talking like she was interested. Probably a delivery driver – looked like one.

Marshall clocked DI Dean Craven over by the window, perched on a stool and looking out.

Marshall sat alongside him. 'Morning, Dean.'

'Rob.' Craven smiled as he sipped from his coffee. 'Gather congratulations are in order?'

Marshall frowned. 'What for?'

'Your promotion.'

'It's just acting.'

Craven scratched the stubble on his chin. 'Not what I heard.'

Marshall hated that aspect of policing – felt like more time was spent gossiping about people and promotions than on solving crimes. 'How are things in drug squad?'

'Same as ever. Doing God's work.' Craven took a dainty sip of coffee. 'Could do with a wee chat about Shunty, if you've got time?'

'Rakesh?'

'Aye. He's in Craigmillar, right?'

'The daft sod has sadly got himself stuck there. Why are you asking?'

'Got a DS gig going, that's all. Think he'd be a good fit?'

'You're probably welcome to him.'

Craven laughed. 'Faint praise, or what?'

'More like I won't be able to get him into my team.'

'Why's that?'

'Because he upset a few people. Or the wrong one.'

'She Who Cannot Be Named, right?'

'No comment.'

'Right.' Craven stirred a sachet of brown sugar into his coffee. 'Heard you're taking over the Hislop case from Mike Mukherjee?'

'Me?'

'That's the rumour, anyway. Mukherjee's being shoved to the side.'

Marshall sat back and laughed. 'Dean, I'm murder squad. Why would *I* be taking over a drugs investigation?'

'And yet you're here, asking me about a drugs investigation...'

'Only because Hislop's come up in a case.' Marshall leaned close. 'Gather you've got eyes on him.'

Craven pointed along the road at St Boswells Hardware. 'Full-time surveillance on his latest enterprise. Used to be an art gallery. We're hampered by the house opposite having a massive front garden, so we can't get anyone in there. Meaning we've got to watch it from an angle.'

'I'm not interested in the investigation, Dean. Just need to ask you a few questions about Hislop.'

'Nowhere enough coffee in the world for that.' Craven finished his cup. 'Can I get you anything?'

'Are you getting another coffee?'

'I might not like drugs, but I do love caffeine.'

'Have enough of it and it's like taking speed.'

'True enough. Is that a yes?'

Marshall nodded. 'Long black, ta.'

'What's one of them?'

'Upside-down Americano.'

'How do you...?' Craven frowned. 'Right.' He clicked his fingers. 'I get it. Water first, then the shot of coffee. Back in a sec.' He walked over to the counter.

Marshall looked out of the window.

Gary Hislop's monstrous car was there, so this lead was checking out. That said, having a brute of a DI sitting drinking coffee in the bookshop window wasn't exactly taken from the advanced covert surveillance textbook...

Craven came back, whistling a tune Marshall couldn't place. 'Just like all his other hardware shops, eh?'

'Except for the name.'

'Right. Not sure why he's broken with that.' Craven pointed over to the counter. 'Maybe this lot don't want him to use it.'

'You'd think people these days would just go online or to the new B&Q at Tweedbank.'

'These shops are on their doorstep. When you're up to your elbows in some DIY project, you just want to get the stuff now, right? And this bookshop's doing well, despite a certain online retailer. Tons of great butchers down here. People like the personal touch, more and more.' Craven winked. 'Besides, B&Q don't give you heroin with your No More Nails, do they?'

'True. So how's it looking?'

'Even though you're not taking over?'

'Even though.'

Craven shrugged. 'Sadly, it all seems legit. It does just look like a hardware business.'

'But you know it's not, right?'

'Well, that's the thing. We do. But it's like he's changed something. Truth is, I don't know what Hislop's game is now. We used to think the distribution for the shops was how he moved the drugs around. Pulled in a few vans, all clean. Weeks apart too. Truth is, it's just how he moves around screws, power tools and bits of wood.'

Marshall frowned. 'Has he actually gone straight?'

'Maybe. Not that he could ever admit it, because he'd have to admit he was ever bent. And he's always insisted he was straight.' Craven sat back as the waitress put their coffees in front of them. 'Cheers, darling.' He poured milk and sugar into his, then stirred it vigorously. 'Best coffee in the Borders in here, I swear.'

Marshall nodded. 'I do like this place.'

'That's the business.' Craven set his cup back down, then looked out of the window, sipping his coffee. 'So, the trouble we've got is—' He frowned. 'My God, that *is* smooth.'

'Trust me, Dean – I know coffee.'

'I'll look forward to having you as boss then.' Craven winked at him. 'We know Hislop's very good at purging people from his organisation, so getting to the bottom of what he's actually up to is pretty much impossible.'

'Surely a guy like you has ways and means.'

'Don't like to brag, but we've got people on the inside, aye.'

Marshall didn't want to go too far down that route. 'I need to speak to Hislop.'

'And not about drugs?'

'Nope. About a murder twenty-five years ago at Scott's View.'

'I heard about that.' Craven took another sip of coffee. 'Hooker found strangled, right?'

'Call them sex workers nowadays.'

'You can call them whatever you like, mate, but we don't stop calling them junkies. You think *Hislop* killed her?'

'Sorry, Eliot Ness, but you won't take him down like Al Capone for tax evasion.' Marshall waited for the laughing to stop. 'Hislop found her body, but he didn't kill her.'

'Still. Prostitution and drugs go hand in hand. Could be young Gary was already in the business. If you find the vestigial limbs of his involvement back then, we could fast-forward to now and see what's what.'

Marshall finally took a drink of his coffee and it was very good. 'Does the name Darren Fox mean anything to you?'

'It's tugging at my synapses. Who is he?'

'Someone who was there that night. A mate of Hislop's.'

'One of those vestigial limbs I could be looking for?'

'If by that you mean some ancient piece of his criminal empire that's otherwise been evolved away, then maybe. Sounds like he was an associate way back when. So if Hislop's been a naughtier boy than he appears just now, then he might lead to something.'

'No, I don't know who he is, but if he's germane to my investigation, then by all means shoot him my way.'

Marshall finished his coffee. 'I came here expecting you to be all weird about me speaking to him, now you're going off on weird tangents.'

Craven grinned. 'I'm just weird about you being my new boss.'

'Dean…'

'It's fine, Rob.' Craven laughed. 'You're okay to chat to him. Just don't fuck anything up. Leave the work to the professionals.'

'Fine. I'll be discreet.'

'Sure you will, *boss*.'

'Come on, mate. You know that's bollocks.'

Craven shot him a crafty wink. 'Do I?'

23

Marshall walked up to the door of St Boswells Hardware but the shop wasn't open yet. 'Typical.'

Jolene knocked on the glass.

Marshall peered in through the window and maybe saw some movement.

The door opened and Hislop scowled out at them. He shifted his focus between them. 'Rob?' He frowned. 'Sorry, bud, but we're not actually open yet.'

Marshall checked his watch. 'It's quarter past ten.'

'No.' Hislop laughed. 'As in, we're not due to open until Monday. Got a ceremony and everything. That local author's going to cut the ribbon. Assuming he remembers to show up.'

'Ah, I get you. Well, we're not here to buy some screws.' Marshall smiled. 'Weird how you didn't call this Main Street Hardware.'

'Bookshop wouldn't be happy about it, would they? Not that I asked them. So I broke with tradition. The one in Duddingston had to be named similarly. Used to be a light shop.' Hislop shrugged. 'It's not a big thing.'

Marshall nodded along with it, like he cared. 'Wouldn't mind a word with you.'

Hislop sighed. 'I really am up against it, mate.'

'Won't be long. And it's nothing to do with your business.'

'Oh?'

'Don't know if you saw on the news about Heather McGill's campaign?'

'That?' Hislop frowned. 'What's happened?'

'We found her body.'

'Fuck.' Hislop went white. 'You're serious?'

'No, Gary, we like to invent murders. Of course I'm serious.'

Hislop puffed out his cheeks. 'In you come, then.' He opened the door for them.

Marshall let Jolene go first, then followed her inside.

The shop looked pretty much ready to go and identical to every other one Marshall'd been in. Maybe smelled a bit more of sawdust and glue. Long rows of shelves with special offer bins at the ends, facing a wide counter.

Marshall gave mock applause. 'Looking good, Gary.'

'Cheers. Like to set them up myself to maintain standards, you know?'

'You must have one in every Borders town now.'

'Innerleithen opens in October. Traquair Hardware, so another break from tradition. And aye, that'll be all of them except for Hawick. Council won't let me open one there because there's already a successful hardware shop in the town. And the bugger won't sell to me.'

Marshall laughed. 'I'm surprised he hasn't had an unexplained fire...'

'I'm not that guy, Rob.'

'Sure you're not, Gary. Sure you're not.'

'Keep telling you lot.' Hislop threw up his hands. 'I'm a legit businessman. And it's working well. Surely you can see that?

I've expanded out wide now – Dumfries, Stranraer and Kirkcudbright in Dumfries and Galloway. This year alone, I've opened in Berwick, Alnwick, Wooler, Prudhoe and Morpeth in Northumbria. Ayr, Troon and Largs in Ayrshire are coming next. Even got approval to open one in Rothesay on Bute. And there's one going in on the High Street in Edinburgh. Had to call that bugger Royal Mile Hardware.'

'Having a network like that must come in handy for moving product.'

'Of course. Means if Kelso's short of screws, I can shift a few boxes from Gala, then send some trowels to Jedburgh for that building site.'

'Not the type of product I meant.'

'I know what you meant but I refute any suggestions to that effect. My business is all legit and always has been. Might've had to chat ever so nicely to someone to get approval here or there, but I'm clean. My businesses bring jobs to a town and we pay very good rent and rates.'

Marshall looked him up and down. 'You're looking healthy.'

'What, after one of your cops ran me over?'

'He wasn't an officer.'

'Potato, potahto. But you're right – physio's *finally* kicking in. Almost regained my full mobility. Been great, actually. I love getting up into the hills for a hike or getting out on my mountain bike.' Hislop flexed his biceps. 'Got a PT at the gym too – go there three times a week.'

'As educational as this is, we're not here to discuss your fitness regime.' Jolene rolled her eyes. 'Where were you last night?'

'Ah, the old alibi question.' Hislop scratched his chin. 'Because of the hassle you lot have put me under, I've learned to document my whereabouts at all times.'

Jolene nodded. 'So where were you?'

'Depending upon your timeframe, I was probably in this

very shop.' Hislop waved over at a camera. 'I've got it on CCTV. Four other people were working here if you need anyone else to back it up.'

'That's very precise.'

'Been a bit of a disaster, to be honest with you. We were in until about three in the morning.' Hislop yawned, then thumbed up towards the ceiling. 'The flat above leaked last week and we had to sort it out in a mad rush. Almost lost a load of good timber, but you'd be amazed what a good dehumidifier can do these days.'

Marshall tilted his head to the side. 'My heart bleeds for you.'

'Sure it does. Does that cover you? I could send you the videos if you want to ogle.'

'That'd be grand.' Jolene handed over a business card. 'You remember much about that night twenty-five years ago?'

Hislop scratched his neck and inspected the business card like he was surprised to be getting called on his bullshit. 'I still feel really bad about what happened to Sharon.'

Marshall frowned. 'Why, did you kill her?'

'No. Of course I didn't.' Hislop laughed as he rested the business card by the till. 'I put some money towards Heather's campaign. Least I could do. Not one to brag, you know? And I wasn't even the one who started shaking that van, but I did open the door and I was first to see her.' He stared into space. 'Can never un-see that, you know? Can still see her lying there…' He focused on Marshall. 'You lot any closer to solving it?'

'Can't say.'

Hislop narrowed his eyes. 'But you think it's connected to someone murdering Heather, don't you?'

'That's not the question I asked.' Jolene rested her hands on the counter. 'Who else was with you that night?'

'A few of us in my car. Eh, Heather, obviously. It was her

eighteenth birthday. And Georgina too... Other car was driven by Sinead. Still see her around. Weirdest thing – she's a taxi driver now. Picked me up in her cab once in Gala from the train. Easier getting a cab there than at Tweedback. Very unsettling, to be honest with you.'

'Did you talk about what happened?'

'Nah. Never that close, were we? Just a bit of "Have you seen Georgina recently?" or "Did you hear Mickey Spence died?" or any of that kind of shite.'

'Who else was with her?'

'Now you're asking...Think she had Kat and Ian and—' Hislop clicked his fingers. 'David. David Limond. He was Sinead's boyfriend. Pair of nu metal goth weirdos. Wore those stupid big trousers, didn't they?' He shook his head. 'What were people thinking?'

'Still in touch with them?'

'Nah. Thing is, Jolene, I was the runt of that litter. The rest of the crowd were Lauder, Earlston and Melrose. Posh towns. Whereas I grew up in a council house in Newtown. They didn't really like me.'

Jolene smiled wide. 'Nobody else with you?'

Hislop stared at her, eyebrow raised. 'Feels like you've an agenda. Out with it.'

'We're keen to speak to Darren Fox.'

'Who?'

'He was there that night with you. In your car.'

'Was he?' Hislop frowned, then he clicked his fingers and pointed at her. 'You know something – you're right. He was Georgina's boyfriend, wasn't he?' Then he wagged his finger. 'Aye, he was. She really fancied Dazza. He was, what, six years older than us? Hanging around to pick on the wee lassies. And Georgie... Talk about a girl with daddy issues... Loved the bad boys.'

Marshall nodded. 'So you knew him?'

'Mate of mine, aye. Lost touch *ages* ago.'

'How many ages are we talking?'

'Got to be ten, fifteen years. Why?'

'We need to speak to everyone, Gary. Just like we're doing here with you.' Marshall smiled at him. 'Could you pass on the contact details you have for him?'

'Sure thing.' Hislop picked up his phone and tapped away.

Marshall's phone rattled in his pocket. He got it out and there was a text from an unknown number, attaching a contact card. 'Thank you.' He smiled at Hislop. 'But I don't remember ever giving you my mobile number.'

Hislop scowled at him. 'Pretty sure you did.'

'New phone. New number.' Marshall held up his mobile and shoogled it in the air. 'Because someone kept crank-calling me. Know anything about that?'

Hislop looked away. 'Nothing to do with me, Rob.'

'I believe you.' Marshall held out his phone, showing the photo of the man at the press conference. 'Recognise this guy?'

Hislop took a brief look. 'Should I?'

'That's not an answer.'

'No, Rob, I don't know him. Who is he?'

'Just someone we need to speak to. If you had any clues as to his identity, I'd really appreciate it...'

'Nope. Sorry.'

'Okay. Let's move on, then, shall we?' Marshall gave him a flash of his eyebrows. 'What do you remember about that night?'

'What's there to say?' Hislop shrugged. 'It was wee Heather's birthday. Two cars driving around. They all wanted to go drinking in Melrose and then to that club in Gala to see some dude from the Happy Mondays DJing. The dancing one. I'd just got my first car, so I thought I'd drive them around. Think I had an early start in the morning, so I was going to Foxtrot Oscar after the boozer in Melrose.'

'Were they drinking in the car?'

'Naturally. But I wasn't.'

'Not really a great idea to have everyone getting sloshed in your car.'

'Hard agree there, Rob, but it's not illegal.'

Marshall nodded. 'Was it just the four of you?'

'Aye. Andi was supposed to be with us but she was ill.' Hislop focused on Jolene. 'That's *Ms* Andrea Elliot née Hardie. Surprised she's still going by her married name after what her delightful hubby got sent down for. After what he did to me.'

Marshall smiled to deflect. 'Okay, so Darren and Georgina were an item?'

'Briefly, aye.'

'And you and Heather?'

'Nope.' Hislop sighed. 'Thought there might be something brewing there but she was a wee bit snooty. St Boswells lassie. Newtown laddie. Like that Billy Joel song, "Uptown Girl". Wrong side of the tracks, me. Well, wrong side of the A68.'

'Even though you had your own car?'

Hislop laughed. 'You'd think, eh?'

'So what made you go to Scott's View?'

'Can't mind why, to be honest with you. We were just driving around, like you do. Met up with the other car, but those guys were even more pissed than Heather and Georgina were. Larking around. Drinking hard. I mean, Ian and Kat were practically shagging. And then we saw the camper van.' Hislop scratched his neck again. 'Old man told me a few stories about that thing.'

'Oh aye?'

'Lassie from Gala used to shag people in it. Working girl, right? So Georgina and Darren started rocking it. I think it was them. Might've been Heather. All happened so long ago, you know? But we soon got bored.'

'Did you join in?'

'Not proud of it, Rob, but aye.' Hislop looked away, a sigh hissing out of his lips. 'Then all hell broke loose. Wee Heather said she saw a laddie leave the camper so me and her went over and had a wee look. Couldn't see anyone, so I went in first. Fuck me. My first dead body.'

'You've seen some since?'

'My first wife died of cancer, Rob, so aye. I've seen my share.'

Marshall winced. 'Sorry, I didn't know.'

'Don't like to talk about it.' Hislop shook his head. 'Heather went inside next and, I have to say, it screwed with her head a bit. She went properly loopy after that. Was quite good mates with her and, like I say, thought something might happen between us… After all, I'd just split up with your good friend and mine, Ms Andrea Elliot.' He smiled, as though just remembering the punchline to an old joke. 'And Heather had just dumped that useless sack of tatties, Mark Henderson.'

Marshall nodded. 'Did any of the others see inside?'

'Think Georgina did. Girl was a total nightmare. Wouldn't wear her bloody seatbelt, the way some laddies won't wear a condom. Never had much to do with her, but she was in there after Heather. Started screaming and crying and making it all about her rather than the fucking lassie who'd died.' Hislop blew air up his face. 'Sinead totally shat it. Just drove off. Took the others with her. Left us all standing there.'

'And you were the one who called it in, right?'

'Only one with a mobile, aye. Bit of a pioneer. Now I hate the bloody things. See my wee lad, he's just addicted to his screens. All these tech CEOs don't let their kids have them until they're eighteen, meanwhile our kids have them from the *second* they plop out of the womb…'

Marshall knew this distraction technique well, but he knew how to handle it. 'You still friends with any of the others?'

'Was, but not after that night.'

'Oh?'

'Like I say, I was from the wrong side of the A68.' Hislop laughed, but it soured like a glass of milk in the sun. 'Bloody hell. They didn't speak to me afterwards.' He scrunched his hands up into balls. 'This whole thing coming up again… Talk about a blast from the past, eh?'

Marshall smiled it away. 'So they just blanked you?'

'Not really. They'd chat to me if they saw me. Wouldn't call me up and ask how I was doing, you know? And then they all just moved away, didn't they? Off to uni. Just me, Mark and Andi left here. And Sinead. Then even Andi left for a bit. Heard Heather came back a few years ago.' Hislop shrugged. 'Heard the news conference on the radio last night while we were working. And now she's dead. Bosses putting the pressure on you, eh, Rob?'

'Something like that.'

Hislop twisted his lips. 'You think it was Marko who did it?'

'Mark Henderson?' Marshall waited for the nod. 'Why do you say that?'

'Well, two things. Marko had been seeing Heather again. I mean, he's no oil painting these days, is he? And she still had it. Heard she just dumped his sorry arse. And he didn't take it well. Whatever the male version of a bunny boiler is, that was him.'

'In what way?'

'Calling her. Stalking her. Trying to get her mates to talk her round. Not cool.'

'And the other?'

'Other?'

'You said you had two reasons you think he might've killed her.'

'Oh, right. Aye.' Hislop lifted his foot onto the counter and stretched it out until it crunched. 'Back then, the cops thought

Mark Henderson killed Sharon. You know, the lassie in the van.'

'Where did you hear that from?'

'Are you serious?' Hislop laughed. 'They fucking interviewed me, Rob. This detective boy. Very intimidating man. Think he had a very obvious wig.' He patted at his neck, just below his left ear. 'Wouldn't stop touching it. Almost made me sick.'

'So someone told the police Mark Henderson killed her?'

'Aye.' Hislop put his foot back down and winced. 'I mean, it might've been me...'

'Might've been?'

'Still feel bad about it, in a way. Marko still services my car to this day and he's really bloody good at it.'

'Why did you tell them?'

'Somebody had to.'

'What? What did you tell them?'

'Heather told a few of her pals he'd gone over the score a couple of times.'

'What do you mean?'

Hislop shifted his gaze between them, his Adam's apple bobbing up and down. 'Way I heard it is he was choking her while they were shagging.'

'A few times?'

'At least once. And she hated it. Not a lot of lassies like it. Pretty much the main reason they split up – Heather was quite a vanilla girl too. Stands to reason Marko might go further with a professional, especially one as notorious as Sharon Beattie.'

'You knew about her?'

'Everyone did. Way everyone talked about her, you could pay her to do anything. And I mean *anything*, just so long as you wore a condom. Or paid double.' Hislop scowled. 'I hate speaking ill of the dead, but that's what people said.'

'People, eh?'

'I worked for my old man, Rob.' Hislop ran a hand down his face. 'He ran the hardware shop here in St Boswells. Shut it when he opened the one in Gala. The reason I named this one St Boswells Hardware is that's what he called it. After I inherited the business, I expanded all this out from there. But he taught me everything. Made me work most Saturdays and Sundays.' He leaned forward on the counter. 'The lads in the storeroom would talk about Sharon. "The hoor in the camper". "If it's rocking, don't come knocking". Wouldn't be surprised if one or two had used her services.'

'Do you know if Mark Henderson did?'

'Maybe. Thing is, all the people in the car were entitled wankers. Except Dazza. All still at school, focusing on their degrees and their careers. And Mark was different.'

'How so?'

'He'd left school by that point, hadn't he? Got himself a job in Gala at that garage. Max Power. All those guys he was working with in his ears all day, every day. Working men, you know? Some of them are absolute animals, you know? No morals.' Hislop grinned. 'Or they talked like they were. Told the sickest jokes they could think of. But most of them are just sad wankers. You can guarantee a couple of them would've been in that camper van with their twenty quid and a rubber johnnie. Or trying to pay her to do it without. And they'd last two pumps, at the most.'

Marshall nodded along with it – he knew the type. All mouth and no trousers, as his grandfather would say. They knew stuff and pretended they knew it first-hand so they appeared to be men of the world. He fixed a glare on Hislop. 'Answer me this, Gary, did you have anything to do with Sharon's death?'

'Never met her.' Hislop shook his head, staying calm and circumspect. 'Besides, paying for stuff I get for free doesn't match my business model, does it?'

'But you shifted the blame to Mark, right?'

'I dobbed Mark in because of how he treated Heather. Didn't think she had the confidence to stand up for herself. Cops needed to know what he was like.'

'Why didn't the cops go further with Mark?'

Hislop laughed, shifting his gaze between Marshall and Jolene. 'Isn't that your job to know?'

24

Marshall sat at his desk, phone to his ear. 'This is Detective Chief Inspector Rob Marshall of Police Scotland, based in Galashiels. I'm looking for Darren Fox, so I'd appreciate it if you could return my call.' He left his number and hung up, then crunched back in his chair and stared through his computer screen, just thinking it all over...

Eight people who'd been there that night. One dead. Two spoken to. A barrage of leads, but whether any of them led to the truth was another matter.

And a DCI chasing down a lead... Aye, maybe not the best idea.

Still, this wasn't just any random person. This was someone on Gary Hislop's radar, someone who'd spilled over into Dean Craven's murky world.

One of those vestigial limbs.

He googled it:

Vestigial limb *noun*: A body part reduced by evolution,

no longer functional but still present – a leftover from ancestral anatomy.

All he could think of was a news story he'd seen about a mutant snake that had grown a leg its ancestors had evolved away from.

Or the saying "as rare as hens' teeth" – they did happen, just vanishingly infrequently. One in a few billion.

Or a Tyrannosaurus rex and those daft wee arms that did nothing.

If he was like Elliot, one of those would become a nickname for Craven...

And he sincerely hoped those rumours were just people having a laugh at his expense, because running a drugs investigation just wasn't him. As much as he wanted Hislop taken down, he didn't have the skills to do it.

Someone knocked on the door.

Jolene stood there, head slightly tilted. 'You okay there?'

Marshall sat back and dropped his pen. 'Fine, why?'

'Look like you're playing chess against a superhuman AI.'

Marshall laughed. 'The trick to playing chess against a superhuman AI is to have your own superhuman AI. Or six of them. Then you choose the best move.'

'Smartarse.' Jolene sat opposite. 'You a chess geek?'

'I've dabbled. That's known as being a centaur. You pick the best of the AI and the human.'

She looked at him like he'd finally cracked. 'O-kay.'

'And now I've let you in on a secret, it's only a matter of time before the rest of the station knows.' Marshall grinned at her, as if defying her to not gossip about his guilty little secret – Elliot would give him a second nickname. Or a third... 'What's up?'

'Ash Paton's speaking to William Carruthers.'

Marshall frowned. 'Who's he?'

'A cop who worked the Sharon Beattie case. One of them.

Retired now, but he's the only one we've been able to get hold of. Wondered if you wanted a wee word with him?'

'Sure.' Marshall grabbed his jacket from the back of his chair and slipped it on as he followed her through the incident room.

She looked around at him. 'Getting anywhere with Fox?'

Marshall held the door for her. 'Just voicemail.'

'Don't believe that's his number for one second.'

'We'll see. I doubt it'll be anything useful for our case, but I don't really want to carry Dean Craven's bags for him.'

'Honestly, I've no idea why Andrea ever went out with Hislop...'

Marshall shrugged as they trotted up the stairs – he wasn't sure if she saw it or not. 'She was young.'

'Maybe. Guess he held her under his spell.' She opened the door to interview room two.

Ash Paton brushed a hand over her clipped scalp and let out a sigh. As modern as she was, the guy facing was the complete opposite.

A total mess in a stained grey suit, still worn despite looking like he retired yonks ago. An old-school copper and he instinctively knew brass and how to treat them – he shot to his feet and thrust out his hand with all the precision of a soldier on parade, or one on deployment. And Hislop was right – his dark hair, in stark contrast to the lines on his face and the ruddiness of his complexion. And the silver at the sides. No subtlety to his wig. 'DC William Carruthers, sir.' He cleared his throat. 'Sorry, ex-DC, given I retired.'

'Pleasure's all mine, Constable.' Marshall used his rank to keep him keen, then shook the hand, getting that tight Masonic grip of the old order. 'Gather you worked the case?'

'That's right, sir. Awful one, that.'

'Then it'd be great to dip into the well of your experience.'

'All part of it, isn't it?' Carruthers took his seat again. 'Rob Marshall, right? Recognise you from the telly, sir.'

Marshall sat next to Ash. 'Thanks for coming in.'

Ash smiled at him. 'We've been discussing Mark Henderson, sir.'

'Shifty bastard.' Carruthers sat back and sniffed. 'Interviewed him. Even held him overnight to put the frighteners on him.' He reached over to pick up the case file. 'Interview transcripts are all in here.' He scratched his neck. 'Henderson refused to answer even the most basic question. And this is pre-Cadder, so you couldn't just "no comment" your way through without the jury being able to interpret that silence as harming your case.' He gave a big laugh.

Nobody joined in.

Carruthers scratched his neck again. 'Still, he just rode it out. Only time he spoke was to claim innocence. Laddie wasn't even eighteen, but he knew how to play us.'

Marshall nodded – he'd seen the sort. 'Did Mr Henderson give you an alibi?'

'Nope. And we had to let him go, didn't we? I wanted to charge him.'

'Because...?'

Carruthers frowned. 'Because his fingerprints were all over her camper van.'

'Hang on.' Marshall looked over at Ash, but she didn't seem to be as confused as he was, so he focused back on Carruthers. 'Henderson wasn't one of the group at Scott's View that night, but you found his prints on the van? And then you just let him go?'

'We had to, didn't we? Boy told us he'd worked on the camper van at his garage for its service that week. Logs checked out.'

'Which garage was that?' Even though Marshall already knew.

'Max Power in Gala.'

'I know it.'

'Right. Place is still there but Max must be getting on a wee bit now. But the theory my boss was running with was Henderson had chatted to Sharon when doing the service and booked her in for a shag, then he went over the score.'

'Why did you think that?'

'The Hislop lad told us he'd choked the McGill lassie while they were rutting.'

Marshall grimaced at the word. 'Did you manage to back up that story?'

'Asked everyone. Henderson denied it. Heather too. Heard it from nobody else.' Carruthers scratched a plook on his neck hard enough to pop it, by the looks of it. He stared at his fingers, then sucked them. 'Actually, that's not true. Heather didn't want to talk about it. Don't blame her, either. Just turned eighteen, right? And two hairy-arsed cops are asking her if she's been choked while doing the nicey-nice with her former laddie?' He laughed. 'Hardly likely to open up, is she? And she'd just seen Sharon's corpse in the camper van.'

'Does that mean you don't believe the story?'

'I tend to go where the evidence leads me, sir. But the fact we couldn't back it up makes me doubt it.' Carruthers pointed to Ash. 'DC Paton here said you found Heather's body?'

Marshall nodded. 'That's right, aye.'

'You think the same guy did both?'

'Be mad not to at least consider it, eh?'

Carruthers nodded, then shifted his focus between them. 'You think the Henderson boy did her too?'

Marshall sat back and made it look like he was thinking through a fresh insight. 'Seems a bit tenuous to me.'

'Eh?' Carruthers frowned. 'Why d'you think that?'

'For starters, Mark Henderson had to get into and out of a camper van to murder a sex worker, while his friends –

including his ex-girlfriend – just so happened to be there and yet they didn't spot him?' Marshall paused until he got a nod. 'And why would he do it? What's his motive?'

'Because he could.' Carruthers leaned forward. 'Tell me this, son – in your time as a cop, as a detective chief inspector, tell me you haven't seen the most heinous shite done because some wee bastard just wants to?'

'Fair enough.'

'You've got the DNA my betters lost. Maybe if you hang on to it long enough this time you can see if Henderson's a match?'

But Marshall clocked him as a follower, rather than a leader. The kind of cop who'd carry the coat for the boss and who'd never challenge the party line on anything.

Carruthers picked up a document and flicked through it. 'Gary Hislop would be Thomas Hislop's boy, correct?'

'That's right.'

'Good kid. But I never trusted him an inch.'

'Thanks for the chat.' Marshall smiled at him. 'I'll leave you with DC Paton.'

'Hope you catch him. For both their sakes.' Carruthers shook his head. 'This is the Borders. We're not supposed to have murders down here.'

'I wish that was true.' Marshall walked over to the door, then led Jolene back towards his office.

Jolene walked alongside him. 'What are you thinking, Rob?'

Marshall scowled as he skipped down the stairs. 'I'm thinking they had bugger all to go on back then.'

'That's pretty much what I got from a scan through the file.'

'And what's *your* take on him?'

'I'm allowed to have a take?' Jolene grinned as she opened the office door. 'My take is I can't help but think Heather's actions have caused Sharon's killer to come out of the woodwork. We were holding off on the public announcement to do it strategically with the new SIO, whether that's you or the Cold

Case Unit, but she jumped the gun and announced it yesterday. She also posted on her socials to that effect.'

Marshall couldn't disagree with any of that. 'I got a world of pain from Ravenscroft over that.'

'Right. Right. Well, I think this is all connected. Heather announced to the world we had DNA evidence belonging to the killer. The joy of strangulation with gloves is you don't leave any prints behind. And if it's outside, then there's no DNA. Sharon's killer got away with it for twenty-five years. But if it turns out his DNA had been found under her fingernails from defensive scratching? Everyone knows DNA's the clincher. Back then it was pioneering, but now it's just basic policing. Stands to reason he'd want to shut down Heather's work.'

Marshall smiled – he'd trained her well, though most of it was her latent talent. 'So what approach do you suggest we take?'

Jolene checked her watch. 'Suggest we get Mark Henderson's DNA and test it. Then we'll all know for sure if he's the killer.'

25

Max Power was stuck up a back street between Aldi and the bus depot, lurking in the shadow of the hill splitting the two main routes through Gala. Well, the main route and the sneaky shortcut locals knew.

Marshall walked over to the garage, keeping pace with Jolene – no parking anywhere near the place, which was surrounded by parked cars.

Clanking sounds came from inside.

Max Power exhaled his cigarette smoke slowly as he looked at them, but they were just people – his hungry eyes focused on the pool car parked on the pavement. Probably saw a few hundred quids' worth of work in it. But he laughed. 'That thing needs a funeral home, not a garage.'

Marshall joined in, but tried to keep upwind of him. 'It's seen better days for sure.'

'Haven't we all!' Max blasted out a throaty laugh, then shot Marshall a frown. 'Recognise you from somewhere...' A deep frown settled onto his forehead. 'Hang on... You sold the young lad that big truck, didn't you?'

'For my sins, aye.' Marshall nodded. 'How's it been?'

'Oh boy.' Max gave a mad cackle. 'Sunk the suspension and put in a new V8 engine. Old one had six of the eight fuel injectors gubbed. Took us *hours*, but we turned a total mess into an absolute monster. Like shit off a shovel now.'

Marshall was stunned by that. 'Thought you were going to say it'd broken down or something.'

'Hasn't had a single issue. Thing runs like a dream. Shane's ecstatic with it. And now I remember who you are. And what you do for a living.' Max wiped his hands and focused more on Jolene. 'Take it this is an official matter, detectives?'

'Afraid so.' Marshall showed his warrant card. 'Looking for Mark Henderson.'

Max Power rolled his eyes. 'What's Marko done now?'

'That implies he's done other things?'

'Good worker, don't get me wrong, but his personal life is ridiculously chaotic. Never seen a laddie with more going on.'

Marshall looked around and spotted Shane the truck buyer – he even got a wave from him. 'Is Mark here yet?'

'Covering the late shift, aye. Which is good, as he was stinking like a brewery when he came in. Face like thunder too. Take it you've already spoken to him?'

Jolene smiled at him. 'Just got a few follow-up questions to ask.'

'Oh aye…' Max gestured through the garage into the office area. 'Have a seat, I'll fetch him.'

Marshall led Jolene into the tiny room, which stank of instant coffee, oil and – weirdly – mud. Two ancient dining chairs sat next to a desk covered in paperwork, rags and a computer even older than the chairs. An engine sat on the floor, so Marshall had to step over to get to his seat.

Jolene took one and it seemed to list to one side, like a yacht in a heavy storm.

Just as Mark Henderson walked in, face smeared in oil and navy overalls struggling to contain his gut. But his eyes betrayed how little he wanted to speak to them. 'Boss said you wanted another word?'

Marshall nodded. 'That's right.'

Henderson glanced at Jolene, then away. 'Andrea not with you?'

'She's involved with another matter.'

'Fine.' Henderson sat behind the desk. 'What's up?'

'I'm not sure if my colleagues mentioned it earlier, but we uncovered some misfiled evidence from the Sharon Beattie case.' Jolene gave a wide smile, like he could help them solve it. 'It'd be great if we could have a DNA sample from you.'

Henderson laughed. 'You want my DNA?' He gave her a sharp look. 'What are you comparing it with? Did the killer leave something behind?'

'Interesting.' Marshall sat back but the chair didn't feel very solid. 'That's the kind of question the killer would ask. Or someone very well-versed in forensics.'

'Come on. You're saying you've only just found evidence from back then? Don't believe that for a second. Stitching me up here.'

'We can't just conjure up DNA.' Marshall leaned forward and the chair felt a bit more stable. 'It'd been misfiled.'

'Misfiled, eh? And you just happened to find it now, eh?'

'Because of Heather's work, yes. And even "lost" things can have a chain of custody. This item fell to the bottom of the evidence box, below the file folders. Given the box was sealed and hadn't been opened in twenty-five years, we know it was put in there on that specific date and it was removed on a recent date. Therefore, it stands to reason it was still in the box during the time between those dates. It's solid evidence and it's admissible in court.' Marshall left a pause, trying to see if Henderson was keeping up. 'So if you're confident it's not you, then you could ride this out. But the thing is, you'd be wasting our time.' He sat back in his chair now. 'So, I guess the question is how confident are you?'

'Not giving my DNA to anyone.' Henderson got back to his feet. 'Heather told me not to trust the cops. You just want a quick result, right?'

Marshall smiled. 'Twenty-five years is hardly quick.'

'Don't get smart with me.'

'I'm serious.' Marshall joined him standing. 'But we could do this in the police station, if you'd rather.'

Henderson sneered at the suggestion, but it seemed to calm him down enough to sit again.

Marshall followed it, then tried a hard look this time. 'The truth is, Mark, we got lucky with this evidence thanks in part to Heather's persistence. This is the chance for Sharon Beattie to get some justice. It's also the opportunity for you to prove it wasn't you.'

'It wasn't me.'

'So prove it. Once and for all.'

Henderson just sat there, shaking his head.

Jolene tilted her head. 'When was the last time you heard from Heather?'

'When she broke up with me.' Henderson gritted his teeth, nostrils flaring. 'Over WhatsApp. Didn't have the courage to do it in person.' He clenched his jaw. 'Don't want to speak ill of the dead, but being treated with that little respect? It's pretty shitty, isn't it?'

Jolene nodded. 'Probably pretty common nowadays, right?'

'With kids, sure. But we're in our bloody forties!'

'But you didn't approach her after that?'

'No. Why would I? I'd got the message, loud and bloody clear.'

'Maybe because you were annoyed she'd broken it off over WhatsApp?'

'I'd called her a few times. You know that. Andi was asking

me about that at home.' Henderson shifted his gaze between them. 'Put it this way, I've kind of got used to Heather breaking up with me and me not having a scoobie why.'

'So she didn't say why she broke it off back in 2000?'

'Nope.'

'Someone ends a relationship and you don't know?'

'Right. Exactly.'

'But you were in a relationship with her recently and you didn't discuss it?'

'Of course we did.' Henderson sighed. 'But not in any great detail. We were both different people back then. Well, she changed a lot after the incident. So she kept saying, anyway.'

'But she never gave you an explicit reason?'

'Said I was selfish.' Henderson looked away. 'And I was. Thing is, I was really struggling at school. And I only stayed on because she'd encouraged me to. I was working part-time here. Most weekends. Old man got me this. Worked here himself. But I just drifted apart from that group. Couldn't manage to keep up with them.'

'Sadly, we can't ask Heather.' Jolene sat back and sighed. 'It wasn't anything to do with you being sexually aggressive?'

'*Sexually aggressive*?' Henderson shot to his feet. 'What the fuck are you talking about?'

'We've had reports of you choking her during—'

'Fuck off!' Henderson jabbed a finger towards her. 'This is fucking *bullshit*.'

Jolene sat back, calm as you like. 'You're denying it?'

'I'm not a fucking strangler!'

'You never did a bit of that even because she wanted to?'

'No fucking way!' Henderson narrowed his eyes and took a few deep breaths. 'When I had sex with Heather, it was straightforward.'

Marshall frowned. 'But you told me and Andrea that Heather was wild, right?'

'I'm very vanilla. Few lads in here are proper shaggers and never tire of telling you.'

'You had sex in her car. That's not vanilla.'

'Okay, but she's wilder than she used to be.' Henderson sat down again. 'And wild for me. Like I say, I'm very vanilla between the sheets.'

'Wild enough to want you to choke her when you're having sex, Mark?'

'No!'

Jolene held his stare. 'We have Heather's laptop.' She pulled out some papers. 'We've extracted a copy of the WhatsApp messages you shared with her.'

Henderson swallowed hard. 'And?'

'Well, your story checks out. You were dumped by text.'

Henderson seemed to relax a bit. 'So why are you still speaking to me?'

Jolene handed over a sheet of paper. 'Have a look at this.'

Henderson stared her down, then reached over to pick up the page. His hands were shaking. He scanned it, then set it down and swallowed again. 'Bloody hell.'

Jolene left a pause. 'You recognise those names?'

'Bit thrown by seeing them again, to be honest. A lot of people I haven't even thought of in such a long time.'

'You ever discuss them with Heather?'

'Not really.'

'Even when you were going out recently? Even when she was running a campaign to investigate what happened?'

'Even so.' Henderson tapped the page. 'Still see Gary Hislop when he gets his cars repaired. Has so bloody many. Doing well for himself. The fucking snake.'

Jolene tilted her head again. 'Why do you say that?'

'Well…' Henderson folded his arms. 'Gather he's been questioned by you lot over the last few years.'

Jolene smiled. 'He told you that?'

'He did, aye. Reckons you lot think he's this drugs kingpin, when he's just a wee fanny with a few hardware shops.' Henderson laughed, but it darkened to a glower. 'It was Gary who told you about the choking, wasn't it?'

Jolene shrugged. 'Can't comment on that.'

'Okay. Thing is, I've sat here and answered your questions, but there's a reason I don't trust you lot.' Henderson snarled at them, like a rat backed into a corner. 'The cops tried to pin it on me back then. Thought I was an easy suspect, didn't you?'

Marshall raised his hands. 'Neither DI Archer nor I were serving back then. We're both younger than you.'

'You seem just the same, though.' Henderson shook his head. 'You *honestly* think I murdered Heather?'

Jolene reached over for the page. 'We just need to know where you were last night.'

'I told this boy here.' Henderson pointed at Marshall. 'I was in the pub, then I had some mates back to mine for some games of Uno. Then I stumbled to my bed. Him and Andi Hardie woke me up.' He prodded the desk. 'I'm not a killer. Why would I want to kill Heather, eh? Truth is, I hoped to get back with her. Might not be much to look at but I really liked her.'

'Okay, but this all goes back to why your prints were all over Sharon Beattie's camper van.'

'I told you lot this. I'd worked on it in here.'

Jolene laughed. 'That's incredibly convenient.'

'I know you lot checked out my story. It's all true – Sharon was a regular customer here. That thing was ancient and broke down a lot. We used to do a lot of camper vans and four-by-fours and that. Only place in Gala that did.'

Jolene nodded along with it. 'So you'd speak to her when she was in?'

'Right. I mean, she was sketchy. Obviously on drugs. But she was nice enough.'

'But you didn't give DNA back then.'

Henderson looked away. 'Didn't have to. So why should I?'

'You could do it now. Get ahead of this. Prove you're not the killer.'

Henderson locked eyes with her. 'I'm not the killer.'

'So why not just clear your name, then?'

'Because you lot took my fingerprints and they matched to the ones in the camper van. And you didn't believe me when I said I worked on that van. Made my life hell. So why the hell should I help you now?'

'To prove you didn't murder Sharon or Heather.'

'I didn't. And you don't have anything saying I did, do you?'

Marshall cleared his throat. 'Mark, your way out of this is to give us your DNA. It'll only take a few hours to process. If you're innocent, then you'll be clear of this by the end of your shift. And for good. We'll never have to speak again.'

Henderson seemed to consider it. 'But if you lot frame me again...'

'We can't. It's a fairly binary thing. It is or it isn't. If it matches, then you'll face justice. And if you refuse, it won't prejudice you, but you can bet we'll be speaking again. Frequently. And we'll be having words with all your pals in the pub. The guys here at work. Anyone you know. Ex-girlfriends to see if they were ever choked by you.' Marshall leaned forward and spoke in a harsh whisper, 'And we can also get a warrant to obtain your DNA.' He sat back, keeping his expression neutral. 'So really it's a choice of now or later.'

Henderson scowled at them. 'You can't do that.'

'It's a big ask, sure, but the odds are stacked heavily in our favour.' Marshall stretched out, acting all casually. 'After all, Mr Henderson, your fingerprints were all over that camper van twenty-five years ago.'

'Mark.' Max Power was waiting in the doorway, wiping his fingers on a rag. 'Can I have a wee word?'

Henderson glowered at them as he got to his feet. He left the office and chatted to his boss, just out of earshot.

Jolene looked over at Marshall. 'If you've nothing to hide, why hide it?'

'Agreed. Some people are right to fear authority. The police aren't exactly squeaky clean these days. Or we're just worse at covering things over and better at identifying corruption.'

Jolene laughed. 'Sounds a bit woke to me.'

'It's just reality. I worked in the Met with some of those people who—'

'Mark!' Max Power's shout was loud enough to hear over the din of the garage. 'I've known you all your life, son. Your dad was a great pal of mine. You're a good laddie. A bit daft, but you've a good heart. But I don't get this. If you didn't kill that lassie, then—'

'I didn't!'

'So give them your bloody DNA to prove it.'

'I don't trust them, Max.'

'Mark. If you don't give them it, then I'm going to believe you killed both those lassies. And that's me and you finished.'

Henderson was quiet now, just the grunt and groan of the other mechanics and the clanking of machinery. The radio playing a Coldplay song.

Henderson came back through, head bowed. 'I'll give you my DNA.' He jabbed his finger at Jolene. 'But I really don't trust you.'

26

Elliot took yet another sip of tea, but she was drinking so much it was like she was on a drip. Seemed like all Barbara McGill did was make tea, drink tea and bake scones – never seemed to eat any, but then grief did funny things to you.

And Elliot knew all about that.

Barbara sipped some of her tea and gasped. 'Thank you for letting me spend time with Heather.'

'Of course.' Elliot lifted her cup but didn't take a drink. 'I'm sorry you had to do that.'

'Aye. Goes against the natural grain of things, doesn't it? You want your kids burying you, not the other way round.'

Elliot looked away.

Barbara shut her eyes. 'Sorry, Andrea – I didn't think.'

'It's okay. Mine have already done that for one parent.' Elliot gave a polite smile, but she stung inside. Her heart and deep in her guts. Everything ached. 'Leye told me the funeral director will be in touch to arrange things in due course but, as this case is a murder, I have to warn you Heather's body won't be released for a long time.'

'I understand.' Barbara nodded. 'Is there anything I can do to help you?'

'Not sure. I'm working on the media liaison for this case. We'd need to—'

Elliot's phone lit up with a call.

Sam calling...

Elliot bounced it and stuffed her phone back in her handbag. 'Sorry about that. Shouldn't have my phone out.'

'It's okay.' Barbara smiled, full of kindness and understanding. 'Was it work?'

'No. It was Sam.'

'Is Sam your new man?'

Elliot sighed – nosiness was a two-way street here. 'Sam's my daughter. She's at uni in Glasgow now.'

'Heavens! University already?'

'I know... Her marks are stellar too. Somehow. No idea where she got that from. She's even got herself a wee boyfriend now.' Elliot yawned.

'Andrea, go home and get some sleep.'

'It's fine. I've got a system, from when I was in uniform. Just get through this shift, then go to bed an hour early.' Elliot yawned again. 'Easier said than done, though.'

'It's tough for you, isn't it?'

'I'm fine.'

'No, Andrea, you're not. You've lost your husband and you're raising three kids on your own. One was tough enough with two of us.'

Elliot took a drink of tea. 'It's much easier now Sam's off to uni. And Mum and Dad help out a bunch.'

'Your folks are good people.'

'Aye, they try to be.' Elliot smiled but it felt hollow. 'So, as I was—'

'I'm worried about—'

They both laughed.

Barbara gestured to her. 'You first.'

'No, you go.' Elliot held her gaze. 'I insist.'

Barbara sighed. 'I was saying, I'm worried about Heather's house.'

'What about it?'

'Well, anyone could break in.'

'We've locked it up and she had a security system. A pretty aggressive one.'

'That's true, I suppose.' Barbara poured out yet another cup of tea. 'I suppose it'll be fine.'

Elliot waited for her to finish. 'Was there anyone who Heather was in touch with in the media regarding these campaigns? Maybe nationally or locally?'

'Not that I can think of.' Barbara frowned. 'Not that she'd tell me, anyway. Why?'

'Just in case we can leverage something she'd placed in the press before. They love follow-up stories.'

'I don't think she'd done much with real papers. You know, newspapers. It was mostly on Instagram.'

'Okay, that's what I figured.'

The doorbell rang, a glorious chiming melody completely at odds with what was happening.

'Better see who this is.' Barbara winched herself up to standing. 'I've got more than enough lasagnes and cottage pies to last me through the next ice age, I tell you.' She shuffled through the house.

Leaving Elliot on her own. She got out her phone and texted Sam back:

Sorry, love. Busy with work. You okay? Mum x

Barbara shuffled back through. 'Look who it is!'

Georgina McAllister was with her. Another of their number from back in the day. And one Elliot hadn't seen in a good while. She'd barely aged a day, but had managed to straighten out that fizzy hair. No escaping that red face, though, made her look constantly sunburnt. 'Hey, babe.' She leaned in for a hug. 'Not seen you for *aaages.*'

Elliot let her hug away. 'Had stuff going on.'

'Tell me about it.' Georgina sat between them. 'So, how *are* you?'

'I'll let you two catch up.' Barbara shuffled over to the mug tree. 'Let me get you a cup of tea.'

'I'm good, Barbara.'

Barbara swivelled around. 'Are you sure? Look like you're fading away, hen.'

'Wish I was.' Georgina reached over and stroked her arm. 'Listen, I'm so sorry about—'

'*Enough.*' Barbara smiled at her. 'Can I get you a scone? I baked them this morning. And some cherry ones from last night.'

'Thank you, but I just had a coffee at the office.' Georgina smiled back, but it faded to her natural sneer. 'Listen, I don't know what to do about the silver anniversary tomorrow.'

Barbara frowned. 'What do you mean?'

'Well, given what's happened, shouldn't we cancel it?'

'What anniv—' Barbara shifted to raise her eyebrows as it dawned on her. 'Oh. You mean what Heather was doing for that Sharon lassie?'

Georgina gave her a double thumbs up. 'Exactly.'

'Heather would've wanted it to go ahead.'

'But it's so soon after—'

'Even so. I know my daughter. I know her mind.' Barbara poured out some fresh tea. 'How about you repurpose it, so it's less of a remembrance ceremony and more of a vigil for Heather?'

Georgina jerked her head back at that suggestion. 'Wouldn't you want to have her funeral?'

'Andrea said we won't get her body for ages.' Barbara pointed at Elliot. 'And we don't need her body to celebrate her life. Heather was well loved in the area. I'm sure loads of people will be there.'

'Are you sure it doesn't feel inappropriate?'

'Nonsense. You have my blessing. You lot raise a glass to her. It's what she'd want. And that's the end of it.' Barbara thumped the table. 'Now, I'm going to put the kettle on, so I'll be making you that cup of tea, missy.' She got up and limped over to the sink with a series of moans and groans, then filled the kettle and put it on to boil. 'Had more than enough tea to see me through the next ice age, so I have.' She shuffled off to the hall, then the toilet door opened and the extractor started humming.

The sharp click of the lock and Georgina exhaled. She looked over to Elliot and whispered, 'Should I leave?'

'To be honest, I think she needs company.'

Georgina grinned. 'She's got more than enough to see her through the next ice age.'

Elliot raised her eyebrows. 'That's a bit unkind.'

'Sorry. Heather said it all the time. Always joked about her mum. All our folks have their little stock phrases, right?'

Elliot smiled at that. 'True enough.'

'I'm going to cancel the thing. It's not right.'

'That's a good idea. I didn't want to say anything to her, but the police side of this aren't too keen on it going ahead.'

'No surprise there.' Georgina sat back and rested her arm on the chair back. 'That why you're here, Andi? To shut it down?'

'No. I've been put in charge of media stuff.'

'So why are you here, then?'

'Because I knew Heather.'

'So they've got you snooping?'

'Come on…' Elliot had known she was a bitch, but speaking to her again made her remember precisely how much of one Georgina McAllister was. 'Truth is, I can't be close to the investigation. I've been asked to track down all the people she knew, starting with who was there.'

'Right, right.' That braying laugh again. 'So you *are* sniffing around.'

'Hardly. I sat with Barbara at the hospital while they brought in her daughter's body.'

'Sorry. That was bitchy of me.' Georgina shut her eyes for a few seconds. 'Must've been awful for her and I'm glad she had someone with her.' She frowned. 'Was Heather murdered?'

'Can't say.' Elliot left a pause, then winked. 'But yes. We think so.'

'Jesus. Is this to do with what happened?'

'I don't know.'

Georgina shook her head. 'She was the best of us, wasn't she?'

'Heather had her flaws, like we all do, but aye – she really was a good person.' Elliot watched her nod along with the sentiment. 'Do you remember Darren Fox?'

'Oh God. Aye. He was good mates with Gary, wasn't he? Worked for his dad. That right?'

'Sounds about right, aye. Trouble is, I don't really remember him.'

Georgina scowled. 'So why the hell are you asking?'

'Because we can't get hold of him.'

'Right.' Georgina looked away.

Elliot raised her eyebrows. 'You went out with him, right?'

Georgina shot her a glare. 'Who told you that?'

'It's true, isn't it?'

Georgina held her gaze for a few long moments, then looked away again. 'Okay, so I was seeing him.' She sighed. 'This was back in my wild days. Look at me now. Own a house outright. Husband with erectile dysfunction. Three kids. Stupidly busy job. Back then, though…' She shook her head. 'Heather and Gary… I thought they were going to get together. Never did.' She jutted out her chin. 'You'd been going out with him, right?'

'Aye, but I'd dumped him. Just like Heather did with Mark.'

'Aye. Such a weird pairing.' Georgina leaned forward. 'You know she was seeing him recently?'

'We do, aye. They broke up, right?'

'Right.'

'Mark told us Heather was seeing somebody else.'

'Oh, really? And you need to speak to him?'

'Right, aye. Obviously not a suspect, but if she was seeing someone, it makes sense to speak to him.'

'So someone told Marko?'

'That's right.'

Georgina gave a mischievous wink. 'I mean, that someone might've been me.'

'Who is he?'

'He doesn't exist.'

'Eh?'

'I was winding up Marko.'

'Why would you do that?'

'Because it's so easy.' Georgina shrugged. 'I love to taunt him. Just a bit of daft fun.'

Some of Jolene's team had wasted time tracking down this guy…

And he didn't exist.

All because Georgina wanted a bit of a laugh at Mark Henderson's expense.

What did he call her?

The arsehole…

No wonder why…

Elliot held that gaze again, but wanted to give her a hard piece of her mind. 'I didn't think you were that close?'

'Course we were. Lived around the corner from him when we were wee. Used to wind him up all the time. Still do.'

'I didn't know that.'

'We moved to Melrose in primary, then he was in my class in high school. Round the time my dad bought that farm up past Lauder.'

'So *you* told him Heather had met someone else?'

'Aye. Some random guy on the internet.'

'And had she?'

'No. God, no.'

'Georgie, we've got people scouring the Borders looking for him.'

'Shite.' Georgina ran a hand through her salon-fresh hair. 'I'm really sorry.'

'But I take it you spoke to him recently?'

'Sure. Look, the truth is Heather just got fed up with him. Marko's one of those guys who hasn't changed since he was fourteen. Maybe even younger. That's all there was to it.' She shrugged. 'Do you know who killed Sharon?'

'We don't, no.'

'Was it the same person?'

'We'll only know that when we solve one or the other.'

Barbara walked back through, then started fussing with the teapot again. 'Sure I can't tempt you with a scone, Georgina?'

'Oh, go on.'

Barbara got out a plate and rested a scone on it, then put it in front of Georgina. 'Got plenty of these, so don't you worry.'

Georgina smiled. 'Enough to see you through the next ice age?'

'Pretty much. Baking's soothing. Feel like rubbish, to be honest, but it focuses me on something that isn't this.' Barbara smiled. 'Butter? Jam?'

Georgina grinned. 'Butter would be smashing.'

Barbara shuffled over to the fridge.

Elliot checked her phone – nothing from Sam. She pulled up the photo on her phone and held it out. 'Wondered if either of you recognised this man?'

Barbara plonked the butter and a knife down, then squinted at it. 'Never seen him in my life. Sorry.'

Georgina started buttering her scone, then inspected it. 'I recognise him… but I can't put my finger on where from…'

Elliot kept holding it out. 'Sure?'

'Definitely know him…' Georgina bit into the scone. 'Who is he?'

'He was speaking to Heather at the press conference yesterday.'

Georgina finished chewing. 'You think he killed her?'

'No, we just need to speak to him.'

'Right. Right. Sorry.' Georgina pushed the plate away – the scone was already gone. 'Lovely scone, Mrs McG.' She stood up. 'I'd better get on.'

Barbara looked at her, all disappointed. 'Don't be a stranger, Georgina.'

'I won't be.' Georgina leaned over to peck her cheek then rubbed her arm. 'I'll check in on you, okay?'

'You don't need to.'

'I want to.' Georgina gave her a hug, then left the room.

Barbara sat down with a contented sigh, like she was catering for a few friends rather than dealing with her daughter's brutal murder. 'Sure I can't get you a scone?'

'I won't want my lunch.'

'Is that the time?' Barbara looked over at the clock to confirm it, then grabbed Elliot's hand across the table. 'Please, make sure that poor lassie gets justice. Heather wanted it more than anything. She was desperate for it. Felt so bad about what they did to the camper van.'

‘I will try, Mrs McGill.’ Elliot held her gaze. ‘I will try.’

27

Duncan drove through St Boswells yet again and the weirdest feeling hit him – it was starting to feel like home again.

It'd been his life at one point, save for going to the school in Gattonside, but it had barely been a thought for a quarter of a century, though now he wondered if he should pop into the Borders Gun Room and have a casual chat about weaponry – never knew when he'd need something. Canada wasn't exactly America with its liberalisation of handguns, but it was much easier to get a piece than over here.

And it'd be useful to be armed with more than a pair of fucking gloves...

He drove past a woman scowling at the world. Not bad looking, mid-forties and with a fringe that she kept sweeping out from the wind.

And it dawned on him – she was a cop, one of the two who'd been at that news conference all over the TV. Not the main one, that was a dude, but what the fuck was she doing here, so close to Mum's house? To him?

He pulled in just past the hardware store and thought about

going in for a nail gun or something, but it wasn't open. Maybe he should go to the new B&Q he'd driven past...

The lady was on the phone to someone now.

Dad nudged his arm. 'She's calling in back-up.'

Duncan rolled down his window and listened hard.

'Sam, I'm your mother, so please don't hang up on me, okay? You can always— Fuck's sake.' She got in her car and raced off through the village.

Sounded like some domestic bullshit. Hopefully nothing to do with him...

But hope had a habit of biting him in the ass...

Duncan checked around him, then drove the short distance to Mom's house.

Mum's, damn it.

Duncan got out and went around to the trunk – the *boot* – for his groceries. Shopping.

Dad was standing there. 'Of course, she could be playing you, son. Making it sound like she's on the phone to her laddie, when really she's just spotted you.'

'Excuse me, pal.' The sharp stab of a Glasgow accent. A man approached him from the lane at the back. Fifties, ruddy-faced, but smiling and very well presented. Looked like he worked out. 'You need a hand with that?'

Duncan returned the grin. 'I'm good, thanks.'

The guy looked at the house. 'You live here?'

'My aunt's house.'

Duncan felt a bit of sweat trickle down his spine – he was splitting the lies here. To the care home, he was Patricia's son; here, he was her nephew.

'Right.' He nodded back along the street. 'You know Barbara McGill?'

'Can't say I do.'

'Just, we heard her daughter died last night.'

'We?'

'Sorry. Declan Harris. Sky News.' He thrust out his hand for Duncan to shake.

'See? You can't stay here. The mother of the lassie you killed last night lives a few doors down. Need to get out while the going's good, son.'

'I'm sorry to hear that.' Duncan shook the journalist's hand, surprisingly weak. 'Heard something about a murder at Scott's View on the radio, but they didn't say who.'

'It's that, aye. Cops are keeping a tight lead on it, but hopefully things will start to drop.' Harris shook his head. 'Freakiest story… The lassie was leading this campaign into what happened there twenty-five years ago, pretty much to the day. Then someone kills her. Talk about messed up, eh?'

'God, aye.' Duncan gave a wistful sigh, then a 'what can you do?' look. 'Anything I can do to help?'

'You know the family?'

'Sorry. Just visiting my aunt.' Duncan grabbed the grocery bags from the trunk and gave him a tight nod. 'Hope you get to the bottom of it.'

'Thanks, pal.' Harris held out a business card. 'Give me a call if you hear anything.' He kept hold of it as Duncan took it. 'Make it worth your while…'

'Sure thing, pal. Anything to help.'

Harris let go, then walked off down the street towards another house.

Duncan took the *shopping bags* inside the house, but that whole exchange fizzed around in his head like a game of pinball, lighting up big scores and bouncing off bumpers, except his flippers weren't quite working. He went straight into the living room and turned on the TV.

Took a while to warm up, but it went straight to BBC News. Mum'd probably had it locked to that channel just before the heart attack and nobody'd touched it since.

The murder of Heather was a low-level story, just rolling on the ticker at the bottom:

Police Scotland investigating murder near Melrose...

The main story was the new Canadian PM giving a press conference ahead of the G7 meeting in Canada the following week.

Dad was in his chair by the window, smoking an unfiltered cigarette. 'You voted for his party at the election, didn't you?'

Duncan ignored him.

The main story cut back to a newsreader in the studio. 'Police Scotland are investigating a murder at Scott's View, a beauty spot in the Scottish Borders, which was the scene of a recent campaign to reopen the investigation into the historic murder of Sharon Beattie in 2000. While they haven't released the identity of the victim, a Police Scotland spokesman had this to say.'

A man stood there in sharp suit, looking calm and rested. Silver hair swept in one of those quiffs a good twenty years too young for him. The caption read:

Det. Superintendent John Ravenscroft

'The body of a 43-year-old woman was found in the early hours of this morning, here at Scott's View, a noted landmark named after the fabled novelist Sir Walter Scott.'

That woman from along the street stood next to him, looking all frazzled. The footage must be a few hours old, then...

Det. Insp. Andrea Elliot.

But Duncan had a name for her... If he ever needed one...

'The victim was Heather McGill, who was the person responsible for leading the campaign to help us solve Sharon Beattie's murder, which occurred in the same location twenty-five years ago. We're urging anyone with relevant information to bring it directly to the police by calling 101 or visiting your nearest police station. It just might be that you saw something that could lead us to finding her killer.'

So the truth was out, then…

Duncan googled her name, but all he got were a few hits from crimes she'd solved. Appeals to the public. Nothing juicy, like who Sam was. Son or daughter?

He opened Twitter and searched but there was nothing of note. Yet. Something needed to catch before it'd start trending. That or it'd been borked yet again now that asshole had renamed it to X. Same thing on both Facebook and Reddit.

Too early.

His phone rang in his hands and he almost dropped it.

Butler House calling…

Duncan sat back, heart thudding, then answered it. 'Hello?'

'Mr Radford, it's April Johnston. Are you okay to speak?'

Something sparking inside him.

Dad leaned forward to tip his cigarette onto his ashtray and exhaled out of the side of his mouth. 'Is she dead?'

'Oh, hi.' Duncan sat back, eyes closed. 'Is Mum okay?'

'She's fine. I'm ringing to say we've received an opportunity to fill her room.'

'Oh, that was super quick.'

'Well, we're in demand.'

'When do you need me to collect her?'

'She's in a wheelchair, so it'll be an ambulance dropping her off.'

'An ambulance?'

'Not an emergency one. A patient transport one.'

'Right. Sure.'

'Would today work?'

'Of course. I mean, this place is ready for her so any time works.'

'Excellent. We could drop her off around five?'

'Five's perfect.'

'Grand. Obviously, we'd need to ship her possessions to you, but we've got a company on a retainer for this kind of thing. How does that all sound?'

'I'd rather just come and collect it, if that's okay?'

'Sounds ideal.'

'I'll come for, what, four?'

'Sure. See you then.'

'Excellent. Bye.' Duncan ended the call and sat back, watching the TV.

He didn't expect things to move so quickly.

But they were starting to happen...

Dad was lighting a fresh cigarette from the tip of the other. 'You might not be listening to me, son, but at least you'll be in control of something...'

28

Someone knocked on the door.

Marshall finished chewing and wished he could take more time over lunch just one day. Always trapped in this bloody office, working away, instead of sharing the time with someone. He looked over to the door with a deep sigh.

'Hey, Rob.' Trev stood there, eyebrows raised. 'Mark Henderson's given his DNA samples to the custody dude.' He clicked his fingers. 'What's his name?'

'Fergus.'

'Right.' Trev nodded. 'Jay's going to drive it up to Howdenhall to process it.' He shook his head. 'Could do with that centre of excellence down here, couldn't we?'

'That's not going to happen.' Marshall sat back in his chair. 'How long will that take him?'

'About fifty minutes, assuming it's a clear run.'

Marshall smiled. 'I mean to process.'

'Oh, right, yeah.' Trev scratched at the back of his head. 'You've missed today's batch, so it'll be tomorrow.'

'But you can do ad hoc work, right?'

'We can. And seeing as how you asked so nicely…'

Marshall smiled at him. 'Appreciate it, mate.'

'Catch you later.' Trev knocked on the wood, then buggered off.

Leaving Marshall with the last bite of his sandwich.

Jolene stormed in, eyebrows high. 'How big a rocket did you fire up his arse?'

'Trev?' Marshall laughed. 'No rocket required. Just be nice to them.'

'Really?' Jolene collapsed into the chair opposite. 'He shot off like a SpaceX launch.'

'Hope he doesn't blow up, then. Especially not before he does what I need him to do.' Marshall smiled at her. 'What's up?'

'Got something. Maybe.' Jolene rested her notebook on the desk. 'My team have been focusing on two prongs. First, the friends and family of Sharon Beattie. Her brother lives in Holland now.'

'Did we know she had one?'

'Nope. Managed to speak to him, though. Not in touch with their dad. Said he's still alive, but reckons he moved to Germany. Mother died in 1994 and left the family camper van to Sharon.'

'Okay, that's good. Tallies with a few things and opens up other avenues. Are the brother or father suspects for Sharon's death?'

'Why not? Daughter embarrasses them. One or both confronts her, then one thing leads to another. Strangling. Then years later, Heather ruffles a few feathers and threatens to use DNA... It works.'

'Agreed, but it feels a bit flimsy.'

Jolene sat forward. 'Ash is going through Heather's laptop, by the way. We've been through all of her WhatsApp messages up to the cut-off, but there's nothing juicy there.'

'And the phone?'

'Still no sign of it.'

Marshall nodded but he couldn't hide his disappointment. 'Okay, but what about stuff sent to her Facebook page? This guy she was going to meet?'

'We're a bit hamstrung on that front. Can't get into her Facebook account because she's got two-factor authentication on. Like when you get a text with a code?'

'I know what it is, aye.'

'Well, Ash reckons it's secured by texts to the phone but we can't get in as we don't have the phone. But we're persistent. Or she is, anyway.'

'And how are we doing with the people in the car?'

Jolene got up and walked over to the whiteboard. 'Okay, so Heather's dead.' She scribbled a name. 'Hislop and Georgina have been spoken to.'

Marshall joined her, but had to frown. 'Who spoke to her?'

'Andrea.'

'When?'

'Just before lunch. She was visiting Heather's mum after the latest press conference and Georgina just happened to turn up.'

'Okay. But we need to speak to her independently, okay?'

Jolene nodded. 'Got two skulls going to her work right now. The big IFA in Gala.'

'How are you doing?'

She turned around, scowling. 'Eh?'

'You, Jolene. How are you doing?'

'I'm fine. Why?'

'It's just, with Cal leaving and Andrea side-lined, I've only got one DI. You. You're only just in the job.'

'Are you saying I'm screwing this up?'

'The complete opposite. You're doing well. Just make sure you shout if you need help.'

'Douglas is good.'

'How good?'

'He's a very experienced DS. Takes a lot of the strain.'

'Okay, good.'

Jolene did some more scribbling. 'Also, Darren Fox is dead.'

'Wait, what?'

'Motorbike accident near Loch Lomond.'

'Brutal. Anything suspicious?'

'Nope. We think he's Gary Hislop's cousin. His mother's sister's son. Lived in Penicuik.'

Marshall nodded. 'Okay, so that's the first car done.'

'Second car also had four in it. David Limond, Katherine McNish and Ian Smith were the passengers. They all moved away and we're struggling to track them down. Crawford's got a team out speaking to their parents, so we should get something.'

'Fingers crossed.'

Jolene tapped on the whiteboard. 'The driver, though – she lives in Newtown St Boswells.'

29

Jolene kept on down the A68. 'I just prefer going this way, that's all.'

The speed limit changed again as the road narrowed and Newtown St Boswells passed on the right, partly hidden across the fields.

Marshall pointed back the way. 'It's surely quicker going through the town, isn't it?'

'I'm driving so we go my way, okay?' Jolene pulled into the right-turn lane. 'See? It's easier to turn, then you're doubling back through the town, sure, but to where we want to go.' She slowed as they passed Gary Hislop's home, four council houses he'd bought and welded together. 'It's on the market now. Think it'll sell soon?'

'I might be in the market, but I won't be buying it.'

'Can you afford it?'

'Probably not.'

Jolene laughed. 'How's that all going?'

'Saw a place in Clovenfords last night.'

'Ooh, fancy.'

'Not really. But it'd do nicely.'

She pulled up outside a house a couple of streets away from Hislop's place. 'Are you going to put in a bid?'

'Haven't thought about it, to be honest. This case has kind of taken over everything.' Marshall got out and let her lead him to the house, a fairly standard suburban semi.

Jolene opened the garden gate and passed a white Dacia with a yellow "Taxi" sign, then knocked on the door. 'Sinead Paton. That's no relation to Ash, by the way.'

'Didn't think she was.'

'Always pays to check around here.'

The door opened and a flustered woman scowled out at them. 'Can I help you?' She bent over to tie up her shoes.

Marshall flipped out his warrant card. 'Police. Looking for Sinead Paton.'

'You've found her.' Sinead frowned as she switched foot. 'What's this about?'

'Wonder if we could do this inside?'

'Sorry, I'm just heading out.'

'We won't keep you long.'

Sinead looked up at him, finally reading his warrant card. 'What's this about?'

'We're detectives. This is about a murder.'

'Sake.' Sinead sighed as she stood up and revealed a web of tattoos up her neck, stopping at the jawline, but she had a couple of Japanese throwing stars on her cheek – Marshall thought they were called shuriken. Both arms had sleeves all the way down, in a confusion of patterns. 'Fine.' She got out a Samsung phone and texted someone. 'I've just messaged my boss, so you've got five minutes.' She folded her arms. 'What's happened?'

Marshall nodded behind her. 'Can we do this inside?'

'No. Place is a shit tip.' Sinead stepped forward and pulled the door until it closed.

They really weren't getting inside, were they?

Marshall smiled at her. 'Gather you drive a taxi?'

'What gives that away? The fact I've got a taxi on my drive?' She shook her head with a fierce scowl on her face. 'I love driving. Always have. Is this about a passenger?'

'No, it's about what happened back in 2000 at Scott's View. When you found Sharon Beattie.'

'Oh.' Sinead screwed up her face. 'Right.'

'What do you remember about that night?'

'Not my proudest moment.' Sinead looked away. 'But the cops spoke to me back then and I told them the whole truth.'

'We're not here to accuse you of anything, Sinead. Just want to know what happened. That's all.'

'Right.' Sinead's lips flickered into a snarl. 'Thing is... When I saw her lying there on that soggy mattress, I just totally shat it. Ran away. Took them with me.' She shook her head. 'Talk about looking guilty, eh?'

'Who's them?'

'Kat, Ian and Dave.'

Marshall nodded, like this was news. 'You still in touch with them?'

'Not really. We all went to uni and just drifted apart. I mean, it was a couple of months after... We all seemed to want to run away. I managed six days at Dundee uni studying geography for some stupid reason. I just hated it. Managed to switch to doing nursing at Queen Margaret in Edinburgh. I hated the actual job, though, so I sort of ended up being a cabbie. A mate needed a hand and I've been doing it fifteen years now. Always loved driving – passed my test the day after my seventeenth birthday. Lots of practice on a mate's dad's farm track.'

'Which mate is that?'

'Georgie. Georgina. Folks owned this big place up near Langshaw? Sold it and moved, though.'

'It's not just Sharon's death we're investigating.'

Sinead frowned. 'Is this that thing on the news?'

'It is. Heather McGill's body was—'

'Fuck. Fuck.' Sinead collapsed back against the door. Her top rode up and showed a giant tattoo of Marilyn Manson on her tummy. Or at least, Marshall thought it was him. 'Heather's *dead*?'

'I'm afraid so. When did you last see her?'

'Few months ago. Heard she'd returned but I had no interest in speaking to her.'

'Why's that?'

'Never really liked her, to be honest. You must know what that's like? Always one or two in a group who you don't get on with, right?' She stood up tall and hauled her top down. 'Not that I want to speak ill of the dead, like. Or that I hated her or she hated me, just... Didn't really get on.' Her lips twisted up. 'But she doorstepped me one day, few months back. Like you pair just now. And she was really pushy, kept on asking about that night. And I really didn't want to speak to anyone about it.'

Jolene gave her a kind smile. 'Must've been tough.'

'Really tough.' Sinead wiped away a tear. 'I... I hate myself for running away.'

Jolene stepped forward. 'It's a completely natural reaction.'

'For a coward, you mean...'

'For anyone. You didn't do anything wrong.'

'I ran away! That whole thing totally fucked me up. I spent years denying it but I was a complete fuck-up. Drank too much. Took too many drugs. Sober now, but fuck... Half my tattoos are from when I was blasted. Spent the last decade covering over the worst ones...'

'You've heard of fight or flight, right?' Jolene held her gaze. 'Birds and cats and lizards do it, not just people. It's natural.'

'So? I should've stayed.'

'You did nothing wrong.' Jolene showed her the photo. 'Do you recognise this man?'

Sinead glanced at it then looked away. 'Fuck sake. Worst fare of my life.'

Jolene frowned. 'So you know him?'

'Gus Beattie... Sharon's dad.'

Marshall felt a fluttering in his chest, like a swarm of butterflies were flapping their wings.

The man who approached Heather was Sharon's dad...

He had to be a suspect... Or just a massive lead – that whole half of the case was a complete zero, so this was a step forward.

Marshall could tell Jolene was thinking along the same lines. 'What do you mean by worst fare?'

'Picked him up at the hospital after a drop-off there. Asked me to drive him up to Langlee. Had no idea who he was and it took him a while to realise who I was.' Sinead looked over at her car. 'He was in the cab of the lassie who ran away from his daughter's body.' She shook her head. 'Gave me such a hard time about it.' She blinked hard. 'And I deserved it, to be honest. But then he got really angry and started threatening me. Fuck sake, I didn't deserve that! It's like he thought I'd killed her. Fuck that. I'm not standing for that shit. What happened to his daughter was fucking awful, but I didn't kill her.'

'What did he do?'

'No idea. I dumped his arse on Galafoot Bridge – he could fucking walk the rest of the way!' She scowled at them again, like they were blaming her. 'We didn't kill her! We found her! Sure, we were dicks, but we were young and daft. If it wasn't for what we did, she would've been a missing person.'

Jolene nodded along with it. 'Do you know what he'd been in hospital for?'

30

Yet again, parking at Borders General Hospital was completely screwed.

Jolene went around the loop again, muttering under her breath, back to the start.

Marshall pointed over to the hospital itself, sheltering away from all the cars. 'Park at the front.'

'*Fine.*' Jolene drove off, but kept on muttering. She pulled into the taxi bay and put out her official police sign, then got out first.

Marshall followed and had to jog over to the hospital entrance. 'Steady on there.'

Jolene glanced at him. 'Why was he speaking to Heather?'

'The million-dollar question, right?' Marshall looked at the photo on his mobile again. 'He doesn't look happy, does he?'

'You'd think he'd be happy with her opening up Sharon's investigation, wouldn't you?'

'Might've thought Heather was prising open old wounds with a crowbar.'

'Fair point, but also makes me very suspicious and I refer

you back to my earlier theory.' She stepped through the revolving doors before they'd finished revolving.

'Could do with speaking to Leye, if we get a moment.'

Jolene glanced over at him. 'Has he done the postmortem?'

'That's what the chat would be about.'

'Oh, here we go...' Jen was standing at the entrance to A&E, messing on her phone. She looked up at them. 'Fucking hell, Rob. You look shattered.'

'I feel it.'

Jolene patted Marshall on the arm. 'I'll see you in a minute.' She walked off towards reception.

Marshall yawned. 'How was the gig, then?'

'Not really my cup of tea, but Cath enjoyed it. Shame you had to bugger off.'

Marshall yawned again. 'Tell me about it.'

'Let me guess – you're working this murder that's all over the news?'

'Sadly, aye.' Marshall yawned some more – he really needed to stop but it was so bloody hot in here. And it was like they pumped the sedative into the air. 'Managed to get some sleep last night, but nowhere near enough.'

Jen folded her arms. 'What are you doing here, then?'

'Here to see someone.'

'Patient?'

'Employee.' Marshall showed her his phone. 'Gus Beattie.'

Jen rolled her eyes. 'Oh. *Him*.'

Marshall kept holding out his phone. 'You know him?'

'Sadly. Why are you so interested?'

'He's Sharon Beattie's father.'

'The victim from twenty-five years ago?' Her eyes went wide. 'Wow. Listened to a podcast about it a few years ago, but I didn't connect the dots. Pretty interesting. I remember it. We were still at school. They reckoned it was someone from Gala Academy who did it, right?'

Marshall winced. He knew exactly who that'd be – Mark Henderson. 'I wouldn't read too much into that.'

'Sounds like you know who did it?'

'No comment.' Marshall looked around the waiting area. Despite the parking situation outside, it was pretty much empty. 'You know where he is?'

'Who, Gus?' Jen reached back to tighten her ponytail. 'Bad luck, Rob – he quit a few months ago.' She rolled her eyes. 'In the middle of a shift too. Talk about unprofessional.'

'You're joking?'

'Wish I was. What a pain that was. I needed to get two patients who'd been in a car crash up to theatre and he didn't show up to take them.'

Marshall ran a hand down his face. 'Any idea where he lives?'

'Gala, I think. Langlee, I remember him saying. I'd need to pass you on to HR.'

Marshall narrowed his eyes at her. 'But?'

'But I heard the reason he left is because he got another job…'

31

Jolene drove along Scott Street in Gala, past Gary Hislop's original hardware store, which did seem to be doing enough of a trade to pass any money-laundering investigation...

Marshall had to hand it to him – his shops were busy enough to look genuine and not a front for his drug running...

Jolene kept it slow behind a Citroen thing doing ten in a twenty. 'What gig was it, then?'

'Everything Everything.'

'Never heard of them. Any good?'

'Quite like them. My sister collects their records on vinyl. She's become a bit obsessed.'

'Jen collects *vinyl*?'

'No, Cath. She stopped drinking and seems to have started trying to collect stuff she doesn't need instead of getting drunk all the time.' Marshall scratched his chin. 'I mean, she owes me a ton of money, but I'm glad she's got a hobby that doesn't require the police attending her property once a week.'

'Weird.' Jolene drove past her street, then headed straight over, instead of taking the right turning back towards the station. The entrance to Butler House was a sharp left, but she managed to secure a place by the front door. She parked just outside and got out. 'I mean, it's all on Spotify, right?'

'It's about possessing a physical object. And tracking down rarities. Or securing a new limited edition release.' Marshall led over to the entrance. 'Besides, I've got a few records myself.'

'Aren't you way too young to have had vinyl growing up?'

'Mum was big on it. Hates change. And then you couldn't really get it anymore and now it's massive again.'

Jolene opened the door. 'Do *you* like it? The collector thing?'

'A bit. It's not the sound or the crackle or anything like that. Something to do with listening to only about twenty minutes at a time. Freshens the ears. Makes it a more mindful experience.'

'You're such a weirdo.' Jolene entered the place and walked up to the desk.

A young nurse looked up with a smile. 'Can I help?' An Eastern European accent, but Marshall couldn't drill down to which country.

'Hiya.' Jolene smiled at her as she held out her warrant card. 'Police. Is the manager about?'

The nurse took the warrant card and jotted down some details. Her name badge read "Zuzana". 'Sorry, I need to be very careful about who we let enter.' She handed it back to Jolene, then looked at Marshall. 'Can I see yours?'

Marshall smiled and handed it over. 'Sure.'

Zuzana jotted down some details then handed it back. 'Mrs Johnston is on her break.'

'It's fine.' Marshall looked around the place. 'We're actually looking for Gus Beattie. Is he working?'

'Ah yes. Mr Gus is in the TV lounge.' Zuzana got up and led them through. She was tiny, less than five foot tall and probably weighed less than either of Marshall's legs. 'Through here.'

Jolene nodded at her. 'Thank you.'

The TV lounge was stuffed full of armchairs, all facing a fancy-looking telly mounted so high up the wall it must've hurt the necks of anyone sitting in there.

A man sat next to an old woman, feeding her something on a spoon but without much success – it was even worse than feeding a baby. She was spilling it everywhere and no matter how quickly he wiped it up, it left stains.

Marshall didn't need to check his phone – this was definitely the guy who spoke to Heather after the press conference.

The old lady pushed away from him. 'I want to die, so stop feeding me.'

'Look, Patricia, you're being moved, so you need to be able to—'

'Not going anywhere!'

'Patricia…'

'Listen, fuck face, if you can't kill me, find someone who can.'

Gus laughed. 'Come on, Patricia, the ambulance will be here to take you to stay with your son again.'

'I've no idea who you're talking about.'

Gus looked over at them. 'Hi there, can I help?'

Jolene smiled. 'Police, sir.'

Patricia looked around at them. 'What have I done?'

Jolene laughed. 'Nothing.' She focused on Gus. 'We just need a word with you, sir.'

'Bit busy just now. Patricia's moving out today.'

'It's pretty important, sir. It can't wait.'

Gus sighed. 'What can't?'

'It's about Sharon.'

Gus sat back in the chair and looked like he was going to start crying. Frowning. Rubbing his eyes. He refocused on Jolene again. 'Has something happened?'

'Sharon's the lassie on the telly. The hoor who was killed!' Patricia broke down crying. 'Oh no…'

Zuzana swept back into the room. 'Come on, Patricia, let's get your favourite show back on, eh?' She caressed Patricia's arm, but she was lost to a flood of tears.

'How about we chat in the office?' Gus stood up, then led them out into the corridor and ran a hand down his face. 'Patricia's... She's suffering from dementia. She doesn't cope well with new people around.' He gave them a polite smile. 'Let's use the office before we incite further outbursts from her, eh?'

32

Duncan took one last look around his mother's room. This had been her home for almost a year and he hadn't even known she was in here...

'Time's wasting, son.' Dad was over by the window, looking out at the trees as he smoked. 'Get away while the going's good.'

Duncan picked up the two old suitcases and carried them out into the corridor. The rest of Mum's stuff must be on the way to transport over.

He took a final look, then shut the door and carried the suitcases through the care home towards the front door.

'This way.' Gus walked past with two people.

Duncan dropped a suitcase and it tumbled down the steps. He made to move after it but only succeeded in dropping the other one.

Mum's old bloomers spilled everywhere.

A big man raced over and picked it up for him. 'Here, let me help.'

Duncan frowned at him – he recognised him from somewhere but couldn't place him. 'I'm fine.'

'Doesn't look it.' The big guy zipped up the suitcase, then helped him outside with it. 'Where are you parked?'

'Over here.' Duncan led down the steps, then crunched over the gravel to the rental – to the *hire car*.

'This is really bloody heavy. What's in it?'

Duncan looked back at him. 'All the stuff Mum's been ferreting away.'

He nodded. 'Are you Patricia's son?'

'For my sins, aye.' Duncan unlocked the car but struggled to lift the suitcase into the boot.

The big guy looked at him like he was a pathetic wretch, then hefted the other one straight up and in. 'We just saw her. I'm sorry you're going through that.'

'Is what it is, eh? Ambulance is going to drop her off back home, but I wanted to make sure I moved her stuff out and got the place ready first.'

'Good man.' He lifted up Duncan's suitcase, straight in. 'It's a big thing to take on. My grandfather's in a home like this. They take great care of him, but it must be a tough job.'

'They do a great job, aye, but Mum hates it here. Well, that's not true. She just wants to die in her own home.'

'Good luck with it.' The big guy smiled. 'I hope it's a long time away.'

Duncan smiled. 'Thanks, but the GP doesn't think so.' A final nod, then he watched him go back inside.

'He's a cop.' Dad was leaning against the passenger seat. 'See? The cops are onto you, you numpty. Get away.'

Duncan frowned at him. 'How do you know he's a cop?'

'Look at him. You watched him talking on the bloody TV about Heather! Don't tell me your mind's going too?'

Duncan looked at him as he climbed the steps into the care home and it all clicked into place.

Detective Chief Inspector Rob Marshall.

Shite…

'They're here to ask Gus about what my wife's been saying, aren't they? They'll put two and two together, son. You need to go! Now!'

Duncan walked over to the building and went back inside.

Zuzana was pottering around by the desk. God, she was tiny. She spotted him and let out a sigh. 'Sorry.'

'You okay there?'

'It's just…' She stepped closer to him. 'There is a new resident taking your mother's room and, of course, I am having to get him set up and I've spent long time emptying her room. And the policemen are here with Gus.'

'See?' Dad was sitting behind the desk, feet up. 'Told you he's a cop. You complete numpty… Go!'

'Sounds rough.' Duncan gave her an understanding nod. 'Why were they talking to Mum?'

'Not her. They were talking to Gus. His daughter was killed.'

Duncan felt his eyes bulge. 'Gus's daughter? Recently?'

'No. Years ago. Sharon. Is on the news. That was her.'

'Go, son. Go. Now.'

Duncan looked around but he couldn't see his mother. 'How often does Gus care for my mother?'

'She is one of his favourites. He has most success feeding her and calming her down when she's agitated.'

'Has she been agitated today?'

'She was… Feeding didn't go well and then the police officers upset her. But she's okay now. She's in the TV room now, watching her favourite show.'

Duncan nodded. 'Got all her stuff in the car. I could drive her home?'

'Best to wait for ambulance.' Zuzana patted his arm, softly and slowly, then looked up with those big eyes. 'I'm going to miss her.'

'Really? After the things she says to you?'

'I try to see through all the anger to the person underneath. Your mother is good person. She's the woman who raised you.'

'That's a good way of looking at it.'

'My grandmother was same. Is hard.'

'I wanted to thank you.' Duncan stroked her arm and felt the old urges return. 'You do a great job here for them.'

'Is nothing. Is just my job.'

'It's not just that, is it? It can't be easy doing this, but you put your whole self into it.'

'Thank you.' Zuzana ran a hand across his cheek. 'Are you up for this, Colin?'

Duncan nodded. 'I am.'

'Caring directly for someone with dementia is very tough. It's what we're trained to do, you know? We have experience.'

'I've done worse jobs.'

'Oh?'

'Back in Canada. Saw a lot of stuff I'd rather I hadn't. Worked in a hospital for a bit.'

'So you know?'

Duncan smiled grimly. 'Oh, I know.'

'I want you to know I feel sorry for you.'

'I don't want anyone to feel sorry for me.'

'No. Sorry. Is…' Zuzana shook her head violently. 'My English is not so good. I just want to help. I can… If the transition proves too tricky, I can help.'

Duncan frowned. 'How?'

'I could come and see Patricia. Maybe help. If she sees a familiar face, it might ease her?'

'That'd be great.'

And he felt the urge to take her life.

So strong, like he could hold it, or at least take it out of his chest and throw it around.

But she'd done nothing wrong. She was a good person.

She'd left her home country to set up a new life here, just like he'd done – and that took guts.

No, he couldn't kill her.

'Are you seriously thinking of killing her when the cops are next fucking door?' Dad shook his head, laughing. 'Focus on getting away, you idiot. Maybe treat yourself to a holiday in the Dominican Republic once this is all over. Let your urges run wild again. But go. Now.'

Zuzana led him through to the TV room.

Mum was happy as a pig in shit, watching some noisy kids' show on the telly.

Zuzana crouched low beside her. 'The ambulance is going to take you back to your home, Patricia.'

Mum scowled at her. 'Eh?'

'Colin's going to look after you, okay?'

'Oh.' Patricia frowned. 'I just want to die.'

'Come on, Mum.' Duncan smiled at her. 'You asked me to do this for you.'

'Did I?' Her frown deepened, then faded to nothing. 'Oh, yes. I've been asking for ages but they said I couldn't leave here.'

'It's okay, Mum. It'll be you and me against the world.' Duncan took her hand and gave it a squeeze, but it was so thin and frail he worried he might snap something. And it was so cold. 'And we'll win, won't we?'

'We always do, son. We always do.'

Zuzana wheeled her through the care home.

Duncan followed her and stopped to look through the window into the manager's office where Gus was talking to the cops.

His heart rate spiked, like someone was drumming on his chest with mallets.

He just had to hope they weren't onto him...

Zuzana opened the front door and led them outside.

The patient transport ambulance was a knackered old Ford

van with a knackered old driver leaning against it, sucking on a cigarette. 'That her?'

Zuzana stopped and nodded.

The driver stamped out his cigarette and left the butt there, then took his time climbing the steps. He wheeled her down the ramp then over to the ambulance, where he locked her wheelchair into some kind of lift thing that winched her up to the side door. He wheeled her in, then locked it in place.

'There you go, Mum.' Duncan smiled at her. 'Be back home in no time.'

The driver shut the door, then folded the lift thing away until Duncan couldn't even see it. He nodded at them, then got in and drove off, just one other passenger in there.

Duncan watched him go, then looked at Zuzana as she followed him over to the hire car. 'Thank you for all that.' He opened the passenger-side door out of habit, then had to walk around to the driver's side.

'You will need to return wheelchair, of course?'

'I will. And I'll get her a better one.'

'This is good car.' Zuzana smiled at him. 'I like you, Colin. You seem like a nice older guy.'

That hurt him a bit. In his head, he was still nineteen. But he tried to return her smile. 'Thank you.'

33

Gus Beattie looked out of the window, scratching at his neck, then he sat behind the manager's desk and let out a deep sigh.

Marshall raised his chin. 'You okay there?'

'Sorry. Patricia's leaving today.' Gus sighed again. 'Pretty rare for them to go out the front door with a loving child, rather than the back door with a funeral director.'

Marshall nodded. 'My grandfather's in a care home like this over in Gattonside. We call him Grumpy, because my mum's dad was Granddad.'

'Grumpy.' Gus chuckled. 'I like that.' He frowned. 'Is he suffering from dementia?'

'No, Grumpy's maybe lost a few of his marbles but he's still pretty sharp. A wily old fox, I have to say. Just has mobility issues. Needs a bit of help with showering and personal care, but he's doing well.'

'Better that way than the other. Dementia's *tough.*' Gus shook his head. 'The more it sets in, the angrier they get. Confusion makes it even worse. Take it out on the ones they love or on their carers. And they're just trapped inside their heads. Awful.'

Marshall drummed his fingers on the desk. 'Thanks for your time. We wanted to ask you a few things about Sharon.'

'So you said. Has something happened?'

'No. But you're aware of us reopening the investigation into her murder, right?'

'I am, aye. This lassie found me. Heather. Told her I didn't want to be included in the campaign.'

'Why not?'

'Don't see it doing any good for anyone.'

'You don't want justice?'

'*Justice*.' Gus laughed. 'If we were going to get that, it would've happened a *long* time ago. Sharon was twenty-one when she died. I wasn't even forty. Imagine that? Being forty years old and your adult daughter's been murdered?' He looked up at the ceiling and let out a deep breath. 'I had her young. Too young, probably. I was a medic in the army, you know? They like us to breed young. Makes us more pliant, probably.'

Marshall waited until he made eye contact before he nodded. 'I can't imagine what you've been through.'

'You don't want to.' Gus gave a bitter laugh. 'The press hounded me afterwards. I'd lost my fucking daughter and they'd be outside the flat or waiting for me when I clocked off at work.' He scratched at his neck again. 'I wasn't proud of what she did. I distanced myself from it. And the guys at the hospital were brutal in those days. "Yer wee girl's a hoor, Gus." "Did you use her, Gus? Mind if I do?" "Maybe get us a discount?" What the fuck do you say to that?'

'That's rough.'

'Fucking tell me about it. It's all just banter to them. Trying to get a rise out of you to… I don't know. Maybe it's their way of showing affection. It's hard with lads, you know? But they did rally around me when it happened. One lad stuck the nut on a reporter who wasn't taking "fuck off" for an answer.' Gus re-enacted the motion, the short violent snap of someone who'd clearly done it himself in real life. 'My wife died a few years before Sharon and both sets of folks are long gone. My boy was in Amsterdam, smoking dope like it was going out of fashion. I struggled. Big time.'

Jolene smiled at him. 'Where did you—'

Gus broke down, leaning forward and resting on his arms. His whole body rocked as he cried.

Marshall looked over at Jolene, then motioned for her to hang back and let it play out.

Gus looked up at them in turn, tears filling his eyes. 'I decided to leave this country. I went to stay with my boy in Holland. Worked with him in a bulb factory for a bit. I'd been based in Dortmund in the army, so I knew a few boys over there. Got me a gig in a hospital there. Loved it.'

Marshall nodded – it tallied with what Jolene had unearthed. 'Why did you come back?'

'I don't really know, to be honest with you. Born here, so I reckon this should be the place I die when my time comes.' Gus inspected his nails now, like this was all okay. 'Truth was, I came back to go to a pal's funeral. Drank himself to death. Well, hit by a bus. Some guys from school were there and we made a night of it after, so I stayed in a pal's spare room. Ended up getting into a thing with a lassie. Decided to come back and get a job in BGH. Of course, that relationship ended not long after I got back. And I've stayed around. Thing is, it's really not bad here, is it? Plenty of worse places, eh?' He looked around the room like he was taking in the view from the top of Three Brethren or somewhere similar. 'Getting too old for this kind of work but I've got nothing else. My pension's not enough to live off. Modern life fucking sucks.'

Marshall nodded. 'Mind telling us where you were yesterday evening?'

'Where do you think I was?'

'Scott's View.' Marshall left it vague to see if Gus wanted to continue his confession.

'I was, aye. Spoke to Heather McGill.'

'Why was that?'

'I...' Gus let out a deep sigh. 'Her campaign was a total pain in the hoop. She's *awful*. Heard I was back in the area and started hounding me. Kept banging on about justice for Sharon. Fuck's sake – that daft wee bint was only doing it because she'd found her body. Felt so fucking guilty, didn't she? Found my lassie...' His bottom lip trembled. 'Every time it comes up, everyone's reminded of how my wee girl was a prostitute. As if that's all she ever was. She dies again every time.' Fury flashed across his lips. 'And I don't want justice, I just want my fucking daughter back. And no matter what Heather achieved with this stupid campaign, that's not going to happen, is it?'

Jolene nodded sagely. 'I totally understand.'

'Right. Aye. Sure you do, hen. If I could wind the clock back, I would. But I'd go even further back. See, my daughter used to be a good girl. Then her mum died and she completely went off the rails and I didn't know what the hell to do. You have a bairn and you think that's you for the rest of your puff, sharing the load with your better half. But see doing it all yourself? Absolute murder, so it is... And I was still a laddie myself. Just a daft wee laddie. With two fucking kids.' Gus wiped tears from his eyes. 'Both ended up running away, didn't they? Him to Holland and her...'

Jolene frowned at him. 'Did she leave the country?'

'Thought she did but one of the lads at the hospital told me she was living in a flat in *Langlee*. Three streets away.' Gus blew out a long, sad breath. 'Visited but she wouldn't come home. Turns out my wee lassie was selling her body for money to buy drugs. *Drugs*. And using her mother's old camper van to... To... I mean, the bloody thing was ancient. Surprised it passed its MOT. Old Volkswagen thing. My wife bought it with her pitiful inheritance from her old man and we were supposed to go all over the Highlands. Over to Ireland. Across Europe. Even had a fanciful idea of getting it on a boat up to Iceland and driving it around there.' He snorted. 'Then a few weeks later, Yvette collapsed in Tesco. Blood cancer. It'd spread everywhere. No hope of anything. Just had weeks with her. Barely had any time to say goodbye.' He banged a fist off the desk. 'The fact someone could just pick up my daughter, *use* her, and then... And then murder her... It completely broke me, you know? I realised I had nothing left, so I had to escape, so that's why I moved away. But nothing solved it, just left this hollow emptiness inside.'

Marshall waited a few seconds to let him recover from that purging of emotions. 'I saw you speaking with Heather after the press conference.'

'She'd persuaded me to meet her there. Thought it was just a wee chat, just me and her. But there were all these journalists and TV cameras there and... Bloody hell. I... Just... She wanted me to speak, but I wasn't having any of it.'

Jolene frowned. 'Where did you go after you saw her last night?'

'Back home. Then to the pub. Ladhope Inn in Gala.'

'And after that?'

'Can't tell you.'

'I'm sorry? It's important we know your whereabouts.'

'You're asking if I've got an alibi for something, right?'

Jolene nodded. 'Heather McGill was murdered.'

'Fuck's sake... She wouldn't listen, would she?' Gus clamped his eyes shut. 'I'd warned her not to go sticking her foot in the hornet's nest, but did she listen? Did she hell. Just kept kicking it, didn't she? Had her own agenda too. I'd put Sharon's ghost to rest, but that lassie... She was ploughing on, wasn't she? And this happens? Jesus Christ.'

'You may have been the last person to see her alive.'

'Wait.' Gus frowned at her. 'Last person? You mean other than the killer.'

'Did you kill her, Mr Beattie?'

'Of course I didn't kill her! Wouldn't harm a hair on her head. After everything I'd been through with my daughter, I'd never subject another human being to that. Of course I didn't kill her...'

'But you won't say where you were.'

'It's not *won't*, it's *can't*. I blacked out, so I literally can't tell you what I did. I got in, put the Scotland match on and opened a bottle of whisky. Drank it until there was none left, then I passed out. Woke up, had a coffee, then came in to work. Still no idea what the score was in the Scotland game.'

Jolene folded her arms. 'We can speak to your neighbours.'

'Good.'

Jolene held his gaze. 'Do you have any idea who could've killed Heather?'

'No, but it stands to reason it was the same animal who killed Sharon, right? She wouldn't let it lie, would she? Kept on trying to drum up publicity. Didn't care the effect it had on people, did she?'

'People like yourself?'

'Damn right. I'm *sore*. I *still* ache over what happened.' Gus grimaced. 'But I didn't kill her. I'm not some idiot masking what he did by pretending to black out.' He laughed. 'Here's a thing. Night of Sharon's funeral was the loneliest I'd ever been in my life.' He looked over at Marshall. 'Hired a girl myself. Not for anything other than company...' He laughed. 'Turns out she knew Sharon and I ended up crying on her shoulder all night, with my fucking clothes on. Name was Thora.' He leaned forward. 'The lassie Sharon was staying with in Langlee. The one who got her hooked on smack. Bumped into her in Aldi a few weeks ago. She still lives in Gala. Had me round for a cup of tea, would you believe?'

34

Duncan couldn't remember ever seeing his mother so happy in her life as when her wheelchair slid down the lift ramp.

She sat there, beaming and soaking up the attention of the neighbours watching her.

'Here we go. Gently.' The driver stopped it at the bottom, then wheeled her off. 'You okay there, Patty?'

Mum looked up at him. 'My son's going to kill you.'

'Mum.' Duncan crouched in front of her. '*I'm* your son.' He glanced up at the driver. 'And I'm not going to kill anyone.'

'You could've been such a good boy.' Mum frowned at him. 'I blame your father.'

'That's gratitude, eh?' Dad was standing in the doorway, sucking on a cigarette. 'After all I did for her.'

Mum looked at the house. 'Where am I?'

'You're home, Mum.'

'Home?'

'You don't have to live in that place anymore.'

'But I liked it there.'

'Well, you'll like it even better here.' Duncan smiled at the driver. 'I'll take it from here.'

'Sure about that, pal?'

'Aye, I've got this.'

'Good luck, pal.' The driver gave a flash of his eyebrows. 'Going to need it, eh?' He opened the ambulance door, then hopped in and drove off.

Five o'clock on a Friday and he was probably tasting the first pint of a long, long session. A whole weekend where he didn't have to drive people in that ambulance that stank of pee.

Mum looked at Duncan with doe eyes. 'Am I going to die here?'

'It's what you want, Mum.'

'Are you going to kill me too?'

'Don't be silly. You're my mum.' Duncan wheeled her over to the steps then spun her around. He got onto the top one and tried to bump her up.

Much harder than it seemed.

He was sweating and aware of all the eyes watching him.

Thing with a wee town like this was everyone watching you…

Watching every little thing you did…

Duncan bumped her up onto the second step now and almost lost his grip, but he managed to hold on. He took a deep breath, then another bump and she was into the house, but Duncan felt like he was going to have a heart attack.

He really needed to get a ramp for this, assuming she wanted to go out for those walks Dr Japp recommended.

'Duncan?'

He looked back along the street, sucking in deep breaths.

The neighbour from yesterday was there, looking at him like he'd robbed a bank or murdered someone. 'Hi, Duncan. Is that your aunt back out?'

Duncan shut the door behind him, locking Mum inside the house on her own. 'It is, aye. I'm going to look after her.'

'Oh, that's good. How is she?'

'Not great. But not awful. It can be better for patients in her state to have familiarity.' Duncan smiled at her. 'Sorry, I've forgotten your name.'

'Alison. Alison McNish.'

'Of course. I'd offer you in for a cup of tea, but she needs to lie down and I've got a ton of stuff to do, not least getting a ramp for these steps.'

'Totally understand that.' She nodded enthusiastically. 'Is there anything I can do to help?'

'Maybe. Let me get her settled and sort out a few things, then I'll pop in for a cuppa.'

'Sounds great.' She smiled at him. 'You're doing a great thing there.'

'Thank you.' Duncan gave her a final nod, then shut the door.

His heart was somehow beating harder and faster than when he'd hauled her up the steps.

Mum was sitting in the middle of the hallway, looking around the place. 'I'm starving.'

'Okay, I'll get you something to eat in a minute. Just need to get your stuff in from the car.'

'I'm hungry now, fuck face.'

Duncan stood there, grinding his teeth. 'Okay.'

'What's your name? You look familiar. Are you my new nurse?'

'It's Colin, Mum.'

'I had to send Colin away.' She whispered, 'But it's a secret.' Then followed it with a childish giggle.

'I know, Mum. It's me.'

She stared at him with searing intensity. 'He didn't mean to kill that girl.'

Duncan chose to ignore her and wheeled her through into the kitchen. 'I went shopping yesterday, Mum. What can I get you? A sandwich? Some soup?'

'Biscuits.'

'Okay, so you want biscuits?'

'Yes, please.' Mum smiled at him. 'Remember when my boy was a wee laddie? We'd eat Jammie Dodgers very slowly. Nibble away until we just had a wee bit of biscuit around the jam. And then he'd gobble it all up!'

'I remember, Mum.' Duncan laughed. 'But shouldn't I get you some—'

'He was such a lovely wee laddie, Colin. So kind.'

He really should give her some of the baby food. Shouldn't he?

'She's going to die soon, son.' Dad was sitting at the kitchen table, tapping off the end of his cigarette into his McEwan's 80 Shilling ashtray. 'Give her what she wants.'

Duncan didn't know if that was right or not. 'Do you want a Jammie Dodger, Mum?'

'Fig rolls.'

'I don't have any in.'

'You don't have my favourite biscuits in? Thought you were supposed to be my son?'

'Well, I am.' Duncan got out the oat biscuits from the cupboard and put two on a plate. 'Here you go. You like these.'

Mum looked at them with a sour look on her face. Then she picked one up and ate it whole.

Didn't chew, just swallowed it right down.

Was that a good idea?

Duncan just decided to play along with it. 'See? You like those cookies.'

'Don't call them cookies.' Mum grabbed his shirt collar and pulled him close, with a deeply hidden strength. 'They're *biscuits*.'

'Okay, Mum. But I've lived in Canada for so long.'

'Aye, because you killed that lassie.'

'Mum. I love you, okay? But you need to stop saying that.'

'You think I've lost my marbles, but I'm still fine. I remember it all. Remember you coming in with that look on your face. Those scratches on your arms. And I knew what you'd done. Made you sit here and tell me everything.'

'Mum. Stop it.'

'Take me back there.'

'Where?'

'To the home. I felt safe there.'

'Look, this is what you wanted, so you're going to have to work with me, okay? You can't go back to the care home.'

'But I liked it there.'

'Okay, but you'll love it here. Nobody can change the channel, promise. You can watch all the news you want.'

'Get me some fig rolls, then. That wee foreign lassie always had fig rolls for me.'

'I'll pop along to the shop in a minute. I've spent the afternoon sorting out your old room, Mum. Do you want to see it?'

'How am I supposed to get up there? Have you somehow installed a stair lift, eh?'

She had a point there.

All that time and he hadn't thought about where she was going to sleep...

'How about I take you through to the telly, eh?' Duncan wheeled her through to the living room and turned it on. 'Got this working again. The internet's not on yet so you're missing some channels.'

Mum grabbed the remote out of his hand and switched it over to Sky News.

The journalist he'd spoken to was doing a piece to camera. What was his name? Declan?

'—and the police named her earlier today. We've spoken to

neighbours of the victim's mother today. This is what they had to say.'

It cut to a red-faced woman in her sixties. 'It's awful. Heather was such a lovely woman. Used to see her mum a few times a week.'

Mum pointed to the telly. 'Awful business this, isn't it?'

'Awful, aye.' Duncan couldn't look at it. 'I'll just take your stuff upstairs.'

'Can I have some more of those biscuits?'

Duncan chuckled to himself. He went back through to the kitchen and tipped another two out onto the plate. A deep, deep breath, then he went back through to give them to his mother. 'Here you go. I won't be long, okay? I'll hear you if you need me.' He went into the hall, then walked outside.

The street was quiet, just a passing car. Nobody he recognised. No signs of cops or reporters.

He grabbed the suitcases from the boot, then shut the lid.

And it was all going so well – but Declan Harris was lurking around. He spotted Duncan and made a beeline for him.

Duncan waved at him with the suitcase, hoping he'd get the frigging message, then went inside. He shut the door behind him and locked it, then carried her cases up the stairs and into her room.

Christ, they were too bloody heavy and there didn't seem to be anything in them.

He opened them and laid them on the bed, then started rooting through them. Clothes and not much else. Didn't look like they'd been washed recently – probably just had a rotation of a few familiar dresses.

The doorbell chimed.

'Bloody hell.' Duncan looked out of the window onto the main street.

Harris was standing by the door, chewing gum and looking into the lounge.

He'd shut the curtains, hadn't he?

Sod this.

Duncan went into his old bedroom and shut the door. Just had to wait it out. He sat on his old bed, feeling pathetic. At least the walls weren't filled with his old girlie posters ripped from *Loaded* and *FHM*. Mum had decorated it as a guest room, with tasteful side tables and lamps. Anonymous decor.

'Help!' Mum was calling from downstairs.

Fuck.

Duncan went back into her bedroom to look out of the window, but there was no sign of Harris.

A deep breath, then he went back downstairs.

The front door was hanging open.

Had she got out?

'Help!'

Duncan raced into the living room.

Mum was in the same place, staring at the telly. 'Those biscuits were shit.'

The plate was empty.

Duncan let his breath go. 'You scared me.'

'Got stuck in my throat.'

'She almost choked.' Harris was over by the window, waving his phone around like he was trying to get reception.

Duncan clutched his chest. 'Shit, I didn't see you there.'

'Trying to call an ambulance for her. Luckily I was just outside when I heard her shouting for help.'

Harris's face was back on the screen.

Mum looked over at him. 'That's you!'

Harris frowned at the screen, then sucked in his gut. 'Aye, that's me. Well spotted.'

'But you're here?'

'Recorded that earlier. You'll see it repeated until the seven o'clock update.'

Mum seemed satisfied by that, though she was deeply impressed. 'Who's killing these lassies?'

'I don't know.'

Duncan stepped closer to him and spoke in a low tone. 'She's just seen the news about the lassie from down the street, which has upset her.'

'Oh, she knew Heather?'

'Is that her name?'

'Aye. Awful business. Just been in with her mum. Poor woman. Lost herself in baking scones. Police named her daughter. It's her. You know her?'

'Not from around here, sorry. My aunt's got dementia. I've just taken her out of the care home. On her wishes.'

'Tough gig, mate.' Harris grabbed his arm. 'My dad's suffering too. Listen, I'll let you get on.' He passed him a card, which Duncan was sure he'd already done. 'Give me a shout if you need a hand. Or if you just want to talk about it.'

'Of course. Thanks.'

Harris smiled at Mum, then left them to it.

The front door slammed, then Duncan watched him go past the window.

Finally, he could relax.

Dad looked up from reading the paper by the window. 'Son, as much as I hate to say this, but you really need to silence that woman.'

Duncan couldn't find anything in him to disagree with that. He'd formulate a plan.

'I really need the toilet.' Mum frowned at him. Then something softened in her face. 'Oh. Too late.'

Then Duncan started to smell it...

35

The number of times Marshall had driven out of Gala this way, heading south on the A7… and he'd never even noticed these houses.

Thora lived in a huge old mansion on a side street climbing the hill, just opposite a park where Marshall had arrested a paedophile a couple of winters ago.

Big walls, bigger gates. Must've belonged to mill owners or at least senior professionals in the trade. Managers, accountants, engineers. Not the swiftest commute down to the mills lining the Gala Water, but they probably didn't all attend every day… Must be the owners, then.

Jolene opened the right-hand gate and led through. 'How do you feel that went?'

'With Gus?' Marshall stopped to consider his response. 'Hard to say, really. He was a guy who had a lot to get off his chest, right?'

'A *lot*. Once he started, he wouldn't stop talking. Barely had to ask a question.'

'That's a great DI trick, knowing when to let them ramble.' Marshall winked at her. 'Does he strike you as a killer?'

'Not sure. He was obviously deeply affected by what happened to his daughter. Seems to have gone completely off the rails. He has the look of an alcoholic.' Jolene held up her phone. 'Jim McIntyre's going to speak to the locals at the Ladhope and see if they can shed any light on him. Could be he's had sixteen whiskies too many one night and confessed to them.'

'Or they could just give us an alibi.'

'Right. Exactly. Or not.'

'Let's see how this plays out, then.'

The main entrance was on the side of the house which, despite the towering walls, had a glorious view across to where the Tweed and Gala Water met just past the town – another mark in the column for it being a mill owner's residence.

Jolene rang the bell and waited, arms crossed. 'Nice place, eh?'

'What's your point?'

'Well, considering...' She leaned in close and whispered, 'What she used to do...'

The door opened and a woman in her early forties looked out. Fluffy jumper and skin-tight blue jeans. Dark hair, sharp features, even sharper gaze – it could slice you open like she had lasers for eyes. 'Can I help you?'

Marshall smiled at her. 'Looking for Thora Scott.'

'That's me.' Her eyes darted between them. 'And you are?'

'DCI Rob Marshall.' He showed her his warrant card and pointed to the side. 'This is DI Jolene Archer.'

Thora wrapped her arms around herself. 'What's this about?'

'Mind if we come in?'

'I do, actually.'

'It'd be easier if we—'

'I've got builders in just now.' Thora unfolded her arms and shoved her hands as deep into her pockets as they'd go, which was barely to the knuckles. 'They're tearing down a wall.'

As if on cue, a big thud came from inside, reverberating through their feet.

'Ah, okay.' Marshall laughed, then looked around. 'Nice place. Been here long?'

'Two years. Finally got fed up of the state of it so we're doing the work we put off when we moved in.' Thora gripped the door handle tight. 'Is there a problem, officers?'

'Why would you think that?'

'Saw you on the news last night...' She shut her eyes. 'This is about Sharon, right?'

'Partly.'

'Feels like a lifetime ago. Seeing you on the telly last night was a bit of a shock. I mean, I haven't thought about her in a long time. Sounds awful as she was a mate. My best mate... But it's true.' Thora swallowed something down – maybe guilt. 'I've changed a lot since then. I've got two kids, for crying out loud.'

Marshall nodded. 'You used to live with Sharon, right?'

'Up in Langlee, aye.' Thora looked over in the general direction of the area, perched on the steep bank the other side of the valley. 'Truth is... Sod it, I might as well tell you it all, right? I was on the game too. We were both smackheads. Heroin addicts. People think you're scum, but I was just lost. Had such a lot of shit to deal with growing up. Just like Shaz had. And I didn't deal with it, so I sought escape anywhere I could find it. I was drinking in the park at thirteen. Doing coke at fifteen. Then smack at eighteen.' She looked like she wanted to punch herself in the face. 'What happened to Sharon was a real wake-up call to me. Number of times I'd gone off with some bloke in a car...' She rubbed at her temples. 'The *only* good thing that came out of that was that I cleaned up. Chucked my phone off Galafoot Bridge, which meant I lost all the contacts on it – even better, they lost me. Those sad wankers... They couldn't text me or call me and ask me to suck their stubby little cocks.' She snorted out through her nostrils. 'Moved back home to my parents in Cloven and went cold turkey. I was one of the lucky ones, you know? I got out. I was able to start over again. Went to college and trained as a hairdresser. Work in a salon in Melrose and I'm married with two boys now. Harry and Tim. And you know what? I'm happy.' She wiped a tear away before it had a chance to form.

Marshall stood there, waiting for her to lead – when the information was flowing, you listened. You paid attention to what was said – but you listened to what *wasn't* said too, then you could double down on that.

Thora took a few moments to herself then seemed to shiver despite the day's warmth. 'On the news, it said you've got some DNA evidence. Does that mean you've got a new suspect?'

'All I can say is it's still early days. We need to go through the forensics carefully.'

'I see.' Thora refolded her arms. 'Okay, so why are you here, then?'

'We gather you're still in touch with Sharon's father?'

'That old waster?' Thora scowled. 'After what he put her through...' She flared her nostrils then puffed out her cheeks. 'You know something? The night of Sharon's funeral, he tried to pay me to have sex with him. That... That was the final straw for me. He just sat there, crying his heart out. I just thought... I couldn't put my dad through that. Or my mum. I had to get out of it. Never charged him, but that changed me, you know?'

Marshall nodded. 'I can imagine.'

'And when you say we're still in touch? Hardly. I mean... I bumped into him a few weeks ago. He was in Aldi, looking at the whiskies, trying to find the cheapest one, I think, and complaining about minimum pricing. And he seemed in a bad way. Felt so guilty. Had him here for a cup of tea, but he just wanted whisky. I can't have anything in the house.' She shook her head. 'Said that lassie had been hounding him.' She bit her lip. 'Heather McGill.'

Marshall nodded. 'Did he say why?'

'Why do you think? Because of Sharon. Heather's the one who found her. This campaign she was running... She felt so guilty about it, didn't she? And I could see it in his eyes how much it pained him.'

'Did you speak to Heather?'

'Of course I did. She was very good at tracking people down, wasn't she?' Thora twirled her hair around her finger. 'And despite what Gus Beattie said to me, the truth is she was doing something good there. I *hate* what happened to Sharon. What I hate worse is we never knew who did it.'

Marshall looked over towards where he thought Scott's View would be, but the three-humped camel of the Eildons was in the way. 'Heather's body was found last night.'

'Oh my God.' Thora looked like she was going to be sick. Her eyes bulged and she covered her mouth with a fist. 'What happened?'

'We're not at liberty to divulge that, I'm afraid, but it was murder.'

'Was it the same guy who killed Sharon?'

Marshall held that steely gaze. 'Do you think it could be?'

'Truth is, I've no idea who did that.'

Marshall nodded slowly. 'Thing is, it'd be helpful if you could remember any of her clients.'

'*Clients*.' Thora gave a bitter laugh. 'We weren't hairdressers. We were *prostitutes*. Hoors as everyone called us.'

'I was trying to be respectful.'

'Respect... Give me a break...' Thora gave him a cold stare. 'Why do you want to know?'

'Well, we could match her clients against the sample of DNA we have from her attacker.'

'I see.' The look got even colder. 'Sorry, but I didn't know them. She didn't know any of mine either.'

'Do you know how she found clients?'

'We didn't have a pimp, if that's what you're asking. I worked in a barbers on Channel Street and I'd get punters that way. Quite easy to identify the ones looking for business. You could tell the second they walked in. The hunger in their eyes. The way they wanted to wait for me to cut their hair rather than Fat Eric. And if I stroked their neck or something... Bingo. I just had to chat to them while I was cutting away and ask them a few questions. After five, I'd know...'

'Did Sharon work with you?'

'Nah. She'd pick up blokes in the pubs in Melrose or Gala. I'd mostly just go in their car. Thing is, most guys just wanted a blow job or a handie. Sometimes they were so desperate it didn't take a lot to pop the cork.' Thora shut her eyes again. 'Unlike Sharon, I had limits. She'd take them somewhere in her camper van. Around here, that bloody thing was more iconic than McDonald's arches. Sometimes one bloke would be showing up as the last one was leaving.'

'Do you know who Sharon was out with that night?'

'Told the cops this – I don't know.'

'Is that a didn't or don't?'

'Didn't. Still don't. I was doing a full shift in the barbers that day. Then I had three evening punters, so I didn't get home until late. I was desperate for my medication. Shot up and just passed out. Then I came to in the morning and Sharon hadn't come back. She didn't have a mobile, but I did. I was going to go to the cops to report it, but I started panicking about my gear. I'd just scored and the things I'd done for that smack...' A shudder ran through her body. 'But then two cops turned up. They'd traced the plates on the van back to the flat. Said Sharon's body had been found. Made me go and identify her.' She couldn't wipe away these tears and let them slide down her cheeks. 'I didn't tell them anything. I couldn't because I didn't know. Like you, they asked for a list of all the names of Sharon's johns. I didn't share any because I didn't know any.'

'Is it possible some of your clients also visited Sharon?'

'I don't know.'

'You said you had limits, but she didn't.'

'Right. She'd take extra to do stuff like bareback and anal... Taking a massive risk with that, for just a few extra quid. Not just AIDS but STDs, you know?'

'Is it possible they wanted things that weren't on your menu but might have been on hers?'

'Huh?' She frowned. 'What do you mean?'

'Choking her. Strangulation. That kind of thing.'

'Maybe. But I can't think of anyone specific. When we weren't doing that or scoring smack, we were just two normal lassies. We'd chat shit about music, telly, you name it. But we didn't talk about our johns.'

'If you remember any, please get in touch with us.'

'I will do.' Thora turned and opened the door, then immediately turned back to face them, wiping away the tears running down her cheeks. 'And I hope you catch the fucker who did that to her. We were both stupid. Fucked up. Lost lassies. But nobody deserves what happened to her. Nobody.'

36

Duncan walked along the street, hands in pockets, trying to ignore the world.

'What a fucking mess, eh?' Dad kept pace with him, hands in the pockets of his suit, cigarette hanging from his lips. Time was, Duncan would've called that a fag, but living in Canada for so long... Some of the word changes weren't that bad. 'Your mother's completely crackers, son.'

Duncan ignored him. He put his fingers to his nose and could still smell shit.

'You knew it wasn't going to be a picnic, son. But did you ever think it'd be *this* bad?'

Duncan slipped into the Morrisons Daily next to the bookshop and grabbed a basket. He took his time walking around the two aisles. He found the biscuit section around the corner. The fig rolls his mother moaned about were there, but they stocked two different brands. He swithered and swithered over which one to get, then he grabbed both.

Then he remembered how she used to love bourbons but it could've been custard creams, so he put both into his basket.

And he chucked in a few other packets.

Rich Tea.

Digestives.

Chocolate digestives.

And some fancy American-style cookies.

'Wasting time here, son…'

Now for the main event.

Duncan sucked in a deep breath, then found the tiny shop actually had an adult diapers section – *nappies*, damn it. And it was surprisingly well stocked. He looked at the different brands and sizes, but he had no idea which one to get.

'Should've got a supply from the home. You've paid up to the end of the month, so it's not like they don't owe you something, is it?'

Duncan grabbed two boxes of them, which he thought should fit, then took the whole lot over to the counter.

A woman in front of him was just paying. 'Enough tea to see me through the next ice age, I tell you, but I'm making scones like they're going out of fashion and I keep running out of milk.' She grabbed her bag, then shuffled off out of the shop.

Duncan waited until she'd left, then politely stepped forward and rested his basket down on the shelf. He smiled at the woman behind the counter.

She didn't speak. Didn't even look at him, just stacked up his shopping.

He spotted a tube of Smarties, so he added them to the basket. One thing about North America he couldn't shake was how their chocolate all tasted like farts. God knows how they achieved that. Or sold so much.

'These are for you?' Dad was behind the counter, inspecting the packets of cigarettes. 'You selfish wee shite.'

The woman tapped the card machine.

Duncan got his phone out to pay.

Dad jerked around. 'Idiot. Don't leave a trail here.'

'Sorry.' Duncan smiled at her. 'Force of habit.' He dug out a fifty-pound note from his pocket, then handed it over.

The server tapped the register – the *till* – but she *still* wouldn't speak.

Duncan couldn't, because he was stunned into silence by the amount showing.

£54.62

How much were those nappies? They must've cost a bomb because the biscuits sure as hell didn't.

He unfolded a tenner and slid it under the Perspex membrane.

He collected his change, then smiled at the woman and left the shop.

'The less time you spend in Scotland, son, the better.' He could almost taste Dad's smoke as he paced away from the shop. 'Like I keep telling you, go. Now.'

Duncan was starting to see the logic in that...

He wasn't cut out for this, was he?

37

Marshall stood at the whiteboard, sipping from his mug of tea. Too much milk in it and he really wanted a coffee more than anything. He yawned and looked over at Jolene. 'Anything else?'

'Not sure.' She shook her head. 'The stuff Thora Scott told us tallies with the old case file and what Gus Beattie told us. Thora was spoken to back then, but she only answered to the effect that she didn't know Sharon's clients.'

Made sense to Marshall.

Heroin addicts were fixated on their next shot. Anything that risked that wasn't something they engaged with. Plus junkies stole from each other: food, clothes, money, drugs.

Still, a sigh escaped his lips. 'Just wish the team back then had been more thorough.'

'They did a good job, Rob.'

'Not saying they didn't.' Marshall gave her some side eye. 'Apart from losing those nail clippings.'

'Well, aye.' Jolene shrugged. 'That's getting processed tomorrow, apparently.'

'Thought it was today?'

'Trev called me. He's a man down due to bloody Covid, of all things. And sadly, that's the man who does the ad hoc biology. Alternative was to send it to Gartcosh, but it would still take just as long.'

'Okay.' Marshall updated the note on the whiteboard to that effect. 'Well, it'll be good to get the results.'

'Speaking of Gartcosh, I emailed the National Human Trafficking Unit based there about whether Sharon or Thora were on their radar. Or any of their predecessors' radars.'

'Good stuff.' Marshall yawned as he gave the whiteboard one last check, then glanced at his watch – how the hell had it got to half past seven? No wonder he kept on yawning. And he shouldn't be drinking tea. He recapped the pen, then set it down on the lip below. 'Let's call it a day there. We've made some solid progress.'

'Solid isn't good, though, is it?'

'No, it's a foundation. This isn't flimsy. We can build from here.' He nodded at her. 'See you in the morning.'

'Sure. You doing anything nice?'

'Updating Ravenscroft. Feeding my cat. Arguing with my sister.'

Jolene laughed. 'So, the usual then?'

'Pretty much. Have a good one.' Marshall watched her go, then grabbed his laptop bag from his desk and left his office.

The incident room was a hive of activity. Half of Jolene's team were huddled in the far corner. She was listening in and he really should give her some cover – one DI wasn't enough, was it? As much as he tried to help...

But it didn't seem like anyone else needed Marshall, so he buggered off while he could.

Back out in the corridor, he spotted a light on in the old forensics lab, so he opened the door.

Ash and Crawford were in there, working away on laptops.

Marshall frowned at them. 'You're both still here?'

'Aye, sorry.' Crawford looked over at him. 'Just about to leave.'

'Just updating Sarge.' Ash leaned back and stretched out, her top riding up. 'I like working through here because it's empty now they're all up at Howdenhall.'

'Don't get used to it.' Marshall perched on the edge of the desk. 'The uniform sergeants are moving in here next month.'

'Well, they're not here now.' Ash clapped her hands, then rubbed at her eyes. 'God, I'm shattered.'

'Just on my way out of the door myself. You guys getting anywhere?'

'Needed to update you and Jo, Rob.' Crawford pointed at his laptop. 'Someone handed in a phone. Wanted Ash to confirm it's Heather's before I told you.'

'And it is.' Ash nodded. 'It's definitely hers.'

Marshall let out a slow breath. 'You get anything from it?'

'Not much.' Ash scowled at her computer like it was its fault. 'Didn't find any dating apps on her phone. I'd checked her emails and there's no sign-ups to like Bumble or Hinge or even Tinder. Nothing.'

Marshall frowned. 'I thought Georgina McAllister had been winding up Mark Henderson?'

'Had she?' Crawford frowned. 'Well, at least we know it's not true.'

'Okay. You need to make sure you're talking to the other teams.'

Crawford nodded, but his eyes betrayed how annoyed he was – probably as irritated as Marshall was. 'Will do, sir.'

Marshall held his gaze. 'Have you found this man she was supposed to meet?'

Ash shrugged. 'Maybe.'

'Go on?'

'Well, now we've got the phone, sir, I've managed to finally get into her Facebook page. There are tons of messages.

Hundreds, really. A total deluge after the press conference last night. And Heather seems to have responded to every single one.'

'That's dedication, I guess. Anything specific jump out at you?'

'Nope.' Ash frowned at the screen. 'Hang on. There's this.'

Marshall looked at it but she was scrolling too fast for him to keep up.

Ash stopped, then circled a message with her mouse pointer. 'Some guy called Jim Smith said he had information about Sharon Beattie's murder.'

'Did Heather reply?'

'She did, aye. He was quite pushy. Said he was only there that night, then heading back to Orkney. Insisted on meeting up. Left a mobile number.'

Marshall read the messages and got the distinct impression it was someone trying to manipulate her. Whether there was anything malicious in it was another thing. Someone desperate to help the cause could justifiably do that to salve their conscience.

And if she'd shared the messages with him, he *definitely* wouldn't have let her attend solo.

'Do you know if she did call him?'

Ash opened another screen, which mirrored Heather's iPhone. 'There we go. I'll run that number.' She yawned. 'The network's given us the full list of calls, but I don't recognise that number. She texted you a while after she'd exchanged those messages, Rob. Sorry, I mean sir.' She scanned through a long page of numbers, then into another screen, which showed dots on a map. 'Seems like she sent that when she was near Scott's View.'

'And where was he?'

'Just checking, sir. Looks like he'd been in St Boswells.'

'Near her mum's house?' Marshall stood up tall. 'Have you run that phone?'

'Aye, naturally. Pay-as-you-go bought at Edinburgh Airport.' Ash looked up at him with a sour look. 'Which screams "burner" to me.'

'And me.' Marshall started pacing the room. 'Okay, so what you're saying is it looks like he messaged her and called her from St Boswells using a burner phone bought at the airport. Then Heather met him that night at Scott's View, around the time she texted me.'

Crawford nodded. 'And that starts to feel more like she was set up by him, right?'

'Very much.' Marshall stopped his pacing and perched on the edge of the desk again. Right on the corner, which dug into his leg. 'Where was it found?'

'Along the road towards St Boswells.' Crawford snarled. 'Looks like he tossed it as he drove off, hoping it'd smash. Careless, really, because Ash is really good at this.' He jotted something down in his notebook. 'We'll dig into this Jim Smith account on Facebook. Right, Ash?'

'On it. I've done a few of these requests and it's fairly routine. Info won't be with me until tomorrow.'

'Have a good night, then.' Marshall stood up again. 'You two are fighting the good fight for me and I appreciate it.' He got up and left the room, then walked back in. 'Listen, I mean it. I'm giving you both acting-up ranks for the duration of this case. Inspector for you, Douglas, and sergeant for you, Ash.'

They both nodded, but it seemed like the case was more important to them than personal progression.

'I'll do the paperwork first thing tomorrow, but I need you to help Jolene share the load while Andrea's not on this case.'

Crawford smiled. 'Will do that, sir.'

Marshall got a nod from Ash, then he left them to it. Whether they'd celebrate or not...

Reception was empty for once, so he stepped outside the station and into thin rain that seemed to be just about stopping. It didn't make him hurry across the car park.

He unlocked his car and dumped his bag on the back seat, then felt the urge to call Kirsten – out of habit. He'd normally do it when he left the station.

But that was his old life – he needed to move on.

'Evening, Rob.' Isla Routledge was getting out of the car next to his, a cute wee Fiat thing in black, parked maybe a touch too close to his... 'Ships that pass in the night, eh?'

'Something like that. Night shift?'

'Still back-shift. And we're halfway through.'

'But you only got off shift at half five this morning?'

'A sergeant's work's never done.' Isla held up a case of doughnuts bought from Asda. 'Got this to boost morale. Most of my team would run through a brick wall for one. Warner would literally try.' She tipped the box towards him. 'Can I interest you in one?'

'Trying to cut out sugar.' Marshall patted his belly. 'Getting too fat.'

'Nonsense. Or if you have, it's clearly working for you.' Isla frowned at him. 'Anything you need us to do overnight?'

'Nah, it's all taken care of. One of those slow-moving cases that is just so very, very annoying.'

'Not something we ever have to face. Well, not the annoying bit, anyway.' Isla winked at him. 'Take it your weekend's knackered?'

'Unless we pull a result out of the bag, aye.' Marshall smiled at her. 'You'll be off your rotation tonight, aye?'

'Oh, aye. I'll sleep for Scotland tomorrow, but we're heading to Sheila's for some drinks. Just as well she doesn't have any immediate neighbours.'

'Did you speak to her and Warner?'

'Gave them a piece of my mind. One of them listened and I'll let you guess who.'

Marshall laughed. 'Have a good one, though. See you around.'

'I'll try to.' She winked again. 'It'll be a lonely weekend otherwise, then back in here for nights on Monday...'

'Brutal. See you later.' Marshall watched her go into the station, then sat in his car.

He drove off, but he couldn't stop thinking about those winks...

38

Saturday

Duncan came to and had no idea where he was.

In a dark room.

Curtains drawn, but street light spilling in.

He flicked the light on. Right, he was in his old bedroom. It hadn't all been a dream, after all...

He checked his watch, but it was charging. He slipped out of bed and walked over to the charger sitting on his suitcase – still ready to go in case he needed to.

Half past three.

So much for getting some sleep now he was back over this side of the ocean.

'Help!'

Mum, calling from downstairs.

Duncan jerked into action. He left his room, then ran down the stairs.

Mum was sitting in her chair in the living room, blankets cast to her feet. 'I'm cold.'

'Mum, it's June.'

'So? It's bloody freezing!'

The living room window was wide open – how the hell had she managed that?

Then he remembered opening it after he'd changed her yet again, trying to get the stench out. Must've forgot to close it.

Duncan pinched his nose. He reached over to shut it.

'Too hot.'

Duncan touched a hand to her forehead and she was freezing. 'Need to get you all warmed up, eh?' He restored the blankets, tucking them into her armpits. The storage heaters were ice cold. 'Could do with getting some HVAC in here.'

'Some *what*?'

'Central heating.' Duncan knelt down in front of the fire.

No wood. No kindling. No firelighters.

Because it was summer.

And the house hadn't been lived in for *months*. And even then, his mother wasn't exactly with it before she went into that home.

Duncan stood up. 'Is there any wood outside?'

'How the hell should I know?' Mum shrugged. 'Should be.'

'Let me get some in.' Duncan grabbed the wicker basket, then went over to his jacket hanging in the hall and put on his gloves. Felt so familiar putting them on. He stepped into his shoes, then walked outside with the laces trailing behind him.

Might be June but it *was* cold. And here he was, standing there in just sweatpants. He shut his eyes. Trackie bottoms. He stomped to the end of the garden, just by the lane at the back. Dad's old wood store was still there and pretty well stocked, but the wood was all damp and rotten, like it hadn't been topped up since he'd gone.

Still, he found a few drier logs at the bottom that'd do for a fire. He filled the basket with them, then went back inside.

Mum was somehow out of her wheelchair and rooting around in the lower kitchen cupboards. 'There's no Rich Tea!'

'Look, Mum, I bought you some earlier.' Duncan opened one of the cabinets above the counter, way out of her reach. All those glasses from over the years filled them, but sixteen packets of biscuits sat at the front. 'And I got you some of the fig rolls you like.' He opened the packet and handed her one. 'Here you go, but you can't just live off biscuits. I'll make you some porridge when I get up, okay?'

'I want those oat cookies, you stupid fuck face.'

'I've got you them too.' Duncan pinched his nose – he was exhausted and this was already too much. And he could smell the lingering tang of shit from her accident yesterday evening. 'Mum, please can you stop calling me that?'

'Who are you?'

'I'm your son. Colin.'

'You don't look like him.' Mum scowled at him as she chewed on her biscuit. 'I need you to wipe my bum.'

'What do you mean?'

'I went to the toilet but I couldn't find any toilet paper.'

'Right.' Duncan stared into space. That explained the smell…

'This is a disaster.' Dad was leaning against the counter, shaking his head as he sipped from his cup of tea. 'So stupid and arrogant to think you could manage this whole thing. Your mother needs professional help, not your shambling amateur nonsense. And you need to leave the country!'

Hard to disagree with that.

Duncan went into the bathroom and saw she'd somehow torn open all of the nappy bags and thrown the toilet rolls all over the floor, like some teenage lads having a right good laugh in the PE changing room.

It wasn't funny to him now…

At least there was a bath downstairs too – he couldn't face

the prospect of getting her upstairs to the one up there. This one would be okay…

'Did you fill your nappy?' He went back into the kitchen, but she wasn't there anymore.

She was back in the living room, trying to get back onto her armchair.

'Mum, let me…' He helped her get settled, then tucked her back in. This must be what having kids was like. Or ten times worse… 'Don't get too comfy, okay, because we need to get you into the—'

'Stop!' Mum looked at him like he was crazy. Or going to murder her. 'My son's going to kill you, you prick!'

'Mum, you need to stop saying that.'

'It's true, isn't it? Fuck face. You killed that lassie!'

'You…'

'Fuck face.'

'*Mum.*'

'Fuck face. You killed that girl!'

'Mum… Seriously, you need to—'

'You're a killer! You killed that lassie! And I helped you get away with it!'

Duncan towered over her, attempting to intimidate her. 'Mum, you need to stop—'

'You useless prick!' Spit dribbled down her chin. 'I wish I'd let you rot in jail!'

Dad was standing by the fireplace, smoking his cigarette. 'You know what you need to do, don't you?'

Duncan did.

He didn't want to, but his needs outweighed hers.

He grabbed her by the shoulders. 'I don't want to do this.' He pushed her down into her chair, then wrapped his gloved hands around her throat.

Dad was leaning against the fireplace. 'This is the first sensible thing you've done since you got here.'

Duncan started squeezing and it didn't take hardly any effort to kill his mother.

He rocked back on his heels and sat there, staring at her. Despite all the people he'd murdered, this one felt different.

Dad was applauding. 'Now get gone!'

39

Marshall woke up.

Something was pinning his legs down.

He reached over to flick on the light, then looked down the bed.

Zlatan lay on top of the duvet, purring away. A king owning his kingdom.

And Marshall's leg was dead from the wee tyke's dominance.

He managed to wriggle free and sit up in his bed.

Took him a moment to realise where he was – back in his old bed in Jen's flat above her garage. At least it was *his* bed, moved up from London by the local removals company who didn't charge through the nose.

He reached over to check his phone.

Six o'clock.

On a Saturday.

And he'd been up till midnight running a profile on their killer – and getting bloody nowhere. Two data points and twenty-five years in between – he knew it was a fool's errand.

He'd better get up. Get in the shower. Get into the station. Start the day.

But he was so bloody tired, so he lay back and shut his eyes. Just a few minutes, right?

His phone buzzed and jerked him awake again.

He picked up his phone and checked the screen.

A text from Jen:

I've been called into work to cover. Assume you're going in? Get you a coffee?

Marshall replied:

Desperate for one. Ta.

He noticed another message that'd arrived overnight.

A text from Isla Routledge, received about two in the morning.

Topless and showing off her breasts.

This what you were looking for?

Fuuuuuck.

40

Marshall struggled to focus on the briefing.

Everyone seemed exhausted, yawning into stale cups of coffee and chewing on staler bacon rolls, filling the room with a sweaty stink.

And he couldn't stop thinking about the photo. He'd deleted it – the right thing to do – but he hadn't responded yet.

What could you say?

Flirting in person was one thing. Discussing personnel matters over text had maybe crossed a professional line, but it wasn't exactly an escalation path to sexting.

Was it?

Marshall didn't know. Dating had been a mystery to him and the rules seemed weird now, especially since the pandemic, not that he'd dabbled. Not that what happened with Kirsten really counted, not in that way. They stumbled into something, rather than seeking each other out on apps.

Bloody hell.

He had his phone in his hands but he didn't know what to type.

Crawford was glowering at Marshall. 'You listening, sir?'

'I am.' Marshall put his phone away and cleared his throat – aye, he'd better let that one sit for a bit... 'Carry on.'

Crawford gave him a judgemental glare, then went back to his notebook. 'As such, we've spoken to eighteen James Smiths across Scotland overnight, including Jims and Jamies. Even a Hamish. None match that account or have ties to Orkney.'

'Okay, that's interesting.' Marshall nodded along with it. 'So we think it's a dummy account?'

'That'd be my assumption, aye. But it could be someone from elsewhere in our remit.'

'And this is on top of him using what appears to be a burner phone to call her, right?'

'Right, exactly. So the odds are stacked in favour of Jim Smith being a fake name. Sadly, too easy to fake social media accounts. There was that case in Edinburgh a few years back.' Crawford gave a steely look. 'We'll get to the bottom of it, guv. Don't you worry.'

'Cheers, Douglas.'

'Don't mention it, sir.' Crawford pointed at Ash. 'I've asked DS Paton to dig into it to give a better digital footprint, but there's no update.'

'Calm down, Doug.' Ash was scowling at him. 'I've only just got in. Might be waiting in my email.'

Crawford raised his eyebrows. 'Case like this, we need to focus.'

'Keep your wig on.'

Crawford patted his head. 'Cheeky.'

'Truth is, I did get in early.' Ash smirked. 'Been working with the big boy digital forensics team at Gartcosh, sir. They think that Jim Smith account accessed Facebook using a mobile with a burner SIM in it.'

Crawford's turn to frown. 'How do they know that?'

'They've got ways and means. Also reckon it was using a VPN, which scrambles the location.'

Marshall jotted that down on the whiteboard. 'Going to some lengths to hide. Which makes it seem all the more suspicious, right?'

'Precisely.' Ash nodded. 'Good news is we know it was sent locally while attached to the wi-fi at Butler House care home.'

Crawford frowned. 'You can tell that?'

'Ways and means, guv. You'd be amazed by what information companies like Facebook and Google store on you. They know what you like so they can advertise rubbish at you.' Ash shrugged. 'And part of that is knowing where you are at all times. VPN or not, they look for other things to connect you to the real world.'

'Okay, so Butler House care home wi-fi makes me think Gus Beattie.'

Crawford nodded. 'We'll bring him in, sir.'

'Let me know how it goes.' Marshall looked around the room. 'Just a bit of an FYI for the rest of the team, but I've given acting-up promotions to DS Paton and DI Crawford for the duration of this case. Congrats, guys.'

A ripple of applause lashed through the room.

Ash stared at the floor, but Crawford basked in it.

Marshall looked at Jolene. 'DI Archer, can you give your update now?'

'Will do.' Jolene made a note on a bit of folded-up A4. 'The only other real update from our side is we've spoken to the National Human Trafficking Unit in Gartcosh about Sharon and Thora.'

'That was quick.'

'Twenty-four-seven operation over there. More stuff done out of hours than within, they said.' Jolene unfolded the page and frowned at it. 'Okay, so that work would've been done by Lothian and Borders back in 2000. Most of their efforts in that sphere were in Edinburgh, in fact virtually all of them. This is around the time they were clamping down on kerb-crawling in

Leith and they started licensing saunas. Or turning a blind eye to what happened in them. But my contact reckons anything down here would've been dealt with as a local crime thing. I was going to speak to anyone still serving to see what we could glean, but I gather it's not much. Again, a blind eye.'

'My mum picked Sharon up a few times.' Crawford nodded slowly. 'Backed up what she told you yesterday. Sharon and Thora were known heroin addicts and sex workers, but vice never formally investigated them.'

'Right. Good.' Jolene nodded. 'Downside is no investigation means no leads.'

'Okay, but that's still good.' Marshall made a note on the board. 'As long as we keep driving everything home, we'll get somewhere with this case.'

McIntyre raised a hand. 'Sir, I've managed to get locations and contacts for the other three who were in Sinead's car.'

Jolene scowled at him. 'News to me...'

'Sorry, ma'am. Been a hell of a day, hasn't it?'

Jolene checked her watch and laughed. 'It's twenty past seven, Jim.'

'Even so.' McIntyre shrugged. 'Been in since four because two are in Australia and the other is in Chile.'

Crawford shook his head slowly. 'They really did want to run away, didn't they?'

'Hard to imagine getting further away, Sarge. Sorry, guv. Local cops in Oz are going to speak to them today. Whatever time it is over there. Chile's proving a bit harder, but I'll keep on it.'

'Cheers, Jim.' Marshall smiled at him. 'That's good work.'

Then Marshall's phone rang.

Trev calling...

Marshall looked around the room, then focused on Jolene.

'Better take this. Jo, can you finish up?' He walked over to his office, then answered the phone as he shut the door. 'Marshall.'

'Great news, Rob.' Sounded like Trev was driving. 'We managed to process the DNA and fingerprints overnight and I've just finished running it against the sample Mark Henderson provided.'

'And?'

41

Duncan sat in the kitchen, watching Sky News playing on mute on the tiny portable telly Mum had bought on a whim in nineteen oatcake. Certainly long enough ago it was still a CRT, but the wee box plumbed in digital telly to it.

The news showed President Trump sitting with the new German Chancellor, Friedrich Merz.

As far as Duncan could tell, nothing had changed since last night, so the same update played. But he wasn't sure what it had been… If he was imagining the stasis.

Duncan got up and picked up the packet of oat cookies, but he couldn't face eating. His gut was churning. Most of the time, he'd finish the packet in one go…

Then the breaking news logo flashed up.

Duncan reached over to unmute it.

'—the case of a murder at Scott's View, a famed local landmark named after the celebrated novelist Sir Walter Scott. A spokesman had this to say.'

Det. Superintendent John Ravenscroft

'We've processed the DNA we recovered from—'

The doorbell chimed, loud enough to drown out the TV.

'—any information to come forward.'

Bollocks – all that time waiting and watching the same loop from last night and Duncan had fucking missed the fresh details.

He turned off the telly and got up, then walked down the hallway, avoiding looking into the living room, and answered the door.

'Good morning, Colin.' Dr Japp stood there, dressed in black and pale as the Grim Reaper. 'Shame to be meeting again so soon.'

'Isn't it just...' Duncan scratched his neck and opened the door wide. 'Thanks for coming out at such short notice.'

'All part of the service.' Dr Japp stepped inside, then rested his bag on the floor and eased off his jacket. 'Where is she?'

'Through here.' Duncan showed him into the living room.

Dr Japp followed him in, then stood there. 'Well, I can see the lividity.' He bent her arm, checking for rigor.

Didn't even lift up her high-necked nightgown.

Didn't wonder why it was clean – after she'd crapped herself, giving Duncan one last indignity as he cleaned up the mess.

He gave a deep sigh. 'What happened?'

'We had a nice evening. She was so grateful to be back in her own home. Even got her playing cards for a while. Spent the evening looking at old family photos, hoping to jog her memory a bit. And she wanted to sleep in the chair here and wouldn't be dissuaded. I checked on her before I went to bed.' Duncan swallowed hard. 'When I got up, I couldn't wake her.' He shut his eyes briefly. 'Only got her out of the home last night. Didn't think she'd go so soon.'

'Sometimes it's the way. Little changes in that condition can lead to huge repercussions.'

Duncan nodded. 'Just seems really surreal, you know?'

'I know, because it is. But it's also very real.' Japp puffed out his cheeks. 'Well, since she's died in the house, I only need to issue a death certificate, then we can get her buried.'

'That's it?'

'That's it.' Japp smiled at him. 'Let's have a wee dram together and I'll sign the form as we sup it.'

'Of course.' Duncan took one last look at his mother – she looked like she was sleeping – then led Japp through to the kitchen. 'Please, have a seat.' He went into the cupboard and found a bottle of his dad's old whisky. He had to wipe away the stoor.

Dunpender Centenary edition

He showed it to Japp. 'This any good?'

'Heavens.' His eyebrows shot up. 'That's too good.'

'My mum's just died. The least she deserves is the good stuff.'

'True.' Japp nodded – the old lush didn't need much persuading, did he? 'Aye… She deserves to be remembered.'

'Doesn't she just?' Duncan searched through the cupboard of glasses, but didn't see any suitable ones. He found another cupboard full of glasses and pulled out two crystal tumblers. He poured out a healthy measure and a tiny one, then handed over the healthy one to Japp. 'There we go.'

Japp looked up from his form. '*Slàinte mhath.*' He sank the whisky in one go.

'*Slàinte.*' Duncan drank his – and almost threw up. It was *disgusting.*

Why the hell anybody could drink that fiery pisswater was a complete mystery.

'Aye, that's the business.' Japp cleared his throat with a deep animalistic growl. 'Braw distillery. Wee place up in Dalkeith.

Had a bit of bother there a few years ago. Found a body in a cask, would you believe?' He signed the form and passed it over. 'There you go, Colin. I'm really sorry.'

'Thank you.'

'That's the local funeral director.' Japp got out a card and slid it over the table. 'I'd give him a call soon, if I were you. Even though it's Saturday, he'll be here soon.' He gazed at the bottle of whisky like others would lust after a woman. 'If you call him now, we could have another wee dram while we wait?'

42

Saturday might be a half day, but Max Power's garage was a clattering noise.

They probably did more work today than the rest of the week. Or it just seemed that way from the customers waiting while their cars were fixed.

Meaning Marshall and Jolene had to stand outside the waiting area.

Jolene was on a call, rolling her eyes at Marshall as she yawned.

Marshall looked at his own phone. He'd deleted the message from Isla, but he could see she was online. Just hadn't messaged him.

What do you say to that?

Pretend it didn't happen?

He'd have to laugh it off soon. That was the sensible choice. Kept her onside, pretend nothing bad had happened.

He remembered their chat last night – her going to Sheila Crawford's for drinks after their shift. Probably got wasted and the Dutch courage made her sext him in the middle of the night.

Fucking hell.

It was... pretty flattering.

They got on well. And he liked her.

But this was way too much...

'What now?' Mark Henderson appeared in the doorway, sneering at them.

Marshall gave him a smile. 'Anywhere we can chat in private?'

Henderson opened the office door and looked inside. 'This is clear.'

Marshall let Jolene go first, then followed Henderson into a store room stinking of rubber. Racks of tyres filled the walls, leaving barely any space. 'Can you shut the door, please?'

Henderson wiped his hands on a rag then tucked it into his pocket. 'Whatever it is, doesn't need any privacy, does it?'

Marshall let out a sigh. 'Thank you for giving us a DNA sample.' He left a long pause. 'It's allowed us to eliminate you from the case.'

Henderson frowned. 'Excuse me?'

'We ran your DNA against the recovered sample and there's no match.'

Henderson swallowed. 'So I'm clear?'

'You're clear.'

'I guess that means you can't frame me anymore, eh?'

Marshall held his gaze. 'It's never been our intention to do that.'

'Right.' Henderson chuckled, then sucked in a deep breath. 'Thing is, I want to help you find Heather's killer. What can I do?'

'There's nothing much you can do.' Marshall shrugged. 'Unless you know who killed her?'

'No idea. I told you lot back then and I'll tell you it again. I was playing my N64 that night. Some people think it's sad, but I've always loved gaming.'

'Of course. But I just wanted you to know personally. And to thank you for your time and your co-operation. But if you hear anything that's helpful to us, it'd be great if you passed it on to us.'

'Right, sure.' Henderson ran a hand down his face. 'Fine. I'll let you know, alright.'

Marshall smiled at him. 'Thanks for your time.'

MARSHALL PULLED into the station car park and took the space by the door. 'Poor guy's been to hell and back over this stuff, hasn't he?'

'True.' Jolene opened her door. 'Guess it means he's kept his job.' She shook her head. 'Old Max didn't seem to be happy with his attitude yesterday.'

'Nope.' Marshall got out into the thin rain. 'And it's understandable. Having someone working for you for over twenty-five years being accused of murder must be a nightmare.'

'For everyone involved.'

Jolene's phone rang. She checked it and groaned. 'Better take this.'

Marshall nodded. 'See you inside.' He walked over to the station.

'Rob!'

Marshall spun around.

Isla walked towards him, dressed like she'd just been to the gym. Or was heading there.

Ah, crap. Exactly what he didn't need right now...

He hadn't had time to craft the perfect response.

He didn't even know what a good one would be...

Totally out of his depth with this – what he wouldn't give for a serial killer. He knew where he was with them.

Marshall smiled at her. 'Thought this was your day off?'

'Aye, but...' She stopped next to him and avoided eye contact. 'Can we have a word?'

'Sure.'

Isla ran a hand through her hair – he'd mostly seen it tied up. 'Rob, I'm *mortified*. Sorry, sorry, sorry.'

'It's okay.' Marshall raised his hands at her. 'I've shared the image with your inspector and half the team.'

Isla's eyes went wide. 'You've *what*?'

'I'm joking. I figured it was a mistake, so I deleted it. Sure your boyfriend would appreciate it, though.'

Isla frowned at that. 'Thanks, Rob.'

'Have a good weekend, okay?' Marshall tapped his nose. 'Your secret's safe with me.'

Isla looked him up and down. 'Appreciate it.' She looked like she was going to say something, but then she scurried away from the station and her well of shame.

Jolene walked over, scowling at him. 'What was that about?'

'Nothing much. Just a staffing issue.'

'Are you trying to bring her over to the dark side?'

'Asked and refused.'

'Really?'

'Some people want to stay in uniform because they like it. She'll be an inspector soon, I reckon.'

'She's good, aye. What was the staffing issue?'

Marshall's phone chimed. A text from Isla:

I'm so sorry, Rob. Thank you xx

He tapped out a reply:

It didn't happen, okay? x

The kiss was a mistake.

Shite, shite, shite.

Talk about digging a hole...

Jolene tilted her head to the side. 'Rob, is there something going on between you and Isla?'

Marshall put his phone away, but he was blushing. 'Isla? No.'

Jolene gave him a long, hard look, but she didn't press him on it. The main benefit of being the guy who'd got you promoted was it bought loyalty – but also discretion. 'So, we've lost our prime suspect. What now?'

'We interview Gus Beattie.' Marshall puffed up his cheeks. 'And we go through the case file again to see what we can shake loose.'

43

Duncan sat in the kitchen and tried to figure out how the hell he could get a good cup of coffee in this house.

Just tubs and tubs of instant, all dried out and stuck to the bottom.

He'd found the bottoms to three glass French presses – cafetières over here – but none of the lids seemed to fit.

No grinder, no beans...

Not even any of the pre-ground stuff.

He should go to the café in the bookshop, but that'd mean leaving the house with her still here...

And he couldn't do that.

Mum was fussing over by the cooker. A bright-yellow apron, marking out scone shapes on a baking tray.

Duncan waited for eye contact. 'You never loved me, did you?'

'Of course I did.' Mum laughed at that. 'When you killed that lassie, you fell to pieces. Told me what you'd done. How you'd murdered her. I couldn't let you go to jail, could I? I was the one who arranged for you to stay with my sister. What's that if not love?' She walked over to the cooker and switched on the oven. 'And did you thank me? No. You called me a few times over the years, but it's like you weren't listening to me. Just so lost in your obsession with killing all those lassies.'

'And he didn't stop killing them, did he?' Dad was sitting at the table, drinking instant coffee from those horrible smoked glass mugs he'd found. 'Once he got the taste for it, he couldn't stop, could he?'

'No.' Duncan sighed. 'Didn't want to.'

Mum went back to pressing out her scone shapes. 'Was it all girls like Sharon?'

'Girls. Women. Sometimes men.'

Dad frowned at him. 'Were they all hoors?'

'Not all, no. Second one was a student. Young lassie in Canada. Just walking home from a bar one night. Total accident, really.'

'Guess it didn't matter whether they were hoors or not, eh? They just had to look you in the eyes and seem open to something, right? Then you'd reward that by killing them.'

'Could've said those words myself.' Mum set down her rolling pin. 'He killed them for loving him?'

'Nobody loved me. Not even you two.'

'I did, fuck face.' Mum prodded her apron with her dusty finger. 'And you fucking killed me, didn't you?'

'I… I had to… You were going to tell someone.'

'Would I? Would I really?'

'You'd already started! Saying I was going to kill people for you. And you didn't even recognise me. How could I know you wouldn't blab to someone?'

'Who would've believed me, eh? You didn't need to murder me like that.'

Duncan didn't have an answer for that.

Dad clapped his shoulder. 'You did what you had to, son.'

'Talking shite.' Mum scowled at him. 'After all I did for him, he couldn't take care of me for one night, could he? I saved him and he couldn't even try for one day.'

Duncan pointed at Dad. 'He told me to do it!'

She glowered at him. 'It's your fault, son.'

Duncan threw the whisky bottle at her and it smashed against the wall.

'Waste of good whisky, that.' Dad looked at Mum. 'Couldn't bear to have him around, could you, Pat? Not after what he'd done. The shame of it. Shipped him off to your sister, then you didn't have to think about the scumbag's actions. Didn't even get to say goodbye to me, did he? I died and he didn't see me.'

'I didn't want to. After all you put us through!' Duncan threw the glass at his dad and it hit the wall behind him. 'You didn't fucking deserve it!'

'Creating such a mess there.' Mum shook her head at him. 'I should've just shopped you, Colin. All those poor people you killed... Their relatives would've had some closure, at least. And you've killed so many since. I know I was selfish and just wanted to protect my laddie.' She rested her fists on her hips. 'But not as selfish as you, eh? Worse than your father.'

Dad raised his hands. 'Leave me out of this.'

Duncan got up and started picking up the shards of glass from his tumbler. A splinter slipped and sliced his palm open.

Fuck.

Dad scowled at him. 'Idiot.'

Duncan dashed over to the sink and ran the wound under the tap. 'You got any plasters, Mum?'

'I've no idea.' She sat opposite Dad. 'I can't remember anything because of this condition.'

Duncan opened the drawer and sifted through the batteries and instruction manuals and sandwich bags and lightbulbs and fuses and more batteries and more sandwich bags, and found some plasters.

'This wasn't my fault, son. My mind wasn't working right anymore. You didn't need to kill me.'

'Of course I did.' Duncan dried his hand with kitchen towel, then wrapped a plaster around the wound. Not easy doing it one-handed and it being all damp and the plaster being ancient. 'You would've slipped. Would've told them I'd killed Sharon.'

'What, I'd tell them you strangled that poor wee girl? Would they believe me?' Mum glowered at him, then laughed. 'Thing is, Duncan or Colin or whoever you want to be... You deserved to get caught, because you're *pathetic*. You had to pay that lassie to have sex with you in the camper van.'

'I didn't!'

'What were you doing there, eh? Playing cards? Chatting about football? Discussing philosophy?'

Someone knocked at the door.

Duncan snapped back to reality, but he could still smell the scones. The smashed whisky was still there. And his hand throbbed under the plaster. So some of that was real.

He covered the bottle over with a bundle of kitchen towel – almost out of the stuff – then walked through the house. 'Coming!' He opened the front door.

A wee man was standing there, jangling keys in the pockets of his red trousers, which matched the colour of his face. Tweed jacket. Hair like the top of a thatched cottage – and probably just as flammable. 'Morning. I'm looking for Colin Radford?' His accent was London, but Duncan couldn't narrow it down from any of the Home Counties.

'That's me.'

'My name's Keith Maguire?' He gave the wide smile of the used car salesman. 'From Maguire & Day? The funeral directors in Melrose? I'm here for your mother?'

'Oh, right.' Duncan smiled as he stepped out of the way. 'In you come.' He looked outside in case that reporter was snooping around. 'Thank you for coming so quickly.'

'Summer's a busy time for us, you know?' Maguire looked around the place, as if pricing it up. 'But still, it's what we sign up for in this game, right?' Jangle, jangle, jangle. 'So, where is she?'

'Right. Sorry. My head's up my ass.' Duncan showed Maguire into the living room.

Maguire stood in the doorway, brushing a hand through his hair but only seeming to make it that bit worse. 'Ah, is that her there?'

No, it's the Queen...

'I knew her, you know?' Maguire looked over at him. 'Proud member of the community, wasn't she? At the kirk every week, wouldn't you say? She didn't suffer too much at the end, did she?'

'Dr Japp said she just... Her heart stopped beating in her sleep.'

'Best way, don't you think?'

Duncan nodded. 'Feels like I should be doing something to help.'

'There's really nothing to do, is there? Take a few months for probate to clear, assuming the will's in your favour? I mean, you could start clearing out her stuff – can be very cathartic, if you catch my drift? Took me months with my own parents when they went and they weren't exactly hoarders, you know? I know a few decent house clearance specialists? I could give you a card?'

'I'll think about it.'

'Of course, of course.' Maguire cleared his throat. 'Anyway, I've got a bit of time today so I'll start work on her this afternoon, if that suits? And the office will be in touch regarding funeral arrangements, as she didn't have anything on file?'

'Mum just wanted a quick cremation.'

'Don't they all?'

'I'll use whatever money I have to get a wee plot with a nice stone.'

'That's a lovely way to remember her, isn't it?' Maguire looked over at the door, where a younger version of him stood. Tall and gormless, with a suit a few inches too short for his gangly frame. 'You haven't met my son, Brodie, have you? We'll be a while here, so you should probably get out and clear your head, if you want to?'

Duncan knew Maguire would be sizing up the contents, but this house was the last place he wanted to be. Maybe he could get a real coffee. 'That's probably a good idea.'

Or maybe he could just cut and run.

Once he'd tied up the final loose end.

44

Elliot sat in her office playing Balatro on her phone, but she didn't have a two pair in her hand and she was all out of discards. Just had to hope a single pair was enough to squeak over the line.

And it wasn't.

Fuck's sake.

Another run gone.

Last time she listened to either son's games recommendation...

But she could maybe have another go at it, couldn't she?

After all, it wasn't like Ravenscroft had any work for her. What was the point in having one of Scotland's best investigators doing *media liaison*? He didn't even let her speak at the last briefing and it took so bloody long to convince him to name Heather.

Reduced to playing games to fill the time...

So she just sat back in her chair, feeling effed off.

She checked her phone for anything other than Balatro and there was still nothing from Sam.

Sod it – she tried calling the wee madam.

And Sam bounced the call.

Sodding hell.

Elliot went back to Balatro and started another run – this time she was going to beat it.

Her phone buzzed.

Busy.

Elliot knew full well what a full stop meant to that generation.

Didn't stop her from calling again.

And *that* didn't stop Sam from bouncing it again.

Buzz.

Text:

TOLD YOU I'M BUSY!

Elliot stared at her phone for a few seconds, then put it away. 'Little bloody madam. After all I do for you...' She sighed and scrunched up her face.

Why the *hell* am I sitting here playing games?

She checked the doodles she'd made for a nickname for Ravenscroft, but they were all bloody awful.

'Right.' Elliot clapped her hands together, then got up and walked out into the incident room. She had a good look around but there was nobody to bully. Or nobody who looked like they needed it.

Light on in Marshall's office, though.

She peered in through the glass.

Ravenscroft was standing over him, hammering home a point by jabbing his finger towards Marshall.

He really did need a nickname...

Cheeky bastard hadn't announced his presence to his *media liaison*, had he?

Elliot nudged the door open.

'—need results and soon. Okay?' Ravenscroft jerked around and locked eyes with Elliot. 'Just a second, Inspector.' He turned back to Marshall. 'What about Sharon's father? You said something about wi-fi at the care home?'

Marshall nodded. 'We've spoken to him, sir.'

'And?'

'A few things. We checked his alibi for Thursday night. While he didn't give one, his neighbours saw him at the time in question. Fell asleep on the sofa. Drunk, they reckon. Must've been lying on the remote because his TV went up really high. Knocked on the door, but no answer. Door wasn't locked, so they went in and turned it off. He didn't rouse.'

'Right.' Ravenscroft snorted, then looked around at Elliot. 'I see. And what else?'

Marshall shrugged. 'Thing is, around the time the message was sent by Jim Smith, we saw him speaking to Heather at Scott's View.'

Ravenscroft ran a hand down his face. 'So it wasn't him?'

Elliot got between them. 'We don't believe so.'

'You don't, do you?' Ravenscroft sneered at her. 'Andrea, have you got something for us? Or can it wait?'

'Me? No, sir.' Elliot raised her eyebrows. 'And I've been told not to be close to the investigation and focus solely on media liaison.'

'Don't get smart with me.'

'Wasn't my intention. Just stating facts.'

'I need a result. And that's on Rob, not you.' Ravenscroft gave a withering look. 'I know you can do it, okay?' He took one last glance at Elliot, then left the office. 'See you both later. Got some calls to make.'

Marshall picked up the file and dropped it onto the desk with a loud thwack, then opened it and started poring through it.

Elliot sat on the edge of the desk. 'You know if you stare into the case file long enough, the case file stares back into you.'

'Right.' Marshall looked up at her. 'Nietzsche said it more eloquently.'

'Who?'

'Never mind.' Marshall shut the file. 'You seem bored. And a bored DI Andrea Elliot isn't a good thing because you find mischief.'

'No comment.' Elliot pointed at it. 'You getting anywhere?'

'Been sitting here for...' Marshall checked his watch then sighed. 'Almost four hours. I've been looking through everything. And I've found the cubic root of bugger all. But don't worry, because Ravenscroft's been in every half an hour to pester me and pile on the pressure.'

'I could do with some pestering, Robbie. You're right – I'm *bored*.'

'Wish I could use you.'

Elliot tried to read something into that. The thought of him using her for his sexual pleasure made her go all funny down below. He was a handsome bugger, that was for sure, and it'd been a long time since she'd had a shag.

Probably just a functional one minute forty-three with Davie...

And Dr Donkey was single these days after he dumped Weirdo...

She nodded at him. 'Did that DNA from twenty-five years ago help?'

'All it said was it wasn't Mark Henderson who killed her.'

'Oh, that's news to me.'

'Sorry.' Marshall stretched out. 'Trev's running the search for a familial match now. The ethnic profile shows a male with a Scottish and English heritage, so no help on that front.'

'Right.' Elliot pursed her lips and stared at the door. 'Ravenscroft needs a nickname.'

'Sure you'll think of one.'

'Thought of several, but they're mostly awful.' Elliot stared into space for a few seconds, but nothing fresh came to mind. 'When did we have to start managing our bosses?'

Marshall folded his arms. 'It's what happens when people get over-promoted.'

'Pringle, Gashkori and now you.' Elliot winked at him. 'At least you know what you're doing. And you probably think you're under-promoted, right?'

'Me as acting DCI isn't under-promoted.'

She should ask him out for a drink, shouldn't she?

Maybe the timing was wrong.

Not like she didn't have a gazillion things in her head, was it?

Or just a bite of lunch, maybe that Japanese place round the corner.

'Catch you later, Robbie.' Elliot got to her feet, then opened the door.

Trev was out there, staring into his phone.

Elliot waved a hand in front of his face. 'Looking a wee bit lost there, Trevor.'

Trev looked up and frowned. 'Oh, it's you.'

'Charming.' Elliot laughed. 'You act like I've been kicked off the force or something.'

'Sorry, it's just…' Trev sighed, then looked around her. 'Rob, I've got a parental match on the DNA from Sharon's fingernails.'

Marshall joined them in the doorway. 'Go on?'

'John Radford.'

'Doesn't mean anything to me. That's the guy's father?'

'So it would appear. Lived in St Boswells.'

'Why is his DNA on file?'

'He got into a violent altercation with a neighbour in 1996. Punched him hard enough to hospitalise him. Not bad form too as he was in his sixties at the time. Had a day in court. Fine and suspended sentence, plus DNA held on record in perpetuity.'

'Still alive?'

'Not sure, but his last-known address is Butler House care home in Galashiels.'

45

Duncan drove his rental along the back way into Galashiels and pulled in outside a hardware shop to let some traffic past. Must've been quite some town way back when – some pretty fancy houses up here and some nice apartment blocks. Plenty of development on the other side of the river too. He looked into the rear-view.

His parents sat on the back seat, like he was taking them out for a leisurely drive somewhere.

'We've discussed it, Colin.' Mum made eye contact with him. 'Your father's right. You should've left me here and gone back to Canada.'

Duncan pulled out, then rattled along the street.

'I would've kept quiet.'

Dad clutched her hand. 'Nobody believed her, did they?'

'Exactly. It was safe to leave me.'

Duncan pulled into the parking lot but the only spot free was under an old oak, the leaves pregnant with rain. He opened the door and planted his right foot on the ground. 'Stay here.'

'How can we go anywhere?' Mum laughed. 'You killed me. We're just figments of your imagination.'

'I mean it.'

'You've really fucking lost it, fuck head. You're a serial killer. The lowest of the low. You kill, and all because you're weak. You're disgusting and pathetic and I really—'

Duncan got out and slammed the door. 'Fuck's sake.'

The rain was chucking down, but he stood there, trying to centre himself.

This was a disaster. Every time he whacked down one mole, another popped its head up.

He took the folded-up wheelchair out of the trunk, leaving his carry-on luggage in there, then carried it through the rain and up the steps into the care home.

Zuzana was behind the desk, talking with the manager.

They both looked over at him.

'Mr Radford?' Zuzana frowned. 'Is everything okay?'

Duncan rested the wheelchair down, then tried to speak but he couldn't. He just shook his head. 'My mother passed away during the night.'

'Oh my.' April clutched the pearl necklace around her neck. 'I'm… That's awful. I'm so sorry.'

Zuzana fluttered those eyelashes at him. 'Are you okay?'

'Got her wish of dying at home.' Duncan shrugged. 'Heart just gave out.'

'A change of venue can cause that.' April tilted her head to the side. 'They become so accustomed to their routines, it's really all they have left. Sometimes transferring from one care home to another or even just changing rooms can do it.' She shook her head as if loosening some cobwebs. 'Still, your mother seemed so vibrant. Always had a wicked sense of humour. But one thing you learn in this business is to focus on today and getting through it.'

'Thank you. We had a great night just looking through old family photos. It meant a lot to us both.' Duncan looked around. 'I just thought you'd like to know. You guys dealt with her every day. You cared for her. And you all did such an amazing job.'

'Of course. I'm so sorry. We'll attend the funeral, of course. It's the least we can do.'

'She'd love that. It'll be a quiet affair, of course. Though I'm not sure she even wanted one. Dad's was quite an ordeal.' Duncan started to feel weird, like he shouldn't be here.

April set her eyes tight. 'We had the police here earlier. Second time in two days.' She didn't look happy about it.

Duncan frowned. 'Oh, I'm sorry to hear that.'

'All this business with his daughter. It's awful. I had no idea he was *that* Gus Beattie.'

'Anyway.' Duncan shifted his focus between them. 'The funeral director's collecting Mom just now, so I thought I'd get out... Clear my head...' He held up the wheelchair. 'I wanted to return this and—'

'—make sure there's no evidence pinning anything on you.' Dad tapped his watch. 'Get the fuck out of Dodge, son.'

'—collect the last of her stuff.'

'It's all gone, I'm afraid.' April frowned. 'You took it.'

'That was *it*?'

'I'm afraid so.'

'Sorry. That's... Okay. I'll get out of your hair, then.' Duncan gave them a polite smile. 'Thanks for looking after her.' A final nod and he left them.

The rain was teeming down now, a proper biblical deluge. So much for it being June.

Duncan hurried across the parking lot.

'That went well, fuck face.' Mum was chasing after him with a speed she'd not had since he was a young one. 'You're such a loser.'

Dad walked alongside Mum, holding her hand. 'You wanted to kill them both, didn't you?'

Duncan hurried over to the car, trying to outrun his parents.

'Face it, son, you should just kill them.' Dad blocked the driver's door. 'April thingy and whatever the foreign lassie's called. Strangle them both.'

Duncan glowered at him. 'Shut the fuck up.'

'Mr Radford?' Zuzana wrapped him in a hug. 'I'm so sorry.'

He hadn't seen her.

And he held her too long.

She was *tiny*. Nothing of her.

She broke off and looked up at him with doe eyes, standing so close to him. 'I'm sorry, but April wanted me to give you this.'

Duncan took an envelope from her. 'What is it?'

Zuzana evaded his gaze. 'It's the bill for next month.'

'*What*?'

'Because insufficient notice was given.'

Duncan felt like murdering someone, that's for sure. 'But you've got a new resident for that room?'

'I'm sorry. It's the rules. Unless she died in the home, sixty days' notice is required or you pay for an extra month.'

'But... She could've fucking warned me.' Duncan looked over at the building, scowling, then shut his eyes. 'It's not your fault. It's just... A lot. And the timing...'

'I'm truly sorry for your loss, Mr Radford. I could see in her moments of lucidity that your mother was lovely.'

'Me? Lovely?' Mum laughed at that. 'You want to kill her, don't you, fuck face?'

Duncan couldn't help but nod. 'That's kind of you to say. I wish you'd met her before.'

'Me too.' Zuzana smiled at him. 'Actually, I've got something Patricia gave me. And I think it's better for you to have it.'

'It's not really—'

'Please. I don't think she should've given me it. My car is

right here.' She opened the trunk of the next car over and rooted around for something.

Duncan looked around. This spot was pretty secluded. A huge weeping willow blocked the view from inside and the fence from most of the rest of the parking lot.

'Kill her, fuck face. Do it now.'

Duncan reached into his jacket pocket and touched his gloves.

'Fuck the risk, son.' Dad stepped forward, slowly licking his lips. 'You've got the bloodlust, haven't you? Let yourself do it... Go on...'

'I can't. She doesn't deserve this. It's not like she was beating you up or anything.'

'Who cares?' Mum leered too. 'You know you want to. That's all that matters here. Just kill her.'

Duncan stepped towards Zuzana and put on his gloves.

'Just a second, Mr Radford. I am sure he is here.'

Duncan grabbed her mouth from behind, then shoved her into the boot of her car.

She weighed *nothing*.

He pinned her down, squeezing her throat with his free hand and keeping her mouth covered with the other.

She started slapping his hand, scratching at his gloves. Eyes bulging. Then nothing.

Far too easy...

46

'What's my thinking?' Marshall hurried across the car park to avoid the rain. 'My thinking is I don't like it.' He sighed as he skipped up the steps into Butler House. 'Colin Radford emigrated to Canada a few days after Sharon Beattie was killed. And we've got a parental match to him. We've got a prime suspect.'

Jolene held the door. 'How easy will it be getting him back from Canada?'

'Not. In the slightest. But let's see what they've got to say here first.'

Looked like nobody was here, despite Saturday presumably being their second-busiest visiting day.

Jolene knocked on the desk. 'Hello?'

The manager looked out of her office, blowing her nose on a hankie. 'Oh. Good morning, officer. Is this about Gus?'

Jolene frowned. 'Why would you think that?'

'Well, it's just...' April smiled. 'Never mind. What is this about?'

'It's regarding John Radford. His last-known address was here.'

'John Radford?' She frowned as she checked the computer. 'I'm afraid he died in 2014.'

'I'm sorry to hear that.'

'It is what it is. Thing is, it's pretty common to have family members visiting their loved ones, then a few years later, they come in as guests themselves.'

Jolene frowned. 'What do you mean?'

'His wife Patricia was a patient here. Sadly, she passed away last night.'

'Was that expected?'

'Well no, but it wasn't unexpected either. She'd actually just left our care, her son was looking after her.'

'Does she have more than one child?'

'To be honest, we didn't even realise she had Colin until recently. He'd been living in Canada since 2000. Only just came back to sign off on her DNR and ended up taking full care of her.'

Marshall looked at Jolene, then back at April. 'He's in the country?'

'Colin? Yes. Yes. Actually, he was just here.'

47

Zuzana looked up at Duncan.

Dead.

Fuck. That was a mistake. He just couldn't help himself.

If the cops were going to be onto him, taking his rental would be a mistake.

Duncan slammed the lid and got behind the wheel of her car, resting his carry-on luggage in the footwell. He slotted the keys in, then twisted them. The engine didn't start.

Only, it had – one of those electric things. Or a hybrid.

'She really liked you.' Dad was on the back seat of this car, smoking away. 'Probably would've let you shag her too. What a waste to kill her.'

Duncan checked his passport was in his pocket, then reversed out into a wide arc. 'You told me to!'

'Stupid prick, you never listen to me. Go. Now.'

'You're one to talk.' Mum took her hand away from his. 'Remember him seeing you put Keith in hospital that time? What did you even argue over?'

Dad looked away from her. 'Can't even remember.'

'Son, are you sure you should take this car?' Mum locked eyes with him in the rear-view. 'It's got a dead body in the boot!'

'He needs the car to get somewhere, doesn't he? They'll find his hire car soon enough. And trains and buses have those cameras nowadays. If he takes this car, then by the time they clock what's actually happened, he can be out of the country.' Dad lit up a fresh cigarette and Duncan could taste the smoke in the air. 'Dump the body somewhere. Not obvious.'

Duncan put the car in gear and shot across the car park. 'I know the perfect place.'

DUNCAN SLOWED as he passed Scott's View. No sign of any police presence anymore. Just a normal tourist viewpoint, like someone hadn't been murdered here a few days ago – or twenty-five years.

Dad sparked another cigarette. 'This where you had in mind, son?'

'Nope.' Duncan kept on down the road. Nothing in the rear-view and he started counting the cars coming the opposite direction. 'You'll see.'

'Thought you were in the clear, didn't you?' Mum lit her own cigarette from Dad's. 'But they're going to arrest you.'

'I would've let her go, but then you'd given her that book, didn't you?' Duncan eased through Bemersyde, a reassuringly old village – a single-track road, most of the homes hidden behind lush beech hedges. Nothing bad could happen here. 'I couldn't let them get that book, could I?'

'Was it worth it?'

'Everything's worth it if you get away with it.' Duncan kept scanning for the car park on the right and there it was – further on than he remembered.

Empty too. And he hadn't seen a single other car.

'Perfect.' He parked rear-end on in the space nearest the path towards the statue, then reached over for the book he'd dumped on the passenger seat.

A load of family photos his mother would pore over daily when he still lived this side of the pond.

He sifted through it, lingering over each page. Loads of photos of himself, including ones with his Aunt Margaret on a family trip to Canada. 'I'd forgotten about this.'

'My sister.' Mum leaned between the seats to look over his shoulder. 'She helped you settle in Canada. Died a few years ago, didn't she? Had her funeral back here in that crematorium near Melrose. But you didn't come back, Colin, did you?'

'I couldn't, could I?' Duncan looked at his dad. 'Because of *him*.'

'Didn't come back for my funeral, either.'

'You didn't deserve that.' Duncan put the book down.

Still no cars had passed.

Just as he remembered, a path led ahead to the statue. Trees on either side, all thick with leaves. A field on the north side. No livestock in there.

Duncan got out into the heavy rain, then walked around the car.

Sharon was waiting for him. 'Killed another lassie, eh?'

Duncan couldn't look at her.

'I was your first, wasn't I?' She looked so young, but not full of life – like life was something to endure, something that impacted you, that killed you slowly. 'But you killed me quickly, Colin. Paid me extra to let you choke me while you stuck that thing in me. Didn't even get the money, did I?'

'I put you out of your misery.'

'That's wasn't your choice to make.' She scowled at him. 'Why are you dumping her here?'

'Why do you think?'

'Because we shagged here a few times? Once where you

paid me to shag me without a condom because you'd never felt that? Is this you trying to close the loop?'

'Something like that.' Duncan took another look around, then opened the boot. He had to move quickly now – he picked up Zuzana and she barely weighed anything. One last look, then he shut the trunk and carried her along the edge of the field, fast fast fast. Despite the rain, it wasn't too hard going.

Dad splashed ahead of him, walking backwards. 'What are you doing?'

'It's symbolic.'

'You need to dump her and go.'

Duncan kept going and soon saw the statue overlooking the river, just through the woods. He stood there, at the edge, and listened to the silence for a minute or so. Listening hard. Might not be any cars nearby, but there could be ramblers around.

Dad tugged at his sleeve. 'What the hell are you doing?'

'This is symbolic. I used to meet Sharon here. In the car park back there. One time we did it here. That time, the time I killed her... we had to go to Scott's View because this place was too busy.'

'You're completely insane.'

'Of course I am.' Duncan laughed. 'I'm talking to my dead parents while I carry my latest victim's body through the woods.' He broke along the edge of the trees, then came to the statue.

An almost cartoonish William Wallace, more Viking and Wagner than Mel Gibson in that bullshit film.

Staring out across the Tweed valley towards Melrose and Gala, like this was his domain rather than all of Scotland.

Sharon stood there, staring at him and shaking her head.

Duncan rested Zuzana's body in front of the statue, then raced back towards the field. 'Now we can go.'

48

Marshall tried the door again but nobody answered still. He tapped dial, then put his phone to his ear.

Still no answer.

So he called Crawford instead.

Unlike Leye, he answered straight away. 'What's up, sir?'

Marshall thumped the door like it'd beaten up his niece. 'Did you get anyone to visit that address in St Boswells?'

'There now myself, sir. Nobody here. We've even been inside and it's empty.'

'You *what*?'

'Back door was open. Credible threat and all that.'

Marshall hoped that was true… 'Can you get forensics there?'

'Trev's just turned up.'

'Good man. We believe his mother died there, so try to get him to focus on that.' Maybe making Crawford a DI wasn't the worst move in the world. 'And can you arrange surveillance?'

'How many skulls you talking?'

Marshall tried to step in out of the rain, but there was

nowhere that wasn't underneath the downpour. So he kicked the door again, even harder. 'Just a couple for a few hours.'

'On it.' Crawford paused – some people were speaking in the background, then it sounded like a bus hissed past. 'We're trying to track a few things down. Got people on with the bus company and with ScotRail and with the car hire company. Trouble is, if he's lying low...'

Marshall tried the door again, but no bugger was answering. 'Okay, keep me updated.' He hung up and called Leye again, looking back across the square to a rain-soaked Melrose, then back up at the sign:

Maguire & Day
Funeral Directors

Leye answered. 'Rob, my friend. What's up?'

'Finally.' Marshall chapped on the door again. 'I'm here, mate. Where are you?'

'Oh, so that was you rattling the door.' The door finally opened and Leye stood there, grinning in the gloom behind him. 'Good afternoon.'

'Who did you think it was?' Marshall hung up.

'Sorry, we were a bit preoccupied.'

Marshall followed him inside, dripping on the floor, then through the funeral home. The place had enough bouquets to operate as a florist, and was less a place for grieving and more a high-end kitchen showroom. Rows of marble and granite headstones in various configurations. Racks of coffins, all stacked end-on and ranging from the Tesco Value basic box to the Harrods food hall, with sheeny varnish, brass handles and gold edging.

A small tweedy man stood in the doorway, grinning away. 'Hi, Keith Maguire, and you are?' Not a local – if Marshall had to guess, he'd put money on Brighton or any of the East Sussex towns along that stretch of coast.

'DCI Rob Marshall.' He shook his hand, all cold and clammy. 'Care to bring me up to speed?'

'I'd just returned here with Patricia's body from the funeral director when my good friend here called, hadn't I?' Maguire nodded at Leye, then focused back on Marshall. 'Do you want to see her?'

'That'd be great, aye.'

Maguire led them through into the back room, much more functional than the rest of the place.

A woman lay on the slab in the middle of the room.

Marshall sort of recognised Patricia Radford from the care home. She looked peaceful now, rather than the violent, confused woman in the last few days of her life.

'When I collected her, she was sitting in a seat and I thought she could just talk to me, you know what I mean?' Maguire passed Marshall some papers. 'Dr Japp signed the death certificate, so I was just prepping her to go to straight to cremation, wasn't I? And I'd only just started washing the body when Leye called, if you can believe that?'

Marshall nodded, but was looking at Leye. 'You know Dr Japp?'

'Sadly.' Leye nodded. 'He's one of those who I just don't think cares anymore. He's been going through the motions so long…'

'I know him, don't I?' Maguire chuckled. 'Can't believe he's still trading, if you catch my drift?'

Leye laughed as he inspected her body. 'You speak to him about Patricia?'

'Saying I wouldn't? Course I did, didn't I? One of those who just kept talking about the family, right? Says he'd had a dram with Colin to mark her passing but you answer me, who bangs on about how good the whisky is when they're doing that?'

Marshall frowned. 'Colin is her son?'

'That's what I said, diddle I?' Maguire shifted his gaze between them. 'Feels like I'm missing something here?'

'You'd be right to think that.' Marshall sighed. 'Her son has been out of the country for a quarter of a century and now he's back we've got two deaths in the Borders in a matter of days.'

'Eh?'

'A murder on Thursday evening.' Marshall pointed at Patricia. 'Then he's taken his mother home to look after her and she dies the first night in his care...'

'And you think Colin killed her?'

'Was Japp there when she died?'

'Japp said he wasn't, right? Colin woke up and found her like that, didn't he?' Maguire shook his head. 'If you ask me, he'd clearly been tucking into the drams since breakfast, know what I mean?'

Leye looked up from his work and pointed at some papers. 'But he confirmed Patricia died overnight. Cardiac arrest.'

Marshall picked them up and read through, but the handwriting was appalling. 'You mean she had a heart attack?'

'No. A heart attack is a myocardial infarction. It's the deprivation of oxygen to the heart muscle. Part of the heart muscle dies and it leads to the heart stopping pumping.' Leye shifted his gaze between them. 'But a cardiac arrest can also be caused by lack of oxygen to the brain, or by cessation of breathing, electroshock, or a few other causes. In this particular case, the heart just stopped receiving electrical signals and hence it stopped beating. No blood for the brain or the organs. Hence death.'

Marshall winced. 'Sounds awful.'

'One of the better ways to go, Rob.' Leye roared with laughter, completely inappropriately for the surroundings. 'Now, you've asked me to confirm what Dr Japp found. GPs are allowed to put a presumptive cause of death on a death certificate without a post mortem. They can also refuse to do so when the death was unexpected or when their physical examination reveals anomalies. Japp skipped that part. I'll have to transfer her to my lab and do the usual to finalise things. Review the patient's clinical history. Then an external examination. Then I'll inspect the heart itself. And we'll conduct laboratory tests. Toxicology, cardiac biomarkers, microbiology. And we'll look at the other organs to exclude non-cardiac causes, such as a stroke or an embolism.' He held Marshall's gaze for ages. Then he kept holding it. And broke into his usual wide grin. 'But I don't have to do any of them for what you need.'

Marshall returned the smile. 'Go on?'

'Her GP signed her death certificate with a presumed cardiac death. Understandable, given her background of a few infarcts already... They'd brought her back because there was no DNR in place and the care home documented them all. Nothing to raise immediate suspicion, at least in his mind.'

'But in yours?'

'I just needed to look at her for a minute to disprove that.' Leye pointed at the throat. 'See the faint contusions across the front and sides of the neck?'

A ring of bruising around her neck; the impressions of fingers around her throat.

Marshall swallowed hard. 'She was strangled.'

'Potential signs of it, yes.' Leye raised a finger. 'The strap muscles in the neck show fresh haemorrhaging. That's not something you see after death, Rob, but it's consistent with force applied while she was still alive. The killer had big hands and stood over her when he strangled her. Given how frail she was and how bad her heart was to begin with, we've only got petechial haemorrhages in her eyes. With younger or healthier people, they fight more and last longer... you'd see petechiae on the face or on the chest as well.'

'And with her, she just went?'

'Correct. The others didn't have time to form.'

Marshall sucked in a deep breath. 'So she was murdered?'

'There's no evidence of a fall, or trauma consistent with an accident and there's no natural disease process that would otherwise account for my initial findings. In short, she could indeed have died from cardiac arrest, secondary to manual strangulation.' Leye raised the finger again. 'But this is my initial assessment. I'll get the full postmortem done soon.'

'Thanks, mate. I really appreciate it.' Marshall smiled at him. 'Any idea whose fingers created those bruises?'

'Once we get the body there, we'll fume the skin using heated cyanoacrylate to preserve and identify oily fingerprints. I'd expect some to match Dr Japp, maybe some from the care home. And from her son too, of course – he'd been caring for her. But none of that is conclusive.' Leye gave him a hard look. 'But I have identified a glove pattern on the bruising.'

'Does it match—'

Leye nodded. 'Same as Heather's killer.'

49

Marshall sat in his office, kneading his forehead. He glared at the weird-shaped box sitting in the middle of the meeting table, like Ravenscroft was in the room with them.

'Sorry, but—' A hiss of static. '—driving through—' More static. '—phone reception's very, very poor.'

Elliot reached over to mute the phone. '*Still* don't have a nickname for him.' She unmuted it.

Marshall shot her a warning look. 'The big update, sir, is we've got a suspect for Sharon Beattie's murder.'

Ravenscroft gasped. 'Who?'

'His name is Colin Radford.'

'And who's he when he's at home?'

'As far as we can tell, he grew up in St Boswells. Went to Heriot-Watt University in Edinburgh, then he worked on the oil rigs as an engineer. Based in Aberdeen, but he used to travel back and forth. We think he went touring from there. Highlands and islands. Bit of a loner by all accounts.' Marshall cleared his throat. 'Radford emigrated to Canada in 2000.'

A long pause while the cogs slotted into place in Ravenscroft's head. 'When Sharon Beattie was murdered?'

'That's right, sir. And he just so happens to return the day someone kills Heather.'

'You think he killed her?'

'We have Heather speaking with someone on a pay-as-you-go phone purchased at Edinburgh Airport on the date we believe Radford arrived in the country.'

'We believe?'

'We're checking with Immigration to determine when exactly he arrived. But the care home confirmed his presence on Thursday, so it could be him. Plus the Facebook message was sent from an IP address assigned to the Butler home.' Marshall took a deep breath. 'He was in the country when Sharon was killed. And now his mother also dies in suspicious circumstances.'

Ravenscroft clicked his tongue a few times. 'Okay, so you're saying he murdered them both?'

'Correct. Solid balance of probability in our favour at this stage.'

'And is he in custody?'

'That's the issue, sir.' Marshall sighed. 'We don't know where he is. His last known location was Butler House care home in Gala, where he returned a wheelchair and informed them of his mother's death.'

'Okay, Robert – this is where you tell me what you're doing to track him down.'

'I spotted that, sir.' Marshall rolled his eyes, making Elliot giggle. 'We've put out a BOLO on Radford and I've asked DI Archer and DS Crawford to do a detailed search of the nearby area around his mother's house and the care home. Trouble is, he doesn't seem to have embedded himself in the community, which is what you'd expect given he's only been back in the country a couple of days. And we don't know where he is.'

'Okay. Let's prioritise finding him. Have we reach—' Static squealed out of the box. '—friends across the pond?'

'I've placed a request through Interpol with Canadian cops to discuss Colin Radford, yes.'

'That'll be the Royal Canadian Mounted Police?'

'Indeed.'

Elliot laughed. 'They cut down trees, they wear high heels, suspenders and a bra.'

Ravenscroft grunted down the line. 'Inspector…'

'Sorry, sir. Just can't take the Mounties seriously.'

'It was the lumberjack who did the cross-dressing, not the Mounties.'

'Oh, right.' Elliot frowned. 'Sorry.' She made a wanker gesture.

Marshall glowered at her, but she wasn't looking. 'We're staking out the house, just in case Radford's stupid enough to return. But we believe he's a flight risk. Primarily to Canada. We're liaising with Transport Police to cover all flights to Canada, as well as the main connecting airport hubs. Heathrow, Gatwick, JFK, Schiphol in Amsterdam, Charles de Gaulle in Paris, you name it.'

'Good stuff.' Another blast of white noise. '—me posted.'

And just like that, the call ended.

'*Such* a dickhead.' Elliot shook her head. '*Definitely* needs a nickname.'

Marshall sat back and shoved his hands into his pockets. 'Can I ask you to go and—'

Elliot's phone rang. She checked it. 'Better take this.' She got up and left him on his own.

Marshall wished she didn't just do that, but then again he'd rather she was out of the room than in it.

This nickname thing needed to stop…

Crawford peered in, pointing back the way. 'Boss. She okay?'

'Not sure.' Marshall got up from the meeting table and walked over to the whiteboard, not that there was anything to update on it. 'You got him yet?'

'No, guv. Sorry. But Ash has managed to connect Jim Smith to Colin Radford.'

'How?'

'We were snookered until we spoke to the care home. He'd given the number of the phone he used to connect to Facebook to send the message. He also got the wi-fi to connect his "cell phone". And the IMEI is a match. International Mobile Equipment Identity. Basically the phone's serial number. Most apps are now logging it as well. Means even if someone pulls out the SIM on a stolen phone, the actual device itself is attached to the data.'

'Okay, so Radford lured her to Scott's View?'

'Looks like that. Then he killed her.'

'Okay, that's great work.' Marshall added it to the whiteboard – removing a mysterious Jim Smith figure made things look a lot simpler. 'Pass on my congrats to Ash.'

'Will do. She's a good officer.'

'She really is.'

And now Marshall's desk phone rang.

Crawford nodded. 'See you around, sir.' He left the room as quickly as he'd entered it.

Marshall picked it up. 'Hello?'

The line was all crackly.

'Hey, it's Detective Staff Sergeant Brad Tremblay of Niagara Regional Police. Looking for Rob Marshall?'

'That's me.' Marshall frowned. 'Thanks for calling, but I'm a bit confused here. Interpol put us onto the Royal Canadian Mounted Police, so how come I've ended up with regional police?'

'Your call got routed to the RCMP as the local reps on Interpol, but the horsemen don't do local policing here in Niagara, meaning they farmed it down to us as the agency of jurisdiction.'

'Does that mean you're the right guys?'

'If I wasn't, bub, I'd be kicking this back to the boys in the red tunics.' Tremblay laughed.

Marshall paused. 'We don't have staff sergeant in our command tree. How does that equate?'

'Think of it as more of a manager at this rank than a police officer. We go detective constable, sergeant, then staff sergeant, then inspector.'

'So, it's kind of like a chief sergeant?'

'Something like that.' Tremblay laughed again. 'So that makes our chief inspector one higher than yours.' Sounded like he was flicking through some pages down the line. 'Anyhoo. This is about Colin Radford, right?'

'Right. Gather he's lived over there since 2000.'

'Sure did.' Sounded like some keys were getting mashed down the line. 'Yup. Got a few local entries for him on Arremess. Ellekayeh is Welland.'

Marshall paused. 'Okay, so you lost me there.'

'Sorry, I'll try to sound less Canadian.' Tremblay laughed at his own joke.

'The accent's fine. It's the words I'm toiling with. Arremess?'

'Whoops, yeah, sorry. R dot M dot S. Records Management System. Everything's an acronym here.'

'Same here at times. Take it Ellekayeh is his Last Known Address?'

Tremblay chuckled. 'Well translated.'

'And what does Welland stand for?'

'It's a town. His LKA was here in Welland.'

'Apologies for my ignorance, but whereabouts in Canada is that?'

'West of the Falls, south of St Catharine's.' Tremblay paused. 'Ontario, the Canadian side of the ditch.'

'So…' Marshall tried to search through his North American geography but didn't really have much. 'Is that near Toronto, Vancouver or Montreal?'

'Actually closer to Buffalo in New York State, but yeah – think of us as near Toronto.'

'What kind of place is Welland?'

'It's about fifty thousand people. Kind of a commuter town now. Used to be industrial, what with the Welland Canal and cheap power, but now most of the factory jobs are gone. Automated away, but some politicians will make you think they've all gone overseas.'

'Same thing happened here.'

'Gotta love globalisation, huh?' Tremblay hammered his keyboard again. 'Pretty affordable, considering we're close to the fourth-biggest city in North America, but it won't be for long. Niagara College is really taking off so there's a huge rental market, which is driving the prices up a bit but we're nowhere near teeoh.' He chuckled. 'That's T dot O.'

'Toronto. Got it.'

'Except we don't say all those syllables, bub. Tron-oh.'

Marshall laughed, but none of that was useful – except a guy with an engineering background would've found work in a town like that back in 2000. 'Does Radford have a record?'

'No convictions. Just a few routine contacts. Couple traffic tickets. Found someone's purse and cell phone a few years back. Got his house B&E'd when he was on vacation in 2002. But nothing even remotely criminal. And nothing on file since after 2005. What's up with this dude, anyhow?'

'We think he might've fled to Canada after strangling a sex worker back in 2000.'

'Shit.'

'Then this week, the person who was leading a crusade to reopen the investigation was, we believe, *also* strangled after meeting Colin Radford.'

'Damn it.'

'It gets worse. His mother died overnight and was taken to the funeral director's here. Died of natural causes, according to the local GP. That's General Practitioner. Our pathologist, however, believes she was also strangled.'

'Holy fuck, that's major. Likes to strangle ladies, does he?' Tremblay thwacked at his keyboard. 'Weird how I've got no hits on the guy since 2005. Not even a speeding or traffic violation. Lemme pull his DL and see where he's living now.' He paused. 'That's driving licence.' He grunted down the line. 'Huh.'

'What's up?'

'We don't get a lot of choking deaths here but... Nah, it's probably nothing.'

'No, go on.'

'It's just... I worked cold cases in 2019. Had this big push for them, so it was all hands on deck. We had an unsolved back in 2001? Ellen something. College student off campus in Welland walking home from a bar. The place she left was on East Main. Lyons runs right off there, so we're talking less than a klick away from where your guy's living. Let me poke around on ViCLAS. Sorry, Violent—'

'We've got ViCLAS too.'

'Beauty. Be amazing if I could crack a cold case here just by answering the phone!'

'That'd be great.' For him... 'Does Radford own that property?'

'Not sure. I'll have to dig a bit deeper. It's a little bungalow. Maybe scoot by and talk with the neighbours or current occupant, see if he left a forwarding.' Sounded like Tremblay clicked something off his teeth. 'If I can get official confirmation from you guys that he's wanted in connection with a series of strangulation murders on your side of the pond, I might be able to stretch it to a warrant for his house here. I'll need to get confirmation from our crown attorney that the grounds would be sufficient, but I don't see that as being onerous.'

'Okay, that's useful. I'll email something through right now. You going to tackle this yourself? Doesn't sound very managerial.'

'Cop first, boss second. I'll let you know how it goes. You going to be there for a while?'

Marshall checked his watch. 'It's twenty past three now, but I can't see myself getting away anytime before midnight.'

'Sure thing. I'll give you a call in a couple hours. Got your cell number here. Pinged you an email so you've got my addy to send that stuff through.'

'Thanks. And I appreciate the help.'

'*No problemo*. If this earns me a trip to Scotland, that'd take an item off the ol' family tree bucket list.'

'Isn't Tremblay a French name?'

'Dad was half Quebecois. Eh-haw-ee-haw-ee-haw!' Tremblay paused, like he expected the joke to land. It didn't, so he coughed instead. 'The better half of him was Scottish and my mother's a hundred percent Scottish, so, yeah – we could be cousins or something.'

How a lot of North Americans thought – needed to create an identity from their ancestry...

'Thanks. I'll await your call.' Marshall ended the call, then unlocked his machine and he had the email already in draft, or most of it anyway. All he needed was to add in Tremblay's name from *his* email, then top and tail it.

As per our discussion...

Look forward to hearing from...

Done.

Marshall sat back and stared up at the ceiling.

Tremblay was more than likely looking to clear his own stats with that cold case rather than to actually help, but still...

Knowing what Radford had been up to before he returned to Scotland would be very useful.

And having someone on the other side of the pond would also be helpful in case he got out of the UK as well…

Then there was a knock on the door.

Isla was standing in the doorway. 'Hey there.' Looked like she meant business too.

Shite…

Marshall smiled at her, but he didn't have time for this… 'Hi, didn't see you there.'

'You looked lost in that. Whatever it is.'

'Doing some good old-fashioned thinky. What's up?'

Isla stepped in and shut the door behind her. She frowned, nibbling her lip. 'Listen, we need to talk.'

'About what?'

'The, uh, picture?' She pointed at her chest. 'I should really explain who it was actually for and how it ended up going to you.'

'I told you, there's no harm done.'

'Rob, I'm really not like that. You must think I'm horrible.'

'It's fine. They were fine.' Marshall coughed. 'I mean you're fine.' He was blushing. 'I mean—'

'Would you like to get something to eat? Maybe chat about something that isn't my breasts?'

Maybe Marshall did have some time after all… 'Well, as it happens, I am fucking starving.'

50

Marshall held the door for Isla, then followed her inside the Gala Tap, pretty busy for a Saturday afternoon. Might be a hipster wanker's kind of place, but it still had sport on, showing some golf on the giant screens, muted – "Heroes" by Bowie blasted out of the speakers.

'Love this song…' Isla stood waiting for a seat. 'Keep forgetting how quiet my gym is on a Saturday. Fairly often my rotation covers the weekend and I'm stuck going in when it's rammed.'

'Wish I had the time to go.'

'That a dig?'

'No. Just… Things have been a bit crazy. Need some stability in my life.'

'I hear you.'

'You got a programme at the gym?'

'Kind of. Two I rotate through. Today was arms, shoulders and back. Leg day tomorrow.'

'I can feel the pain just listening to that.'

'Hey you.' Cath leaned in for a kiss. 'You get home okay on Thursday?'

'After a fashion. Had to get an Uber.'

'Ooof.' Cath gritted her teeth. 'Gig was great, by the way. Even bought a couple of vinyls I didn't have.'

'Vinyls? Aren't they called records?'

'I don't care.' Cath smiled at Isla. 'You guys just in for drinks?'

'And some food.'

Cath narrowed her eyes, clocking a cop. 'Follow me, then.' She led them over to a booth right underneath a speaker and dumped some menus onto the table. 'Be back in a minute for your order.'

Isla sat down, then watched her go, eyebrows raised. 'She's a bit familiar.'

'She's my sister. Well, half-sister.'

'Oh, right.' Isla laughed. 'That explains it. So, your mum or your dad's first kid?'

'She's actually a few years younger. My dad's a complicated guy. Really complicated.'

'Haven't been in here before.' Isla looked around. 'Not the kind of place we get called into.'

'Been in here a few times. My dad's favourite place.'

'Right. I usually go out in Melrose.'

'You live there, then?'

'Melrose Gait, so it's not really in Gala but it's definitely not Melrose. But it's not that far to walk to either. Few miles along the cycle path.'

'But it's not that close, either.'

'True. You live in Melrose, right?'

'Used to. I'm between homes just now, so I was staying with my mum in Melrose for a bit, but she got fed up of me, so now I'm back at my sister's.'

Isla pointed to Cath, chatting to the barman. 'Her place?'

'Other sister. See what I mean about complicated?'

Isla laughed. 'Thought my life was chaos, but bloody hell.'

'Actually looked at a place in Clovenfords the other day, but I'm not sure.'

Isla frowned. 'Why not?'

'Because it's a massive place for one bloke.'

'Was there a Mrs Marshall?'

'Nope. I was in a relationship for a couple of years with—'

'Aye, heard that ended.'

'That's right.'

Cath came over. 'What can I get you guys to drink?'

Marshall smiled. 'Pint of soda and blackcurrant, ta. No ice.'

'Oh, I'll have the same.' Isla grinned. 'With ice.'

Cath jotted it down. 'Be right back.'

They sat in uncomfortable silence, just looking at each other. Marshall wanted to look away, but he was drawn to her.

Isla leaned forward. 'Do you actually want to get some food?'

As if on cue, his stomach gave a deep rumble. 'I need it.'

'When did you last eat?'

'I had a coffee first thing.'

'And actual nourishment?'

Marshall had to think. 'Had a sandwich about eight o'clock yesterday.'

'Right, then – you're eating. Sergeant's orders.'

'Fine.' Marshall gave her a cheeky salute. 'Sarge.'

Isla sat back, grinning. Then rolled her lips over her teeth. Then leaned over to him again. 'Rob, I'm so sorry for sending that photo.'

'It's okay.' Marshall held up his phone. 'I did delete it.'

'I want you to know something.' Isla ran a hand through her hair. 'I'm not the kind of girl who sends nudes to random people, okay? It's usually five or six steps before you start that kind of shit, isn't it?'

Marshall paused. 'And yet you did.'

'And I'm so, so sorry.'

'Who was it meant for?'

Isla looked away. 'Nobody.'

'That doesn't ring true to me. Remember you're dealing with a detective here. One with a PhD in criminal psychology.'

Isla blew out a deep breath. 'Here's what happened.' She sighed. 'I was in the gym after I got off back-shift the other day. Go to this place over by Aldi in an old mill building. Spit and sawdust kind of deal, but it's twenty-four hours. You access it using an app on your phone. So I go in there after my shift a few times a week. Keeps me sane to just plug away at my programme, right? And it's busy at like six o'clock before everyone goes to work, then after about three until eight or nine. But I went in at midnight and I was there on my own. Don't mind being on my own.'

'Right, so you took a topless photo in the middle of the gym?'

She raised her eyebrows. 'Rob, I took it in the toilets.'

'O-kay. I didn't look at the background.'

'It's…' Isla grimaced then sat back.

Cath put their drinks down in front of them. 'You ready to order food?'

Isla gave her a smile as she picked up the menu for the first time. 'Give us a couple of minutes?'

'Sure.' Cath returned the smile. 'Today, I'm recommending the blue cheese burger. Assuming you like blue cheese, of course. And burgers.'

'Who doesn't like burgers?' Isla frowned. 'I'm a veggie.'

'We do all the burgers in fake-meat versions.' Cath winked at her. 'I'm vegan and that's *primo*, though the vegan blue cheese is rank.'

'I'll bear that in mind.' Isla nodded. 'Sod it. I'll have the veggie blue cheese burger.'

'Sweet potato or normal chips?'

'Sweet potato.'

Cath jotted it down. 'Rob?'

'I'll have the same. But the meat burger.'

'Coming up.' Cath strutted off towards the bar.

Isla watched her go, then grabbed his hand. 'I'm mortified, Rob. Seriously.'

'It's okay.'

'Thank you for being so decent about it.

Marshall held her stare. 'Trouble is, it could've gone to anyone.'

'I know.'

'I mean it. You're a cop. You've got to be very careful, okay? I've got the numbers of some right rogues on my phone. I don't want yet another cop being blackmailed. Especially a good one like you.'

'You think I'm good?'

'Lot of detectives like to pretend you uniforms are idiots, but it's a tough job. I'm not cut out for it. And you do it very well.'

'Thank you.' She sipped her drink. 'I've deleted the photo on mine too and I've no intention of even taking any more nudes.'

'That's good to hear.' Marshall took a long sip of his drink. It had ice in it... 'But I'd rather hear the truth.'

'Okay, so what I said about the gym... I was in there on Wednesday at midnight, just after my back-shift. I'd just deadlifted ninety kilos, which is my personal best.'

Marshall raised his eyebrows. 'That's more than I can manage.'

'Seriously?'

'I mean, I've never done a deadlift. Couldn't tell you what one is.'

'It's like a squat, but you pick up a barbell with weights. Arms hang dead, hence the name, and you lift with your legs. Women are pretty good at deadlifting, supposedly.' Isla took a long sip through the straw, maintaining eye contact. 'And I thought I looked like I *slay*, as my niece would say, so I decided I should probably take a boob pic, just in case. At my best, not one when I'm on my period or just after a shift rotation.'

'In case of what?'

'In case... Rob, I've been out of the dating scene for a long time... The younger lassies in the station, the ones who are on the apps, they say it's all about texting, then sexting, then photos. Right?'

'Take your word for it. You're younger than me.'

'Not by much.' She took her drink below halfway.

'I still don't see how a photo of you ended up on my phone.'

She stared deep into her drink and sighed even more deeply. 'Last night, after our rotation, a few of us went to Sheila's house in Selkirk for drinks.'

'You told me you were planning to.'

'It was brutal. Just the girls in our rotation, so eight of us. We got *smashed*. And we ended up talking about who we'd smash in the station. Couple of them were saying that Doug guy in your team. Only later I found out he's Sheila's son and they were saying it to wind her up. Joke's on me. Because I earnestly said you.' She shrugged. 'Because I would.'

'You said that in front of seven other cops?'

'So? Rob, I've enjoyed flirting with you, okay? There's something between us. Right?'

Something fluttered in his stomach.

Marshall shrugged. 'I think so, aye.'

'It was on my radar to maybe one day approach you now you're single again. So that was most of it.'

'So the photo wasn't to use on the apps?'

'God no. Makes me feel sick, to be honest. You use them?'

'However sick it makes you feel, multiply that by ten.'

'Good. Way someone described it to me is you're on the

apps whether you want to be or not. Speak to someone in the bar and they're probably on them. So you're sort of involved.'

'Can see the logic.' Marshall took a big gulp of his drink – just not quite enough cordial in there. 'So, what, they dared you to send that photo?'

'I'm not like that, Rob. I swear.' Isla pulled at her hair. 'What happened was... God, this is *so* embarrassing. One of the girls thought it'd be funny to jump the queue, so she sent it to you while I was in the toilet.'

'She just happened to have your phone, eh?'

'Talk about a forensic interview, eh?' Isla shook her head. 'I'm mortified here, Rob.'

'It's okay. I'm not judging you.'

Isla looked at him like she didn't believe that for one second. 'I'd left my phone unlocked because the music was coming out of it... This cheesy playlist. Sheila's barely got a CD player, so it was wired into her stereo.'

Marshall smiled. 'Okay, I'm starting to buy this.'

'Really?'

'Who sent me the photo?'

'Teigan Morrison. She's young and daft. Spends half the time in the gym. Looks more like a model than a cop. But she really cannot handle that amount of booze and Sheila was chucking it down her throat like she was on her hen night.'

Marshall nodded slowly. It all made sense. 'You'd smash me?'

'That's what the kids say.' Isla finished her drink. 'So here's my situation, okay? I divorced my ex and I've been through such a shitty couple of years. He's a total prick. Thought I was in love, but then I found out he'd caught an STD off a slapper from Musselburgh.' She raised her hand. 'I've been tested. We never had much sex toward the end, anyway.' She looked away. 'Well, turns out he did. Just not with me.'

'I'm sorry to hear that.'

'The divorce papers came through a few months ago, so I'm single again. Been using my maiden name for a while.'

'Routledge?'

'Right.'

'Take it you had kids?'

'Nope. Should make it easier, right, but he was such a prick about it all. Made me glad I hadn't bred with him.' She pushed her glass away. 'Do you have any?'

'Just a cat. Zlatan.'

'Cute name.' She smiled. 'Well. I want you to know it's not because you're the first bloke to show interest in me, Rob, but you're the first one I trust. I've got a pretty fucking high bar now. And you seem like a good guy. Thing is, I'm single, Rob. And you are too.'

'How did you know?'

'I'm a cop. Everyone talks.' Isla laughed. 'I heard Kirsten didn't want to move in with you or something.'

'That's right.'

'Mind me asking you why?'

'I don't want to be that guy who talks about his ex on a date.'

She raised an eyebrow. 'This is a date?'

'Feels like it.'

'Well, I've just talked about my ex, so it wouldn't be fair, would it?'

'Things had been strange with me and Kirsten for a while. She started to get cold feet and it took me a while to notice.' Marshall took a bracing sip of his drink. 'Weird thing is, I just heard she's got a gig at Gartcosh. Pretty ironic given I was based there for a bit.'

'You were in forensics?'

'No. DCS Potter's direct report teams are there rather than at Tulliallan. I headed up the Behavioural Sciences Unit, which sounds grand but it was just me and a part-time PhD student.' Marshall snorted. 'Basically, money drove a wedge between us.

I sold a flat in London for a decent profit. And Kirsten was struggling to sell her place in Gorgie.' He pointed over at Cath, serving someone else but noticing his gesture. 'Also, I didn't consult her when I gave Cath a loan.'

'Really?'

'It wasn't *too* much – I'm not stupid because I doubt I'll ever see it again, but it's helped her set up a hair salon. Doing well, apparently. Reckons she'll soon be able to stop working in here too.'

'Well, that's pretty good of you to do that.'

'Really? Because Kirsten kind of lost her shit over it. I should've talked to her about it, but she'd just never...'

'It's your money, Rob. If we were in a relationship, I'd want you to talk to me about anything.'

'Do you think I wouldn't?'

'I'm saying I've been in a relationship where I *couldn't*. Once contempt sets in, the whole thing's fucked. And if I get into something with you, Rob, I want it to be completely open and honest. Okay?'

'Okay. The thing that ended it was Kirsten wanted to be...' Marshall scratched his ear. 'Friends with benefits.'

Isla screwed up her face. 'But you didn't want that?'

'No. Of course I didn't. I just want to be with someone who wants to be with me. And that's the problem. In the end, she didn't want to be with me. She'd felt hemmed in for ages and hadn't said. I mean, it was nice spending time together but it wasn't enough for me. And I'd given her what she wanted. Holidays together and sex when she liked. But it wasn't enough. I thought we were moving forward in the relationship, but clearly we'd gone farther than she wanted to. And so it was time to move on.'

'That's rough.'

'So that's why I ended it. No one's fault really, just a failure to communicate effectively about the things that really mattered.'

'Sounds like you're better off out of it.' Isla sat back. 'Did you like what you saw?'

Marshall finished chewing. 'Hard to say no.'

She shuffled around and sat next to him. Then held his hand. And leaned over to kiss him.

Marshall had never been kissed like that before in his life.

Her hands everywhere, burning with passion and fire.

Everything he wanted.

'Okay, guys.' Cath stood there, holding their food. She plonked the plates down on the table. 'Think I've got them the right way round.'

Isla frowned as she shuffled back. 'I can't eat—'

'Relax, honey. See the wee V on the flag...?'

'Ah, okay. Thank you.'

'Can I get you any sauces?'

Marshall nodded. 'Just vinegar.'

'And you?'

'I'm fine, ta.'

'Back in a sec.' Cath frowned at her brother, then scurried off.

Isla was staring at him. 'You're such a good kisser.'

'Me? That was all you.' Marshall took a big bite of his burger and it slid down so bloody well. He was *starving*. 'So, when I'm off shift, would you like to—'

And right then, Marshall's phone started ringing...

Ravenscroft calling...

51

Elliot turned up at the car park and it was already filled with cars. She'd wanted to be among the first, but it felt like she'd be among the bloody last...

Tired and a bit grumpy.

And starving. Mr Fancypants Marshall buggered off with his new piece, leaving her to man the fort...

But she also realised she was pretty fucking giddy. This was her own case and a fresh murder at that – a chance to get away from Dr Donkey, at least for a little while. Run a team again, show Ravenscroft what's bloody what.

She got out into the downpour and it made her think of that old song about dancing naked in the rain. She giggled as she walked across the car park.

McIntyre and a few others stood around, drinking tea and seemingly doing bugger all. He thumbed behind him 'She's over there, ma'am.'

'Good stuff, Constable.' Elliot looked at his mates but didn't recognise any of them. 'How about you show me?'

'Of course.' The big lump led her along the common

approach path. 'I got your call as I was doing some canvassing in St Boswells for DI Crawford, so I wasn't too far away.'

Crawford was a DI?

Since fucking *when*?

Still, Elliot didn't really care, so she gave him a professional nod as she walked. 'We got an ID?'

'Not sure. I've been waiting for you.'

'But Trev's here?'

'Right. Full forensics services team, aye.'

'Thank you.' Elliot trudged through the puddles and just didn't care about the mud splashing up her legs because she was back in the saddle again. 'Great being able to lead an investigation again…'

McIntyre scowled at her. 'Even though some lassie's been killed?'

'Well, no. Not that bit. But I'm glad for the sake of her family it's me investigating and not some two-bit loser. Thing is, Jim, I'm just not cut out for media liaison. Waste of everybody's time.'

McIntyre stepped aside to let a CSI bustle past them.

Elliot nodded at them, but she couldn't for the life of her remember the guy's name. Or if he was a guy. 'Ravenscroft said the victim's a nurse. Been onto BGH?'

'I think someone was heading there, aye.'

'You think or they are?'

'I'll have to get back to you, ma'am.' McIntyre stopped near the stupid big William Wallace statue. 'This is it.'

Elliot had always hated the place. It looked so daft, and wasn't Willie Wallace based in Stirling or something?

Plenty of Borders folk you could celebrate instead, that's for sure. Like Walter Scott or Doddie bloody Weir.

Still, better than the one of bloody Zeus or whoever it was down at the river.

That prize pudding Stish was guarding the inner locus,

though he was having to re-stick the crime scene tape back together. Warner's mate, though not quite as daft – and Elliot thought that battle-axe sergeant had split them up.

Isla...

Marshall's new flame...

McIntyre started signing them in. 'Couple of ramblers found the body.'

Elliot took a Tyvek suit from the pile. She hated the bloody things, but at least this way she'd look like she was the SIO on her own investigation. 'Are they suspicious?'

'Nah. Two old duffers in some rambling club. Probably had a heart attack when they saw her.'

Elliot got her left leg into the suit's trouser, then spotted someone leaving the tent.

Trev pulled his goggles and mask free from his face. 'Andrea?'

She stuck her right leg in, but had to take it back out because her heel got stuck in there. Like doing the bloody hokey cokey, this. 'No, I'm the Queen of Sheba.'

'Are you running this case?'

'You say that like I've never run a murder inquiry in my puff.' Elliot glowered at him. 'Robbie Marshall asked me to, aye. He's sort of SIO and I'm deputy, but he said I'll be largely autonomous.'

'That's good.'

Elliot stood up tall. 'Tell me about it. Best investigator in Scotland and I've been side-lined.'

Cheeky sod looked at her like he didn't agree. 'Well, we've got an ID on the body.' Trev pointed inside the tent. 'Zuzana Svoboda. Works at Butler House care home in Gala.'

'Ah, shite.' Elliot sighed and felt the whole thing crumble away to dust. 'This is bloody connected to the other case, isn't it?'

McIntyre grinned at her. 'So much for getting your own case, eh?'

52

Just like a few days ago, Marshall had to drive past a car park and find a space along the road. At least there were no cameras or reporters this time, certainly not that he could see.

He got out and tasted a burger burp, checking his phone as he walked over.

A message from Isla.

A photo of her in the gym.

Wish you were here x

Wish this was the first photo you'd been sent from this phone x

Marshall put his phone away and started to feel a bit uneasy about this whole thing.

Sitting there, it felt natural and real. And right. But Jesus, they'd kissed once and she was back to sending these photos.

Still, it actually counted when you kissed and you were both sober. Didn't it?

Nobody to talk to about it. And he was feeling completely out of control. And seemed to be in a new relationship.

Maybe he should speak to Jen about it. Or Jolene.

Neither was ideal – Marshall needed an app for finding confidantes.

And maybe he should let himself enjoy it. Isla was really good-looking and a good laugh and seemed to want the same things as him. Seemed to be an actual adult. And she'd leaned on him for some important professional things – he'd asked her advice on some too.

Fuck it, they got on really well – you didn't message someone that frequently if you didn't.

Maybe it was time to lose himself in a new relationship?

Marshall got his phone back out and called Isla as he walked.

Isla answered it straight away. 'Hey, there.'

'Hey. Thought you weren't going to send any more explicit photos?'

'Well, I can make an exception for you, Rob. At least you can't see my nipples in this one.'

'Almost.' Marshall laughed. 'Listen, I'm sorry we had to curtail that lunch. I was really enjoying it.'

'I could tell. You're such a good kisser.'

'I'm just sorry it had to stop at kissing.'

'You'll keep.'

'Thanks for being so understanding.'

'It's the nature of the beast, right? Thing about us cops is we understand.' Another thing going for her – she totally *got* the job. 'Is it a murder?'

'Aye. And it seems to be connected to my case.'

'Oh, so I'm not going to see you for ages?'

'Probably not.'

Isla paused. 'But when you're off this case, we're getting a drink. You. Me. Soon.'

'Sure. Just let me get this case put to bed. These cases.'

'Might be a while, then?'

'Aye, but I'm a patient man.'

'Sounds perfect.'

'I better go, Isla. Have a good night. Okay?'

'I'll try to.'

Marshall ended the call and walked down the path, actually feeling like he could float there.

Maybe it wasn't such a bad thing to let his feelings guide him for once.

Stish was guarding the crime scene and had found a rare Police Scotland brolly from somewhere.

Elliot was standing next to him, scowling like she'd just lost a winning lottery ticket.

Marshall locked eyes with her. 'Got your voicemail, Andrea.'

She looked away. 'Aye. Doesn't look good.' She pointed to the side.

'Ah, Rob – we meet again.' Leye and his team wheeled the body past on a trolley. 'Do you want to take a look?'

Marshall frowned. 'Can I?'

'Of course.' Leye opened the body bag.

Sure enough, it was Zuzana.

'That's her alright.' Marshall looked at Leye. 'Are you able to run her PM tonight?'

'I'll try but failing that, it'll be Monday. I don't work on a Sunday. Mrs Anotade doesn't like me dealing with the dead on a Sabbath.'

'Thanks, mate.' Marshall nodded. 'Any idea what happened?'

'Strangulation. And I usually hate to bow to pressure from your team, Rob—' Leye gave Elliot some serious side eye. '—but I'd say this is a match for the other two. Same indentations, which makes me think it's the same gloves.'

'Thank God he didn't chuck them after killing his mother.' Which made Marshall think they probably had psychological significance to the killer. 'So what you're saying is Colin Radford has murdered a *third* victim in, what, three days?'

Leye nodded. 'That's what it looks like, yes.'

'A spree killer already…' Marshall stepped out of the way. 'Okay. Have a good one tomorrow.'

'I shall endeavour to.' Leye led his team away.

'Thought I was getting my own case there, but nope.' Elliot was leaning against a tree, arms folded. 'Back off to media liaison I fuck.'

Marshall smiled at her. 'Just brief Ravenscroft for me. Then we'll chat. Okay?'

Elliot sighed. '*Fine.*' She scurried off back to the car park.

Jolene appeared, looking back the way. 'Andi? You okay?' She came over to Marshall. 'She alright?'

'She's Andrea Elliot. When is she ever alright?' Marshall frowned. 'Take it you've not found Radford?'

'Nope. Last spotted at his mother's old care home. We found a hire car there.'

'Did anyone notice her missing?'

'Zuzana? Thought she'd buggered off. She was already staying late on her shift, apparently and the news about Patricia Radford had rattled her.' Jolene winced. 'Her car's not there. Or here.'

Marshall frowned. 'So he's got it?'

'Maybe.' Jolene shook her head, trying to process the sheer enormity of it all. 'Well, he's not at her house.' She looked over towards St Boswells. 'We've got it under surveillance, but I can't see him returning, can you?'

'No.' Marshall blew air up his face. 'I asked forensics to tear the house apart. Any update?'

'Trev was moaning about it, said he didn't think they'd find anything.'

'Still worth looking.'

'Of course. Why did he dump her body here?'

'Where people dump bodies is the weirdest thing. Can mean everything or nothing. Zuzana's been dumped here, but we've no idea where she was killed. Heather, he just strangled and pushed over the side at Scott's View. Maybe someone drove past and spooked him into running. Maybe not. His mother, he pretended she died naturally. Didn't even have to dump her. And Sharon Beattie, he was spooked by those kids rocking the camper van back and forth after he'd killed her. This is a marked departure from his MO. He blitzes them and leaves them in situ. No conversation, no victimology, no abduction, no relocation, no chance for DNA. This is how he's been able to get away with things for twenty-five years – he's prolific and by now quite refined.'

Jolene looked around. 'So you think this place has some significance?'

'Maybe. It's another beauty spot. Only a mile from Scott's View.'

'But why's it significant?'

'I don't know and that's the honest answer. Could hold particular significance, or it could just be that he's on the run, so this is on his way to somewhere.'

'But if he's heading north or south, wouldn't he take the A7 or A68 from Gala?'

'Not if you wanted to avoid ANPR cameras.'

Jolene nodded. 'Assuming he knows about ANPR.'

'He's avoided detection for twenty-five years. You don't do that without knowing certain things about law enforcement.'

'Could just be lucky.'

'Twenty-five years isn't luck.' Marshall sighed. 'But I take your point. This is a back road. If you go over to Kelso, then you can fly down the A697 to Newcastle or go up to Edinburgh. Plenty of other back roads there too. By the time he's on a main road like the A1, meanwhile, we're still looking around here for him.' He glared up at the dark skies and tried to conjure up some inspiration from somewhere. 'Okay. So. We've got Colin Radford coming back into the country. He kills Heather McGill. He kills his mother. Now he kills the woman who looked after his mother.'

'That's about the size of it. Thing is, Rob, he left the country and got away with it for all those years. He thinks he's invincible.'

'But he's not. Nobody is.'

'True.' Jolene looked as lost as Marshall felt. 'Got a call from Immigration. We've got no record of Colin Radford entering England, Scotland, Wales or Northern Ireland.'

Marshall nodded. 'So he's travelling under a fake name?'

'Must be.' Jolene shook her head. 'The manager at the care home said his mother had been prattling on about her son being a killer, but they'd chalked it up to dementia. You think he's killed her to stop her blabbing?'

'Maybe. But the irony is they thought it was just her condition – otherwise Police Scotland would need a unit just to investigate the ramblings of everyone in a care home.'

'But maybe coming back to the country and hearing her saying that made him freak out…'

'Not a bad suggestion at all. Okay, so that's four victims we know of. Meaning he's technically a serial killer, plus one to spare. The timing of these three means he's also a spree killer. Both are different flavours of the same bastard. And maybe my laughing Canadian buddy can conjure up another case to go along with these.' Marshall shut his eyes for the duration of a long, slow exhale, then locked eyes with Jolene. 'The upshot is I need to put my thinking cap back on and return to my old profession so I can conjure up a profile.' He looked around, and the emptiness of the landscape really pissed him off. 'Where the hell is he?'

53

Duncan couldn't believe he'd made it this far.

He pulled up his hoodie, which stank of petrol and smoke, then grabbed his carry-on bag from the floor by Dad's feet, got off the Gatwick Express train and followed the thin crowd through to the terminal building. He was far from an expert, but he thought his glasses and face mask would clear him of their snooping.

Hardly anybody else around, but then again it was evening on a Saturday – after the rush of the day and all the weekenders would already be gone.

He wheeled his case after him through to departures, looking around for anyone following him. He walked over to the terminal building, clutching his passport, then joined the queue at the BA ticket desk.

Sky News played on a row of flat panels above the desk, covering the upcoming G7 summit and their reaction to Israel attacking Iran.

The attendant smiled at him. 'How can I help you, sir?'

Duncan smiled at her, trying to keep cool. 'Need a single ticket to Toronto.'

'Okay. Just a second.' She checked her machine. 'The flight takes off at five to ten.'

Duncan checked his watch. 'Cool. It's seven now. Plenty of time to get there.'

She smiled. '9:55 tomorrow morning, sir.'

'Oh, right.'

Dad was leaning on the desk, yawning into a fist as he watched the news. 'If the next flight to Canada is tomorrow, then don't fucking go there.'

Duncan cleared his throat. 'When's the next *indirect* flight there?'

'You could go via Amsterdam, JFK or Heathrow?'

Dad laughed. 'Avoid the States – those fuckers have the death penalty for what you've done.'

Duncan smiled at her. 'How long's the layover in Amsterdam?'

'Six hours at Schiphol overnight, followed by a flight at six.' She checked again. 'Heathrow... You'd need to be there in an hour to clear international security. Or wait until six o'clock.'

Duncan smiled. 'Keen to get in the air soon.'

The screens showed a police cordon outside his mum's house in St Boswells.

Fuck.

'—are tight-lipped about their presence at the house on Main Street in St Boswells in the Scottish Borders.'

Duncan was blushing. He tried to snap to, but he was focused on the screen and what they were saying. What they knew...

Mum was getting in on the act. 'If they're onto you for what's gone on here, it's only a matter of time before they piece together the stuff over there. Turning yourself in might not be the worst idea in the world, Colin.'

'No way. He's got this far.' Dad laughed. 'Son, you need to head where there's no extradition...'

'Just a sec.' Duncan looked over at the board and scanned down it. 'Got it.'

54

Marshall sat at his desk and tried to log into Microsoft Teams.

Bloody hated all these apps and how they insisted on updating just as you tried to get on a video call. Zoom and Teams and Google Meet, which sounded like a lab-grown burger when you said it out loud.

And Teams – why they had to change it from Skype into *this*...?

His laptop sat there, thinking it through, so he checked the BOLO – but it didn't show any hits yet.

How could Radford steal a car and just disappear like that?

He tapped out a text to Isla:

> Really sorry about this but I don't think I'm getting away anytime soon. Going to pull an all-nighter to knock together a profile. Hope you enjoy your film x

He went back into Teams and the screen was filled with a young-ish face, but with silver hair.

Brad Tremblay

'Hey there, Detective Chief Inspector Marshall.'

Marshall smiled at him. 'Good evening.' Then he got lost in a huge yawn.

Tremblay laughed. 'You sure you're okay to do this, bub?'

'No. I'm not. Just caught another murder we think is Radford's.'

'Oh, shit.'

'Aye. A nurse from the care home his mother was staying at.' Marshall gave a bitter smile. 'We set up surveillance on his mother's house, but he's long gone. Give me some good news, Tremblay.'

Tremblay paused so long Marshall thought the connection had frozen. 'Mind if I call you Rob?'

'Not at all. It's Brad, right?'

'My mother calls me Bradley, but nobody else does.' Tremblay coughed. 'Listen, remember I mentioned that cold case to you earlier, right?'

Marshall nodded, but there it was – Tremblay *was* focusing on his own case. 'The strangling back in 2001, right?'

'Right. Ellen Fraser. Sadly haven't picked up anything tying it to Radford.'

Marshall sat back in his chair. 'I didn't expect much.'

'Doesn't stop us over here. Had my team out canvassing regarding this Colin Radford dude. Spoke with a neighbour who says Radford's been living in that place for a couple decades now. Pretty much since he moved here. Quiet guy, keeps to himself. Not married, never seemingly in a relationship. Hasn't been seen since the weekend.'

'That tracks with everything I've got. You got any idea where he went?'

'Works at Atlas Steel as an engineer, so we spoke to his boss

– reckons he took family leave to sort out his mother's condition back in Scotland.'

'He said that?'

'His mom? Sure. Why?'

'It's just, we've got conflicting reports of him pretending she was his aunt and he her long-lost nephew.'

'Huh. Well, the story seems straight this side of the Atlantic. We've got the CBSA looking for Radford.' Tremblay raised a hand. 'Sorry. Canada Border Services Agency. Trouble is, they don't have him leaving the country.'

'Meanwhile *our* immigration don't have a log of him entering the country.'

'Huh. So he's using a fake passport?' Tremblay winced. 'Are we dealing with some Jason Bourne dude?'

'No, we're not.' Marshall snarled. 'I saw him with my own eyes and he's no super-agent.'

Tremblay frowned. 'You met him?'

'Bumped into him during the investigation. Wouldn't pin him as Jason Bourne or James Bond. Just a normal guy. So if there's another passport, it's not—'

'Just one second.' Tremblay sat back and spoke to someone on mute.

Marshall sat there, trying to steel himself to the probability of Radford slipping through his fingers.

The sound crackled and Tremblay reappeared. 'Got an update for you.' He clicked his tongue and held up a sheet of paper. 'My guys just spoke to another neighbour. Dude recalled how Radford used to be Colin but changed his name after his father died.'

Hope surged in Marshall's stomach. 'Go on?'

'Sounds like he didn't have much love for the old man and decided to put his whole legacy into the past. Dude reckons Radford calls himself Duncan Brown now. Apparently Brown was his Aunt Margaret's married surname and Duncan is Colin's middle name.'

Marshall felt an urge to move. 'Okay, so we need to do all the same stuff for Duncan Brown, right?'

'Already on it.' Tremblay shook his head. 'I'm going to send you the relevant case file for my strangulation. Your scientists there can read our DNA report and see if it jives with what they've got. Sorry it's not exactly helpful in tracking him down...'

'Still, you just never know. I'll see if we've got Duncan Brown coming into the country. More importantly, if he's flying out under that name, we can block his exit. This could be just the break we need.'

55

Duncan sat on the plane and couldn't stop his leg from jigging up and down.

Still on the ground, but he was on board. But would they suss him and haul him off?

Wedged between two giant men – big dudes with soft bodies and sharp elbows, and right beside the toilet too. That's what happened when you got the last seat on the flight.

This was going to be a *looooong* flight.

Assuming he was allowed to take it.

And they'd been sitting here a while, hadn't they?

'Ladies and gentlemen, this is your pilot speaking. Sorry, but we're experiencing a slight delay on our scheduled departure to Punta Cana. Just liaising with ground staff here at Gatwick. We're expecting to be on our way in approximately fifteen minutes and I'll keep you updated as soon as I know more. Thanks for your patience and understanding – we'll do our best to get you in the air as quickly and safely as possible.'

Fuck...

Had to be the cops.

They were going to ground the flight, weren't they?

They were going to arrest him.

Drag him off the plane in handcuffs and throw him in jail forever.

It was over.

He was so close…

Fuck.

'Left it too late, haven't you?' Dad was standing in the aisle, looking down at him as he smoked. 'Should've listened to your old man and left days ago. This has been a complete disaster.'

Duncan just shut his eyes. Everything shut down inside his head. Whatever was going to happen… Let it happen…

The jolt of the plane moving backwards.

Felt like a kiss.

'Ladies and gentlemen, some good news for y'all – we've now received clearance to depart. At this time, please ensure your seatbelt is fastened, your tray table is stowed and your seat is in the upright position. Thanks again for your patience, and we'll be on our way shortly. Cabin crew, please secure the cabin and cross-check.'

Then the plane started rolling across the tarmac.

Duncan stared away, looking out of the window. Watching the green expanse of the airport, then the runway.

Just a few seconds now.

Duncan stared straight ahead, focusing on the information display on the seat back. The map of the northern hemisphere, with the arced flight path from London down to the Caribbean.

He'd watch it all the way.

He just wanted them to let him do that…

And not have anyone meet him at the far end.

'Such a waster.' Dad tapped his ash onto the carpet. 'Such a bitter disappointment to me and your mother.'

The plane rumbled as it rocketed forward, then that sharp pressure backwards as it took off and soared up into the sky.

Dad laughed. 'You think you're free now?'

Duncan took his gaze away from the seat back to lock eyes with him. 'I am free, Dad. I am.'

56

Sunday

The plane hit the tarmac and sent shockwaves riding up Duncan's legs. He gripped the armrests, nudging his neighbours back for once, but still stayed focused on the display on the seat back in front of him.

The flight was now over a small dot in the Caribbean. One he knew very, very well – his playground.

'Ladies and gentlemen, welcome to Punta Cana International Airport where the local time is twelve thirty-five. Outside, it's a chilly twenty-nine degrees or, for our North American passengers, that's a sweltering eighty-four.'

The passengers around Duncan laughed.

But he just sat there, sweating and trying to ignore everything except the display and then getting off this flight.

'Just give us a couple minutes to taxi you over to the terminal where you can then disembark. Thank you for flying with Edwards Air and, on behalf of myself and the crew, I hope you have a wonderful stay here on the beautiful island. For your safety and the safety of others, please remain seated with your seatbelt fastened until we have come to a complete stop at the gate and the seatbelt sign is turned off. Thank you.'

Duncan let himself sit back in the chair now.

He was on the ground now – shouldn't he feel safe?

He didn't.

He wouldn't.

Still had one last hurdle to jump.

He looked outside at the airport lights shimmering in the haze and, even at this time, he could almost feel the heat seeping in through the thick glass.

The aisle passenger smiled at him. Dude looked like a kind uncle with one of those beards that'd make you sweat in heat like this. 'Never seen anyone rawdog a flight like that before.' English accent. Refined.

Duncan looked over at him but didn't give any emotion. 'I didn't have a choice.'

'Oh?'

'Here for a funeral. Had to rush through. Didn't even have time to buy a magazine or book.'

'Worse places for it, I guess.' The passenger stroked his beard. 'Could've loaned you a novel or something?'

'It's fine. I have a lot of thinking to do. It was my son who passed.'

'Oh, I'm so sorry.'

The light went off and everyone started doing their thing. Getting up, getting in the way. Sitting there, being in the way.

His neighbour hoisted himself up and reached across the aisle for his bag, but he couldn't quite reach so he had to step over.

Allowing Duncan a gap he could slip into. He grabbed his carry-on from the overhead locker above his head, then shuffled through a few places. Not too far to the door. 'Excuse me. Got a funeral to get to.' He slipped through the emerging gaps until he was right at the door.

First to get off.

Just had to wait now.

Minutes passed as he stood there – all he could think of was the local police waiting for him.

He tried looking out of the door, but it was just dark out there, punctuated by the steps being driven over.

No signs of any cops, but...

The flight attendant smiled at him with a kindness and warmth that made Duncan want to just strangle her there and then.

No, he needed to wait.

He reached into his coat pocket, his left hand touching the passport, but then the gloves.

Dad's old work gloves. He might've been a complete bastard, but something in the fabric kept Duncan rooted to the past. Made him feel centred. He had nothing else from his early life in Scotland and he wasn't ready to get rid of them now.

Something thunked.

Then again.

A light switched on the door, then the flight attendant opened the door with an even wider smile.

Duncan stepped off the plane onto the steps down and the heat was like stepping into an oven. But it was the humidity that winded him. It was the same every time he came back to the Dominican Republic, his second home – third, if you counted Scotland, but he had no intentions of ever returning there.

Fresh sweat trickled down his back as he descended the steps towards the bus.

He looked around for cops, but saw nothing.

Maybe they'd be in the terminal?

No sign of Mum or Dad on the bus.

Duncan stood there, trying to gauge whether this would be

the first side to get off, but ultimately it didn't matter. Nothing mattered.

DUNCAN LEFT the airport and stepped into the burning night. The darkness seemed to sweat and seep and ooze.

Punta Cana.

He was safe again.

He was still free.

He hailed a cab swinging in and the dude got out and nodded at him.

Duncan handed him his bags and named the resort on autopilot, a large fraction of the Spanish he knew, then he got in the back and let himself relax.

In half an hour, he'd be in the resort. Check in. Dump his stuff. Shower. Then he could grab a cab out someplace with a late licence. Or maybe even just find someone in the hotel bar or casino.

After all that stress, he really needed to let his bloodlust spend itself.

Because it was back with a vengeance and nothing was going to stop him from killing again.

57

At the end of the morning briefing, Marshall looked around the room. Everyone looked tired and exhausted – almost as bad as how he felt. He didn't dare yawn, in case he just fell asleep on his feet. 'Okay, so our main focus is to track down Colin Radford, AKA Duncan Brown. I've been working with a contact in Niagara police in Canada but we really need to shake down any contacts we've got, both locally and nationally.'

McIntyre stopped sipping from his coffee long enough to frown. 'As in Niagara Falls?'

'Sure. And that's on the US border. But this is in Canada. Radford AKA Brown lived in a town called Welland in Ontario. About fifteen miles away.'

The main door clattered open and Crawford rushed in, panting for breath.

Marshall tilted his head to the side. 'Douglas, you okay?'

'Oh aye.' Crawford stopped to breathe deeply. 'Just got word back from North Yorkshire police.'

'What? Why?'

'They've recovered a burnt-out car from a village called

Nether Poppleton. Place just outside York. It's registered to a Zuzana Svoboda of Galashiels.'

Marshall frowned at him. 'York?'

'Right. Looks like he drove her car all the way there.' Crawford stood up tall and wiped his forehead. 'Spoke to the DI, who's going to co-lead on it as a murder inquiry. No chance of us getting any evidence from it.'

Marshall frowned, trying not to get too excited – or too disappointed. 'Okay, good. Good. So we've got Radford in York.'

'Nope. Transport Police have him catching the train to King's Cross, then the Thameslink from St Pancras to Gatwick.'

'Which is next door... Definitely Gatwick and not Brighton?'

'Right. Got off there.'

'Which means he's *probably* getting a flight from Gatwick. Do we have anything backing that up?'

'Not yet.' Crawford shook his head. 'Transport Police are running CCTV for me inside the terminal, but on the initial pass we think there's someone who could be him. Just need to check it myself to confirm.'

Marshall tried not to get his hopes up. 'Do we know where he could've flown to?'

'Waiting to hear back on that. They had some system issues last night, meaning some flights got delayed. Flight manifests are on their way to the local police and they'll share as soon as they get them.'

'Okay, good.' Marshall nodded his thanks. 'Did we get anywhere with forensics here?'

'Spoke to Trev just before this.' Jolene looked at her notebook. 'House looks fairly clean. The chair where he killed his mother is being processed. They also found a smashed bottle of Dunpender whisky and a broken glass. It's got some blood on it, so Trev's running it through. Odds are it'll be a match for Radford.'

'Good stuff. Okay, we're building a very robust case here,

but our main task is still to locate him.' Marshall looked around. 'Please speak to your direct superior officer for guidance on all tasks. Okay. Let's do this.' He left the room and slipped into his office, then collapsed into his chair.

He could've gone to sleep, but instead he stared up at the ceiling and felt like they were getting further away from catching him, if anything...

A flight from Gatwick...

He could be anywhere. Plenty of destinations and a lot of them without extradition treaties.

Not to mention plenty of connecting flights to similar places...

All he could do was focus on what he could achieve, so he unlocked his laptop and looked at his profile – an early stab in the dark that'd cost him most of last night.

Who needed sleep when there was a killer out there?

His email flashed up.

DSS Brad Tremblay.

Marshall clicked on it.

Hey Rob,
Hope all's good there. I'm still in if you wanted to confab? Same Teams link as last time. I'll jump on now.
Regards,
Brad

Marshall found the old email, then clicked the link and drank some water while the laptop did its thinking.

At least it didn't have to update this time...

Then Tremblay appeared. Dark windows in the background, the lights down low.

'Good morning.' Marshall gave him a broad grin. 'Assuming it's still night over there?'

'Morning here, alright.' Tremblay yawned. 'Three o'clock in the blessed AM.'

'This could've waited until later.'

'Case like this? No way. Besides, I figured you'd be in by now.'

'Been working most of the night, anyway.'

'Oh, right.' Tremblay coughed. 'So, uh, I got your email. The DNA from our cold case was a match to your case, so we've got us a suspect. Let the games begin. We got approval to get inside his home. Place is spotless. He's professionally cleaned the place before he left, so it feels to us like he's cut and run over to you. Forensically inert is how my guy described it.'

'Figures. No computers or anything?'

'No, nothing. We're breaking down drywall to see if he's got a stash of trinkets hidden somewhere, but the place just looks like you could move straight in. Sterile.'

'Be a shame to knock those walls down, eh?' Marshall's grin faded to a frown. 'So, you think he was planning on running?'

'Or at least being open to the possibility he wouldn't go back.' Tremblay shrugged his shoulders and threw up his hands. 'Or maybe this is how the guy lives. A strict regime of deep cleaning constantly means he's less worried about his past catching up with him.'

'That might not be a bad shout.' Marshall scribbled a note on the first page of his draft profile – that was good and opened up a few doors. 'You ever watch that film *Heat*?'

'Sure. Pacino and De Niro? Stone-cold classic movie. Why?'

'De Niro's character was a bank robber and he had a bag ready at all times, so he could run if he needed to.'

'Got you. Imagine living like that?'

'For some people, the thrill of the chase is everything. And it seems like Colin Radford is that person. Or at least partly.'

Someone chapped on the door.

Crawford, eyes narrowed. 'Guv, Transport Police just got back to me. They've got a Duncan Brown boarding an Edwards Air flight to the Dominican Republic, landing in Punta Cana.'

'Great.' Marshall made another note. 'Is it definitely Radford and not just some random Duncan Brown?'

'Oh, it's Radford. CCTV from Gatwick checks out. Can see him buying the tickets. See him at security. See him waiting for his departure, then at boarding – in the final cohort to get on the flight but he stood the whole time.' Crawford passed over a sheet of paper. 'His Canadian passport got scanned several times. Definitely our guy.'

Marshall stared at the photo and it was definitely Radford, just maybe five years younger.

So he felt a bit of relief.

But also a sting of pain – he'd got away.

Crawford glanced at the screen then at Marshall. 'I'll leave you to it, guv.' And he even shut the door behind him.

'Thanks.' Marshall looked at Tremblay. 'You hear that, Brad?'

'Your guy said he's in the DR?'

'Well, he's boarded a flight there. Whether he's still there remains to be seen.'

'Sure. I know the DR well.' Tremblay grinned. 'We call it Punta Canada, given the number of Canadians who go there over winter.' He laughed. 'Practically an extra province, although with the state of things right now it's probably not a good time to be joking about taking on new territories.' But the humour slipped away from Tremblay's face, replaced by a deep scowl. He leaned forward and rested on his elbows. 'Thing is, we asked the neighbours about anything weird or unusual about Radford. One neighbour remembered there being a murder down in Punta Cana while he was there. Reason it stuck out is Radford hadn't even heard about it. I mean, it was a national story here and would've been next to impossible to miss it if you were down there.'

'So Radford was there when it happened?'

'On vacation, yeah. Went a couple times a year. Sometimes as many as four. Neighbour had recommended a resort down there and reckoned Radford was a creature of habit. Kind of dude who goes to the same place every year.'

Marshall made another note – if that was borne out by other facts, it'd add something very juicy to his profile.

'Anyhoo.' Tremblay sniffed. 'The victim was another Canadian. Name of Sylvie Bouchard from Montreal.'

'Okay. So...' Marshall looked up from his notes. 'Are you saying he's been killing when he's on holiday?'

'Looks like it. Things are a lot looser down there than here. Same deal with where you are. Plenty of people vacationing so it's easy to get lost in the crowd. And this might be our lucky break, Rob – maybe this isn't a needle in a haystack job.'

Marshall smiled. 'No, it still is, but at least we know the haystack.'

'Well, we know which haystack to start in.' Tremblay winced. 'Keep thinking he could have a second back-up passport and be headed back to Toronto. Or be on a boat to the US or Venezuela or *anywhere*. Bunch of islands down there he could hole up in for years and nobody would find him.'

'Told you, Brad, we're not dealing with James Bond or Jason Bourne or Jack Bauer or any of the JBs. If he's a creature of habit, like you said, then Punta Cana is a familiar hunting ground for him. He's probably stressed out of his mind, having had to murder three people, including his own mother, before escaping the UK.' Marshall shut his eyes briefly. So bloody tired. 'But given the Dominican Republic is practically an extra province, I take it you have some contacts down there?'

'The Policía Nacional Dominicana.' Tremblay shuffled some papers. 'Already spoken to them. Turns out Sylvie

Bouchard was strangled. No signs of sexual activity. Killer wore a pair of gloves.'

Marshall shut his eyes again. 'Like my crimes and your cold case.'

'Give that man a cigar.' Tremblay shot finger pistols with both hands. 'I've asked for the autopsy report to be sent up.'

'Still, I'll be able to match it against our cases. He left an imprint on all four victims as he strangled them. Could be he's got a pair of lucky gloves.'

Tremblay laughed. 'Lucky gloves, huh?'

'Never underestimate the power of certainty with a serial killer. He knows them. They reassure him.' Marshall made another note – and one he thought was pretty crucial. 'Feels like we're closing in, Brad, but he could also just escape. What can we do? I'm not even sure there's an extradition treaty between the UK and Dominican Republic.'

'Well, if Duncan Brown is in PC, sure – you guys can't extradite from there, so he thinks he's safe.' Tremblay winked. 'But we can.'

'You guys have a treaty?'

'Oh, hell yeah. Like I said, there's a huge tourist pipeline between here and there. Nail him for our crime and we can always add Scotland to his dance card once we get him back to Canada.'

Marshall didn't want to hope too hard, but he felt himself doing it anyway. 'Will they play ball?'

'The DR cops? I think so. I shared the DNA profile with the PND for the murder of Sylvie Bouchard and they're going to get a local scientist to look into it. I'll warn you, Rob – they're not quick. Or well staffed or well equipped, but they *have* offered to assist us in apprehending Duncan Brown if we produce a valid Canadian arrest warrant.'

'And have you got one?'

'Well, the reason I'm still up is I was waiting on our scientists to finish comparing the DNA your dude sent through. Trev Pienaar, right? And it seems like we can connect Sharon's murder to my college student in Welland.'

'You've got a match?'

'Yep. Happened a long time ago, Rob. 2001. He was maybe less careful than he is now.'

'Fuck. He's been doing this for twenty-five years, hasn't he?'

'Might not be Jason Bourne, in your estimation, but he thinks he is. Kind of guy who can kill with impunity.' Tremblay fixed him with an intense look. 'Level with me here, bub – have you absolutely nailed him to those murders?'

'If he was still here, he'd be in custody. We've got a BOLO and a warrant for his arrest. All we're missing is him.'

'Okay, but how forensically tight is it?'

'We've got his parental DNA on file. Both of them now. Whoever killed Sharon Beattie is their child. And we only know of one person.'

'A genetic link between the killer and Radford/Brown is the piece of the puzzle our crown attorney was looking for.' Tremblay drummed his fingers on the table. 'You up for a trip to the Caribbean?'

'Eh?'

'I mean, we can compare notes on the case over Teams all you like, Rob, but with you having seen him in the flesh, you'd be much more likely to spot him than I would based off of an old photo.'

Marshall paused, trying to not get too excited. 'I need to run that past the boss.'

'Do it. But do it quick. Most flights from the UK to DR connect through Toronto Pearson, so we could catch the same flight.'

58

Monday

Marshall wandered through the strange airport, yawning. He'd no idea what time it was. Or what day. But the giant curved roof made him think of Stansted or London Luton. One of the two; he couldn't tell them apart, at least not in his head. He stopped to check the departures board but the connecting flight wasn't showing yet.

That, or he couldn't figure out which code he was looking for.

'Rob?' A man was walking towards him. Silver-haired, baby-faced. Shorts and a brown T-shirt Marshall couldn't read the dark text on.

Marshall grinned at him. 'Brad Tremblay, as I live and breathe.'

'C'mere.' Tremblay wrapped him in a hug and slapped his back a few times, then broke off. 'Man, it's good to see you in the flesh.' He looked him up and down. 'They putting your luggage on the flight?'

Marshall looked down at his paltry cabin-sized suitcase. 'No, this is it.'

'You not planning on staying long?' Tremblay raised his eyebrows. 'Man, you must be confident.'

'Not at all. Just don't have a lot of beach clothes at home. Last time I was on one was in Eyemouth.' And that name meant less than nothing to Tremblay. 'Figured I could get some in Punta Cana.'

'Sure, sure.' Tremblay led Marshall through the terminal. 'Got a gate for our flight, so let's grab a coffee.' He walked at such a fast pace, like he didn't exactly need any more, and trundled a hard-shell suitcase behind him. 'Your flight okay?'

'Not bad. Managed to get on the direct one from Edinburgh. Slept most of the way.'

'Didn't fancying going via Gatwick?'

'No. Hate flying domestically in the UK. So much waiting around – if I'm going to sit in an airport for a few hours, I'd rather it was in a seemingly exotic airport.'

'Pearson ain't exotic, bub.'

'Feels it compared to anywhere in the UK. Besides, the Gatwick flight our quarry took only flies once a week, so I didn't have a choice.'

Tremblay turned around to smirk at him. 'Our quarry, huh?'

Marshall laughed. 'Don't know why I said that.' He yawned. 'Tired, I guess.'

'We'll get some java in you. Local stuff's as good as the beer.'

'That's not exactly praise.'

'True.' Tremblay laughed. 'But both are world-class.'

Marshall checked his watch and sort of calibrated it to local time. 'The flight's in half an hour, isn't it?'

'Always got time for Tim Horton's, bub, and there's a stand right next to it anyhow.' Tremblay looked over to him as they walked. 'How you feeling, Rob?'

'On edge, I guess.' Marshall sighed. 'I'll level with you here,

Brad. When I wasn't asleep on that flight, I was thinking about how we've found our killer, only for him to get away.'

'And that's the shittiest of shitty feelings.' Tremblay stopped by the coffee shop. 'Cream or sugar, Rob?'

'Just black, thanks.'

'Man after my own heart.' Tremblay ordered but the place was so loud, Marshall couldn't hear anything. He tapped his phone to pay.

'Thanks for sending through both files. I've coupled it all together with what we have on him and got a loose profile.'

'You got a profiler working the case?'

'Me. Used to be one.'

'You're a regular Clarice Starling, huh?'

'Was.' Marshall took his coffee from Tremblay and relished the heat in his hands, then followed Tremblay over to their gate. 'Anyway. Upshot of my work is Colin Radford was a nice kid. Intelligent but bullied by an alcoholic father. Mother was religious but meek and mild. Had a temper in her latter days, when she suffered from Alzheimer's, but not while he was growing up. Bottom line, Radford had a need to control his situation to make up for the lack of control he had as a child. Abusive father, ineffectual mother, so he asserts himself on those he perceives as being weaker. The only evidence we have of any sexual activity was with Sharon Beattie, a known sex worker.'

Tremblay stopped by the gate, but nobody was even boarding yet. 'His first victim, that we know about.'

'Right. He'd been known to tour Scotland when he was onshore from his job on the oil rigs.'

'So there could be more?'

'Always can be. But I'm speculating that Sharon was his first.'

'You think something went wrong during the act of intercourse and he felt his manhood challenged in some way? And it made him snap?'

'No. There was no intercourse. The DNA came from under her nails. For him, he had a lack of power and control in his life and overly religious restrictions from his mother. Power, domination and control. If something went wrong, he wasn't equipped to deal with that and he overreacted. Rage kill, blitz and immediate flight. It's quite possible that the kill became almost the same as a sexual release for him. I suspect he was impotent or asexual. Fast forward to now and there was certainly no sexual component to Heather or with his mother. And it's early days analysing the final victim, but Zuzana Svoboda was strangled too. Found fully clothed. No overt signs of sexual activity.'

'And that tallies with my college girl and with Sylvie Bouchard. So it's anger-motivated, huh? Dominance, control and excitement.'

'Right. Exactly.' Marshall sipped his coffee through the lid. 'He's educated to degree level at Heriot-Watt in Edinburgh. Engineering. So he's smart, resourceful and capable.'

'Are you really sure he's not a Jason Bourne type?'

'Sure. He's details oriented, methodical, clean and organised. He only breaks that pattern when he's killing. So having his house neat and sterile matches that profile, as does visiting the same resort year after year. We'll only know for sure if we find him there. Let's focus on the fact we've successfully tracked our quarry.'

And right then, the ground staff invited them to start boarding the plane.

59

Marshall had his headphones on, listening to Cath's Everything Everything playlist on Spotify. And finding himself getting into them more and more. Those deep electronic beats with live instrumentation coupled with vocals you had to focus on but which were so vivid and rewarding.

The perfect soundtrack to a flight filled with touching up a criminal profile of both a spree and serial killer.

A hard judder rattled through him as the plane touched down.

Tremblay jerked awake and looked like he'd just been shot.

Marshall pulled off his headphones and paused the music.

'Welcome to Punta Cana International Airport where the local time is twelve thirty-five. Outside, it's a chilly thirty degrees, or for our North American passengers, that's a sweltering eighty-six.'

The passengers laughed.

Marshall groaned.

Tremblay sighed. 'Every time...'

'Just give us a couple minutes to—'

Marshall powered off the headphones, then put them into the travel case. He gathered together the files spread across his lap, then stuffed them into his laptop bag on top of his computer. 'That was some sleep.'

'I'm like a baby. As soon as I'm in a moving vehicle, can't keep my eyes open.'

'I'm still wired from that coffee.'

'Lightweight.' Tremblay sat back, waiting while the plane taxied across the tarmac. 'Six of them a day just to keep my focus.'

Marshall looked across Tremblay towards the hot morning. Heat haze everywhere, distorting the parched grass and cracked tarmac.

'We'll be off the plane soon, bub.' Tremblay grinned at him. 'And we'll catch him.'

'Purpose of your stay?'

Marshall smiled at the immigration officer. 'Business.'

'I see.' He frowned. 'And what business is that?'

'I'm a police officer.' Marshall showed his warrant card. 'From Scotland in the UK.'

Tremblay stepped in. 'We both are.' He showed his own card. 'Here to meet Colonel Valentina Garcia.'

'I see. Well, enjoy your stay.' The immigration officer stamped Marshall's passport, then Tremblay's.

'Thank you.' Marshall collected his papers and his passport, gave the guy a nod, then walked through into arrivals, where the air conditioning seemed to be off.

'This way.' Tremblay strode off, dragging his luggage behind him.

Marshall had to jog to catch up, but the heat was sapping his energy.

Tremblay led him outside into the searing heat.

Marshall felt like it could strip the flesh off his bones. 'Not used to this temperature.'

'I can tell.' Tremblay looked Marshall up and down. 'It gets hot back home in summer because we're so far from either ocean, but it's nothing like down here.'

'Scotland only gets anywhere this hot once a decade. And that's for half a day. At most. Before it rains.'

A police car pulled up on the kerb and a woman got out of the driver side. Not the tallest, but she wore a hard military uniform in a hot climate and didn't seem to be sweating. And her gaze was hardcore – if the heat didn't sear away his flesh, her look would. 'Tremblay?'

Tremblay raised an eyebrow. 'Colonel Valentina Garcia?'

'That's me.' Garcia shook his hand, then gripped Marshall's like a python smothering a rodent. 'And you are?'

'DCI Rob Marshall from Police Scotland. Pleased to meet you.'

'I've been to Scotland once. Far too cold.'

'And that's probably just in the summer.' Tremblay rested his luggage at his feet. 'You're going to help us track down Duncan Brown AKA Colin Radford. Right?'

'We shall see.' Garcia glared at them in turn, but Marshall seemed to get the longest burn of that glare. 'I'll tell you the same thing I told Bradley over the phone. You are both here under my authority.' Her Spanish accent was subtle – this was a woman who was clearly well educated and used to being in charge. 'You may be police officials at home, but here you are tourists with badges. Are we clear?'

Marshall nodded – he was in no mood to mess with her. 'Of course.'

'Good.' Garcia opened the back door for Marshall. 'In here, Chief Inspector.'

Marshall got in the back, but felt like a wee laddie while his parents were up front.

Tremblay wedged himself in the passenger seat and grabbed the handle above the door.

Garcia drove off, really fast.

'So why were you in Scotland?'

Garcia glanced around at him. 'I went to university in the United States. We had a visit. So I went and I've never been so cold. I only lasted two weeks.'

'What time of year was it?'

'July.' Then she started talking to Tremblay and the open windows meant Marshall couldn't hear what she was saying.

She passed through a giant roundabout, then hit a long road through a lush green landscape, mostly unspoiled, but it was fast enough and quiet enough.

She wound up the windows and Marshall could hear them talking now. 'I mean it, Tremblay. Why do Canadian police need help from England?'

Marshall leaned forward. 'I'm from Scotland, not England.'

Garcia shot him a glare but didn't say anything.

'It's part of the UK, but it's very different from down south.'

They drove in silence and the road started winding to the side.

'Um.' Tremblay coughed into his fist. 'The reason Rob is here is because he's actually seen Brown in the flesh. That's infinitely better than relying on a picture and my eyesight.' He added on a laugh for good measure.

It didn't land with Garcia. She locked eyes with Marshall in the rear-view mirror. 'And he frequented this resort often?'

'Creature of habit.' Tremblay glanced around at the back. 'As far as we can tell, Radford always came back to this place in Punta Cana, year after year. Few times a year. Mar Glorioso.'

'As you said.' Garcia gave a brief smile. 'I passed this information along to the local officers, but there are thirteen hundred rooms and over four thousand people at the resort. The surrounding resorts each have a similar number.'

Marshall nodded. 'So that's a pretty big haystack, but not huge.'

Garcia frowned, then looked at Tremblay. 'Sorry, I don't understand what he's saying.'

Tremblay grinned wide. 'He said, that's a pretty big haystack, but not huge.'

She didn't seem to know what he meant by that. 'We have spoken to several people who just checked in, but we have not found this Mr Radford yet. Or Mr Brown.'

Tremblay gave a cheeky glance towards Marshall. 'So he could be here under a different alias?'

'No offence, but distinguishing between one *turista blanco* and another isn't an easy task for us.' Garcia turned off to the left along a coastal road. 'Especially based on a seven-year-old passport photo.'

Marshall laughed. 'I'm sure he'll stick out like a sore thumb when he gets sunburnt.'

'Hardly. Pink skin is common for visitors here.' Garcia indicated to overtake and swept past a sports car with the top down. 'Thing is, Mr Marshall, I cannot afford to have my officers guarding rooms on a ten-years-old cold case. And our scientists have not established a link between your suspect and our case. We are assisting out of courtesy only.'

Marshall nodded. 'There are three recent murders in Scotland.'

'True, but you have enlisted my help on this cold case in Canada. My country does not recognise yours for the purposes of extradition. That's where I start and where this ends for you.' Garcia looked back at him. 'Besides, by now everyone knows the police are looking for someone, so I suspect your suspect has fled.'

'And we shall test that hypothesis.' Tremblay smiled at her. 'Look, thank you for the help so far.'

'Do not mention it. But that's all we can do.' Garcia sighed. 'My men will be busy. We have had a murder in Otra Banda, a few miles away. A young teenaged male. Local. We are having to direct our resources there.'

'Wait.' Marshall frowned. 'So you can't help?'

'I am helping to the extent of my abilities. You are not my only priority. I am driving you both to the hotel and warning you to stay out of trouble. If you find this Colin Radford or Duncan Brown, then you must call me. You do not approach him yourselves. Are we clear?'

'Okay.' But Marshall was pissed off – wasting all that travel time and money on a wild goose chase. And Ravenscroft would have his balls in a vice if there wasn't a result here.

Or was it just that he wanted to be the one taking Radford down? Was he really a glory hunter?

'Here you go, gentlemen.' Garcia pulled up outside a sprawling hotel. 'You wander around as tourists and if you spot him, you let me know.'

'Of course.'

'There are twelve thousand guests in this cove alone. That's my job to police, not yours. You don't have jurisdiction here over my officers. Am I clear?'

'Very clear. But the dude always comes here. Rob's a profiler and his experience says he'll be here.' Tremblay patted his stomach. 'My gut tells me it's our best bet in finding him.'

'I personally think you are both wasting your time here, but I just cannot afford to devote resources on a mere hunch.' Garcia sat there for a few moments, then looked around at Marshall. 'But I wish you good luck.' She gave a tight nod. 'He sounds like a bad man and I hope you catch him.'

'Thank you.' Marshall grabbed his luggage from the

footwell and got out into the searing heat. Seemed to be even hotter down on the coast, despite the breeze from the sea.

The beach was golden sand being snogged vigorously by pale-blue water, which spread out into the depths of the Caribbean. Sunbathers draped themselves on towels and loungers, barely any of them in the shade. Not that there was much.

A whole world away from the Scottish Borders, even the bits on the coast. Or maybe even further from those.

Tremblay joined him on the pavement, staring up at the sun in a state of sheer bliss. Like this was a holiday. Or a *vacation*.

Marshall caught Tremblay's door and peered back into the car. 'Hopefully I'll be calling you soon.'

Garcia nodded. 'I am not holding my breath.'

Marshall shut the door, then watched her car roar off past a giant bank of solar panels. He picked up his suitcase. 'We got a plan?'

Tremblay shrugged. 'Check in. Get changed into beach clothes. See you back here in twenty.'

60

Marshall looked in the full-length mirror and tried to decide if he was ready. Fancy shorts he'd bought during the drought in May but hadn't worn since. Cream polo shirt. White socks. Walking trainers.

Sod it, it'd do.

He grabbed his keycard from the machine, then went out into the main area of the hotel.

Tremblay sat by the fountain, fannying about on his phone. Backwards baseball cap, swimming shorts and a shirt flapping in the breeze. He looked up and raised his eyebrows. 'I said twenty minutes, but I swear you took longer to get ready than my daughter at her prom.'

Took Marshall a few seconds to realise the print was of Bob Marley. 'Okay, so where do we start?'

'Nu-uh.' Tremblay looked Marshall up and down then laughed. 'We need to sort you some more appropriate attire, bub.'

Marshall raised his hands. 'What's wrong with this?'

'I came prepared, whereas you didn't seem to fathom the kind of heat we get here.'

'It's not like it's any worse than Greece or Spain at this time of year.'

'True, but you don't look like the kind of dude who goes to Greece or Spain. And if you do, are you really wearing that get-up?'

'Tend to go to Northern Europe in the summer. Heat's for winter. And that's when I go anywhere.' Marshall laughed. '*If* I go anywhere.'

'Workaholic, huh?'

Marshall looked away. 'Something like that.'

'Join the club, buddy. Look, you're here to fit in, not stick out like a cop on a half-assed stakeout. C'mere.' Tremblay grabbed Marshall's sleeve and dragged him towards the shop.

MARSHALL STOPPED LATHERING high-factor lotion onto his arms, then took another look. He was now dressed and ready – long board shorts, shirt and crocs, the kind his sister swore got her through a double shift in the hospital way back in the Borders.

He hated it, but at least he looked the part – if the part was that of clueless tourist.

Sod it – he left his room again and found Tremblay sitting in a chair this time. He gave Marshall the same up and down, but this time he raised both thumbs. 'Now we're cooking.'

Marshall looked away. 'Feel stupid.'

'You look a lot less stupid, bub.'

Marshall laughed. 'Says the guy in his forties with a backwards baseball cap.'

'We both look the right kind of stupid to fit in. Which is the whole point of a surveillance operation.' Tremblay passed Marshall a small bag. 'Here you go, buddy. A local SIM card for your cell. Should be able to fit two into your phone, assuming you have the same ones we do.'

'Thanks. And you mean mobile.' Marshall sat down and used the little hook thing to prise open the SIM slot, then slotted home the new card. Took a few seconds but it connected to a network name he couldn't even read, let alone pronounce. A text from Jen popped up but he pocketed his phone. 'So what now?'

'Now, we wander around and try to fit in. See if we can't spot this dude.'

MARSHALL LAY ON THE BEACH, just in his shorts. The sun was thudding down on him like a physical weight. He took off his sunglasses and checked his torso – all looking a bit pink down there. He lathered up some more suntan lotion, but it was probably a lost cause.

His phone dinged and he reached over for it, trying to avoid smearing the screen in lotion.

TREMBLAY

Check out the guy in the red. Same size and age as Radford. Move in a little closer and see if it's him.

Marshall took his time, trying to act naturally. He looked over and spotted Tremblay, spreadeagled in the sun.

Further past him was a guy in red shorts.

Could it be him?

He'd only seen Radford briefly at the care home, just a couple of minutes while he helped him out with his mother's luggage, but he had to admit this guy was a good match. Late forties, early fifties. Average height, average build. Leaning over his iPad and hiding his face.

Sod it.

Marshall got to his feet, grabbed his towel and sat next to the suspect.

The guy looked up from his iPad, shielding the sun with his hand. 'Can I help you, buddy?' American accent, but Radford lived in Canada for years.

'First day here.' Marshall smiled at him. 'Didn't expect it to be this hot.'

'I'm not interested.' He went back to his iPad.

'Excuse me?'

'Said I'm not interested.'

'Just friendly.'

'But you coming over here dressed like that and chatting me up?' He pulled on a black MAGA hat, then started drying himself with a towel bearing a Confederate flag. 'Fuck off.'

It wasn't Radford – that much was obvious.

Marshall shrugged. 'Sorry, I thought I recognised you, that's all.'

'Well, you don't, asshole. So go fuck yourself.'

Marshall scowled at him, but decided getting into a fight probably wasn't the best idea, so he grabbed his stuff and walked back into the hotel.

So nice and cold inside, like being in the chiller section of a supermarket, but the whole place was like that.

His phone pinged.

Not from Tremblay, but from Isla.

Another photo of her, wearing her cap and blowing him a kiss.

Just got off shift x

How's the Dominican Republic? xx

Marshall started tapping out a reply.

'Not him, huh?'

'Nope.' Marshall casually put his phone away and looked over to Tremblay. 'Let's head back out.'

'Nah. We won't find him now.'

'Eh?'

'It's getting dark soon. And it's like a light switch here. Click and it's night. Besides, Rob, you said it yourself in that profile you pulled together – Radford's MO is hunting during the day, then pouncing at night. Assuming he hasn't found some new —' Tremblay made some rabbit ears. '—"quarry".'

Marshall looked away. 'Not going to live that down, am I?'

'Not by a long shot.'

Marshall let out a deep sigh. 'I want to keep going.'

'Dude, it's time to eat, drink and regroup. Besides, you can't extradite him, so this is technically my case. And you might be a couple ranks above me, but I reckon that means I'm actually in charge.' Tremblay smiled. 'You worried about the budget?'

'More our lack of success today.'

'I'm not.'

'Really?'

'This is the case that's going to get me promoted, bub.' Tremblay clapped his shoulder. 'Besides, DR's dirt cheap, not like some of the other islands. Can stay in this hotel for a week, all inclusive, for twelve hundred bucks.'

'That's... Hang on...' Marshall frowned. He opened his phone and tapped in "1200 CAD to GBP". 'Six hundred and fifty quid, give or take.'

'That sound cheap to you?'

'That's pretty much what you'd pay in a crappy resort in Greece or Spain.'

Tremblay looked around them. 'But this is a *nice* one.'

'True.' Marshall sighed again. 'But you don't have a transatlantic flight to account for. And one you booked just before the plane took off, so it wasn't exactly cheap.'

'Dude, I get it. In my world, murder and money both start

with the letter M. If I can solve one with the other, then I'm a hero. Being able to name the guy is one thing but slapping the cuffs on him and dragging his sorry ass back home for some justice – that's priceless. But we've drawn a blank for now. The guy's probably hiding out here. Knows you're onto him, so he's likely to be getting his head down. Bit of room service, watching the news. So let's try again tomorrow, okay? This is a marathon, Rob.'

'It doesn't feel right.'

'No, it doesn't. But all work and no play makes Rob a dull boy. We'll catch him. Doesn't have to be on the first day.'

'Suppose.'

'He's here. Feel it in my gut, bub. But let's start back up again tomorrow morning. Besides, I'm starving and could do with a few wobbly pops.' Tremblay walked off in the direction of his room. 'See you in the bar in thirty. Text me if you're going to be later.'

'Sure thing.' Marshall went the other way, trying to console himself with the fact they'd have a whole day of it in the morning rather than less than half. He swiped into his room, then lay down on his bed.

Thank God for air conditioning – maybe six hours of this and he'd start to feel less than melting.

How did people actually enjoy this?

He looked down at his body again – his legs and chest were more than a bit pink, even with the high-factor lotion.

Bugger it.

He took a photo of his red arms and sent it to Isla.

61

Marshall walked into the bar, dressed this time in some other clothes he'd bought in the store. Felt a bit more natural than the beach ones, though nowhere near as natural as the ones he'd brought himself – but hey, the objective was to fit in.

Tremblay stood by the bar, grinning as he sipped from a glass of beer – not a pint, maybe two thirds at best. 'Hey there, Rob.' He looked at him again and winced. 'Oof. You look like someone's put you on a grill.'

Marshall touched his arm and felt the heat. 'That lotion didn't cut it, did it?'

'Saying you need higher than factor ten?'

'*Ten*? I need at least a fifty.'

'It goes higher than thirty?' Tremblay laughed. 'Lightweight.'

'No wonder I look like a lobster.'

'Well, they might not have lobster, but they've got crab in the buffet tonight. Won't last long.' Tremblay led over to a free table, like he'd already booked it. 'Looking sharp there, Rob.'

Marshall glanced down at his trousers. 'Look like I had a tough session on the back nine.'

'You fit right in, though.' Tremblay laughed. 'Heard they got some good courses in Scotland.'

'The best, apparently.'

'You a golfer?'

'Nope. Tried it once. Couldn't work out whether I hated it or it hated me more.'

'Well, they got some real good courses here. Promise they won't bite.'

'Take your word for it.'

'Maybe that can be our cover.' Tremblay frowned. 'Two dudes on a golfing trip.'

'I'll never pass that. Besides, does Radford golf?'

'We asked, but the neighbour back home didn't know. It's kind of a country club kinda deal back there.'

Marshall gestured towards the bar. 'What can I get you?'

'Drunk?' Tremblay laughed. 'Dude, this place is all inclusive, so strap on the feeding bag.' He chuckled. 'You a fan of beer?'

'If it's an old-fashioned one that tastes like vinegar, then no. But one of those hop-heavy modern IPAs, sure.'

'Man. I love me an IPA, but it's not a thing down here in the islands yet. Got just the ticket, though. Back in a sec.' Tremblay lumbered over to the bar. He looked every inch the cop, though. Something about men of a certain build that attracted them to the job. Or maybe it was something the job did to you.

Marshall checked his phone – he had a reply from Isla:

> Sexy. Wish I was there xx

> Looks like you've not so much caught the sun as smeared it all over you. Get some after-sun on you, you madman! xxx

Marshall felt something – even if it was just being wanted, it was nice.

No, he wanted her too. Something deep in him.

He'd not really felt that with Kirsten, or hadn't in a long time. They'd kind of stumbled hard into things and he hadn't been prepared for it – he'd been so green, living his life like a monk.

Then things got so difficult. Or just... hard to process.

Things seemed easy with Isla. No barriers or stuff getting in the way. Sure, it was early days, but that lack of friction felt hugely appealing.

Marshall tapped out a reply:

It's a lot hotter than I expected! x

Tremblay came back over with two glasses of beer, still those small ones. 'Here we go, bub.'

'Cheers.' Marshall took a sip and it was a very basic lager. 'Lordy, that's awful.'

'Isn't it? And *Lordy*?'

'Like in that Moby song.'

'Bit before your time, isn't it?'

'Thing with old music is you can listen to it after it comes out.'

'True.' Tremblay sipped his beer and grimaced. 'So, how old are you?'

'Buy me a drink and ask my age...' Marshall laughed. 'I'll be thirty-nine in September.'

'Huh. Good going to be a DCI already.'

'One rung lower than your guy, right? How about you?'

'Forty-six.' Tremblay sniffed. 'So, you been a cop, what, seventeen years? Twenty?'

'Twelve.'

'How the hell did you get to that rank in *twelve years*? I've got twenty-five in. We go to thirty. But I've been stuck at staff sergeant for the last eight.'

'I was direct entry.'

Tremblay snarled at that – like he only just realised he wasn't dealing with a real cop and felt all cheated now. 'They do that in Scotland?'

'Not anymore. But mine was in the Met.'

'The Met, as in London?'

Marshall nodded. 'Best part of ten years, aye.'

'Never been. On the same bucket list as a trip to Scotland. It must be an amazing place.'

'It's a huge city. Tons and tons of things to do there. I used to love it. Then I lived there and worked there, so now I just like it.'

'But you're not based there anymore?'

'Nope. A case brought me back home and I stayed. Have to say, I prefer the relative peace and quiet of the Borders.'

'Country boy, huh?'

'Something like that.'

'Man after my own heart.' Tremblay grinned. 'Same relationship I have with Toronto. Based there for eleven years. Uniform in 52 Division. Downtown. Right in the thick of it. Made a shit-ton of OT, then got assigned to street crime, then CID and eventually homicide detective.'

'And now you're in Niagara?'

'Wife wanted the quiet life. I didn't disagree. Great place to raise kids. In Ontario, you can move from one police service to another without losing your pension. The experience I had in Toronto made me a shoo-in for Major Crime in Niagara. Promoted twice since I patched over, even though we didn't solve that strangling. So I guess it's been worth it. Just wish I could step up again before my time's up, you know?'

'I get that. Still, that's a while you've been there, right?'

'Long-ass time. Real nice place too. Probably a lot more built up than you're used to in Scotland.'

'Where I live is the complete opposite of built up. I cover a huge area geographically but it's mostly hills filled with livestock. Biggest two towns are barely thirteen thousand people, but there are quite a few of them dotted around.'

'Huh. Got you. Toronto's pushing six million and Niagara's closing on half a million.'

'Bloody hell. That's bigger than Edinburgh.'

'Edinburgh's six million?'

Marshall laughed. 'No, Scotland itself is only five on account of everyone buggering off to Canada.'

Tremblay bellowed with laughter.

'No, Edinburgh is like half a million. London is twelve. Greater London, anyway.'

'Right, right.' Tremblay took a sip of beer and seemed to hate it as much as Marshall did. 'Why did you leave the Met? There a Mrs Marshall wanting the quiet life?'

'Nope. I just felt it was time to return home. Like I said, a case brought me back and I could've gone back to the Met and kept doing what I did. Truth is, it's been great. Reconnected with my family. Found a few family members I didn't know about.'

'Oh?'

'It's complicated. But I had… stuff going on before. It's why I left home in the first place. But I feel much better for it now.' Marshall took a long drink of his beer and it didn't get any better-tasting. 'So, we're going to catch Radford, right?'

'I hope so.'

'You're the expert here but don't you fancy our chances?'

'It's a long shot, I gotta admit. But like I said to Garcia, my gut tells me he's here. Not just that, but your whole profile on him backs it up. You were doing that in London?'

'Nah. I joined the Met because I hated the profiling stuff.

Couldn't stand being so passive. Just standing back and having to consult and advise on stuff, you know? I wanted to do stuff, which is why I became a cop. Not that I ever stopped doing the profiling, you know? Thing is, we don't like to talk about having serial killers on account of it upsetting the public. It'd be like saying there's a vampire plague or something.'

Tremblay chuckled. 'I hear you.'

'So aye, that's me.' Marshall stared into the fizzing bubbles in his beer. 'Does your gut tell you Radford's been killing here over the years?'

'Don't see why not. He killed in Scotland twenty-five years ago, then fled the country to live in Canada. Add in my cold case and you've got two murders in subsequent years.' Tremblay leaned forward. 'And we know Radford came here regularly, so we can surmise he killed Sylvie. And we can also surmise she might not be the only one.' He held up his phone. 'While you were getting your duds on, Garcia emailed me a few unsolved cases she's pulled from over the years with matching or at least similar MOs. For her claiming she didn't have the time to help us, she's been busy on the back end. Maybe Colonel isn't her resting place in rank either. We should look at them when we get a minute.'

'Got a few hours just now, Brad.'

'All work and no rest...'

Marshall smiled at that, but he'd rather solve the case than get wasted. And he wasn't sure Tremblay was thinking along those lines... 'I thought Garcia didn't seem interested in those older cases.'

'Sure, but that's because she's got enough on her plate with current crimes. She'll feel differently when the DNA is a match.' Tremblay took a drink of his beer and dribbled a bit over the side. 'Thing is, I had a word with her earlier when you were getting changed into your beach gear. She said she'd look into the old cases and *voila*, she's produced a list for us.'

'You can be very persuasive, can't you?' Marshall winked at him. 'Got me to travel all this way for starters.'

'Right. Explained to her how Radford's been able to get away with it here. You heard the woman – policing a resort ain't like a town or a city, where you've got a static population and any changes get noticed by the locals real quick. Here, the tourists vastly outnumber the locals and a transient population is just about impossible to police.' Tremblay waved a hand around. 'Think about it. Everyone here will be gone in two weeks.'

'Makes sense.' Marshall saw the logic in it. 'You're saying this is a perfect hunting ground.'

'Right. Exactly.' Tremblay finished his beer and gasped. 'Radford's killed in Scotland, like you say, then he fled to Canada, where we think he's done it again. And both times he's got away with it. But he's obsessing about it. He needs to kill again. He needs to keep killing again and he must've seen how tough it'd be back in Canada. Don't shit where you eat, that sort of thing. So he comes here and he's been able to do it with impunity. So he has no reason to stop and every desire to keep going.'

'Could've said those exact words myself.' Marshall waved around the space. 'You come to Punta Cana much?'

'Used to. Prefer Curaçao these days.'

'Where's Curaçao?'

'Dutch island just off the coast of Venezuela. Name's Spanish, obviously, but let's not get into that. Much smaller than here. We discovered it about ten years ago and just fell in love. We're building a house there in Grote Knip. Absolute paradise.'

'Nice. Planning to retire there?'

'Still at least five years away from that. Got to get my thirty in and Mrs Tremblay's a teacher, but she won't be able to retire for a few. She's a bit younger than me. We'll probably do the snowbird thing. Spend the winter months down there, then head north again to maintain our citizenship and free healthcare. Rent out the place on the island when we're not there.'

Tremblay spun his glass around in his hands. 'So there isn't a Mrs Marshall back in Scotland?'

'Nope. Used to be a future Mrs Marshall, but she's no longer on the scene.'

'She a cop?'

'Forensic scientist.'

'Oh, interesting.'

'Why do you ask?'

'Trust me, never date a cop. We're all nucking futs. The shit we see as detectives, like us, or those dudes out on patrol... it totally warps your mind. Mrs Tremblay keeps me sane, despite her kids making her feel crazy. Or as close to sane as I can get.' He laughed then held up his empty glass. 'Makes us rely on stuff like this to preserve what sanity we've got left. Here.' He got out his phone and showed Marshall a picture of him with a blonde-haired woman and two teenaged kids, all doing the Mickey Mouse pose in searing heat at Disney World.

'Beautiful.' Marshall thought of Isla and whether she was nucking futs.... 'I just started seeing someone back home.'

Tremblay raised an eyebrow. 'And she's a cop?'

'Right. She's...' Marshall took a sip. 'She's one of the good ones. Uniformed sergeant in the same town as me. Good team leader. And I get on really well with her.'

'Man... Working in the same station. It'll feel claustrophobic, won't it?'

'We'll see.'

'It sounds complicated.'

'I'm complicated.'

'Do tell?'

'Long story.'

'Got all night, buddy.'

Marshall finished his drink. 'Sounds like we need another. Same again?'

'Despite my buddy's recommendation, that beer is a crime against humanity.' Tremblay looked over to the bar. 'Get me a CC and cola.'

'Yet another of those abbreviations.'

'Canadian Club. It's a rye whiskey they stock here for us Canadians. Locals know a rye and coke is one of them to us.'

'I'll get two of them, then. Need the toilet first.'

Tremblay tilted his head to the side. 'You're not getting out of that long story, y'hear?'

'Wouldn't expect it.' Marshall got up and walked off towards the sign for the bathroom. Like everyone else, he checked his phone as he walked.

A message from Isla, another seductive photo of her in her bed.

Missing you, Rob. Good night x

Marshall pocketed his phone and held the door for the toilets, grinning like a total idiot.

A guy came out, also checking his phone.

Then another.

And neither thanked him – the way he was dressed, they probably thought he worked there or something.

Marshall looked back the way, towards Tremblay – maybe Isla was nucking futs, after all.

But maybe Marshall was too.

He looked into the casino.

Colin Radford was sitting at a fruit machine, sipping a beer as he pumped the handle.

62

Marshall sat back down at their table.

Tremblay looked at his empty hands then up at him. 'Where are the drinks?'

'Radford's here.' Marshall nudged his head back behind him. 'Playing on the fruit machine in the casino.'

'Fruit machine?' Tremblay scowled. 'Oh, you mean a slot.' He glanced over, subtle as you like, then back at the empty beer glasses. 'How sure are you?'

'It's him.'

'Okay. You have him as a gambler in your profile?'

'It's compatible. Extreme risks. Thrill of the chase. Obsessions.'

'Okay. So here's the plan – you approach him, confirm it's *definitely* him. Maintain eyes on him while I call Garcia.'

'It is him, zero doubt. And what if he makes me?'

'Good point. I'll go and play on the slot next to him, while you call Garcia.' Tremblay got to his feet. 'Same again?' Deliberately loud. But not subtle.

Marshall nodded. 'Sure.' He looked over to the casino again. Radford was just leaving, clutching his beer glass.

'I got this.' Tremblay got up and walked over to the bar. 'Two CCs and cola.'

Marshall took out his phone and found Garcia's number. He hit dial and put it to his ear, keeping an eye on what was unfolding.

Radford approached the bar slowly, watching everyone, but smiling like he knew them all. Tremblay made eye contact with him, then he started chatting back to him.

Marshall felt his fillings rattle in his mouth, but they seemed to be getting on okay – Radford was engaging like he was a regular dude and not a cop trying to snare him.

'Who is this?'

'It's DCI Rob Marshall.' Marshall leaned forward. 'We've got eyes on Radford.'

Garcia paused. 'Where are you?'

'Hotel bar. He was in the casino. Tremblay's speaking to him right now.'

'I *told* you not to engage. Stay there and do nothing.'

Radford looked around the place as he laughed at a joke Tremblay had made, then he did a double take. His eyes pulsed as he focused on Marshall.

Shite.

Tremblay spotted it and jerked forward, reaching for Radford.

Too slow – Radford shoved him in the chest, pushing him backwards. Tremblay caught his legs on the barstool, then tipped right over, cracked his head off the bar top and landed on the solid floor.

Radford shot off through the bar area.

Shite.

'He's made us!' Marshall pocketed his phone and sprinted after Radford, following him into the dining area.

Radford turned around and spotted Marshall. He grabbed a plate from a waiter and hurled it right at him.

Marshall ducked.

The plate missed him but the steak slapped him in the face like a jilted lover.

He had to wipe the fatty stuff off his face.

Meanwhile, Radford hopped onto the buffet table and jumped right over, then bombed it out of the room, into the pool area.

Marshall weaved to the side, then had to dodge around a queue of diners. He raced out onto the pool area, the lights all bright and glowing.

Somehow Tremblay was right behind Radford. Not as quick a runner, but he was a straight-line bulldozer. He closed on him and leapt forward, trying to rugby-tackle him.

Radford dodged Tremblay's reach.

Tremblay slipped, bounced on the floor, then tumbled right into the pool.

Marshall stopped. Should he help?

But Radford hadn't stopped – he raced around the pool and hopped up onto the karaoke stage.

He couldn't let him get away. 'Stop!'

Radford spotted Marshall, then grabbed a microphone off the stand, unplugged the cable and hurled it towards him.

Marshall ducked this object and avoided it completely.

Judging by the scream, it'd hit someone behind him.

Marshall didn't have a chance to check – Radford was running again, through the exit and out onto the beach.

Marshall chased after him, but running on the sand was tough going.

And Radford seemed to be quite a bit fitter or just more experienced at this kind of thing.

But he seemed to be running in a curved arc around the beach and heading towards the main road through the resort.

Marshall spotted a shortcut – a path leading up a set of steps to the pavement, which would surely get him there much quicker. He took it and kept an eye on Radford at a safe distance.

Radford reached the road and stopped dead. He spun around, searching. Then he seemed to relax – maybe thinking he'd lost Marshall.

Marshall charged up the steps, then hit the road, but he'd lost sight of Radford in the heavy night-time traffic.

Shit, shit, shit.

He sped up but had to keep stopping to search for him.

And not finding him.

Then he saw why – Radford was jogging across the road, right in the middle.

'Stop!'

Radford swung around and locked eyes with Marshall.

Then everything happened in slow motion.

A lad on a motorbike careered towards him, honking his horn and screaming as he hurtled towards Radford.

He slipped into a skid and went low.

Then Radford disappeared.

Shite!

Marshall raced over to the centre of the chaos. 'Police!'

The biker lay on the ground, rolling and screaming.

Radford lay behind him, completely still. His face was white, his jaw clenched. Both his legs were trapped under the bike. He tried to push it away, but it was locked in place.

At least he was alive.

Tremblay joined Marshall, dripping wet from his dip.

Radford screamed again.

Tremblay moved forward to haul the bike off.

Marshall held him back. 'We need to wait for Garcia.'

Tremblay shifted the bike free, then pointed at him. 'I don't think he's going anywhere.'

Radford's legs lay at weird angles, both clearly broken.

63

Marshall sipped ice water, so cold and clear it tasted like it'd come straight from a glacier. The police station was baking, despite it being in the middle of the night. 'So bloody tired.'

'Not surprised.' Tremblay's golfing gear was bone dry now. 'Your body must think it's, what... Morning?'

Marshall checked the clock again and tried to remember the correct sums. 'Three a.m. No, four. Hang on. Actually, I think it's five a.m. for me.'

'Man.'

Marshall looked over at him. 'Your hunch paid off.'

'My gut's legendary back home.' Tremblay patted his belly and gave a deep laugh. 'You'll be calling me Inspector Tremblay this time next year. Be the same rank as you, right?'

'Give or take, aye. Just glad we've caught him.' Marshall frowned. 'Are you going to extradite him?'

'The request's been made.'

'Think they'll accede to it?'

'Hard to know. Depends on what the DNA shows. If he's a

match they may want to keep him. If not, they'll be happy to get rid of him.'

The office door opened and Garcia beckoned them into the room. 'Gentlemen.' She sat behind a desk. No computer, just stacks of paperwork.

Marshall followed Tremblay in but didn't want to sit down. Despite the time difference and exhaustion he'd felt a few moments ago, he was now fizzing with energy.

Tremblay sat. 'You spoken to him?'

'In hospital, yes.' Garcia flared her nostrils. 'Both legs are broken, but he's been able to talk to us.'

'And?'

'There is good news. He matches the description of the prime suspect in the murder in Otra Banda.'

Marshall frowned. 'The local teen who was killed?'

'Yes. Mr Brown is now talking about it. Painkillers tend to loosen a person up, so we now have a suspect for our case.'

Marshall raised his eyebrows. 'Is that going to be admissible?'

Garcia looked at him as if he was crazy, then focused on Tremblay. 'We will take a closer look at the cold case involving the murder of the young woman from Montreal. Happened so long ago, but this new case is a good break for us.' She shifted her gaze between Tremblay and Marshall. 'This is very good for all of us. We can clear up two cases in one go. And there are the others too, the ones I sent you, Tremblay.'

'That all sounds positive.' Tremblay nodded. 'What about my case back home? And Rob's cases?'

'Those shouldn't concern you.'

'What do you mean?'

'Our cases have priority. We'll prosecute him here first.'

Marshall sat down now. 'I can't just let him get off.'

'If this concludes as expected, Mr Duncan Brown will do at

least twenty years here. Minimum. Thirty, if he did any of these other murders. And we believe he has.'

'So Brad and I catch him, but we don't get to bring him to justice for murders back home?'

'Chief Inspector, you should not worry.' Garcia narrowed her eyes. 'In this country, we do not coddle our prisoners like you do. It will be a very *hard* twenty years, if he even survives that long. And he will be an old man by the end of his sentence. Which he will serve in full.'

Marshall tried to seek some consolation in that, but would Gus Beattie? Would Barbara McGill? Would Zuzana's parents back in Plzen? 'How confident are you of securing that conviction?'

'We have a saying here. Close enough is good enough. Our judicial system is not founded on letting guilty people go like it is in Canada and England.' Garcia put her cap on her head and got to her feet. 'You two aren't the only ones with ambition. This will add a significant boost to my career as well. Now, I have much work to do to progress this. I will be in touch. I suggest you get some sleep.' She left the room.

Tremblay watched her go. 'You buying that crap?'

Marshall sat there for a few seconds and tried processing it. Maybe it was the water he'd been drinking, but he had an ice-cold burning in his gut. He tried to flip it around and see the positive side of things – she was pretty Machiavellian in her thinking, so maybe they should be. He looked over at Tremblay. 'Maybe close enough *is* good enough. We can't close off our cases completely, Brad, but we can put them to bed.' He let out a tight breath. 'And he'll suffer in the prison here, right?'

'Trust me, you don't want to be in jail here. Bad things happen.'

'Then I think I can live with that. I can't be arsed with chasing the promotion carrot, but this seems like a result no matter where it happens.'

Tremblay nodded his own acceptance to Radford's fate. 'So, what now? You want to stay for a few days? Take your own crack at interviewing Radford? Taste the crab at the buffet?'

'Not a fan of sea insects, I'm afraid.' Marshall yawned into his fist. 'Got an open return when I booked, so I'll see if I can get back in the morning. And it's almost morning to me.'

'It's lovely here.'

'Aye, but I'm not.' Marshall grinned. 'I can't stand the heat so I'm getting the hell out of the kitchen.'

64

Duncan opened his eyes and everything hurt. Everything. Not just his legs, which felt like empty spaces where bone and muscle should've been. His back, his arms. His skull.

And it was so hot in this room.

Those two cops were sitting there.

Duncan thought the Scottish one was called Marshall. The other one was American. Or Canadian.

The one who'd approached him at the bar.

And then he'd clocked Marshall and just knew he had to get away.

And he had.

But here he was, more trapped than ever. Stuck in a hospital bed. Bright blue sky out here.

Fuck.

'Glad to see you're awake, Colin.' Marshall sniffed. 'Or is it Duncan?'

Duncan didn't say anything.

'Don't suppose it matters, does it?' Marshall shrugged. 'Okay, so we're here to have a wee chat. See, I'm booked on the next flight home, back to Edinburgh. That means this is the last time you'll see me. Probably the last Scottish person you'll ever see, in fact.'

Duncan just sank his head deep into the pillow. 'That supposed to encourage me to talk or something?'

'Just wondered if you wanted to give your side of things.'

'My side? This is all nonsense.'

Marshall nodded slowly. 'You don't want to say anything to Heather McGill's mother? Or Sharon Beattie's father? Or Zuzana—'

'No.'

'Ellen Fraser. Sylvie Bouchard.'

'No idea what you're talking about.'

Marshall stared at him and it was like looking into the sun. 'You killed them all.'

Duncan looked away from him. 'You confident of that?'

'I know you did it.' Marshall nodded, then gestured between him and the Canadian cop. 'We know you did it. And at least one in Canada.'

'Plus a few others on this island, right?' The Canadian leaned forward. 'Tourists, locals. Doesn't make any difference to you, does it?'

Duncan stared at him for a few seconds, then leaned back and shook his head as much as the pillow would allow. 'Saying nothing.'

'Interesting.' Marshall raised his eyebrows. 'Is that how you really want to play it?'

Duncan focused on him. The drugs and pain bit at him but he could see the guy was the wrong side of a tan. All red like a Coke can. 'You should've worn some after-sun.'

'Okay, we're done here.' Marshall got to his feet and walked over to the door.

'On you go.' Duncan rolled his eyes. 'That trick won't work with me.'

Marshall opened the door and laughed. 'I'm glad to have solved those cases, though.' He turned back around. 'I mean, you're not going to be pampered in a place like Barlinnie or Saughton back home.'

'Eh?'

'Our penitentiaries are pretty tame compared to what you're going to endure here too.' The Canadian got to his feet and joined Marshall over there. 'First-world problems. Third-world poverty.' He chuckled. 'I mean, they never really mention the second world, do they? But you'll know all about it, very soon.'

'You can't scare me.'

'That's not our intention.' Marshall smiled at him. 'I didn't expect you to admit anything. I just need to visit Gus Beattie and Barbara McGill and Thora Scott, just need to be able to look them in the eye, honestly, and tell them the man who murdered their loved ones is facing justice.'

'You'll never know who did it.'

'Don't kid yourself.' Marshall sucked a deep breath through his nostrils. 'We've got evidence, Duncan. We know it was you. We know exactly what you did.'

'Well, why don't you—'

Marshall left the room.

The Canadian gave him one last look. 'Don't even care about getting you on the record, bub. We've got you where you're not getting out.' And he left too.

Leaving Duncan alone.

His parents were both in the room, sitting on the chairs.

Sharon was over by the window.

Heather too.

Zuzana was by the door, shaking her head.

'Waste of space.' Dad leaned forward and popped a grape in his mouth. 'You could've got away with it if you'd fucking listened to me.'

65

Tuesday

Elliot pulled up outside her home and checked the text that'd arrived while she drove.

From mum:

> The boys are all settled. Probably better stay here. Mum x

Nobody wanted her, did they?

Snap out of it!

She typed a reply:

> If you're sure... Thanks for looking after them Ax

Elliot put her phone away, then got out of the car and trudged over to the house. Took all she had to get the key in the lock and open the door.

Acting DCI Rob bloody Marshall...

He didn't think about the impact his insane obsession had on others, did he? She was sick to the back teeth of carrying

Marshall's bags while he swanned off to the bloody Caribbean. In the station until eleven o'clock, managing his team for him... And just so he could grab the glory over in... Wherever he'd gone to.

And that wee uniform hussy was doing her head in, marching around the station like she was the boss. Just because she was Marshall's new piece.

Where did he get off?

Aye, and it was nothing to do with her feeling like she stood a chance, was it?

Her phone buzzed with another text.

Not a problem xx See you in the morning xx

Elliot dumped her phone on the side table, then kicked off her shoes and stood there, desperate to get out of this horrible new bra.

Weird being here without the cacophony of arguing kids. Even without Sam, those two laddies would make the racket of three.

Wine.

She walked towards the kitchen.

And heard something from upstairs.

Was that someone grunting?

The boys were at her parents and Sam was at uni, still bouncing her calls.

Wait...

Had Gary Hislop sent someone to invade her home?

After all, the cops spoke to him the other day and she'd never escaped his radar, had she?

Elliot sneaked over to the hall cupboard and eased one of Davie's old golf clubs out of the bag.

She heard it again. Deeper.

Someone was *definitely* up there.

Fuck.

Well, whoever it was... They were going to pay. Big time.

She put her foot on the first step and started climbing, one by one. Slowly and softly, skipping the third step which creaked...

She stopped on the landing and waited, listening.

Nothing.

Had she just imagined it?

There – the same grunt.

It came from Sam's room.

Elliot stepped over to the door, then listened carefully.

What the hell were they doing in there? Did Hislop think that's where she'd stashed all that money?

Elliot raised the golf club, then snatched at the handle and launched herself into the room.

Sam was sitting at her desk. She looked over, wiping at her eyes.

'Sam.' Elliot lowered the club. 'You terrified me.'

'Sorry, Mum.'

Elliot rested the club on the bed. 'Are you okay?'

'No. I'm really not.'

'What's happened?' Elliot walked over and ran a hand up Sam's back. 'Why aren't you in Glasgow?'

'I've been suspended from uni.'

66

Wednesday

Marshall wheeled his case back into his office and, of course, there was nobody there.

No sign of Ravenscroft, as promised. Typical. Bloody typical...

He checked his watch. Six o'clock. British Summer Time. God knows what that translated to in Dominican time – one? The changing time zones, jet lag and the layover in Amsterdam were melting his head.

He slumped behind his desk and started getting his laptop to sync with the network. He yawned deeply and just wanted his bed.

Elliot walked in and wolf-whistled. 'You look like a lobster in a pink costume. Not so much tanned as painted yourself pink. This a Pride thing?'

Marshall ignored her. 'Could've done with a few extra days, but it's not really my scene. Way too hot for my liking.'

'Typical Scotsman.' Elliot sat down and shook her head at

him. 'Me, I crave the heat. Worship the sun. So, you just flew straight back?'

'No, I teleported.'

She rolled her eyes at him. 'Ha, bloody ha.'

'Yes, Andrea, I flew back. KLM to Schiphol but I missed my connection over to Edinburgh through no fault of my own, so had to wait another five hours. And when I landed, Ravenscroft wasn't there to pick me up at the airport like he promised.'

'Oof.'

'Aye. So I had to get a taxi here, on top of that Uber on Thursday night and the flights, so my credit card is a wee plastic puddle. And my headphones had run out of charge, so I had to listen to the cabbie moan about how they've changed the airport parking yet again.' Marshall stifled a yawn. Almost. 'Still, my body clock isn't *that* broken by all that globetrotting.'

Elliot smiled at him. 'The crow.'

'Eh?'

'Ravenscroft's nickname.'

'It's not one of your best ones, I have to say.'

She clicked her tongue.

'And seriously, you need to quit it with that. It's not your best look.'

'Right, well, it's good to have you back, Robbie. I'm going home now so I'll see you in the morning.'

'Thank you for holding the fort.' Marshall smiled. 'Everything been okay?'

'No, Robbie, it's all a total disaster. But I'll cope. I always do.'

'You sure you're okay?'

'Not really.' Elliot looked away, then let out a deep breath. She nibbled her thumbnail. 'Sam told me she's been suspended from uni.'

'Oh, shit. I'm sorry.' Marshall frowned at that. 'You should've said. You shouldn't be here.'

'It's fine. I can handle this.'

'She needs you, right.'

Elliot shrugged. 'Maybe.'

Marshall leaned forward. 'What happened?'

'Her coursework got flagged for potential ghostwriting and potential AI abuse. She's been suspended while they investigate.'

'Had a mate go through that hell at Durham.' Marshall nodded. 'Didn't have AI back then, but we had plenty of post-grads willing to write your essays for you. Turns out some of them were lazy and the lecturers kept copies of old ones.'

'Trust Dr Donkey to know.' Elliot dug the heels of her palms into her eyes, then gasped. 'Thing is, this isn't a permanent expulsion yet. But Sam feels like it is.'

'Totally understandable. What happened?'

'Her essay got flagged by some app called Turnitin. It checks for AI use and plagiarism and stuff. Thing is, the match score was inconclusive and she told me she does use ChatGPT. They all do, but she says it's just for research and checking her stuff afterwards but not for writing the bloody essay.'

'If it's inconclusive, I don't understand how she got suspended?'

'Because they got a tip-off from another student. Said they overheard Sam talking about "getting help online" which they're taking to mean hiring a ghostwriter over the internet.'

'Did she actually say that?'

'She can't remember. Might've done.'

'So it's not AI?'

'It might be. The ghostwriting service might just use it.'

'Did she buy the service, though?'

'She won't admit it.'

'But you think she did.'

Elliot stared at him with eyes glazed by tears. 'I just don't know, Robbie.'

'What does she say?'

'Completely denies it, but her head's a total mess. Poor thing.'

'Okay, so you need to attack it, right? Most word-processing software shows the amount of time spent on something, right? Can't she also show the number of revisions and rewrites she's done?'

'She could.' Elliot nodded, then her lips twisted into a snarl. 'If her laptop wasn't missing.'

'Oh. Shite.'

'Aye.'

'Was it stolen?'

'It's what she says, but it could've fallen off the side of a ferry, you know?' Elliot dug those palms deep again. 'I'm focusing on what she's not saying, Robbie. I might have to scrape her up off the floor and have her living with me longer than I anticipated.'

'You'll support her. You've been there for her for her whole life.'

'Right. Suppose so.' Elliot clamped her eyes shut. 'It's so hard doing this on my own.'

'Is Sam okay?'

'She's at her granny's, so she's getting spoilt rotten.'

'Good. You should go and be with her. And if there's anything I can do to help, I'm more than happy to do it.'

'Thanks, Robbie.' Elliot slowly got up then left the room, but she seemed to drag her heels, like she had something else to ask him.

Marshall hoped he'd been supportive enough. Hard to tell with her.

And he'd no idea how things had actually been with her, Jolene and Crawford in charge.

But that was for tomorrow…

Marshall got out his phone and tried calling Ravenscroft, but it got bounced. At least he was still alive.

What did he need to do now?

Ah, right.

He found the email from his lawyer, the arsey chaser, then typed out a reply:

> Hi George,
> Sorry for radio silence. Been away on business. Yes, please put in a bid for the house in Clovenfords. I think we'd discussed the price, so go for ten grand over asking. If you feel we need a specific bid because of competition, then please call me.
> Cheers,
> Rob

That felt good. A step forward. Maybe not in the right direction, but movement was good.

He tried Ravenscroft again while he checked his work emails and got bounced yet again. And his inbox was a biblical flood of shit.

Elliot seemed to have emailed an update every hour, on the hour, as much to cover her arse as anything productive – after all, the case happened to have moved to the Caribbean.

Tremblay had sent him a selfie, sitting at the bar with a bottle of CC, a can of Coke and a big thumbs up.

But there was an email from the HR system.

SUBJECT: Update processed

What the hell was that?

Marshall double-clicked on that.

> Rank updated, effective 2025/06/11 16:23:56.
> Was: Acting Detective Chief Inspector (Detective Inspector)

Now: Detective Chief Inspector

Marshall sat back in his chair and let out a deep breath. What a weird way to find out he was now a full DCI.

He forwarded the email to Tremblay and added in:

RESULT!

He picked up his desk phone and called Ravenscroft, but it he still got bounced.

So he texted Potter:

Hi Miranda, hope you're well. System says I'm now a full DCI. Is that right?

'So you are back?' Isla stood in the doorway, all dolled up.

Marshall put his phone down and looked at her. All those photos and texts they'd shared while he'd been away... Seeing her in the flesh made his stomach flip over. 'Aye. Had to get a cab down from the airport.'

'Rob! I could've collected you.'

'You were on duty.'

'So?' Isla smiled as she sat down. 'Got a table booked in 1953 for our date.'

'Thank you. You fancy getting a drink first?'

'Perfect.' She grinned. 'Just not in the Tap.'

'Well, my sister's not working tonight. At least I don't think so. Is it Tuesday?'

'Wednesday.' Isla smiled. 'How did it go over there?'

'Radford's in hospital with two broken legs, but they're still questioning him. He's not getting away.'

'You got a result, though, right?'

'Right. The police over there are sharing Radford's DNA samples with the forensics teams both here and in Canada. If Radford does manage to get out of jail, then he'll face charges in Niagara and here. It's possible he's killed eighteen times in the Dominican Republic.'

'Holy shit. *How*?'

'Went there two or three times a year for over ten years. They've got a minimum of one unsolved per trip they think matches. And there are possibly more – it's a resort, so they have tons of missing persons every year.'

'Bloody hell.'

'He'll do thirty years minimum over there. We might not be able to prosecute him directly, but we've got him. And he's fifty-six – he won't see daylight again as a free man. Besides, the prisons down there are pretty much second world. He'll *pray* he was in Scotland or Canada.'

'You must feel proud?'

'Not sure pride is how I feel, but we've got some closure. Just need to start briefing people. Gus Beattie and Barbara McGill.'

His phone rang.

'Sorry.' He checked the display.

Potter calling...

He looked over at Isla. 'It's the boss's boss. Do you mind?'

She gestured for him to take it. 'Go for it.'

Marshall nodded his thanks then answered it. 'Miranda... That was quick.'

'Sorry, Rob. Been a hell of a day. Yes, you're a DCI now.'

'Thank you.'

'You're welcome. I hope you'll be having a glass to celebrate?'

Marshall looked over to Isla. 'Planning on going out, aye.'

'A double whammy, eh? That and the case. John said you got a result.'

'Been trying to get hold of him.'

'Ah, that's my fault. Sorry. He's just prepping a press release on the news. On your result.'

'Not the result I expected, but close enough is good enough.'

'All's well that ends well.' Potter sighed down the line. 'But we've got to square the positive aspect of him facing some form of justice with the lack of a prosecution this side of the pond. John's going to spin some guff about leaving an active arrest warrant on our system in the event things fall through in the Caribbean and then again in Canada. Window dressing.' She cleared her throat. 'But going back to your new rank, John was supposed to brief you and get you to sign a new contract.'

'A new contract?'

'We're extending your tenure, Rob. Another ten years.'

'Wow, that's a long time.'

'We can't get rid of you that easily. And it's not unheard of in areas of strategic importance.' Potter's sigh rasped down the line like a broken speaker. 'Listen, John was supposed to brief you on this. The reason for the promotion is we're expanding your remit.'

'Oh?'

'Gary Hislop's opening High Street Hardware on the Royal Mile in Edinburgh. He's really going for it, Rob. And we want you to lead the operation.'

So Craven's rumour was right.

Marshall locked eyes with Isla. 'Doesn't that sit with the drug squad?'

'It does currently, but they've had over three years and we don't see much progress. The rumours have been flying around for some time, so I know you've heard them.'

'I'd be lying if I said I hadn't. But with all due respect, my strength is with serial killers and—'

'Rob, your strength is *actually* in leading very effective investigations. Your conviction rate is the best in Police Scotland.

Hell, it's up there with anyone in the rest of the UK. Besides, what is Gary Hislop if not a serial killer? Might not have killed them with his own hands, but so many in his organisation have disappeared since we started looking into him. Rob, the Hislop investigation is yours. Partly because of the geography but mostly because you've had many dealings with him. Don't worry, I know you'll take him down...'

'No pressure, eh?'

'Nope. Listen, let's catch up and focus on strategy once you've caught up with your sleep.' Click, and she was gone.

Isla looked over at him. 'That all sounded positive?'

'You're looking at a full chief inspector.'

'Wow. Congratulations.' Isla frowned. 'But?'

'But I've just stepped in somebody else's mess.' Marshall walked over to her and pushed the door shut, then wrapped her in his arms. 'I've been meaning to do this for a few days now.' He kissed her deeply.

And for once, everything felt right.

67

Elliot let the engine rattle to nothing and felt no compunction to get out. She looked over at the house and could see Mum was still there with her boys in the living room. Playing that stupid VR game with the daft helmet on her head, bashing those sticks in time with music nobody else could hear – Mum didn't care how daft she looked and the boys loved it.

Sam's light was on upstairs. Blinds drawn despite it being a glorious summer evening.

Elliot sighed.

What a fucking mess.

Her phone chimed with a text message.

Scott's View. Now.

She knew who it was from.

And she knew she couldn't ignore it.

~

Elliot pulled up next to his car.

A graphite grey Maserati sat there. Expensive and fast – no cop cars could catch it in a pursuit.

She opened her car door but didn't get out.

Gary Hislop got out of the Maserati, then carried a box of wine over to her. 'Mind if I get in?'

'Of course I do. Whatever it is you've got to say, you're saying it there.'

'Charming.' Despite that, Hislop got in the passenger seat and rested the wine in the footwell. 'Remember being here twenty-five years ago and finding that body over there.' He swallowed hard. 'Heard they got the guy who did it?'

'Is that what this is about?' Elliot kept her door open. 'Because if that wine's for me, then it should go to—'

'Nope.' He handed her a bottle from the case. 'Still, you deserve these for what you've achieved. It's good news for Sharon's family, right? Good news for the rest of us who were there.'

'This wine's very familiar.' Elliot took the bottle. 'Last time I saw a case of this, it was sitting on that seat with a set of photos of my family resting on top.'

'No idea what you mean.'

'Is this another threat, Gary? Or was it just one back then?'

'Andi, don't you think it's time we buried the hatchet?'

She handed the bottle back. He didn't take it, so she dropped it in his lap. 'Does that mean you don't feel guilty about Davie anymore?'

'Why would I?' He rested the wine on the floor. 'You shouldn't either.'

'You don't feel bad anymore about having my husband killed?'

'Nope.' Hislop gave her a hard stare. 'Because I didn't do it.'

'Of course you did. You got someone to follow the van from—'

'It wasn't me.' The stare got even harder. 'You were on a rampage to pin Davie's death on me, Andrea. Then you stopped. Why's that?'

Elliot looked away. Another car pulled up, so she shut the door now. 'Because I've got to get on with living my life, don't I?'

'Sure it's that?'

Elliot ran a hand through her hair. 'Gary, why are you really here?'

'Helping.'

'Right.' Elliot laughed, all bitter and cold. 'You're something else.'

'It was useful having someone like Davie on the inside. Meant I knew when I was being unfairly targeted.'

'Unfairly?'

'Just an innocent businessman. And I knew when I was being watched.'

'We're going to get you.'

'Nothing to get me *for*, Andi. My business is very clean.'

'We know all of it. Everything you've done.'

'Whatever you think you know is wrong. My operation's one hundred percent clean. I'm completely legit and it's time you lot faced the truth.'

'That's complete bullshit.'

Gary laughed. 'Sucks to fail, doesn't it?'

'Go.' Elliot pointed to his car. 'Leave. Now.'

'Nope.'

'What do you want from me?'

'I want my money, Andi.'

'What money?'

'I know you found it. I want it back.'

'I assume you're talking about the money you paid Davie?'

'Right.'

'Gary, I've told you – I don't have it.'

'You do, Andi. I know you do. And you need to stop lying to me. We paid him a ton of money. He's dead. Ergo, you've got it.'

'I don't have any money. I'm a cop. I'm skint. My pension's good but the income's crap.'

'You've got his life insurance, right?'

'Which I spent on clearing a huge chunk of my mortgage and on a holiday for my grieving kids.'

'Well, that's not ideal, is it?' Hislop licked his lips. 'The way I see it, Andi, your husband fucked me over and now you're due me that money, so I've got no choice but to fuck you over.' He leaned in close enough she could smell his aftershave. 'That plagiarism investigation into young Sam could just go away.'

Elliot shut her eyes. 'What?' Her mouth went dry. '*You*?'

'Me.'

'*How*? How the fuck?'

'Someone who may or may not work for me submitted an anonymous report to the university, complete with supporting evidence. It's pretty persuasive, if not fully convincing. But the clincher was someone else who may or may not work for me pinching young Samantha's laptop so she can't prove she wrote the essay. And the ambiguity means it's just going to drag on even further for the poor lass. Months and months, right? But it can all just go away like that.' Hislop clicked his fingers. 'She could magically find the laptop. Give her the proof to overturn it.'

Elliot sat there in silence, fizzing.

And she realised pretty quickly that she was screwed. And very, very badly.

How the hell could she choose between Sam and the money?

It wasn't a choice.

She leaned her head back against the headrest. 'What do you want, Gary?'

'My money, Andi. Then this all goes away, if you pay me it back.'

'I don't have any money.'

'I want a third of what I paid Davie. That's all. That's a very good deal. And I'll give you two days to get me it, Andi. Put it in the recycling bin at the back of St Boswells Hardware, all wrapped in Bacofoil. Or own-brand equivalent. Otherwise poor Sam's going to have to drop out, isn't she?'

'I don't have your money.'

'You really mean that?'

Elliot shut her eyes and didn't say anything.

'I knew you had it.' Hislop opened the car door. 'Two days. One third. For your daughter's future. That's a very good deal.' He got out and left the case of wine on the seat.

Elliot watched him drive off in that graphite grey cock replacement.

She was fucked.

She'd get home, go into the garage, move the dryer and get the money out of the fake brick.

Dump it in the bin behind his shop.

Then it'd be all over.

Sam would be okay.

Everything would be okay.

Wouldn't it?

AFTERWORD

Thank you. I mean it. Every person who reads my books gets a big thumbs up from me. I genuinely hope you enjoyed this one, I think it's my favourite...

As ever, thanks to a few great people.

James Mackay, first and foremost, for helping develop a terrible idea into a great book. Brutal honesty is so important... And for helping the Canadian and Dominican breathe.

Huge cheers to John Rickards for copy-editing witchcraft and to Julia Gibbs for proofreading wizardry.

Massive thanks to Angus King for taking time out of his summer holiday to narrate the audiobook in time for the release window.

Greatly appreciate a few authors keeping my sane during what's been a ridiculously busy decade which is actually only six months – writing two Marshall books, editing the first four Police Scotland books, writing something else new and I'm sure I've missed another stupid project. Oh, and some more heart surgery but I'm all great now. So raise a glass to Fiona Cummins, Mark Edwards, Susi Holliday, CL Taylor, Liz Nugent,

William Ryan, Derek Farrell, Tony Kent and Neils Lancaster and Broadfoot – if you see their books in a shop, buy them!

Marshall will be back later in the year with *Cuts Both Ways*, which will be a bit of a departure as it'll focus on what's going on up in Edinburgh, and it won't be long to wait...

Thanks again for reading – please leave a review on Amazon as it massively helps indie authors like me.

Cheers,

Ed

Scottish Borders, July 2025

MARSHALL WILL RETURN IN

Cuts Both Ways
Early 2026

Sign up to my mailing list to be first to know when it's out...

ABOUT THE AUTHOR

Ed James is a Scottish author who writes crime fiction novels across multiple series and in multiple locations.

His latest series is set in the Scottish Borders, where Ed now lives, starring **DI Rob Marshall** – a criminal profiler turned detective, investigating serial murders in a beautiful landscape.

Set four hundred miles south on the gritty streets of East London, his bestselling **DI Fenchurch** series features a cop with little to lose and a kidnapped daughter to find..

His **Police Scotland** books are fronted by multiple detectives based in Edinburgh, including **Scott Cullen**, a young Edinburgh Detective investigating crimes from the bottom rung of the career ladder he's desperate to climb, and **Craig Hunter**, a detective shoved back into uniform who struggles to overcome his PTSD from his time in the army.

Putting Dundee on the tartan noir map, the **DS Vicky Dodds** books feature a driven female detective struggling to combine her complex home life with a heavy caseload.

Formerly an IT project manager, Ed filled his weekly commute to London by writing on planes, trains and automobiles. He now writes full-time and lives in the Scottish Borders with a menagerie of rescued animals.

Connect with Ed online:

Amazon Author page

Website

ED JAMES READERS CLUB

Available now for members of my Readers Club is FALSE START, a prequel ebook to my first new series in six years.

Sign up for FREE and get access to exclusive content and keep up-to-speed with all of my releases on a monthly basis.

https://geni.us/EJM1FS

Printed in Dunstable, United Kingdom